JACOB'S TROUBLE 666

TERRY JAMES

Jacob's Trouble 666
Terry James

CKN Christian Publishing
An Imprint of Wolfpack Publishing
6032 Wheat Penny Avenue
Las Vegas, NV 89122

Paperback Edition

ISBN: 978-1-64119-463-1

Library of Congress Control Number: 2018968052

JACOB'S TROUBLE 666

PROLOGUE

The seeds were there all along for parenting the fruits that would sweeten the mouth but quickly grow bitter in the belly. The inevitable came like a flood following the dissolution of the U.S.S.R. Powerful money brokers' fanatic zeal for ever-widening margins of profit, coupled with consumers' appetites for increasingly opulent lifestyles, exploded in an orgy of uncontrolled credit spending by individuals and governments.

A super computer innovation networked the entire planet in a geometric progression when internationalist powers-that-be determined to preempt feared global economic disaster. This resulted in a radically changed worldwide monetary system of electronic-funds transfer.

Magnified by these advances, disparity between the haves and have-nots ripped civilization apart. Unprecedented terrorism and civil anarchy ensued, making cooperative police controls necessary on a global scale.

New, incurable, untreatable diseases brought on by human excesses ravaged the earth. Droughts, floods, earthquakes and other phenomena struck more frequently and with greater devastation. Still, mankind, through exponential growth in knowledge and quantum leaps in science, seemed to maintain control.

That same technology, however, ignited man's basest lusts--enslaving millions within the cyber-space realm of virtual reality by creating addictions rivaling even those caused by the mind-searing drugs that saturated every culture on earth. Western Judaeo-Christian precepts were all but absorbed by Eastern metaphysical theosophies, based on spirit guidance, reincarnation and inner-self search for knowledge, truth and power. Despite all the talk of peace, wars flared, then died to live again in other places. Israel and its neighboring Arabic nations agreed to a cessation of hostilities, and there was prosperity for a season.

Then came the truly cataclysmic events: The Russian coalition war machine totally destroyed in a single day; the inexplicable disappearance of millions of people in a fraction of a second; and the demise of America as a superpower.

Unified Europe, already a powerful entity within the New World Order, rushed to fill the vacuum, promising resolution to chaos created by the catastrophes. This became a promise kept, but better left unfulfilled.

Each generation, while those people live their given increments of history, compares its circumstance to circumstances of those before, and speculates about those who will come after. Jesus assessed the lot of a future generation when He said:

"For then shall be great tribulation, such as was not since the beginning of the world to this time, no, nor ever shall be."

Jacob Zen, deeply engrossed in the old book, and contemplating the torrential calamitous events that had engulfed his miserable existence, judged that this must surely be that time. His lips moved as he read the words inaudibly.

"And I stood upon the sand of the sea, and saw a beast rise up out of the sea..."

"... And all that dwell upon the earth shall worship him..."

"... no man might buy or sell, except he that had the mark, or the name of the beast, or the number of his name..."

"... and his number is six hundred, threescore and six." Revelation 13

"Alas! For that day is great, so that none is like it: it is even the time of Jacob's trouble..." Jeremiah 30:7

Jacob closed the thick volume while moving, almost without thinking, to the other side of the room. He lay stretched full-length on the hard plastic sofa and shut his eyes, gently massaging his aching temples with his fingertips, anticipating the only pleasure Interface had not taken from him: his memories.

His memories of the past — a time when he could envision only right and justice, and a future filled with promise at the side of the young woman who made it possible.

While his thoughts probed into the past, the ever-present foul smells in the room gave way — fading slowly, then more quickly — becoming the calm, crisp autumn scents of a Massachusetts countryside, during that earlier time......

CHAPTER 1

"These things never work out, Jabbo."

"Sure they do."

"Never have for me."

"How many times have I fixed you up? Look, when Jabolonski does something for a friend, it's usually a masterpiece."

Jacob smiled, knowing his stocky friend's self-assuredness, his most pronounced and, at times, his most annoying trait. Rasnick Jabolonski really believed what he was saying.

"She's no Cinderella, but, if nothing else, you'll enjoy talking with her. You two are a lot alike, you know... have a lot in common."

"You mean we're both human?" Jacob cocked an eyebrow to show his skepticism.

"I know. I know! That's the same line everybody uses to pre-sell a blind date. But in this case, it's a fact. She's involved in some government stuff. You know, the kind of stuff you like."

Jacob mentally pictured the female his friend's wife picked for him—a homely, bespectacled Ichabod Crane of womanhood, sitting snootily and shapeless in gray, drooping wool. The depression deepened when he remembered the pile of work he left at his Boston office, the most important work of his young career. He would spend the whole evening smiling and nodding in agreement with Beth, Jabolonski's former college roommate, and would never hear her words.

"She's great, Jake. C'mon! Relax!"

"How long have you known her?"

"Well..."

"Well? What's so hard about that question, Jabbo?"

"Okay, so I haven't met her. But I trust Beth."

"Sure you do. You're not the one being fixed up."

Soft yellows, greens and reds blanketed the undulant horizon, which was less brilliant than the foliage that whisked by just outside the Volvo. Jacob sat on the passenger side, staring past his own sharp features reflecting in the raised window. Something about the neglected work weighed on his thoughts. It wasn't the time line set by the National Security Council chairman. That could be met with little effort. Too, the thrust of the work he was doing in the project seemed right for tackling the problems facing the United States, Europe and Japan. He sensed instead, an undercurrent that tugged his intuition toward some deeper source of worry.

"Hey! Where are you?"

"What? Sorry." His thoughts dissipated with Jabolonski's interruption.

"I said, she works with some group in D.C. that has something to do with national security."

"Who?"

"Come on, Zen! What's the matter with you? Karen Mossberg, that's who!"

"I'm sorry, Jabbo. I was thinking about the work I have piling up."

"Forget it for tonight, okay? Everybody's got to unwind sometime."

"National Security, huh? Just about everything in Washington these days has something to do with national security. Which agency?"

"I don't know. Ask her yourself. It'll give you something to talk about," Jabolonski said while he steered the Volvo onto State 114, northwestward to Middleton.

She was not at first glance a girl of arresting good looks. Not like those he knew who made and lost careers intertwining themselves within Washington, D.C.'s society and officialdom. But she instantly made him forget the work on his desk, and drew him from his self-imposed introversion. She was, he considered while lighting a cigarette, quite simply the most appealing woman he had ever met.

"You don't need that," Karen Mossberg admonished softly, her pretty face portraying genuine concern. The silence that followed and her unyielding gaze made him uncomfortable.

"I've been meaning to quit."

"Yes. I know all the clichés, Mr. Zen: 'I've been meaning to quit'; 'They're killing me'; 'It's just that I have to do something with my hands.'"

"Yeah. Something like that, I guess," he said, grinning. "Rasnick tells me you work in government."

"Change the subject. She'll get off my case," she said, reaching to take the cigarette from his mouth. Then her tone was gentle. "Please don't. They are killing you, you know. You're much too nice to kill yourself with these, Jacob. And if you need to do something with your hands, here, hold mine." She took his right hand and held it between her hands.

"My work involves government, but I don't work for any agency," she said, continuing to hold his hand. "We're interested in policing the National Security Agency, in particular-- at least for the moment, that's our primary area of concern."

"We?"

"P. A.L. — Preservers of American Liberty."

"Clever," Jacob said, Karen Mossberg thought, just a bit smugly.

"You've heard of us." The defensive irritation in her voice and narrowed brows above her intense brown eyes told him to soft-pedal.

"I only meant it's a clever name. Actually, we've spent so much time researching the NSA, I guess we haven't earned a reputation yet. But I assure you we will be heard from shortly."

Her tone was soft again and he sensed she had to struggle with herself to keep it at that level. But the passion and the quick intellect were still there in the eyes--those lovely, dark eyes that sparked reflected light when she made her points.

"What about you? What exactly is your contribution to our benevolent keepers?"

"Nothing quite so stimulating as fighting to preserve our civil liberties, I'm afraid. It has its rewards on occasion, though. For lack of a better title, I guess you could say I'm an assistant consultant to the administration in international economic affairs."

"To the President?"

He was inwardly pleased that she brought up the question, and that she seemed duly impressed.

"Indirectly. My boss does the *vis-a-vis* stuff with top White House people. I'm relegated to rear echelon duty."

The expanded explanation was ego-deflating, but he saw her appreciation for his truthfulness. She reached to touch his arm.

"Being a junior G-man at your age isn't all that bad. You've got a lot of time."

"You people talking business?" Jabolonski entered the patio area of his home carrying meat prepared for the grill.

The evening ended too soon for Jacob. Friendship had grown into pronounced interest by eleven o'clock, when it was time to return to Boston and the horror of his desk. A quality, an indefinable something, drew him to Karen--traits that separated her from the others. Although he was uncertain of her appraisal of him, the look she gave before they parted with a wave and her agreement to get together in Washington told him the relationship held promise.

A shrill scream pierced his skull and reverberated over his brain, causing his eyes to pop open in a transfixed stare. His mind, as always, obeyed its masters instantaneously. He hurried to his position, as commanded.

Bright amber computer data flashed on the rectangular Interface screen when the old woman stepped beneath the Decodscanner.

"Look up!" commanded the stern woman across the counter, her black eyes leering from sockets surrounded by dark, sunken flesh.

The woman obeyed nervously, turning her puffy, age-creased face upward.

The screen displayed:

INterface Response Unity

U.S. SECTOR 781

PROCEED — INPUT

The checker herded a few canned grocery items onto the conveyor, then pressed a button located at waist level behind the counter.

Fumbling through her cracked vinyl purse, the older woman retrieved a tissue and applied it to her cold-infected nose.

"Look, lady! There are other citizens besides you in the P.C.," the checker said icily. "Move along!"

Her eyes betraying fear, she gathered the sack into her arms, coughed into the tissue, and exited the Product

Center under the suspicious glare of a black-uniformed controller.

An old man shuffled tentatively into the checkout lane, avoiding the gaze of the checker. His broad head was bowed as if he sought to hide beneath the upturned collar of the ragged gray coat he wore. "You got an IN, mister?" Her question cut the air in a tone of disgust.

"Yes... Yes... See here." The man let his eyes meet hers fleetingly while he pulled back the sleeve on his right arm and moved his hand to a position beneath the countertop Decodscanner, activating an ultraviolet light which made visible a bar code tattooed on the back of his hand. At the same time, the number appeared on the INRU screen:

5DD197920-J

Looking at the screen, the checker pushed a button, and data was added to the display.

5D019792O-J IN5DR - O - CREDIT LINE - D

"You don't have any drawing rights, Jew! Take these and put them back where they belong!"

The little man shrunk deeper into the oversized coat, although he made a meek protest. "Please... but madam... I..."

"Just get these things back on the shelves, Jew!" She shoved the items roughly at him, cursing beneath her breath. Her outburst drew the attention of others in the Product Center and caused the controller to stiffen to alertness from his position near the exit.

While all eyes were on the frightened man, he moved from the counter and nervously replaced the foodstuffs on their various shelves. His face taking on the bloodless look of a man terminally ill, his only wish was to be gone from the Product Center.

"Are you Jew?" The controller collared him, snarling the question through clenched teeth.

"Answer me, old man!"

He slammed the smaller man hard against a nearby wall, then pushed his elbow into the captive's throat. Unable to answer and growing dizzy because of pressure exerted on his windpipe, the man ceased to struggle against his powerful captor, who jerked and ripped at the overcoat, sending buttons flying when the coat tore open.

The controller pulled the coat apart, exposing a yellow, thread-stitched Star of David on the gray, tattered shirt.

"Why are you hiding this?" the angry policeman demanded, jabbing his finger into the center of the symbol. "You know it's forbidden to conceal being Jew!"

A crowd had gathered, the people's faces reflecting collective hatred.

"Please, sir! I didn't mean to conceal it. It will not happen again, sir."

His plea, in a heavy Slavic accent, brought mumbled cursing from the mob. The controller smiled stiffly while pushing the terrified man through the doorway and onto the concrete walk area in front of the Product Center.

"It won't happen again, because there is no more 'again' for you, my kike friend," growled the bigger man.

"Please, sir..." The prisoner's voice cracked with emotion.

"This is IN Controller Unit six, eight, two, two, two," the policeman said, talking into a hand-held communicator and holding his captive with his other hand. "Dispatch a Decap Unit to seven, seven, zero, one-hundred forty-fifth, J... uh..." He jerked the man violently toward himself, ripped open the prisoner's shirt, and read the number tattooed above the man's left breast.

"Make that five, zero, zero, one, nine, seven, nine, two, zero, Jew." The female operator at the other end of the transmission replied, "Affirmative, Controller six, eight, two, two, two. Dispatching Decap Unit now." The crowd grew larger and was demonstratively pleased with the proceedings.

Several among them shouted obscenities at the prisoner, who tried to hide behind the controller like a teased or frightened child might hide behind his parent.

In less than five minutes, a white van rounded a corner in the distance, then stopped seconds later in the middle of the badly deteriorating street near the mob. Two men in uniform similar to that worn by the controller exited the vehicle and walked to its rear.

One of them opened a panel on the right rear portion of the van and pushed a series of buttons, causing the back doors to swing open. He pressed another, activating machinery that swung out through the rear of the van and unfolded a section at a time, forming, finally, a large metal platform.

Two thick telescoping poles erected from the floor of the platform and extended upward six feet before stopping. A rectangular box-like device emerged from the center of the platform, rising three feet before halting between the two vertical poles. Within seconds, a large contrivance appeared from within the van's body and whirred to a stop between the poles at their highest points. The rectangular device opened and appendages extended from either side to make attachment to the vertical beams. A glistening, chrome-like blade of knife-sharp metal descended slowly from the device's lower position. Another projection ascended from the box on the floor of the platform, three feet wide, three inches thick and notched at its center, a half-circle bite having been taken from it by its machine-creator.

With the process completed, everyone present studied its grim appearance, then looked to the controller, to the little man who was his prisoner, and to the van operator who now helped drag the prisoner up two grated metal steps and onto the platform.

The man made no protest when they pushed him to his knees and forced his neck downward into the concave notch.

Another device descended. It, too, was notched--opposite in configuration to the lower notch--so that when fitting over the back of the prisoner's neck, it locked to form a perfect circle with the bottom notch, trapping the man's head.

The two Decap Unit specialists stepped off the platform, one of them returning to the panel housing the various buttons that controlled the van's ominous machinery. The man remained motionless and silent in his pathetic kneeling position on the platform, supporting his weight on the palms of his hands. When the operator pushed a black button, the shimmering metal blade descended slowly with a mechanized droning sound until it reached the back of the condemned's neck. It slowed almost imperceptibly while pinching through the first layers of flesh, then into the muscles. It continued to slice through vertebra, spinal cord, arteries and trachea, completing its journey with a clank against the bottom of the lower notch.

Blood spurted from the severed carotids, the head plopped heavily into a metal container, the body stiffened, then lay jerking in spasmodic death throes on the platform. The executioners hurriedly removed the corpse to the cheers of those gathered at the scene and heaved the body into the van through a side disposal chute. Another mechanized unit whirred from within the van and made several sweeps across the platform, shooting high-pressure streams of precisely directed water that forced the dead man's blood to run onto the street and into a nearby sewer drain.

"On your interface Response Unit, you have witnessed which of the following? Press the response key for the answer you think is correct.

A. Injustice to a citizen of Interface.

B. A misunderstanding, leading to the unfortunate death of a citizen.

C. Proper punishment for a questionable entity who broke a law to the detriment of Interface Unity.

D. Punitive action for an offense against interface which should have called for a milder disciplinary response."

The questions and the choices posed by the computer voice popped on the screen one line at a time in bright yellow characters against a royal blue background. Jacob Zen's attention darted swiftly from the legal pad on his lap to the screen, then to the key recessed in the right arm of his chair. He jabbed the key and the INRU screen displayed the "C" answer, which flashed on and off several times before the screen snapped to solid blue in preparation for the next question.

"Do you feel Jews deserve equal treatment to that given other citizens of interface, in any or all of its aspects?

A. Yes

B. No"

Jacob Zen pressed a button on the panel, generating the letter "B" and the word "No."

"If you responded B, which of the following most accurately reflects your meaning?

A. The governing of all Jewish entities should be conducted as it currently is under Interface Commission Policy 666 -- I.OOO.

B. Jews should have increased rights.

C. Jew entities should have decreased rights."

He responded to the hollow, synthesized voice after a quick glance at the graphic; the "C" answer pulsed brightly on, then off, then on again.

"Ethnic Inculcation Session 6662E19 is ended. Responses will be programmed into INterface Response Unity and consensus views incorporated into INRLJ Law to the degree

14

those views are deemed beneficial by TRINITY and the Commission of Ten."

Before rising from the chair, Jacob Zen placed the old book on the floor, taking care to hide it from the Scanner Eye. He knelt before the big screen, bowed his head, and drew his right arm to his body, pressing his clenched fist against his chest while militaristic music assaulted his senses, setting in motion brain undulations that moved his thoughts feverishly in whip-like fashion along the full length of his cognitive spectrum. Each run through that dark cerebral inner space would, it seemed, take him over the end, or through the barrier, or into hell's vortex.

But there was no hell, he managed to remember, forcing his oscillating mind to stabilize somewhere near the center of his brain—only heaven, only love. Master Manya and TRINITY said so.

INterface Response Unity was salvation! INterface was the nucleus, the matrix of Universal Truth.

"To Caesar that which is Caesar's and to God that which is God's! TRINITY speaks!" announced the computerized voice, which was at first three separate voices slightly out of synchronization with each other, but which then blended, finally becoming one cavernous voice that was TRINITY'S.

"INterface Response Unity is the New Earth. You are either IN or you are lost. Mankind cannot serve two masters. INterface is salvation. TRINITY loves you."

Jacob Zen lifted his face to see the INterface Response Unit screen fill with a triple image, three distinct faces revolving around and moving through each other, merging, then locking into a single image.

"TRINITY forever!" said the computer voice of INterface.

"Six Ways to Law! Six Ways to Order! Six Ways to Peace! Six! Six! Six!"

The words echoed in his head, although the screen was

now black, the speakers silent. Struggling to his feet, he felt two decades older than his 42 years. His throbbing knee joints and tension-knotted back muscles wreaked barely endurable pain on his stiff, convoluting mind. Looking into the mirror did nothing to roll back those unlived years, seeing the yellowish flesh and the creases branching in multiple valleys from the corners of his eyes and mouth. Hair once dark and thick was now graying and sparsely covering his scalp.

From the only window in the tiny room that had become the one world left to him, Jacob watched the haze-shrouded, deteriorating concrete below, where a squad of controllers stormed into a tenement building. Then he heard the moaning children, the haunting cries of the children.

He dropped heavily into the chair and tried to force the skull-crunching atrocities from his mind, his thoughts returning to the image on the INRU screen--to the black, soul-piercing eyes, the stark face-image which commanded instant obeisance whenever and wherever it appeared. He retrieved the legal pad and the book from their hiding place and, after reading a bold underlined passage in the volume, copied the words:

"And he hath power to give life unto the image of the beast, that the image of the beast should both speak, and cause that as many as would not worship the image of the beast should be killed..." Revelation 13:15.

Soon would be the time of INterface. Time, under pretext of becoming one with TRINITY, to help them account for their victims.

Time again to prove one's self loyal to the Father, Son and unholy Spirit.

Existence at the merciless hands of INterface was possible only because, to fulfill his pledge--that the masters would know retribution as vengeful as that with which they crushed anyone who resisted their incalculable evil--he must remain alive.

But how could he judge evil, considering his own record? How could he escape the fact of his own sin? The man's face when he plunged the 8-inch blade beneath the sternum, thrusting it upward through the heart. The issue of liquid warmth, the blood he could not wipe from his hands even now, while sitting before the INterface Response Unit awaiting TRINITY'S seeing, knowing intrusion into his misery.

Jacob Zen closed his eyes and tried to drive the stifling demons from his mind. His thinking must be clear for INterface, it must! But could it ever be erased, those bugging, dying eyes? The man's gasping, clutching effort to keep his life?

What of Jacob Zen's soul? Would the nightmarish image follow him forever during his eternal run through perdition?

"TRINITY Loves You!"

The electronic voice jerked his attention abruptly to itself and to the INRU screen.

"Six Ways to Law! Six Ways to Order! Six Ways to Peace!"

The screen was alive again, the triple image of the face swirling, crisscrossing, then locking into a single frame.

"Six! Six! Six!"

Subtle movement and noises told him the INterface Eye was active, making its central terminal-controlled adjustments in preparation for INterface.

He must perform the hated ritual for a time longer. Until he was ready to deal with TRINITY and with INterface his own way.

"Now is the time for joining spirits
For becoming one --
Time for committing the ultimate
trust, one to another --

To INterface in love."

Jacob Zen sat back in the console chair, his posture erect, motionless. The Eye atop the INRU whirred and clicked when he pressed the button recessed in the chair's right arm panel. A thin stream of light beamed from the camera, forming a circle on the skin of his forehead. At the same time, a tubular device swung from beneath the right arm of the chair and moved electronically to a stop above his right hand. Data appeared on the INRU screen, glowing yellow characters against the blue background.

JOHN I GARVER

66E-IN-3- 1888271,br> SECTOR COORDINATOR 55O

"Read the following pledge, one. eight, eight, eight, two, seven, one."

He read aloud a copy, which appeared on the screen when the computer voice completed its directive.

"I, six, six. six, I N. three, one, eight, eight, eight, two. seven, one. am one with INterface, as are all within Sector five, five, zero. We have and shall have no other allegiance."

"Prepare for print ident. Seize print plate," ordered the voice of INterface Response Unit.

He complied, placing his right thumb and index finger on the glass plate of the armrest's console panel. The screen display changed to:

AFFIRM -- JOHN I GARVER

SECTOR 55O

COORDINATOR — BBB-IN-3- 1 88827 1

"INterface accepts. IN are you."

The screen went black, the Scanner deactivated, and the apparatus above his right hand droningly returned to its position beneath the chair.

Relaxing, Jacob stared for a moment at the darkened, silent screen, thinking of the absurdity resorted to by history's most advanced technological state. The ludicrous play on words employed to inform the lucky citizen that he was a legal entity within the computer network society. "In are you through the INRU."

He wanted to laugh at their silly official slogan, but there was nothing funny about INterface totalitarianism. The numerical dehumanization imposed by mankind's latest and greatest attempt at Utopia had exacted its toll. If not for his all-consuming purpose, this personality crushing end-product of the quantum evolutionary leap would long ago have driven him to self-destruction. No doubt he would die at the hands of this perfect society; the probability of being discovered increased hourly. But he would do his utmost to have his satisfaction before it happened. Perspiration beaded on his forehead and streamed down his thin face. A cold, unhealthy sweat bubbled up from his core being, the manifestation of the torturous remembrances always with him. Karen, sweet, lovely Karen, their one victim for whom they would pay as great a price as he could extract.

Now he felt the monster closing in on him, its insidious, constricting, grasp squeezing life from him. Yet there remained the cerebral path to take him, if but for a sanity-preserving moment, away from the present.

CHAPTER 2

I
t had begun differently. So differently. He closed his eyes, tilting his face toward the ceiling. The sickness in his stomach eased, memories of those earlier times mercifully taking him from his unbearable present.

"I've known you now for months and yet I don't know you, because all we talk about is me. You're not top-secret like that precious work you guard so jealously, are you?"

"You've known me in the biblical sense; that's all that matters, really," Jacob teased.

Karen Mossberg punched Jacob with her fist, mock horror on her face. "You are a clod for saying so! And that little arrangement can change at any time!"

"You know life wouldn't be worth living without me around to--how shall I say it?--to stimulate your temperament once in a while."

She struggled to a sitting position on the bed, trying to pound him with both hands. Her long, dark hair lashed wildly, whipping his face in their struggle before her resistance melted into submission, both of them feeling passion rise, bringing them together, finally, in a flesh-coupling armistice.

Thirty minutes later, Karen tried and failed to take the cigarette from his mouth while he took his first drag. He held her at arm's length and she gave up. "Go on then! Kill yourself!" She sat in the middle of the bed, her arms folded, staring at him. "But not before I learn more about you." She again lunged for the cigarette, but again he was too quick, moving it out of reach.

"It all began when I was born..."

"Snakes in the grass aren't born; they're hatched," she interrupted his facetious narrative, snuggling her cheek against his chest.

"Rattlesnakes are," he corrected.

"Enough with the pedantic. Get on with the biographical."

"My father died when I was three. Moriah Zen. He was 26."

"You never really got to know him," Karen said in a more serious voice, propping on one elbow to see his face while they talked.

"I remember the beach. When I think of him, I think of a beach... the orange kind, with the sand packed hard. Funny, isn't it? The things you remember from childhood--bits and pieces of things. I can recall the time when I was about five, running down a little hill near our house, and I fell and cut my leg on a broken shoe-polish bottle. Can you imagine? A shoe-polish bottle! I remember that tiny detail, but I can't remember what my dad looked like. Oh, I have a mental image from all the pictures Mother kept. But him? Really know what he was like, who he was... I can't remember. Seems like you'd remember something that important, doesn't it?"

She watched him, seeing the distant look. She knew he didn't want her to answer, and let him have his moment of philosophical self-pity, but she felt deeply for the little boy she saw who would give his soul to know the man who sired him.

"When I was six, Mother and I went to live with Uncle Conrad, Conrad Wilson. No kid could hope for a better father."

Karen watched Jacob study his fingernails; talking about that early part of his life, perhaps dredging up memories of his father, obviously made him nervous.

"Uncle Conrad wanted to marry Mother, but she wouldn't go along. A Hebrew sticking point. Oh, she loved him--slept with him to prove it, but she wouldn't marry him because he was Gentile. Isn't that an interestingly twisted bit of morality and theology? He wanted to adopt me, he really cared for us both, right up until Mother's accident."

"And he was able to get custody?"

"My mother's sister, who could barely afford to keep her own five kids fed and clothed, accepted Uncle Conrad's request to keep me with him. He had been my father for more than four years anyway. She wouldn't let him adopt me, wouldn't let him have any legal holds. She didn't want me to have the Gentile name; said Mother wouldn't have wanted that. But he took me on her terms. I didn't understand it all at the time, but I did know I didn't want to stay with Aunt Frenka and Uncle Jorba Swenke in Brooklyn. They were staunchly orthodox, and I mean you toed the mark or felt the wrath. If Uncle Jorba didn't take the skin off your backside with a yard-long stick for breaking one ordinance or another, then, Teddy—Theodore Hertzl Swenke, my 200-plus pound cousin with a gestapo mentality, would beat a tattoo on your face when you refused to give up whatever you might have that he felt he needed."

Karen laughed, enjoying Jacob's lighter frame of mind. "Sounds like one of my cousins — Anna Daygan. She took great delight in pinching you until she got what she wanted... or just for the fun of it. I could never figure how somebody so fat could run that fast."

"You're familiar with the problem then," he chuckled. Then his intonation became more somber. "Anyway, I was relieved when Aunt Frenka let me stay with him."

Karen stood from the bed and stretched her arms toward him. The gesture made him feel once again like a man rather than the boy he had become during the brief remembrance — a time when Conrad Wilson began molding him into what Jacob hoped to one day become for his foster-father's sake. She bent to kiss him, holding his face tenderly with her slender fingers. The cool feminine touch he must never lose. To do so would be to lose himself. Desire he thought spent began its ascent, though it was an unconsciously beckoned desire he tried to discourage. Sensing his renewed awakening, Karen, he was almost glad, subtly moved away. "How about lunch?" she said.

"Sure. What would you like?"

"Pizza?" she suggested from the bathroom.

"Fine. Want to go out?"

"No. Let's have it here," she shouted to be heard, because she knew he had walked into the den. He came back into the bedroom, pausing to light a cigarette before retrieving his wallet from his pants on a nearby chair. Thumbing through the various papers and photographs, he found a half-metal, half-plastic card, returned to the den and sat in front of the small computer unit in the corner of the room. After inserting the card in a slot just above the keyboard, he depressed a key that activated the unit. When he manipulated other keys, the display screen lit up with information he had input. Five seconds later, the input data was electronically swept from the screen and new information appeared, confirming that his electronic funds were sufficient for transaction and informing him that the telecommunication had been completed between his computer unit and the business with which he wanted to transact. At the same time, the system alerted the business that he wished to interface and that the electronic funds currency units were sufficient for transactions up to 5,079 for Jacob Zen, 771-68-1794-6, Boston, MA TERMINAL 31 BB.

He pushed a button on the right side of the keyboard and the audio-visual connection was made to Broglio's Pizza Bar, serving pizza which was, the pretty girl reminded him, "Thicker and quicker!"

"They'll be there in 10 minutes, sir," the teenager answered when he completed the order; the display screen informed him that the appropriate number of electronic funds currency units had been moved from his account to the account of Broglio's.

"They'll be here in 10," he said to Karen, who entered the den, toweling dry her hair. She came to him and bent to kiss him. "Hope you like shrimp," he said.

She took the half-burned cigarette from between his fingers and crushed it out in an empty coffee cup. "I like you, don't I?"

"Funny!"

He pulled her into his lap and jostled her in a moment of playfulness that gave way to more serious intentions. She stood and resumed drying her hair with the towel.

"The pizza's coming, remember?"

"Yeah. Wish I had told them to bring it later."

"You know that wouldn't work. Everything is on a neatly packaged schedule these days. We must fit into the mold. Cooperate with the methodologies of this New Age, or be left behind. I believe that's how your Ambassador Wilson put it. Not too long ago, there would've been plenty of time."

"Right now, I'll agree with you, but it's my glands talking, not my good sensibility. In a more rational mood, I'd say things like 'we must put aside our personal and national interests for the good of everyone' or 'only when we pull together can we advance to our ultimate destiny!'"

"I'm glad you're not rational right now, because I really wouldn't want to hear that garbage."

"Seriously," Jacob said, watching her brush her wet hair into long, straight strands. "What's to be said that's so great about the good old days? You had to phone the order in, look for money to pay for it--most of the time you had to cash a check or write one--and, of course, you had to drive in ungodly traffic for 30 minutes to pick up the order, or else wait an hour-and-a-half for the pizza, which was always cold by the time it got to you.

"Now, we pay without the hassle of keeping up with coins or paper, and all we need is our UNIVUSCARD for everything. We know exactly where we stand without having to worry about figuring out balances, mailing bills and all the rest. We have more time to do other things, and we save tremendous amounts of fuel and money by ordering through UNIVUS and having the merchandise delivered from the product Distribution Centers.

"And, we have the option, if we choose to be archaic, to do things like we did back in those good old days."

"But not without Big Brother and everyone else knowing our business and scolding us for our lack of cooperation. What about the privacy we've forfeited? And how long do you think we will have a choice about whether to join in?"

"Forfeited our privacy? How?" he asked, incredulously.

"Come on, Jake! We are recorded from birth to death, and I mean every detail. It's all there in the UNIVUS memory banks for anybody who cares to dig deeply enough."

"There are protections. Since the biochip, UNIVUSCARD

can't be used without the thumb and fingerprints of the person who owns the card. There are other features."

"There are no overrides? No ways to break the codes and the safeguards?" Karen questioned in a knowing tone.

"We have to trust something, Karen, or else we're all lost anyway. Of course there are the ultimate overrides, as there have always been, even in your good old days. But they're the province of only a very few at the top level of government. The same guidelines of confidentiality apply to UNIVUS as have always applied to, say, matters involving nuclear and space technologies."

"And they've always been compromised, too," she broke in. "What makes you think this type of top-secret information will be different?"

"I'm sure there will be adequate redress for people when they're caught in the middle of theft of data or accidents or tampering. Especially as the system grows and improves... becomes more efficient."

"Meanwhile, what about the one who suffers the loss, and has to absorb it? Maybe loses everything? Or the person who is sitting in prison somewhere waiting for the system to eventually discover the error and vindicate him?"

"Karen, there will always be mistakes and injustices under law. Every civilization that's ever existed has had to face that. That doesn't mean we just fold up and stop progressing."

"Growing into our Utopia?"

"Well, we certainly haven't gotten there through the old ways of doing things. We've never had the technologies to try something better until now. Look at the improvements in the economies of the world. Hunger is not as great in Third World countries; the common electronic currency has stabilized much of the trade problem and has completely done away with the currency fluctuation nightmare. There's a lot better understanding among the peoples of the West. Before long, we will link with the Middle and Far East, and the language barriers will be bridged by the new translation capabilities."

"But Jake, this is all at the price of individual liberty. Is the pipe dream of having one world worth that cost?"

"We'll have to sacrifice some individual liberties. And the time is coming when we will have to set the example by putting aside national interests to some extent."

"Dr. Marchek calls it the 'Babel Syndrome.'"

"Babel Syndrome?"

"The story in the Scriptures about people trying to build the tower to heaven. They were all of one mind and one language, and God says in His Word that they could eventually do what they set out to do, and He wasn't ready for that. So He confused their communication by introducing many different languages while they were in the process of building the tower. They no longer understood each other, became terrified, then got mad and began fighting, forgetting all about the project."

"Fascinating story, Karen, but so is 'Alice in Wonderland.' You don't believe that nonsense, do you?"

"Of course not. But I do believe this will lead to more problems than it will solve. I agree with the dear old man on one point. The whole thing can lead to dictatorship, by its very nature. Jonathan Schell was right in *The Fate of the Earth*, when he wrote that whether a one-world order should come through fear or through love, either path will lead to the same destination. Dr. Marchek thinks, and he's not alone in his opinion, that the destination will be global tyranny."

"More of his biblical wisdom?" he bantered.

"I don't agree with him because of that, but because of what I see happening. We're relinquishing ourselves more and more to something we don't understand. The majority of people don't want to try to understand. They just don't care. Just trust government; it will do what's best for us."

Jacob reached to her and pulled her onto his lap. She curled her arms around his neck and yielded to his lips when he held her to himself.

"I want to meet this Hugo Marchek. I'm not sure I care for you thinking so highly of him," he said, nibbling the velvet skin of her cheek. "I think the relationship bears watching."

"He's old," she said, laughing, but enjoying his mock jealousy.

"So are half the codgers in Washington, with their nieces at their sides every evening."

"Dr. Marchek is also one of the most moral men to be found anywhere."

"So is Senator Hosfelt, Justice Brendon, Secretary Martin. All of them are extremely moral men who can prove it by convincing you that their concept of morality is the right concept of morality."

"Dr. Marchek's is Judaeo-Christian. He would never approve, for instance, of our sleeping together."

"Who sleeps?" He kissed her. "If that's all that would bother him, he'd have nothing to worry about."

"I think it's cute, his old-fashioned view of marriage and loyalty to one woman."

"What about to one man?" Jacob asked, after she returned his kiss.

"He's really against homosexuality, and I'm not so sure I'd like to share you with a man — call me old-fashioned." She laughed, kissing his neck and hugging him playfully.

"I don't think I'd like this guy, Marchek. There's something basically un-American about that kind of narrow-mindedness."

"With everyone thinking and talking about getting rid of

nationalism so we can all come together, I should think you'd be pleased with anything that's not American in its philosophy, or theology, or whatever."

"Actually, my dear, I can abide internationalist thinking, or any other kind, so long as it's strongly rooted in American precepts."

"Weren't some of those precepts family, home, and sexual fidelity to one's legal, God-ordained mate?"

"Want to get married?" He was facetiously serious.

"What? And give up all my men? Don't talk insanity!"

"Solomon is my hero... my example. Seven-hundred wives..."

"And concubines, too, don't forget," Karen added. "I'm content with the New Age renaissance way of things. It makes more sense. Freedom means the right to make your own choices. You can't do that when you're tied to a dogmatic philosophical or theological contract. I just don't know whether I could get to like your Hugo Marchek."

"You could find out if you go with me tomorrow night. The PAL staff is having a small party at Dr. Marchek's home at seven. A get-acquainted thing for the newer people."

Jacob nudged her from his lap, stood, and lit a cigarette. "I have to put some finishing touches on the project paper. We have three days left, and Uncle Conrad needs me there tomorrow so we can pull everything together. It goes to the President on Monday."

"Sure... some other time, then," she said. But he saw her disappointment.

"I'll do my best to get away by nine. No. I will be there by nine-thirty." Her smile, this time, was genuine.

* * *

CONRAD WILSON PACED the burgundy-colored carpet of his

study, his silver-white mustache twitching typically beneath his thin, peculiarly down-curved nose, the exaggerated exploitation of which had been the delight of political cartoonists for four decades. He dictated to his secretary of 15 years in a burst of inspiration after sipping from a glass half-filled with scotch and ice.

"America has, more than any other national entity, led the way in international reorganization and cooperation in order to make life better in the free world. The VNIVUS and VNIVER electronic currency systems are based on the former U.S. dollar — later assisted, of course, by the contribution of the euro. Middle-Eastern peace was established largely because of the United States' support of and continuing guaranteed protection for Israel. And we neither discount nor forget the magnificent contributions of Mr. Krimhler in that historic process.

"Indeed, in addition to providing most of the funding for the telecommunications and computer technologies that link us, the United States, as always, continues to provide the nuclear umbrella which ensures the future for all of us.

"These and many additional factors give this nation, in this panel's view, not only the right but the common-sense duty to assume the dominant position within any universal governing format."

It was classic Wilsonese, wrapping months of intensive work in a cocoon of precise extemporaneous analysis; in this verbal art, he was without peer.

Jacob sipped his own scotch, watching the old man walk back and forth in front of Alexandra Fitzwell, whose face, when her shorthand had captured the words, glowed with admiration.

"What do you think, Jake?" Conrad Wilson questioned the younger man in the smooth baritone made famous through hundreds of speeches and interviews.

"Wish I'd said it."

Wilson laughed heartily while walking to the small bar in one corner of the study. He poured a drink, then held the decanter in an offering gesture toward Jacob.

"No, thanks. I have a ways to drive tonight."

"Oh, yes! Your young lady. You are quite taken with her, I can tell."

"Oh?"

"This is the longest I've known you to lavish such attention on any one girl," Wilson said, smiling. "And, through our conversations of late, I've come to detect your concern for her. Care to talk it over?" His tone became fatherly. "That will be all this evening, Alexandra."

The woman stopped at the door before exiting the study. "You take your medication," she ordered sternly. "Promise..."

"Yes! Yes!" Wilson retorted gruffly. "Now leave us in peace!"

He turned his attention back to Jacob when the woman closed the door behind her. "She's a jewel, but a bit on the pushy side."

"You would've never gotten along without her all these years, Uncle Conrad. Do what she says. Take your medicine, okay?"

The retired diplomat waved off his foster son's exhortation, wanting to get off the despised subject of his failing health. "Getting back to your young lady, Miss Mossberg. Is the problem between you two something I can help with? Now, I'll admit straight off: my motive in offering to mediate the crisis is largely selfish. I would like to be a grandfather one day," he said semi-seriously, patting Jacob's shoulder he passed by on his way to a large wingback chair directly across from the younger man.

"There's no crisis, really. But there is something. Something I can't put my finger on. You know... the feeling of impending something or the other."

"Yes. I always get that feeling when I'm about to meet with the Russians. I've always called it 'mild intimidation,'" Wilson said with a chuckle. "It's the same with women. They'll get the best of you now and again if you're not on your toes."

He sat forward, smoothed the crease of his trousers, then leaned back, crossing one lanky leg over the knee of the other. "When you were 12, Jake, you assured me that girls existed only to make you and Joey Framington, and all other boys, miserable. Then, at about 18, they were for talking with on the phone from dawn to dusk and for being out with from dusk to dawn. Now they're back to making life miserable. Women, bless their beautiful, black hearts, can be like getting caught in a revolving door when you get involved too much."

"She doesn't make life miserable. Karen's... she's given me new perspectives and insights. Not because of any philosophy or theology she espouses. As a matter of fact, we disagree considerably in most of those areas. It's something that kind of sticks like flypaper to your thoughts. You can't shake it loose."

"That, my boy, is one of the best descriptions of what we used to call 'love' that I've ever heard. Now it's 'mutual self-realization' or 'higher mind unity' or whatever else this generation is calling it," the old man said with amusement; but then he became reflective.

"Whatever you call it, your mother and I had it," he said, his eyes becoming moist. "Don't be afraid of it, Son. It might only come once."

"It's more than that though. Her work bothers me. I'm afraid she's tied to something that's somehow going to get her into trouble. She could disagree with me forever on almost anything and I'd never let it affect the way I feel about her. But this cynicism she has... it almost seems like an obsession with her. I just don't want her involved in something that might hurt her. I think that's at the bottom of my apprehension."

"What's she cynical about?"

"Particularly, about UNIVUS--about the control she feels the National Security Agency has over people--about what the man she works for calls the 'Babel Syndrome.' He says that mankind is going the way of the people described in the Bible who tried to build a tower to heaven. They were a kind of one-world order, I take it. God supposedly took away their common language and scattered them."

"Yes. I'm vaguely familiar with all that malarkey," Wilson said. "Sound's like your young lady is mixed up with one of those Bible-thumping fundamentalist types."

"He's not a minister. He's an eschatologist, she says. Someone who researches biblical prophecies and how they relate to present time."

"And Karen? How does she feel about it?"

"She loves the old man. Thinks there's no finer person in existence. She doesn't go along with the prophecies, the Second Coming, and that sort of thing. But she's convinced that all these tremendous strides we've made will lead to totalitarianism on a global scale. His name's Marchek... Dr. Hugo Marchek. She's part of his organization, because she feels it's the only vehicle available to carry the message of alarm to the public."

"Fanatics have been screaming 'The end is coming' since the beginning of time, but where is it?" Wilson stood to pace in front of Jacob, waving the empty glass while he talked.

"I'm sick of all these self-serving, self-righteous morons who think they're the only ones with the answers! To sit still is to regress. We would be consumed by the evolutionary process. Our technology and our will to go on are all we have to hang our hopes on. We must unite, or else blow ourselves to pieces, or breed and degenerate and pollute ourselves into oblivion."

Wilson calmed and refilled his glass from the decanter. "We've done pretty well pulling ourselves out to this point." He took a drink, grinned, and spoke more softly. "The old boy still has some of the demagogue in him, I suppose."

Jacob returned the smile—understanding--remembering the time three years earlier when a United States senator had used the term in lambasting Wilson. Conrad Wilson was, at the time, defending an administration position calling for a national-identification-computer-system-interact card to replace the Social Security card for each U.S. citizen. UNIVUS had been adopted and the cards issued, but not before one of the most intense battles ever waged in the chambers of Congress had taken place. Wilson was a powerful influence in the winning effort, and those on the winning side had never ceased praising their champion. The losers had never stopped proclaiming at every opportunity that Wilson was the man who had, more than any other, put every citizen at the mercy of the dehumanizing computer network.

"Anywhere there's civilization, the people are, by necessity, under governing authority. Now, for the first time, we have the technology and the good sense to use it for making government optimally benefit the individual. But these idiots would have us crawl back into our caves of ignorance!"

Wilson calmed again and became reflective, rolling the glass between his hands. "There's something afoot that's evil, okay. It's in that dangerous kind of thinking that promotes fanaticism--anarchy under the guise of religious freedom. There's the real enemy to worry about."

"Maybe I should have you talk to Karen," Jacob said, half-seriously. "Here I am involved in some of the very things she's so concerned about, and I can't discuss them with her — to help her understand that these things are for the best."

"She'll know in time, Son," the old diplomat said comfortingly. "Everyone will reap the benefits of the new ways of doing things, and still be able to keep most of the values that matter to us. That's why we've worked so hard, you and I and the others on the project."

"Project Eagle has to succeed. Then all the Orwellian fears can be put to rest for good," Wilson said, then finished the scotch.

* * *

KAREN CHECKED her watch against the antique grandfather clock that stood on an equally ancient, multi-hued oriental rug in the rectangular foyer. Hugo Marchek appeared in the arched, oak-framed doorway that provided entrance to his den. "Come, come, my dear Karen. There are others besides Mr. Jacob Zen in this world." The small, balding man of 78 years peered over the wire-rimmed glasses riding low on the bridge of his thin nose. "Come. We've much to discuss tonight. Mr. Zen will be here in time," he said, his Polish-accented English rendered with good-natured inflection.

She checked her watch a last time before following him into the room which was alive with diverse conversations carried on by men and women in their late twenties to middle forties.

"Your attention, please!" Marchek clapped his hands several times and the room quieted.

"Thank you," he said, adjusting the glasses with his right hand while straining to see the words on the single sheet of paper he held in his left.

"I have before me a memorandum of a highly confidential

nature, which a friend managed to bring out of a certain file. It is disturbing, I am afraid, because it confirms our fears that the new controlling machinery is in place, and that we are very near the time it will be put into use in this nation.

"Details are quite sketchy. The information from this single document, of course, does not tell all. It is self-evident, however, that it was authorized in high places, and that makes it doubly significant. It reads:

"A universal standard of law and order being our ultimate objective, the United States must begin now to put aside provincial interests of all kinds and move into the New paradigm— socially, culturally, politically, and religiously. We have the technology for bringing us into that brilliant future, and we must provide leadership in marching to that future- Only those who can accept the required changes, only those who can adapt to the mix of policies capable of nurturing the New technologies, will achieve a place in the world that is to come. We will do whatever is necessary to claim our portion when the time is right. We must not fail, We shall not fail.."

Marchek's voice trailed off wearily while he removed the glasses, shut his eyes, and rubbed the reddened indentations they left on his nose. "The document is directed to a number of this country's most influential people in business, government, and the media. It is signed by the President of the United States."

* * *

"INTERFACE RESPONSE UNITY is the New Earth. You are either IN or you are lost. Mankind cannot serve two masters! Mankind must serve mankind, because mankind is one with God! Mankind is God. We are one through INterface Unity. INterface is salvation! TRINITY Loves You."

Jacob Zen struggled to his feet upon hearing the mechanized proclamation that snatched his mind from his semiconsciousness. His head spun, his vision blurred and went dark before clearing enough to see the screen and the image of the face.

"TRINITY forever!
Six Ways to Law!
Six Ways to Order!
Six Ways to Peace!
Six! Six! Six!"

The INRU Scanner Eye was alive, panning the room in search of anything not within INterface tolerance. He sat in the console chair holding the back of his head rigidly against the slotted headrest.

"Now is the time for joining spirits. For becoming one with TRINITY. Time for committing the ultimate trust, one to another, to INterface in love"

He performed his required functions when the computer devices had completed theirs, obediently reading aloud the message on the screen: "I, six, six, six, I N three, one, eight, eight, eight, two, seven, one, am one with INterface, as are all within Sector five, five, zero. We have and shall have no other allegiance."

With his thumbprint and index fingerprint confirmed, the Identifier deactivated the INRU. Jacob groped under the console chair with his right hand for the hidden writing pad and book, and, finding them, he thumbed through the old volume and copied the passages quickly.

"How art thou fallen from heaven, O Lucifer, son of the morning! How art thou cut down to the ground, who didst weaken the nations! For thou hast said in thine heart, I will ascend into heaven, I will exalt my throne above the stars of God; I will sit also upon the mount of the congregation, in the sides of the north,I will ascend above the heights of the clouds, I will be like the Most High. Yet thou shalt be brought down to Hell, to the sides of the pit" Isaiah 14:12-15.

"And the woman said unto the serpent, We may eat of the fruit of the trees of the garden; But of the fruit of the tree which is in the midst of the garden, God hath said, Ye shall not eat of it, neither shall ye touch it, lest ye die. And the serpent said unto the woman, Ye shall not surely die; For God doth know that in the day ye eat thereof, then your eyes shall be opened, and ye shall be as God, knowing good and evil" Genesis 3:2-5.

Now was the worst time--the time after being in the half-dream, half-memory state when Karen again traversed his thoughts, dynamic with life. Always, the emptiness raked at his guts, a hollowness that slowly filled with the urge to end it all.

But he must survive TRINITY'S soul-exposing machinery, whose power he witnessed now, the INRU monitor again alive and displaying INterface society at its totalitarian worst. The faces looked the same. Emaciated faces of the dying, like those on the archival films of the Holocaust many decades earlier. But these — in ghastly color. He fought the urge to retch, seeing tiny, naked children, their ribs straining to punch through pasty-white skin, eyes bulging hugely from their sockets. Past hunger. Awaiting the final convulsive throes of what would for them be blessed relief.

"Jewry has brought its plight upon itself. They are plunderers and usurpers! Now they are reaping the bitter harvest of their own making. They have created their own hell, these Jews who defy INterface."

The screen continued to display barely alive people who stared unblinkingly into the panning cameras. "Even these subhumans, who have perpetrated conflicts around the world, even these have a place in the Six Ways Plan.

"TRINITY speaks from Jerusalem at the appointed hour of six!"

The Six Ways Plan — the ever-evolving social, political, and religious blueprint of INterface's reach for perfection. There would be more didactic barrages about the Universal Mind, the need of Oneness with the great Cosmic Organism of which every individual spirit was a cellular part. More assurances that the indwelling Spirit, the God within each person, would guide the Whole to the ultimate Evolutional Apex of Ascension.

Evidence that perfection was not yet attained burned now into his realization, while the scenes of the "Apostate Amputation," as TRINITY termed it, continued with a baby being torn from its mother's arms by a black-uniformed controller. The infant's head then bashed into a bloody, shapeless mass against a concrete wall moments before the mother was herself decapitated. But TRINITY would make it all understandable; TRINITY would explain the reasons for the "Amputations" — why babies and mothers must be butchered for the good of all.

CHAPTER 3

Withdrawal clutched at his intestines. Craving for the drug superseded any other need, even the need to escape through the mind-tunnel into his former existence, and it called to him now from across the room, dark and oval and bitter.

Citizens of INterface were promised relief from the abrasive atmosphere through use of the chemical. Relief from throat disorders which brought on painful spasms, paralysis of the larynx, and even death from respiratory system collapse. The drug's primary by-product, however, was the personality-changing effect it produced; like everything INterface offered, Trachetrol II was designed to contribute to the process of subjugation.

John I. Carver was luckier than most, being part of the controlling apparatus provided generous access to the drug. The average citizen could claim a ration of no more than a dozen capsules each 30-day period. Jacob Zen had vowed to keep his use to a minimum, but the gripping pain of addiction more and more frequently drew him to the walnut-veneered cabinet and the bottle with the liquid-filled capsules.

He opened the container and downed one of the dark maroon Trachetrols, grimacing because of its bitterness and his difficulty in swallowing it. He partially filled a glass with water from the tap, the liquid brownish with impurities because those in charge of the system were unable to keep the pumps and filters functioning properly. His stomach calmed within seconds after the water washed the capsule down, his nerves steadying, but his mind becoming surrealistic in its ruminations. He cursed beneath his breath his lack of willpower.

From the wall above the INRU, the gray-black clock's amber readout, displayed:

"5:50 p.m. ... TRINITY speaks at six."

Jacob shook his head and tried to loosen his body with light calisthenics, moving his arms, head and legs to get back some of the feeling the Trachetrol II was withholding from him. Of all people under INterface tyranny, it was most imperative that he have full command of his faculties; the slightest error, the most minuscule deviation from the routine or unanticipated tasks thrust upon John I, Garver by INterface, would bring a face-to-face investigation by the controllers, discovery, and the end of Jacob Zen. The terror police were too busy most of the time, rounding up uncooperative Jews, to investigate minor officials with INterface.

Only a mistake would stimulate a half-biological, half-machine cell somewhere within the brain of the ever-vigilant computer network, alerting one of the controllers that the matter must be seen after. Soon, though, the Jewish problem would be cleared up to TRINITY'S satisfaction; all other facets of INterface would then be dealt with. He would be found out and eliminated. Meanwhile, his safest bet was the assumed identity and the job that went with it. There were ways to use the machinery at his command to manipulate the hated enemy. The trick was to know when to pull out in time to save himself.

"Interface is the New Earth!

You are either IN, or you are lost!

Mankind cannot serve two masters-Mankind must serve INterface to be one with God!

Master Manya is one with TRINITY!

TRINITY is INterface God!"

Jacob Zen's mind cleared with the forceful words that assaulted him from the INterface Response Unit, different words that grabbed his thoughts and shook them into sudden realization. He was now to equate Master Manya with TRINITY! Part of the INterface Godhead!

"To Caesar that which is Caesar's and to God that which is God's! Master Manya speaks!"

What did it mean? The scene of the INRU screen, too, was different. Instead of the revolving, crisscrossing triple image of the face he expected to see, the slow camera zoom drew his attention toward an illuminated edifice surrounded by the black night sky.

It was, he determined in the next instant, the recently completed temple atop Mount Moriah in Jerusalem, sitting beside the Moslem Mosque of Omar. The rebuilding of the temple was allowed as part of the peace accords between Israel and the neighboring Arab nations. The Jews had given up much for the privilege of rebuilding on this holy site. Israel had agreed to disband her army--at the time the third-most powerful in the world--in return for guaranteed protection by the North Atlantic Treaty Organization, a guarantee that was forgotten the day Russians stormed into Palestine with all the others.

The scene dissolved to another—inside the temple, he surmised, sitting forward in the console chair, straining to see details with drug-affected eyes that worked against each other in the attempt to focus. The camera drew him down the empty corridor that narrowed in perspective, the hallway bounded by high granite walls made eerie by light from a single point which etched stark shadows around and between the walls ornately carved and scrolled surfaces.

"Master Manya loves you," the voice of INterface said solemnly, while yet another dissolve took place on the screen —to the innermost room of the temple, the Holy of Holies.

"The hour is six! Master Manya speaks!"

Indistinguishable at first, a silhouette of a man gradually became identifiable. The several cameras focused on the figure, giving the viewer different angles through a series of dissolves, the camera directly in front of the standing figure finally claiming exclusive possession and drawing it toward the viewer's screen. Still, the draped man was not completely distinguishable, the contrasting shadows obscuring his facial features.

"I and the Cosmogonal Mind, Father of all but the Jew, are One. Those who are IN are One with me, as I am One with the Father. All are parts of the Universal Body of pure existence, linking cells which comprise the great Cosmogonal Organism within which I am eternally at work, taking each of you upward to the supreme level of universal mind-consciousness."

Unlike TRINITY'S mechanized preachments, the words were softly spoken and reassuring in tone.

"The Six Ways Plan edicts that these must be excised. They are as lesions on an otherwise healthy organ, malignant and parasitic, draining the whole's vitality, keeping mankind from reaching the highest order of evolution.

"The disappearance mystery was part of that excision, carried out by natural evolution, similar to dissipation of illness and fever in the body as one becomes whole again.

Part of the disappearance was glorious for those involved. A quantum evolutionary leap to the highest Universal Mind Order by those who earned that existence through their many incarnations, always using their time on earth for the good of their fellow man. Each citizen of INterface who follows the examples of selfless devotion to humanity is even now in the evolutionary process of becoming one, in the eternal sense, with God, with Master Manya."

The camera angle changed, the figure taking on a more ominous appearance; the voice became angry.

"The greatest act you can perform, in earning your elevation to the higher evolutionary order, is to devote yourself to eradicating all who are not IN! From this moment make this your consuming desire! Find them in their nests, wherever they are.

"Kill them! Or call controllers to their places of hiding. Only when this scourge is wiped from our midst can there truly be heaven on earth!"

A cold wash of fear soaked Jacob's thought processes while he watched and heard the call for genocide. How he hated them.

Karen... beautiful Karen. To see this beast die for what it did, whatever it did to her. To see it dead—as dead as the rabbis, whose bodies were being shown now, minus the heads which were already within the white Decap Unit van.

"The leadership of these parasites has been eliminated! Witness their bodies! Soon their disciples will follow them."

Two front-end loaders driven by controllers scooped the robed bodies and dumped them into a chute that closed to form an outer wall of the van. Other black-uniformed men clubbed and kicked men and women, herding them through a small opening into another van. Many who took the blows lay where they fell and were hit repeatedly until they either got up or were bludgeoned to death. "We must do our part in the Amputation begun with the dissipation! The two great commandments from this evolutionary moment forward are:

1. Thou shall worship the Lord, thy God, Interface. E.

2. Thou shall kill illegal Jews and all other enemies of Interface."

The screen again filled with the shadowy image of the self-proclaimed deity, the three cameras in the Holy of Holies taking turns showing Master Manya from different angles through a series of dissolves. The INRU screen went black, returning to life momentarily with a still shot of Master Manya's darkened form. Etched in bright yellow characters above the image were the words:

"MASTER MANYA LOVES YOU!"

Below the image were the Roman numerals:

"VI VI VI

Six Ways to Law!

Six Ways to Order!

Six Ways to Peace!"

Paralysis gripped Jacob and he sat transfixed. It was madness beyond even the insanity he always knew festered at the core of INterface! When he again became aware of the screen, it was dark and inactive, and his automatic reaction was to look to the Scanner atop the INRU to determine whether it was betraying his temporary lapse. One was expected to be active; inactivity allowed time to think, breeding discontent. Watchers became instantly disturbed when they observed thinking; they became especially disturbed when a Sector Coordinator was caught in the act of inactivity at times other than the permitted periods of rest.

The Scanner's smoke-gray convex lens was, for the moment, motionless. He moved from the console chair, watching, although not too overtly, to see if the camera's eye followed him about the room. It did not. His body ached, and he stretched to limber its stiffness, contemplating things he had just seen. Memories emerged to the surface of his conscious thought, drawn by the horrors he had witnessed. He retrieved the old Bible and the legal pad from their hiding place beneath the console chair, then moved to near the room's only window. If the Scanner was activated by Controller Central, the lens would have to swing sharply to put him within its view, giving him time to get the materials out of sight, and to become active.

After a final glance at the snooping camera, he began thumbing through the old book, checking first its concordance. Then, turning to the passages of his search, he copied the Scriptures:

"When ye, therefore, shall see the abomination of desolation, spoken of by Daniel the prophet, stand in the holy place (whosoever readeth, let him understand), Then let them who are in Judaea flee into the mountains; Let him who is on the housetop not come down to take anything out of his house; Neither let him who is in the field return back to take his clothes. And woe unto those who are with child, and to those who nurse children in those days! " Matthew 24:15-19.

He quickly flipped pages to another section of the book, then transcribed the words:

"Let no man deceive you by any means; for that day shall not come, except there come the falling away first, and that man of sin be revealed, the son of perdition, Who opposeth and exalteth himself above all that is called God, or that is worshiped, so that he, as God, sitteth in the temple of God, showing himself that he is God" 2 Thessalonians 2:3-4.

The ancient predictions, in light of Master Manya's claim to Godhood and INterface's genocidal intentions toward Jews, would have at another time chilled his sensibility. But he was too fatigued now, too numbed by Trachetrol, to wholly assess the Six Ways Plan and how it might fit within the prophetical scheme. The drug was pushing him from the present. He saw, with his swirling memory, the thin, bespectacled face of the man who had warned of the coming system that now bedeviled him.

He fought against the drowsiness, standing, doing calisthenics, then splashing his face with water taken from the tap near the window. He sat down again, his thoughts returning to that night. He failed to see the Scanner come to life and oscillate slowly, first toward the right side of the room then toward him. He saw only the face of Hugo Marchek and heard only the cacophony of voices in conversation, coming from somewhere in Marchek's home...

* * *

"YOU MUST BE MR. JACOB ZEN," said the old man in a voice melodious with good humor. Marchek had to look upward to see Jacob while he reached to his guest's offered hand.

"Yes, sir. Sorry if I've caused any problems by being late."

"Nonsense, young man! Come! Someone is going to have a fatal attack if she does not see you."

Marchek held Jacob's elbow, gently towing him toward the conversational noise. "And did you get your business taken care of?"

The question, offered lightly, was obviously not intended to pry.

"Yes. All taken care of."

"Marvelous! Now maybe our Miss Mossberg can smile again. She has had on her longest face all evening--I presume because you have not been here."

They entered the living room, Jacob looking over the milling guests. Marchek called for their attention and got it.

"Karen. Introduce to us your guest, please," the old man

said, pushing Jacob forward into the arms of the girl, whose smile spoke her feeling for the party's latest arrival. She pulled Jacob aside when the introductions had been made and the others had returned to their various discussions, her eyes flashing a mixture of anger, concern, and relief.

"You could've returned my calls," she said in an irritated whisper, glancing nervously at the other guests, hoping she had not scolded loudly enough for them to hear. "I called your cell four times. I've been worried."

"You mean you're mad because I didn't get here exactly when you thought I ought to, and because I didn't call to check in like you thought I should," he said teasingly.

"Don't tell me what I thought! Or what I mean!" her face reddened and her words spilled angrily into the ears of those nearest them. She didn't care.

Jacob pulled her by her arm to near a corner to get away from the others. "I'm sorry about not returning the calls. There's something wrong with my cell phone." He moved them a few feet farther from the crowd. "What is wrong with you, Karen? Since when do you make so much of a joke?"

Tears trickled in slow, thin streams down her cheeks and he stopped questioning her, pulling her to him and whispering while her face lay against his chest.

"What's wrong, Kay? My being late couldn't have upset you this much."

He pushed her away, holding her firmly by her shoulders and looking into her eyes. "Tell me what's wrong."

She said nothing, but reached into the right pocket of her slacks, took out a wadded piece of paper and handed it to him. He smoothed the paper and silently read the message typed on it.

"YOU AND THOSE YOU LOVE CAN BE ELIMINATED AT ANY TIME. THIS IS TO ADVISE YOU TO CONVINCE MARCHEK TO LEAVE MATTERS VITAL TO NATIONAL

SECURITY TO THOSE WHO KNOW BEST, OR YOU WILL PAY THE CONSEQUENCE OF HIS MEDDLING."

The small piece of paper had markings, he discovered through examination.

It had been ripped from what must have been an 8-1/2" x 11" sheet of white bond, two sides having ragged edges. The type was light and the letters broken in places. The non-uniform crispness of the elite characters told him they were struck with inconsistent pressure due, most likely, to varying degrees of strength in the typist's fingers. The machine must have been an old manual.

"It's just some over-zealous staff member of the NSA. Or it could be from a lobbyist who has investment interests in the UNTVTJS system."

"No!... No!" She shook her head in vigorous disagreement. "That's not all. Come with me."

She led him into the foyer then down the hallway and into Marchek's study. Reaching into the upper left drawer, she withdrew from Marchek's desk a manila envelope and handed it to Jacob. "The note was clipped to this. I found it lying on the valet seat when I stepped out of the shower."

"It wasn't there before?" He opened the envelope and spread its contents about the desktop.

"No. I put my jeans across the seat before I went into the shower, and the envelope was lying on top of them when I came out."

"They're photographs." He spread them farther in order to better make sense of the color prints which were obviously taken with a long-range lens. Each of the prints was marked with black circles, each circle drawn within another circle. A vertical line crossed a horizontal line at each target's center. He looked beyond the simulated telescopic rifle sight to the subjects in the photographs. One showed Hugo Marchek walking in a downtown Washington, D.C. setting with a briefcase under his arm. The others were of Karen leaning over a desk, and of himself, reaching for the driver's-side door of his Volvo.

He studied the prints for several seconds, then put his arms around Karen. "Whoever it is, is just trying to frighten you. They probably figured Dr. Marchek wouldn't react as strongly as you, so they wanted you to find their little package."

"They were right. It worked," she said, holding him tightly.

"As crazy as it sounds, this sort of thing isn't all that uncommon any more in D.C. What some elements can't get in more civilized ways, they'll try to get any way they can. Usually, things like this are done by cowards who operate like rats. They don't have the guts to face someone directly or to follow through on their threats. This is probably the last we'll hear from them."

His words sounded good, but whoever had been in Karen's bedroom had let himself or herself in and out in a professional manner. The photographs had been professionally done, assuring Jacob in his own mind that this was not simply a lightweight attempt to scare off Marchek's group. He saw in her trusting expression that she didn't suspect his fears, and that his bravado had at least somewhat allayed hers.

There was a knock at the study door, and it opened slightly. Hugo Marchek stuck his head through the crack. "I didn't mean to intrude on your privacy, but perhaps we need to discuss the matter which I see you have before you."

"Yes. I agree completely," Jacob said, releasing Karen and turning to face the eschatologist.

"Would you mind, my dear, seeing to my guests?" Marchek said to Karen, hoping to convince her that his need of help in the matter was genuine. She knew it was not, but, after getting an agreeing nod from Jacob, she left the room.

"There is no finer young woman, Mr. Zen."

"I agree. And she is very capable of handling this sort of thing, I assure you, Dr. Marchek."

"Of course she is. But please hear me out." The old man moved to a coffee server which sat on a table near the floor-to-ceiling window of his study "May I pour you some coffee?"

"Yes, thanks."

The task accomplished, he handed Jacob the cup, his pleasant smile dissolving into a look of concern. "You see, Mr. Zen..."

"Please, Jacob."

"Jacob. Karen concerns herself far too much with my welfare. She worries whether I have eaten enough, that I am too thin, that I am lonely, that I work too hard... I wanted to talk with you alone, because, as the one who is closest to her, I feel you will want all the facts possible, to see that she is protected from worry and..."

He let the thought die, returning to the server. He poured himself coffee and sat in the old brown leather chair behind his desk. Jacob sat in a chair directly across the desk from him.

"I have not confided to Karen what I am about to tell you, because I am afraid it would overly concern her. I tell you now only because of my fears for her safety—because she is well known to be involved in our organization, and because there are those who wish Preservers of American Liberty, and me, silenced."

"She told me about these." Jacob pointed to the photographs spread across the desk. "And showed me the note."

"No... No! The things I am speaking of now are things she

knows nothing about. I was praying they would not involve her, but, as you can see, they have."

"They?"

"Those who would silence us. I am not certain myself who they are. They have introduced themselves to me very bluntly, nonetheless."

"They've threatened you before?"

"Three nights ago, two gentlemen came in through the door at the side of my house--the kitchen door. I was working in my study. Large men, dressed in heavy coats, who made no effort to hide their faces. One with black, thinning hair, one with reddish hair and a mustache. The words were, 'Stop meddling in matters which concern only those who know what is best for this country. Quit stirring up trouble for those who are working to keep this the greatest and strongest nation on earth.'

"I replied that, in my opinion, the people have the right to decide for themselves what is in their best interest; that they also have the right to not be intruded upon by persons who illegally enter their homes and make threats against them.

" 'Let me clear that misunderstanding up now,' the one with the mustache said. Then he hit me like this." Marchek demonstrated the attacker's right, back-handed blow. "This is the result," he said, pulling his glasses from his face and turning his head so Jacob could see the deep cut above his right ear, a wound, Jacob guessed, probably caused by a large ring.

"The man who hit me then said that he did not like misunderstandings. That he was leaving his mark to prove that he deals in actions, not words only. The next time, he said, he will not leave me a head from which to bleed. He handed me his handkerchief and said something about how he had always believed that old men were the wisest of all men, and he hoped I did not destroy this belief by failing to do what he and his friend advised. I was, needless to say, wise enough to keep my mouth closed at that moment."

"Did you call the police?"

"I did. They said they would come to make an investigation on the incident when they had taken care of more pressing criminal matters. As I said, that was three days ago. I still have not heard from the police, although I have called several times since, only to be told that a Captain Emory Jackson handles such things in my area of the city and that he has been tied up in other things."

"You can't let this sort of thing go by without getting action taken on it."

"There are ways, of course. I could take it directly to the media, or to some acquaintances in Congress. But to do that would be to use valuable ammunition in shooting at small game. It would be just a tiny personal matter, and that is not what I wish those in the media or my congressional contacts to focus on. It would merely give our detractors reason to offer what they would claim was proof that I am only concerned with furthering my personal ambitions for publicity or whatever. And, too, Karen would be upset terribly — as would the others in PAL. No. I will see that the matter is brought to light when it can be combined with other incriminating data, at precisely the right time."

"But meantime, your life might be in danger. These people sound like the kind you can't fool around with. And Karen... what about her? How long will it be until they do something like that to her? Or worse?"

"This is why I am confiding in you. Your contacts within government are much greater than mine, and can be undertaken with less notoriety. I do not know the ins and outs as you do. Perhaps if you could find where this pressure is coming from, someone of your acquaintance might persuade them to leave Karen alone."

Jacob could see in Marchek's expression, and hear in his gentle tone, that the old man's concern was genuinely not selfish, but was totally for Karen.

"If it's coming from anywhere in any agency I know about, you can believe I will," Jacob said.

"I have tried to persuade her to leave PAL so she will not be a target of this... this attempted extortion. As you might expect, she will not do so."

"And she shouldn't have to, should she? What's it all about, anyway? We still have freedom of expression, don't we? So long as it's done in a legal manner. No, Dr. Marchek, it's these thugs who are a threat to the nation, not your organization. I don't agree with everything you espouse, but you have the right to believe it--to express it, too. I'll get to the bottom of it if there's any way..."

"You refresh an old man's memory with a joyous lesson I learned when I first came to this great country. Maybe, despite working so closely with freedom, I, for a brief moment, forgot our young lady's right to express her thoughts, also. You are right, of course; there have been many people die for that right. We cannot give in to them, no matter what the cost."

Jacob stood and moved to the window before turning to face Marchek. "What I find hard to believe is that anyone would concern themselves enough with your activities to use such strong-arm methods. Forgive me, Dr. Marchek, but from what I've learned my talks with Karen, I don't see your cause, or your capabilities, as posing a significant threat to anybody. I just can't figure why whoever's doing this would go to so much trouble."

"No offense taken, Jacob," Marchek said, a knowing smile crossing his face. "You will not perhaps, grasp my explanation of why my tiny organization looms so largely in the eyes of certain elements — not only in Washington, but in other capitals, as well — why I pose such a threat to them."

"You believe that it's you, personally, they're after? Not the ideology you represent? Not the resistance you throw in their way?"

"It is me they want eliminated, because I am one among a very few who have insight into their master plan for bringing their kingdom into being. And I am, perhaps, the only one who is trying to fight the evil intention of our adversary through political and governmental institutions. How long I will be permitted to oppose them through these channels, I cannot say."

"You're talking about some conspiracy to establish dictatorship?"

"Precisely."

"But, such an undertaking, no matter who did the planning, would be humanly impossible — if you're talking about a western or global dictatorship. The divergent political ideologies, the differences in cultures, the religious differences, the social and national animosities that have been going on for generations—some for centuries. Such a one-world dictatorship couldn't possibly hold up. There wouldn't be enough soldiers on earth to enforce such a system."

"You said the key word, young man. 'Humanly,' you said. It would not be humanly possible, you are right. I assure you, however, it will be inhumanly done. More precisely, it will be supernaturally accomplished. It will be a one-world hell on earth, presided over by the devil himself in the form of a superhuman dictator. This is why they want me eliminated, because I know these things, and because I am dedicated to postponing the establishment of their hellish order."

"And how will that be done?" Jacob inquired.

"Just the babblings of an old religious fanatic?" Marchek asked with a tolerant smile. "Well, this scenario of a final world dictatorship, I cannot claim credit or blame for. This ending to the greatest of all dramas was written by the hand of God himself.

"To answer your question, how will it be done? How shall we accomplish the postponement of Satan establishing his Antichrist government? I am not at all certain it can be done. Notice I said 'postponement of,' not 'stop,' its establishment. I only know I must try to do my part to hold it off as long as possible."

"If it's inevitable, why fight it?"

"For the greatest reason there can be. The salvation of souls. The reason Jesus Christ came to earth."

"Now you've lost me for sure," Jacob said. "What does this... this dictatorship thing have to do with whether a soul obtains salvation?"

"Original sin is at the heart of it all. Eve first fell prey to Satan's deception, then offered the forbidden fruit to Adam, who also partook. Thus, man's fall from grace, from God's perfect righteousness--the only state of existence God can accept in order for His creation to be in perfect harmony with Him. Sin came into the world; therefore, mankind could no longer walk perfectly with his Creator. All people need a Savior, you see."

"Jesus Christ shed His blood on the cross at Calvary. He is that Savior."

"Satan was the author of that imperfection, that sin, and is still its chief encourager, its instigator. Antichrist will be Satan's chosen man to wreak havoc upon all human beings who are left upon the planet when millions of people suddenly vanish from the face of the earth. This is known in the Holy Scriptures as the rapture of believers in Christ."

"Apocalypse will then soon bring hellish terrors after Israel's leadership signs a security covenant with the satanic world leader."

"Times will get so bad during the ensuing seven years of Tribulation that people who accept Christ for the salvation of their souls will suffer greatly. They will be in constant danger. Antichrist will murder them by the millions. And the satanic creature, who will hate Jews because God chose to send the Savior, the Messiah, into the world through the Jewish race, will make Hitler's slaughter of these people seem like child's play by comparison."

"My mission then, Jacob, is to spare as many people as possible from enduring the coming years of holocaust, by calling them to salvation... now. To accomplish this, we must try to buy time through fighting the developing Antichrist system--politically, and every other way possible."

Jacob contemplated the old man's words for a moment, then spoke. "You paint a rosy picture," Jacob said. "Being Jewish, it's doubly rosy."

"There is still time for you, Jacob."

"Yes. Well, as you said, it's a scenario. I prefer to concoct my own."

"It is a scenario in the semantic sense, only. All but the very last of the prophecies in God's Holy Word have come to pass. Studies made even by secular historians reluctantly concede this. We, as human beings, are slavish adherents to scientific empiricism; we pride ourselves on our logic. Is it not logical to conclude that since so many of these prophecies have come to pass, and in such minute detail, the remaining prophecies will also be fulfilled?"

"I haven't seen or heard of the studies you're talking about. I still believe man has to work out his own salvation. I'm afraid I'm a hopeless existentialist."

Marchek's smile betrayed his disappointment. "I am sorry for that, Jacob. But God made us creatures of free will. I must respect your right to believe as you wish."

"You believe, then, that the reason for these threats is that your knowledge of the prophecies threatens this would-be dictatorship? That it's supernatural rather than simply political?"

"You make me sound like a sort of mystic, but I assure you these facts can be learned by anyone who cares to carefully read this book."

Marchek picked up the worn, black, leather-bound volume from one corner of his desk. "It's all here--the answers, from beginning to end."

"I must admit I've never studied the Christian Bible. For that matter, I've seldom looked through the Hebrew texts."

"Your analysis is essentially correct. It is my belief that these people want me eliminated because the knowledge I possess is from the one Being who is more powerful than the master they serve. I am, perhaps, the most vocal, the most directly confrontational opposition to their goals of world totalitarianism. Every moment we can postpone them reaching their objective buys time in which souls are saved from Satan's grasp. He will not tolerate this. His consuming desire is to put as many of God's supreme creations into Hell as quickly as possible, and to put his own throne above the throne of God. Slowing his quest for absolute world domination infuriates him. I believe that at this moment I am the human being who is perhaps the greatest hindrance to him."

"Surely you can't believe that, Dr. Marchek. You seem like a rational man."

Marchek chuckled. "I thank you for your compliment. Most who are kind enough to hear me out are not so kind once I am finished."

"I'm sorry, sir, I didn't mean to imply that you are irrational now that I've heard what you believe."

Marchek smiled broadly and waved in a gesture meant to belay Jacob's embarrassment "Do not concern yourself, young man. There is no offense. I know much of what I have said must sound crazy to one who receives it for the first time." He became more serious. "I do not believe that I am chosen of God for passing judgment on this generation, in the same sense of, say, Moses or Noah. I do not hear the literal voice of God telling me to say this or to say that, or to do this or to do that. No... no. I simply believe that I am fortunate to be in a position to warn of what is coming, according to this."

He held up the Bible. "The words, the truths which God has given to mankind. Anyone who reads can learn the truths. Since I have read and prayed and sought the Holy Spirit's guidance in these matters, I believe I have been given a certain amount of understanding of apocalyptic events, which I am therefore obligated to share with my fellow human beings.

"And because I know these things, I must do what I can to postpone Satan's establishing his kingdom on earth. It is all supernatural, yes; but the supernaturalism is between God and the devil, or, if you will, between good and evil—not between myself and those acting as Satan's agents in threatening me.

"If you think it's Satan who's threatening you, why are you not afraid? Why, if there is a devil, and if he's so powerful, why doesn't he just wave his pitchfork or whatever and destroy you?" There was no sarcasm in the question, rather, genuine puzzlement.

"Because, as I said, my Master is greater than their master. My life, yours, Karen's, anyone's, cannot be taken until the God who created it allows that to happen. 'Christ,' as the Bible says, 'holds the keys to death and hell.'"

"And the others in PAL, do they share these beliefs?"

"You, of course, know Karen does not share my faith in Christ, so naturally she cannot believe as do in the things prophesied in the Bible. At least not the supernatural aspects of what is prophesied. The others, unfortunately, are as skeptical as Karen in these matters. They do, however, see the inevitability of the coming totalitarian state, and we agree that there are a select few who will control it. The natural conclusion, forgetting biblical forecasts, is that one person shall emerge as supreme in that coming world order."

"Why does it have to be a dictatorship? Haven't we come far enough to know how to avoid letting the gangster elements have their way at the top levels of government? If good is more powerful than evil, can't those with honorable intentions control such a world government?"

"What would be the first prerequisite for the establishment of a western bloc, one government union? I mean, a global society which is totally unified, such as, for example, the Unified European States?" Marchek queried.

"The primary prerequisite would probably be for all national entities to agree to relinquish governmental control in favor of a central government comprised of representatives of former national governments."

"And what would this mean in terms of its effects on individual citizens of these many nations? Would they not be forced to relinquish at least some of their former ways of interacting socially, politically, economically, and religiously?"

"I don't know about religiously," Jacob said with a frown of concentration. He walked the distance from Marchek's desk to the big window, then turned, rubbing his chin in further consideration of the question. "Of course they would have to give up some aspects of their former ways of life. But what's the point? The people of this country had to change, too, when they decided to form it. That doesn't amount to dictatorship. It's worked out pretty well, I think."

"Ah, but has the final word, historically speaking, been written on the United States? Do you believe there are lessons to be learned, for benefit of the future, by studying the past? Obviously you do, because a moment ago you made reference to our having learned from past mistakes when you asked if we have not come far enough to keep--how did you say it--gangster elements from having their way in the top echelons of any such world government."

"Yes. I agree that we must learn from past mistakes," Jacob said.

"Then, since the final word is not in on the United States--that is, what will be its fate for good or for evil--would we not be wiser to look in the past to other experiences in analyzing what the actual prospects might be for a future governmental entity of such magnitude as our hypothetical western bloc?"

"Yes. I will concede that."

"Of all the great empires that we could look back to, shall we pick Rome? Ancient Rome?"

"Okay, ancient Rome it is."

"My point is, Jacob, Rome, although beginning as an honorable system administered by and represented by honorable men, degenerated through a series of dictator-ships. The people lost more with each succeeding step in Rome's decline. One man, or at very best a small group of men, almost without exception self-servingly evil, lay at the heart of these successive governments. The same thing can be said for every major empire before and since, with the exception of the British Empire. But, like this country, the final historical word has not been written in the British Empire, which, of course, is no longer a true empire."

"Considering past experience, can we logically conclude that another major empire, undertaken with no matter what honorable intentions, will prove different? Have we ever really learned from the past and applied the knowledge for the benefit of the people? I think not. Lord Acton said it correctly: 'Absolute power corrupts absolutely,' and, I must admit, empirically speaking, Darwin was right; the strongest survive."

"And, equally unfortunately, the strongest is always the most carnivorous, the most evil, because since mankind first fell prey to Satan's great lie--that now man can be his own god--man has tried to become exactly that. He has left God out of his affairs. Therein lies the reason man-made government will never, can never, be ruled over by truly benevolent leaders. That is why God must bring the Messiah into the world at the Second Advent. Then there will be a world government that will, for the first and only time, work for the welfare and peace of all people. It will be the theocracy presided over by Jesus Christ."

"If all that is true, how do you expect anything I say or do to help get these evil forces off your back? I can help fight corruption--but the devil, himself? Even I would have trouble with that one," Jacob said lightly, trying to relieve the somberness Marchek's words engendered.

"Postponement. That is what I seek, my young friend. As Jesus said, 'With God all things are possible!' In the process of your investigation, you will come to your own conclusions about this evil force, as you call it. If your efforts do nothing else, they may benefit you personally, convince you that the only hope is the Messiah. If so, that alone will make it worthwhile to me. But, also, the expression, 'God helps those who help themselves,' applies here. God uses human agents to carry out His work, sometimes willingly on their part, sometimes without them knowing it."

"Working for God, huh? Can't climb much higher than that on the ladder of success."

"Indeed," said Marchek, smiling. "And since you might very well be carrying out a mission for the Supreme, I suggest you study His written orders—the instructions He has left for the world to read and follow."

The eschatologist stood from behind the desk and reached to offer Jacob the Bible. "I would like for you to have this, Jacob. It is a friend who has been with me for many years."

Jacob took the book and thumbed quickly through it. "I don't want to take this. I know it means a great deal to you. I can get one."

"It does mean a great deal to me, but it means a great deal more to me that you make a sincere study of it--that you understand its truths. Consider the prophecies while you try to learn what is happening all around you."

Jacob handed the Bible back to the old man. "Thanks. I'll pick up a copy, I promise."

"Remember, my young friend, 'trust in the Lord with all thine heart, and lean not unto thine own understanding. In all thy ways acknowledge Him, and He shall direct thy paths.'"

CHAPTER 4

J acob sat up, startled, trying to get his bearings. The staccato pounding between his unfocusing eyes, combined with the ultra-shrill screaming inside his skull, forced him to grab his head in an attempt to quell the pain.

He was on the floor near the window of the small room. He had fallen from the chair! The Trachetrol! Had he overdosed?!

The vivid thoughts, or dreams, or whatever they were, of Karen and Hugo Marchek, were driven from his brain by the squeal produced by the biosensor grafted next to the bone at his forehead. He must have been away from the console past the allowed time! Controller Central would increase the intensity of the vibration until the proper response was made or until the skull shattered! Already, the level of pain almost incapacitated him, and his body quivered and spasmed while he struggled to his feet and stumbled toward the console chair. He collapsed to his knees before reaching it, the sharp contact with the rock-hard tile making him feel his kneecaps were crushed. Still, the pain in his head increased with each second that passed, overriding the pain in his knees, and he managed, through an inner strength he somehow found, to pull himself up by gripping the right arm of the INRU console chair.

He fumbled to find the right response key, his index finger barely steady enough to locate, then push it.

The INRU screen came to life; the agonizing throbbing in his forehead stopped instantly.

"John I. Garver, six, six, six, IN, three, one, eight, eight, eight, two, seven, one.

Prepare for Ident. Watcher eight, three, seven, seven."

When the computer voice completed the command, the official symbol of INterface, the sparkling transparent pyramid, with its golden Roman numerals DCLXVT superimposed over a photographically realistic blue and white planet Earth, disappeared and was replaced on the screen by the live image of a dark-clad controller.

The man was a hulking figure whose broad, puffy face looked unnaturally swollen, the billowy jowls made more so by the stiff collar that pinched the fat which spilled over it to form a huge double chin. His heavy brows, above slitted eyelids that barely permitted the tiny black eyes to be seen, slanted downward to the point between his eyes where they co-mingled angrily, creating a constant frown of hatred. He glared into the camera in front of him and leaned forward to within inches of the lens to punch keys, giving Jacob, at the other end of the transmission, a fisheye distortion of the Watcher's face against a backdrop of hectic activity at INterface Watcher Facility 500.

"You are tardy, Sector Coordinator five, five, zero. I hope you enjoyed our little reminder that you must be attentive," the fat man said with pseudo-pleasantness, his sickening smile magnifying greatly when he again reached forward, his fare coming to within inches of the camera lens.

"Sir... it was the Trachetrol... it affected me badly this time," Jacob said timidly.

"Perhaps we should put you on rations. Maybe that would help you learn self-discipline. Or should we eliminate Trachetrol altogether and give the position to one who can appreciate its opportunities and its responsibilities? Perhaps I should call out a Decap Unit and let you join these Jews! Yes... maybe dying is the best way you can serve!"

Any response would only damage his case. Would the Watcher send a controller team for him? Few ever returned from a Controller Facility once they were taken there. What were the chances of avoiding the dragnets should he be able to flee the INRU room without detection? He would have no chance to escape the Allegiant pressed against his forehead, at least not until out of its range. But secretly located monitoring stations were scattered about. It was impossible to know where they were — impossible to escape the Allegiant device. Still, there was the other way, the contingency plan...

"Prepare for Print Ident. Seize Print Plate." said the voice of INterface.

Jacob complied, and the video displayed the results through yellow characters generated a line at a time:

AFFIRM — JOHN I GARVER

SECTOR 550 COORDINATOR — EEE-IIM-3- 1 88827 1

The voice announced,"INterface accepts. IN are you."

With the identification process finished, the video changed again to the Watcher, whose huge face continued to present a surrealistic, convex image because he constantly moved in close to the camera lens to manipulate his control board.

"INterface computer says you are IN five, five, zero. But the final decision on that is up to me," said the man while he continued to tinker with the control board. "How long you will be IN is..." Something on the control panel in front of him interrupted the Watcher's words, and he handled the problem before returning his smug gaze to the camera.

"You will be at Inculcation Room seven, seven, three, Facility Five-Hundred, at twenty-two hundred hours, Sector Controller five, five, zero. Do you think it is within your capability to follow that simple instruction?"

"Yes, Watcher eight, three, seven, seven. May I ask the nature of the matter?"

"You may not!" the INterface Watcher responded angrily. "It will not become your business to know until you are here!"

Jacob watched the bloated face fill the INRU screen, the man's fat arm stretching forward to hit a switch. The screen went black.

Jacob stood from the console chair, his thoughts replaying the abbreviated conversation with the INterface officer. Rarely did a Sector Coordinator, or anyone else, get called to a Watcher Facility. AH business was transacted through INterface Response Unity, except in the instances when Watcher Control wanted to deal in personal matters. Such occasions almost always meant that the one called in would vanish--that all records of his having ever existed would be erased from the perfect memory of INterface Response Unity.

Was this the time to try? To try--despite the Allegiant, the dragnets, the impossible odds--to escape? To go underground if possible and continue the research, linking up with others who still believed something could be done? The fat man told him to come to Facility 500, apparently without escort. Could he use the opportunity to make his try for freedom? But, there was no freedom. They would watch him from the moment he stepped from the INRU room and follow him every step of the way to his rendezvous with...

The Scanner was following his movement around the room! Did the Watchers intend to monitor his every movement until the time he had to leave for Facility 500? Did they want him to sweat it out? Worry about the reasons for his being called in? Was it punishment for his earlier lapse in obedience?

The question of whether to bolt was now moot. He would not get farther than the street if he did try to run.

He wanted, needed, another Trachetrol II fix, but he dared not take one. The danger of the drug's possible effect on his level of consciousness outweighed the raking urge to give in.

Looking toward the cabinet near the window, he gritted his teeth and turned his back on the drug's beckoning. There was still a chance, he fought to convince himself. Still time to run, to get lost in the underground sewer caverns or the hundreds of dilapidating buildings. There were too many hiding places for the controllers to cover without an extensive dragnet, and John I. Garver was not that much of a threat to INterface. Too, the possibility existed that he could talk his way through it. Although his rhetorical abilities suffered from years of nonuse, the basic talent remained. He could, like an athlete, shake off the years of mechanical response in front of a video data terminal, away from contact with other human beings, and recoup enough to verbally dazzle them.

He forced his thoughts from their heights, recognizing them as euphoric after-effect of the Trachetrol high from which he was descending. Next would come depression and total lack of confidence in himself--in everything. Then a return again to euphoria. There was no time for giving in to the manic-depressive swings of the drug's lingering influence. He must ignore them and go on with whatever had to be done. If he must face death at the hands of the controllers, it would not be a slow death, not the kind of death they enjoyed inflicting.

It was 18:26 hours, still time left in the allotted rest period. Good! Still time to prepare for the worst eventuality he might confront at Facility 500.

He glanced again at the digital clock above the Scanner to assure himself his burning eyes had not misled him, then moved to the gray plastic sofa. Glancing over his shoulder, he saw the Scanner's lens follow his movement.

Long ago he had planned for such a contingency. He was, if nothing else, a man who compulsively planned for contingencies, he fleetingly thought, while kneeling to pull a heavy blanket from beneath the sofa. The remaining time left of the rest period, from which the Watcher had called him, would provide opportunity to put his plan into effect. Carefully spreading the blanket across the sofa, he put his body between the Scanner's eye and his work. Yes. There it was. The thick belt he placed there seven months ago, along with the four round, hard objects and wires. He slid between the blanket and the sofa, at the same time pulling the plastic belt from its taped position against the blanket. The squirming to get comfortable--so far as the Watchers monitoring his activity should be concerned--allowed him to secretly slip the belt around his waist and attach it securely by squeezing together its plastic mesh clasp. He felt for the battery-pack and the wires that ran through the plastic belt covering and into the explosive material, to ensure they were still in place. He then ran his index finger along the pouch containing the batteries until he found the snap. Unsnapping the flap, he probed for the metal clasp that covered the tiny button which would, when depressed, force the wires in the explosive to make contact with the battery terminals. The resulting explosion should take out anything and anyone within 15 feet.

He clamped the button's cover shut. They would not only be deprived of the pleasure of watching him dance the death-dance to their tune, they would be dispatched into the deepest reaches of eternal hell, as well. He pulled the uniform jacket-shirt over his waist, concealing the explosive belt. The bulkiness of the jacket would hide the belt during a quick frisking by the controllers, but a more ambitious search would betray the secret. By that time, though, the button would be pushed.

In less than three-and-a-half hours, his lifetime of wondering about death, eternity, God, might be answered. Hugo Marchek's beliefs about afterlife proved—or—disproved. Or, nothingness... Anything had to be better than this, and the thought, strangely, provided relief. A single tear rolled slowly down his cheek while he lay with his back to the INRU and the still-activated Scanner. He didn't know why. Anger? Anticipation of what he faced? Separation from Karen? ...sweet, lovely Karen. That night, Karen's look of disgust had amused him while they turned from Hugo Marchek's sharply dipping driveway, the front bumper brace of his car crunching against the concrete curb. She had been mad, and his favorite thing to do when Karen was mad was to keep at her until her anger turned to laughter. He had tried for the first two miles, but she had maintained her solemn expression.

* * *

"SENDING me out of the room like a stupid schoolgirl!" she said, finally breaking her silence. "And you! You went along with it!"

"Come on, Kay. He didn't want to worry you. You knew I'd tell you all about it later."

Her mood mellowed while she studied her fingernails.

"Worry me? What does he think? That I'll fold like some over-protected plantation owner's daughter out of the antebellum South? I think I can handle anything you can handle."

"That's what I told him, but he's from a different time, Karen." He touched her chin and turned her face toward him. "The women were to be protected from the Yankees. Did it hurt so much to humor the old guy?"

She pulled from his grip and again studied her nails for a moment before looking at him. "It's one of the few things about him I don't like."

"You're a granddaughter to him... to be protected. He loves you very much, or he wouldn't go to the trouble."

"I know."

"That makes him one of my favorite people," Jacob said.

"I knew you'd like him," she said, sounding happier. "I'm glad you do, Jacob. You both mean a lot to me." She leaned across the console to kiss him on the cheek.

"Friends again?" He held out his hand, offering to shake hers.

"That won't do." She slapped his hand aside and moved as close to him as the console would allow, then kissed his neck. "Can't wait to make up," she whispered in his ear.

She turned serious again. "I know about Dr. Marchek's visit from those hoodlums."

"How?"

"His transcriber. He left his dictation from that night on the machine. He sounded like he was still woozy from what those animals did. The first thing I do when I get to his study in the morning is check his transcriber, because he leaves random notes recorded. Most of them, he forgets about. I was going to tell you about those men when we were in his study, but he came in and you two ran me out."

"I should've known nothing gets past you."

"He was right; it did worry me. He doesn't lie, you know.

He told me he fell down and bumped his head, which I'm sure was true. He fell after they hit him."

"You can't blame him for wanting to keep you out of it."

"But I *am* in it, and he has to have somebody."

"He does have somebody," Jacob said. "He has us."

She kissed him and there were tears in her eyes.

"He asked me to look into who might be harassing you. Who those two goons might be — what agency they might come from."

"We must be getting close to something, but I can't figure what can be so important that they'd do these kinds of things. There are all kinds of lobbyist groups with more clout than PAL."

"I agree. So does he."

"Then who?"

"He attributes it to Satan," Jacob said, smiling.

"He would! Yes. Satan, to him, is behind all of it," she said, shaking her head incredulously. "He really believes that, too."

"He wanted to give me his Bible to study... said all of the answers are in it," Jacob chuckled.

"What if he's right?" Her question was offered only half-joking.

"I hope he is, because the good will win out in the end, if that's the case."

"On the other hand," she continued the banter, "a lot of people could be in pretty serious trouble, considering that book's judgments on premarital and extramarital sex, homo-sexuality, occultism, and all the other things it condemns that this world loves so much."

"But look at it this way, if both heaven and hell have voting privileges in some eternal election process, hell will hold a majority, I'll wager."

"Gambling's a sin."

"Yeah? Guess my party affiliation is a foregone conclusion, then."

"He has a point," she said, her tone serious again. "He believes that the devil's human agents, that is, the agents the devil has used to his best advantage, are the money powers. 'The love of money is the root of all evil,' he always tells me and anyone else who'll listen." She tried to imitate Marchek's accented speech.

"Greedy money interests have been at the bottom of a lot of conflicts. I'll concede that."

"He's absolutely convinced that Satan has controlled the minds of the huge banking houses and conglomerates right up to the present giants of finance. He believes that is where the nucleus of the movement toward a diabolical world order can be found. They, with their knowledge and control of developing computer and communications technologies, are behind it all."

"For as long as I can remember, as a student and since I've worked in government, I have heard of conspiracy by a select group of financiers. The Trilateral Commission, the World Bank, the Council on Foreign Relations, all the others. It's just like the Second Coming. Everyone talked about it, but where is it? Big money interests have always been part of the overall problem, but we can look to politicians, to the military, to the media, to each one of us, individually. We've all helped create the problem of money controlling the affairs of men."

"That strengthens his contention that these people who know the ins and outs of high finance have the greatest potential for controlling, should a world government be formed."

"Yes. They've always controlled, and always will as long as people put so much importance on material things," he agreed, glancing into the rear-view mirror at the bright headlight beams closing fast on them. "But I don't believe the top people in finance have deliberately set out to control the world in any destructive way, any more than I believe that they are satanically controlled, or that there's a superman who's going to rule any such government." The lights moved closer and were blinding him, and he reached to adjust the angle of the mirror.

"What's wrong with those people...?" Karen's words were interrupted by a crunching jolt.

The Volvo leaped violently forward, causing Jacob to nearly lose his grip on the steering wheel. The car swerved across the white stripes separating the southbound lanes of State 355 before he managed to regain control. His lower back spasmed with pain; he felt as if his entire body had been compressed. He looked at Karen. She was struggling to rise from the floorboard. He looked into the mirror to see the vehicle closing again. A huge, broad vehicle, its glaring lights too high to be those of a car. The raging machine struck again, more violently than before, throwing the girl against the dashboard, but having less effect on him than did the first impact.

Jacob planted his feet firmly and gripped the wheel tightly to prepare for the next jolt.

"Karen!" He looked quickly to see her body's involuntary lurching movements caused by the car's careening. The interior of the Volvo brightened with the beams--then contact. Karen's unconscious body jumped against the dash, then thudded onto the floorboard.

Jacob swerved hard to the right, and the right front of the pursuing vehicle missed the Volvo's left rear fender by inches. He jammed the brakes, and the truck shot past in a blur of light and roaring engine noise.

Karen was hurt! He couldn't stop to help her now; the maniac would crush them! He hit the brakes again, coming to a complete stop, then he stomped the accelerator to the floor and at the same time whirled the steering wheel sharply to the left. The car shot forward, leaving the truck where it had come to a stop in front of its intended victim.

Jacob had a good lead, but was headed north now--the wrong way in the southbound lane--with no way to get off, because both sides of the highway were bordered at that point by high concrete retainer walls. No chance to get off for at least four miles! The thought ricocheted through his mind while he glanced into the mirror to see the headlights far behind.

"Karen!" He tried to help her onto the seat, but she would not respond. He could see a bloodied abrasion high on her forehead and thought he saw her eyes open, then shut again. Her seat belt! Why had she not buckled up?

No time now to attend to her. The Volvo could easily outrun the heavier machine. He would cross the median where the retainer walls ended. The maniac could not keep up then; the Volvo, with its superior cornering and handling, would have the advantage.

The maniac! Until now, Jacob's panicked brain had only considered the dilemma in terms of random circumstance--someone gone berserk on drugs, or drunk at the early morning hour of two o'clock on a deserted highway. The distance he had put between himself and the would-be killer permitted him to consider the more logical probability. Was this act somehow connected to things discussed just before the attack? The Marchek contentions? Was this the time Karen had been warned of, when she and those she loved would pay the price for interference? Jacob felt a vibration. The car's engine was running erratically, causing it to slow down, then speed up once more as the motor faltered, rallied, then performed smoothly again. "No!"

The headlights were closer! He looked at the gas gauge.

More than half full. The collision had jarred something loose--maybe the fuel injection system. Still two-and-a-half miles or more before the walls ended, and the headlights were brighter--the hunter closing in on its prey!

The Volvo's motor chugged erratically and sputtered down, sounding as if it were missing on two cylinders, then caught again and raced to full power. The engine was running more roughly by the second! The car lurching now, sputtering back to life... running more smoothly now... almost dying!

Brilliant light again made it difficult for him to distinguish anything in the rear-view mirror. The big vehicle was three-quarters of a mile back, but still its lights blinded him! What were the alternatives? Only two. Limp straight ahead and try to reach the end of the retainer walls before the on-storming machine caught up. But even if he could make it, his car's loss of power would allow the heavier vehicle to catch up. The Volvo might die, probably would die, if he didn't keep the accelerator fully depressed. The other alternative...stop, quickly get Karen from the car and over the wall, and hide from the attacker. But the truck was much closer now. Karen's limp body would be almost impossible to handle in the time required. Nothing but open space in the neatly mowed ditches outside the concrete walls. No place to hide!

Headlights topped an incline in the distance, sitting high off the ground...possibly the lights of a large truck. Maybe a bus, its lights blinking off and on rapidly, warning Jacob he was traveling the wrong way. The approaching vehicle was within 100 yards, the truck pursuing had closed to within 90. A third alternative! The indecision effect! It was selfish — if it worked. If the oncoming vehicle was a bus, and if it did work, many might die.

Put it into effect at the last possible second! Use the

strange human mental quirk to advantage. Like times when people meet face-to-face on a sidewalk and fall into the indecision effect, not knowing whether to move right or left-- finally breaking into a slow, foolish dance until one steps to the side and allows the other to pass. Would it work similarly with vehicles coming toward each other? Would it work now?

Time only for the one move that might save them, save Karen. The attacker was within 50 yards, the oncoming vehicle much closer... Time to execute!... Only one chance!... *Now!*

Jacob swerved the Volvo to the left, putting it directly in front of the onrushing machine. He saw in that terrifying instant that it was a gigantic tractor trailer rig. Seventy yards... sixty! The Volvo rushed forward, sputtering and lurching toward the deadly lights. The beams of the pursuing machine were offset to the Volvo's right rear, still in the right lane. The oncoming truck swerved to its left, into the lane with Jacob's nemesis, trying to avoid colliding with the car. The attacker cut sharply into the left lane behind Jacob, and closed to within 30 yards of the Volvo's rear.

The huge oncoming truck was weaving, its driver trying to recapture stability. At the precise moment his instinct told him to act, Jacob whipped the car across the dividing line and directly in front of the massive tractor. There were no more than 70 feet between them. The diesel's driver, equally out of instinct, jerked the wheels of the rig hard to his right and the truck crossed the white line into the lane with Jacob's pursuer.

Looking into the side mirror, Jacob watched the tractor-trailer miss him by less than a yard. His attacker had neither the time nor the reflexes to swerve to the right. The darkness framing the hulks of metal gave him clear view in the mirror when they came together in a night-rending flash. The maneuver had worked! He saw the exploding vehicles scatter and carom off the concrete walls and into the deep ditches beyond.

He brought the car to a stop and pulled Karen into the seat. She was regaining consciousness and he smoothed the hair from her forehead to better see the wound. The abrasion was superficial, but the discoloration around it indicated a deep bruise.

"Karen! Are you okay?" He whispered the words and dabbed the wound gently with his handkerchief, wanting her to regain her senses calmly.

"Yes... I think so."

"It's okay, Sweetie. Just sit still."

She sat upright with his help and touched his fingers, which held the handkerchief over the wound. "Is it bad?"

"No. I don't think so," he lied, thinking there could be a concussion. "But we're going to have it looked at just to be safe."

The brightness in the car made her curious about the source of light and she looked around to see the burning wreckage. "What happened?"

"Whoever was trying to run us down got what was coming to him. He hit a semi-rig head on. I'd better go see what I can do for them. Stay here, and keep still. Do you think it's okay to leave you for a few minutes?"

"I'll be okay," she said, smiling weakly.

He trotted from the car, looking back to see several sets of oncoming headlights. He wanted there to be, by some miracle, something he could do for the driver of the diesel, but the heat of the wreckage quickly proved too intense, and he backed away. Both drivers were either killed instantly by the impact or burned alive while their mangled, mashed cabs held them prisoner. He hoped--at least for the sake of the driver of the big rig--that the end came quickly.

Blue and red lights whirled now near where he left Karen. State troopers ran toward him, along with curious travelers who had stopped.

"You see this happen?" one of the officers asked. "Is that your Volvo back there?"

"Yes to both questions."

"Why is your car pointed north, sir? This is a southbound lane."

"I know it's the southbound side," Jacob said, irritated by the trooper's suspicious tone.

"Then why is your car headed north?" The man moved nearer and looked more closely at Jacob.

"Because I couldn't get by the wreck. I turned around so I could go find help," he lied.

"They're finished, Sarge," a trooper who walked back from near the wreckage informed the officer questioning Jacob. The sergeant nodded acknowledgment.

"May I see your UNIVUSCARD?"

Jacob handed him the card, and the man looked at the photograph, then eyed Jacob warily. "You been drinking, or taking some other substance, Mr. Zen?"

"No, I haven't."

"Why is your car so beat up in the rear? Those dents look fresh."

"It happened some time earlier... last night. Somebody hit it while it was parked at a friend's house."

A helicopter thumped overhead and the sergeant looked up, as did Jacob, seeing the chopper's brightly lit belly hovering almost directly above them. The trooper removed a walkie-talkie from his belt and pulled the antenna to full extension.

"Looks like a seven-sixty three, sir. You want a zebra on the zero? Over!"

The communicator squawked in response. "Negative. Over and out!"

Jacob watched the bird whirl away, its red and green position lights rapidly shrinking, then vanishing into the blackness.

The man handed him the UNIVUSCARD. "We've blocked off 355 at the end of the walls. You'll be able to get on the access road there."

Jacob started to call to the officer, who had walked away toward the wreckage and begun talking with two other troopers. He thought better of it. Something rooted deeply in his subconscious reasoning troubled him, and made him know the best thing to do at that moment was to get Karen away from there. He didn't know what lay at the bottom of his worry, but the apprehension-- maybe even fear--weighed heavily on his thoughts while he turned to have a last look at the holocaust scattered across State 355, and at the three uniformed men silhouetted against the flames. At the charred frame of the machine that had nearly killed them.

The full impact of the past minutes hit him, and he began to shake. The dark outline within the blazing mass was clearly that of a heavy tow truck, its semi-molten skeleton twisting in the flames like black, groping fingers reaching from the bowels of hell.

Karen sat groggily beside him while they crossed the Potomac on the Theodore Roosevelt Memorial Bridge, the drug given her by the emergency room doctor 30 minutes earlier doing little to ease the throbbing in her head.

"We'll stay at Stone Oaks for a couple of days. There's always a doctor on call for Uncle Conrad since he's been helping the President. The doctor said you need watching for 24 hours or so." Jacob kept to himself his thoughts about the small army of Secret Service and military guards at the old mansion; her safety would be ensured there.

"We've got to call Dr. Marchek!" Karen sat up with the sudden realization that the old man might be in danger. She grimaced and laid her head back gingerly against the headrest.

"He's all right, Kay. I called him while you were on the table getting patched up. He said to tell you not to worry about him."

The lie was best for her at the moment. He would, in fact, call Marchek when there was time.

Her pretty face reflected lights from approaching traffic, and he saw his words had calmed her. Despite feeling more relaxed himself since the early morning rush began along George Washington Memorial Parkway, Jacob nonetheless kept a nervous watch in the rear-view mirror for the lights he could never see again, but which he would not likely forget, headlights now part of an incinerated heap being trucked to some distant refuse dump. Those who died in the tow truck, though, had friends, and Stone Oaks would provide haven for Karen while he found out who those friends were.

* * *

AT THE SAME HOUR, Jacob and Karen could not know that Hugo Marchek stood looking out his huge study window into the stillness of the early morning at what would in spring be a garden of flowers bursting with color. Now, the grounds lay dark and gray and lifeless, with only a faint, misty illumination to prove they were more than nothingness. He looked but saw little, his mind on the ancient, musty volumes piled atop the scarred table at the center of the room.

An antique lamp with a single 40-watt bulb barely dented the darkness of the study while the old man began thumbing studiously through the books, squinting at the tiny print. He occasionally had to use a magnifying glass, drawing it near, then pushing it away from his face to make readable the words on the yellowed pages.

A small fire, now in its final stages, flickered within the smoke-blackened fireplace, its embers growing darker and collapsing in their degeneration to ashes.

Marchek slowly raised his head, sensing the presence nearby of someone or something in the old home. His eyes closed in a deeper squint, the age wrinkles becoming valleys in the sparse light, when he tried to pierce the darkness of the hallway.

"Saryeva! Is that you?" he called, then stood from the table, craning his neck to hear noises he thought might be coming from the kitchen, the area through which his sister must pass in order to enter. He glanced at his pocket watch. It was most likely not Saryeva; she would not be traveling about, alone, at this hour. Besides, she was spending the weekend with her sister, Katherine, at Silver Spring. Marchek's watch read 5:08. No, it was not Saryeva he heard.

Negotiating the distance from the study to the kitchen was easy for him. His vision, growing worse by degrees over the past few years, forced him to incorporate feel as part of getting around in areas not completely free of obstacles, and though the totally dark hallway made two turns, he moved swiftly and surely, stopping only after he reached the door to the kitchen to flip one of the several light switches on the hallway wall.

Something exploded in front of him, causing his heart to leap. The floor and cabinet, the air around him, swirled with an opaque whiteness. He strained to see through the cloud.

"Isaac!"

He smiled downward at the big tomcat, who stared up whitely from the floor, his yellow coat covered with flour.

"So, old friend, I am getting senile. I did not remember to put you out for your evening's carousing."

He lifted the feline from the floor, holding it at arm's length to brush the powder from its fur. "I guess I subconsciously want you not to disgrace your good biblical name. Lord knows what goes on out there with you and your friends." He held the cat close to him, scratching it behind its badly scarred ears and examining a recently acquired wound. "And to make matters worse, you missed the mouse, yes?" He walked from the kitchen stroking the animal, stopping to switch off the lights before walking down the hallway. "We will put you out in the garden. How will that be?"

Now he could move without following the oak runner along the wall with his fingertips. The lamp in the study, despite its limited output, gave enough light for him to stay centered in the walkway. The cat purred easily against him, moving its head to take maximum advantage of his human friend's massaging fingers. Suddenly the animal stiffened, causing Marchek to lose his grip on the cat. It emitted a low growl, then a nerve-racking scream! It dug its claws into Marchek's arms and abdomen, then into the side of his face, the animal lunging upward onto his shoulder. It ripped viciously into his back, when it let its bottom half reverse toward the floor to break its fall. The old man shrieked, grabbing his lacerated face.

His glasses had been knocked to the floor by the animal's violent action, and he searched the dark hallway for them in sweeping movements of his hands. Finally finding them, he put them on his nose, then stood, dazed, nearly staggering from the experience. The cat was gentle; it had never reacted in this manner before.

He touched his face and felt the warm, slick wetness of his blood, smelling its cupreous odor. The feeling returned; he was not alone in the house. Something cold, unspeakably sinister...something he had long known to exist but had never experienced through his natural senses until now. Chills spread across his body, tightening the skin on the back of his neck and his scalp while he made his way along one wall of the hallway.

"Dear God, give me grace," he whispered just before step- ping into the opening to the study. The light from the lamp flickered, then went out. He stood stiffly in the arched entranceway, his eyes drawn to the fireplace embers that suddenly rekindled to flame, which grew until it seemed he was looking into hell itself!

A warm calm flooded his mind and body. All fear was gone. He could face the intruding force with courage and dignity.

"So," he said in a strong voice, his eyes darting from behind the thick glasses to see into the shadows around him. "You have at last been allowed to come to me!" He moved to the center of the study, then turned slowly to see his nemesis.

"Take my life. But it is I who shall live again to judge you!" He shouted the words with hatred. "The sentence will be everlasting death--yet eternal pain. Death without its peace! Do with me what you will. I shall, through Jesus Christ, prevail!"

* * *

McLean looked good to him in the mistiness of dawn, when he nursed the badly missing Volvo through a shopping district and past the sprawling, immaculately groomed estates, finally coming to the one belonging to Conrad Wilson. Jacob was home, and like the times he had come before, from camp or college or dates, it was expansively welcoming, the massive oaks and hickories holding out their now almost leafless, black arms, beckoning him through the gate and into a home warmed as much by the man he loved like a father as by the hearth always ablaze this time of year with fire especially prepared for the homecoming.

"Hello, Mr. Zen," the man in the dark suit said with a tight smile.

"George." Jacob nodded and handed the Secret Service agent his and Karen's UNIVUSCARDs.

"Thank you, sir. You have some trouble?" the agent asked, seeing the girl's bandaged head and the car's damaged rear portion. "Just a rear-ender. We're okay," Jacob said.

The agent walked back into the guardhouse after returning the cards. Karen marveled at the elaborate television equipment, the many monitors on the guardhouse walls and the television cameras sitting at different points along the top of the thick concrete and stone fence rimmed with wrought-iron spikes. "I heard the President once say in a press conference that Conrad Wilson was a national resource, but I thought he was joking. Just look at this!"

"It's been like this since he began taking on jobs for the Administration. He doesn't want it this way, but they insist."

The heavy sculptured iron gate swung open and Jacob urged the chugging car onto the brick drive and toward the old mansion 100 yards in the distance.

CHAPTER 5

Karen rested her cheek against the side of his chest and used a tissue to dry her tears. Jacob held her close and looked past her, out the dark window of the funeral limo, seeing the small white mausoleum in which Hugo Marchek's body had 20 minutes earlier been entombed. Now, only the minister and a few family members stood near the crypt while a caretaker locked its iron-barred door-gate. Light rain fell from heavily overcast skies and ran in many rivulets down the window. Karen's body suddenly shook and she began to cry bitterly.

Jacob's forehead vibrated with the shrill call: INterface Watchers putting all Sector Coordinators on notice that there were duties to perform. It was the gentler prodding by the masters, calling him not from the forbidden over-dosed state, but from the authorized time of rest. Two opposite emotions kneaded his dulled senses while he struggled to fully know his present circumstance. He was pleased he did not have to relive Karen's agony over losing the old man she loved even more than she realized. This was a loss which he, too, felt with great pain. But, at the same time, he ached with the realization that he was not with her.

No time for regret, for remembrance; there was time only to do that demanded of him. He could afford no further slip-ups if he was to survive to kill some of the enslavers and himself. Feeling the belt of plastic explosives brought him fully back to reality. He pulled the hip-length jacket over the belt and smoothed the material before removing the blanket and standing from the hard sofa.

Electronic impulses again vibrated his skull, and he saw the INRU Scanner's lens rotate, following his limping move-ment to the console chair, his knees bruised and aching from his fall. What did they want of John I. Garver this time? It pleased him to be able to think clearly enough to separate himself from the assumed identity--something he had found hard to do for many months, thanks to Trachetrol II. Could it be that this call was a pardon for the earlier sin of having not instantly answered his master's beckoning? Not likely; INterface was, if anything, unforgiving. Watcher Control most likely figured to use him until the time of his erasure from the system, simply because it was not expedient to send another Sector Coordinator to do the required surgery on behalf of INterface.

When he pressed the appropriate key, the screen, which had displayed the pyramid symbol, changed to a map of Sector 550, each of its 66 geographical portions graphically represented, separated by black lines drawn on a field of bril-liant yellow. The computer voice informed him:

"John I. Garver -- six, six, six, IN, three, one, eight, eight, eight, two, seven, one.

Identification will not be effected. Video Scanner perceives -- IN are you. Prepare to receive visual.

Subject: Enemies to be excised from INterface Response Unity. Respond."

Excision! How he did hate them! How he wished to have all the perverted, abscessing monsters within range of the explosive! Should he defy them? Refuse to do it? Sickness burned in the pit of his stomach, in his soul—if such an entity existed.

How many must be excised this time? Cut off from all food, medical help, and clothing by a mere flick of a finger, erasing them from INterface Response Unity. Cut from the computer's memory—the children, no older than three or so, born after the great disappearance, the dissipation that took all the other children.

"Respond!" the voice demanded, interrupting the tortured thoughts of what complying with the order would mean to the poor creatures at his mercy—people already crazed with worry and hunger and disease. He had no choice; he had to respond as commanded. They would come and do the job themselves, otherwise, and his chance to carry out his plan against the murderers would be lost.

He looked at the digital clock above the Scanner's lens "13:21." He pushed the key on his console.

"Response noted," said the synthesized voice.

He computed silently. It was 7:21— 2 hours, 39 minutes until the confrontation at Facility 500.

Much of the nerve-twisting guilt feeling left him; hatred for those forcing him to commit the atrocity consumed it. Justification for his action would come when he sacrificed himself at Facility 500 to avenge what he must now do.

"Identifier Numbers belonging to enemies within your Sector are being file-interrogation programmed."

"Acknowledge feed."

Jacob pushed a key on the console board and gave the verbal response called for. "Feed perceived."

"Filemark -- Now!" the computer said.

The screen filled with hundreds of Identifier Numbers

belonging to enemies, who would shortly be deprived of access to the INterface computer network.

"Filemark noted," Jacob said.

"Sector 55D infection coming visual -- Now!"

The Response Unit's screen again displayed the black-outlined, yellow map. Hundreds of red points of light flashed, showing Jacob and Controller Central the precise location of every person to be cut from INterface Response Unity. Each subject had the biosensor implanted beneath the skin of the forehead or on the back of the right hand, the sensor programmed with data that included his or her Identifier Number and a Universal Product Code, which, when scanned by a Product Decoder, gave access to commercial computers throughout INterface for transacting day-to-day business. The need to carry easily stolen or lost cards was thus eliminated. Jacob's action would instantaneously destroy the Universal Product Code portion of the Allegiant implanted within each person selected for excision. The Identifier Number would not be affected, but would remain activated, enabling the state to keep track of the excised subject until his or her death.

"Execute!" the computer voice commanded.

He pressed a red button above the Interact keys and saw on the monitor the results.

"Excision completed," he reported, seeing the flashing red lights change to steadily glowing green ones. Hundreds of them, each representing a human being who was no longer 77V.

"Lock toggle guard before end of Interact," the voice warned with dispassion equal to its previous order.

He pulled the red metal guard to a covering position over the Excision Button to prevent accidentally eliminating commercial computer access for loyal citizens.

The clock above the Scanner Eye displayed 19:35 hours,

which was only 25 minutes until, possibly, his own elimination. He was more fortunate than those he had seconds ago victimized.

One shattering instant would send him and as many as he could take with him at Facility 500 into eternity. What about eternity? Would it be an improvement? He did not know why he considered such things at this moment, but the words written in the book ran swiftly through his mind:

"...And that no man might buy or sell except he that had the mark, or the name of the beast, or the number of his name..."

Why remember the words so clearly? He had not memorized them. Was it some preternatural phenomenon? The eschatologist calling to him from the grave? No. Marchek would say he was not in the grave. His essence was some other place—Heaven? Was Marchek reaching out to him from Heaven? Marchek's spirit nudging Jacob toward some deity-directed conclusion?

"Watch after Karen... sweet, lovely Karen," the voice urged, as if it spoke within the echo chamber that was his skull. The voice... Marchek's... The mental image... Karen's beautiful face. He had finally lost his reason.

He stood from the console chair, sweat streaming profusely from his face and body. He did not notice the perspiration, feeling instead the terrible cold of his isolation.

It was the drug, or rather the lack of it, he thought, shaking off his depression, suddenly desperate to go to the Trachetrol. Wanting to turn the bottle's bottom to the ceiling and down as many of the capsules as he could swallow. To die in a state of drugged self-immersion—to be baptized into the black, bottomless waters from which there could be no return. No INterface, no Master Manya--no excisions to perform.

He stopped his downward cerebral plunge. Such a death

would be one of defeat. There was enough of his spirit left to see his plan through to the end that he chose... not one that the grisly computer-state chose for him.

The Trachetrol's call to him eased, but he moved from the console chair toward the cabinet, as if defying its pull with direct confrontation that would fortify his resolve to beat the addiction. He stood peering through the window, its panes stained by the pollution-saturated atmosphere that engulfed the entire globe. Below, on the deteriorating street, several people walked to whatever destination each sought, most holding cloths to their mouths and noses to prevent inhaling the filth rushing toward their lungs with each labored breath. A bicycle bumped along one pocked street, its rider, his head down, watching for the biggest of the holes in his path. He seemed, along with the black Decap Unit that passed by the bicycle, to personify life within INterface society. Symbolized in hybrid purity, the oppression of all tyrannical states to which mankind had ever been subjected. What life had, finally, come down to.

Suddenly a 20-foot section of facade broke free from the rim of the building directly across the street from his window and shattered into a thousand pieces against the sidewalk and street; the man and the bicycle were instantly crushed.

The Decap Unit slowed, the controllers watching the cloud of dust billowing behind them, then continued on its way at its former speed.

Jacob thought of the Trachetrol in the drawer of the cabinet at his side. How he did want the Trachetrol! Had he, like the world around him, degenerated to this? Forgotten humanity? Turned from even a hint of concern for human plight, like the controllers who drove uncaringly away from the poor devil lying squashed beneath the rubble on the street? Like Jacob Zen had turned from thoughts of the crushed man to thoughts of fixing his craving for the drug, which the monster-state provided so the inhumanity could continue with as little opposition from its victims as possible? He wanted to be sickened and repulsed by his own insensitivity to the man's dying, but all he desired, in fact, was to swallow the capsule.

He managed, after watching the tremendous dust cloud thin then become a part of the already thickened, to turn his thoughts to the first time he saw the deadly tentacles of the monster break out of its cocoon of technological promise.

"I assure you, Jacob, the thing defies the imagination, even to someone as inventive as Horstz Buckingham. He got so hyper the first time he saw it, I thought he would have a stroke on the spot. Couldn't praise it enough."

"The same Buckingham who never liked anything done by anybody except himself? That is saying something for it."

"It's that critical striving for perfection that's made him the top U.S. scientist in these developing international linkage technologies," Conrad Wilson said.

"His endorsement makes me even more anxious to have a look. I'm honored that you've let me come along."

"It was the President's idea, not mine. Your hard work and ability earned you this trip."

"I hope I can contribute something."

"If you couldn't, he would never have asked you to come with me. Relax, and remember our motto: "The race can't be won, by a man who won't run and go till it's done!'"

Wilson was obviously happy to see the smile come on Jacob's face when the old man quoted the saying the two of them used often during the younger man's childhood.

Filling the student's head with such apothegms was part of the Wilson methodology, and it pleased Jacob that his mentor still took delight in tutoring him.

"I remember another little gem... "Nobody loves a conceited fool, but the fool who is himself!"

Wilson laughed. "Yes, I suppose I always have had one for most all occasions, haven't I? And, as I recall, that one was well placed."

"And taken to heart," agreed Jacob. "It was tough learning that I was not, in fact, the finest quarterback ever to play at Middlebrook Prep."

"The coach said you would in time be a good one, but that first you had to learn to forgive the trespasses and dropped passes of your teammates..."

"I thought I was a real leader of men back then," Jacob interrupted. "Coach Dibetto was quick to point out that I was slightly off in my evaluation of one Jacob Zen. But you know what?" He looked at Conrad Wilson. "What bothered me most, I should say, what really brought home to me that I had erred, was: 'No one loves a conceited fool, but the fool who is, himself!' It was the first time I had seen you disappointed with me."

"You were as good a son as a man could want," the old diplomat said, patting Jacob's knee. "Still are!"

"I determined right then to shut my mouth and concentrate on making Jacob Zen somebody you wouldn't be ashamed of. I didn't always stick to it, but it did make me a bit more humble, I think."

"Your gifts are considerable, my boy. And it's time for you to put self-doubts aside, where your value to the President and Project Eagle is concerned. We've got quite a job ahead of us. This trip to Brussels is absolutely crucial to our getting a governing handle on terrorism and the economic problems, but it's much more critical that we get the upper hand in this Euro-American unification process. Now, you certainly wouldn't have been chosen for something so important if you weren't qualified—no matter what kind of pull you have."

Jacob said nothing, but felt his nervousness growing. He wished he had confidence equal to the ability with which his foster father credited him.

"Miss!" he called to the hostess, who had just served a passenger several rows forward. A drink seemed in order.

Thirty-seven minutes later, he had managed to calm himself. The captain's voice, announcing the approach to Brussels, startled him out of what was on the verge of becoming a sound sleep, and he straightened, rubbing his eyes.

"There it is, over there," Conrad Wilson said, motioning with a nod of his head; Jacob looked out the window next to him. What had centuries before been a city of symmetrical, pentagonal configuration with a sparse population now sprawled mightily, looking to Jacob like a giant amoeba.

"A real paradox—Brussels and the European Union," Wilson said. "It's one of the most disruptively divided cities in history with an almost feud-like hostility between the Flemish and Walloons. Sort of the whole of European disunity in microcosm. Yet the EU, and now the organizational nucleus for an even more pronounced effort at unification, resides in this very city, as well as in European Rome. It's a case of split personality. On the one hand, they adhere religiously to local governmental sovereignty and linguistic autonomy, divided between chiefly Flemish and French-speaking folk. On the other hand, Brussels seems to possess this mysteriously magnetic force that pulls all of Western Europe, and now the entire trilateral sphere, toward free-world union.

"Only it's not really so mysterious, I think. The real power is economic power. There are more than 500 U.S. companies in the city, not to mention the hundreds of major European and Japanese corporations represented here. Last count, there were some 39,000, employing more than 700,000 people. That doesn't take into account the thousands of subsidiary jobs like craftsman-type people working in the tourist and luxury trades."

Jacob's thoughts had turned to other things, and Wilson saw he had lost him. "Thinking about Karen, huh?" he said after studying Jacob's face for several seconds.

Jacob nodded, looking out the porthole. Wilson gripped his arm. "She's going to be okay at Stone Oaks, Son. You know we have a security force second to none. The vice president wondered out loud last time we visited if there weren't more security people around Stone Oaks than around him--torqued his jaws just a bit, I think," Wilson said, trying to lighten Jacob's mood. "Secretary Laxton won't even talk to me anymore because of it," he chuckled.

The tactic worked; Jacob smiled. "I know there's nothing I could do if I were there, any more than is already being done. But at least she'd have me there to hold on to."

"You heard me instruct those Treasury men. They'll be with her around the clock." Wilson grinned, a thought coming to him. "Maybe you had better worry, come to think of it. There are some mighty fine-looking young fellows in that group. And she's a beauty!"

"If that's all I had to worry about, there'd be no worry. Some things in life are irreplaceable."

Wilson laughed heartily. "Time for another talk about conceit and fools," he said, happy to see he had made Jacob feel better.

"She'll want to get out of there and go back to work for PAL," Jacob said, turning serious again. "I hope she waits until I get back."

"If not, it's going to look like a presidential motorcade

every morning, because those agents have orders to stick with her."

"Taxpayers wouldn't like it," Jacob joked.

"That's one good thing about today's world, Son. The taxpayers are too busy having a good time—spending as much on credit as they can, then worrying about how to pay for it—to concern themselves with how their tax dollars are being spent. So long as we can keep crime from overrunning their neighborhoods and terrorists from blowing everything up, the good citizens will let us do whatever we think necessary with their money."

"I guess that's what we're going to Brussels for, to keep the madmen of the world from blowing it up a little at a time until we more civilized types decide to blow it up on a grand scale."

"Project Eagle will deal with terrorism and crime, of course. What really matters is experience in controlling nuclear weaponry. The U.S. absolutely must be in the leadership position for that very reason. The Europeans and the rest simply do not have the practical experience to deal with issues involving nuclear weapons."

"We haven't done an exactly superb job, ourselves."

"Maybe not, but we're still here, aren't we?" Conrad Wilson said.

"For how long? The Russians are looking pretty hard at the Middle East."

"An even bigger reason why America must be perceived, right from the start of these unification meetings, to be clearly in charge. The Russian coalition respects the nuclear sledgehammer we've always protected our interests with. They would be tempted to test any European who controlled nuclear deterrence to see how far they could push before such leadership would tell them to stop, or risk losing everything. The Russians are definitely watching to see how things go in Brussels, believe me."

The plane's shaking startled Jacob, who never got used to the turbulence generated by the lowering of flaps. The big aircraft smoothed out and dropped rapidly, the buildings near the runway passing swiftly. The pilot cut back throttle to the five engines and pulled the nose slightly toward the sky, then allowed the rearmost tires to settle on the concrete.

"Juice has run checks of every conceivable sort," Wilson said, looking out the limousine's window while they moved along Boulevard De L'Empereur, past Grand Place, then turned right on Rue Du Lombard. "He can't find a hint of who might want Marchek and his organization silenced— not enough to employ such violent methods."

"All I know is that he's dead, and Karen and I were almost murdered the same night. It's more than just coincidence. Whoever they are and whatever their reasons, it involves higher stakes than merely wanting to knock some little religious man off his soapbox," Jacob said with irritation.

"I didn't mean to imply that the matter should be dismissed, or even downplayed, Jake."

"Of course you didn't. I appreciate everything you've done. It's just that I'm here, and she's there, and whoever's responsible is free to sit back and wait for the chance to try to get at her again."

"The Director has taken a personal interest in the murder, and he's put some of the Bureau's best men on it. Everything was almost totally consumed in that wreckage. They've only been able to determine that the smaller truck was probably one stolen from a wrecker service somewhere in Maryland."

The Mercedes turned left on Avenue De Stalingrad and rolled past Manneken-Pis, where the statue stood of the little boy known affectionately to the people of Brussels as the city's oldest citizen. Neither man acknowledged seeing the historic figure, while the black car picked up speed in its journey to the hotel which they would call home for the next five days.

Hotel Clemenseau was all Wilson had promised before their flight to Brussels. The three rooms of the suite were huge, with furnishings Napoleon himself would have found fit for an emperor. Every aspect of the building's design remained faithful to the ornate architecture prevalent throughout the old city, yet the hotel was less than three years old, Wilson told him.

Jacob looked for the telephone in his own portion of the suite, letting estimated figures on the cost of such an under-taking--the ancient architecture at today's prices--run through his mind. He let the thought pass when he spotted the French white and brass telephone on a small, white, gold-leafed table in one corner.

"Miss Fitzwill?" he said, finally able to make the connection after 10 minutes of trying. "This is Jacob."

After answering questions about Conrad Wilson's health and the old diplomat's faithfulness to his medication sched-ule, Alexandra Fitzwill turned the connection over to Karen.

"There's something you've got to see, Jacob," she said when the perfunctory greetings were ended. "I... I've been to Dr. Marchek's home... I don't think I should talk about it, but I've got to tell you."

There was fear in her voice, and he wished video phone was available. At least, then, she could feel he was closer to her. "What's wrong? Why can't you talk?"

"He knew more than he told either of us, Jake. I shouldn't say anything over this phone-- I'm afraid someone might be listening. I know it sounds paranoid, but that's what you thought before we were nearly killed and Dr. Marchek was... murdered."

"Karen, we don't have any choice. I'm an ocean away. We're going to have to take a chance.

Tell me what you've found out."

She was right. She could be in danger! If the lines were monitored—if Treasury had done the killing, protecting what they considered national security, or some other agency. The Bureau... CIA... NSA... they would just as quickly eliminate her.

"I drove to his house this morning. I wanted to collect some of the things I knew meant the most to him--to keep people from taking whatever they wanted, once the relatives are allowed in. I came across a note. It was a reminder to himself to tell me about what he called a 'secret place' where he kept some things that he hadn't told anyone about... not even me. Jacob, he never had time to tell me or to finish the note. He died the night he started writing it."

Jacob was silent while Karen regained control of her emotions. "Oh, Jake... I found the secret place and the things he was talking about in the note!"

"Calm down, Kay. It's all right. Everything is okay. Now... what did you find?"

"I found out the reason he was murdered!"

"What?!" He could hear her sobbing.

"I found out they killed Dr. Marchek because he learned that this country, that is, some people at the top, have..." There was a click. She had been cut off!!

CHAPTER 6

He was not in Brussels—had not just talked to Karen. He was no longer Jacob Zen, but John I. Garver, Sector Coordinator 550.

He felt for the belt of explosives. Yes! Still there. He sat on the edge of the sofa and, though drowsy, had enough presence of mind to smooth the waist coat over the belt. The digital clock read 21:18. The INterface Response Unit's Scanner beneath the clock was active and swept the room like a slowly oscillating fan, then stopped to train on him. He gave the snooping device as disinterested a glance as he could, not wanting to appear apprehensive, yet wanting to know how intent the Watchers were on monitoring his movements. To appear bothered by the camera would be an admission of hiding something from them, and might give Watcher Control incentive to undertake a personal search.

What difference? He rubbed his face with the palms of his hands, trying, with the performance, to convince the Watchers that he was only trying to revive from the rest period. The difference was, he reminded himself, if they came here to the Sector Coordination Terminal, there would likely be no more than two controllers. There would be many more at Facility 500, meaning the explosion would do much greater damage. For the few minutes left to Jacob Zen, John I. Garver must remain a loyal citizen of INterface, a dedicated servant, and a cautious one.

Thirty-seven minutes until the meeting at Facility 500. Why was he summoned, if not to present himself for elimination? Sector Coordinators, once they breached Interact procedures, could not be forgiven like ordinary citizens who made slips and were forgiven on occasion. Sector Coordinators were summarily executed by one of several methods available to Controller Central, and their bodies incinerated; their records of existence were electronically expunged in an instant from INterface Response Unity. But Carver had been told to come—not that he would be escorted by a team of the black-uniformed INterface policemen. Might it be a test to see if he would bolt? Was that why the camera constantly watched him? To garner proof that he was indeed an enemy of the great Utopian order?

Time felt different; it *was* different! The sky had changed with relationship to the hour. Looking out the window, he studied the horizon above the decaying structures across from his building. It glowed eerily in a seemingly perpetual dusk. For months, it had been neither truly night nor day, but an iridescent red-orange, which changed in brightness and hue only moderately when the hour grew late.

At 9:30 p.m.--21:30, as INterface would have it—the sky would have, in former times, been black, the stars points of brilliance against the backdrop. Not a hazy orange that contrasted with the jagged, dilapidating structures to form the silhouetted illusion of a Halloween graveyard scene. In a way, the reality was much more nightmarish than such a ghoulish fantasy could ever be, he thought, starting out of habit to reach into the cabinet beside him for the Trachetrol

II. No! He must not give in to the drug's pull. The chemical might aid him in his desire to do what he had to do by giving him courage, but its debilitating effects would decrease the chances of his success.

There was a problem. His replacement would be at the door in 10 minutes. How to get the Bible and notebook from beneath the console chair with the Interface Eye constantly on him? He had to get them out before the shift change; the next Coordinator would be no more tolerant of the book nor of his note-taking than would Controller Central.

Before, it had been a simple matter; he had folded the old volume and the pad into the blanket he always brought with him. Watching for variation from established patterns was a basic technique used in INterface surveillance, from the time they moved him from the remote Coordinator Center to the inner-city. John I. Garver had brought the blanket with him. They searched it for the first dozen or so times and found nothing. He brought the blanket still—he told them, for the rest periods—and, as he had suspected, they had examined the blanket periodically for months. But for the past few months, they had not inspected the blanket at all. So he had decided to take a chance and had begun bringing the Bible and notepad. Later, he taped the explosives to the blanket, and had brought the belt with him to the Sector Controller Room on a daily basis since developing the contingency plan.

Today's events changed things. The Scanner Eye had watched his movements from the moment he stirred on the sofa following the rest period. There remained a chance, the remote possibility, he thought while again looking out the pollution-soiled window, that he might somehow survive the interrogation at Facility 500. Why, though, would he want to live on in this miserable existence? Perhaps because the will to survive fought on even when less sturdy instincts succumbed to emotion. At any rate, if the Bible and the notepad were discovered, the matter would become academic. INterface would, without hesitation, forget John I. Garver and replace him with a more deserving member from among its ranks. With blazing suddenness only a mind pushed to desperation could generate, inspiration hit. He smiled, his back to the camera, and almost laughed out loud when the thought struck. He would put on a show for the INterface fools. Whether it would work was not important; that was the beauty of it. The reason, perhaps, that the ploy had a chance for success. Yes! It was made more workable by the confidence gotten from his attitude of fearlessness!

Walking from the window to the sofa, he picked up the blanket and slowly folded it as he always did before leaving his shift. Tucking the blanket under his arm, he walked back across the room, stopping to put the blanket on the table by the right arm of the console chair, then walked to the cabinet. He poured a glass of water from the server and took a sip, turning to face the Scanner, looking over the glass to see that the camera was focused on him. He moved back toward the console chair, drinking from the glass while he walked. The camera, he noticed, turned with his movement, and, like he anticipated, the lens was zoomed out, framing for the Watchers the upper portion of his body. Good! The plan should work.

In the next instant, the water erupted from Jacob's hand, the glass shattering against the hard floor. The table next to the chair tipped and crashed onto its side when Jacob's body made contact. The heavy metal lamp bounced crazily across the floor, while he managed, with his hand, to brush the blanket toward the front of the console chair. Sitting on the floor, apparently stunned, he glanced quickly at the camera lens, which seemed to go crazy with confusion, sweeping the room, first across then up and down, the Watcher controlling it obviously trying to make out what the commotion was about.

Jacob cursed loudly for the benefit of the policeman at the other end of the teletransmission. The camera finally stopped its frantic gyrations to point in his direction.

He sat for a moment, wanting to appear confused, himself, then he slowly regained his feet and stood, wiping water from his clothes and looking around at the mess the faked accident had caused. He cursed again, getting a handful of paper towels from a drawer of the cabinet near the window, then returned to the chair. Kneeling with his back to the Scanner, he picked up the nearest pieces of broken glass, then mopped the water.

Even INterface allowed for human clumsiness—had no choice but to tolerate physical ineptitude on occasion. The INterface devil, even he must have enjoyed his underling's comical mishap, if for no other reason than that it offered a brief respite from the Watcher's own misery. He hoped so, while he sopped the last of the water from the floor; someone, maybe the Watcher, would pay for the performance with his life.

With several wet paper towels, he wiped the slivers of glass into a neat pile, picked them up and deposited them in the metal trash receptacle to his left. He carefully calculated, then put into action his move to a position more directly in front of the chair, thus more securely blocking the Scanner's view of the bottom of the chair and his true activity. With the glass removed, he began what the Watcher would think was a straightening up process, first the table, then the blanket. He reached beneath the console chair's right side with his left hand and in one smooth motion pulled the Bible and the notepad across the floor, while at the same time moving the blanket in front of him with his right hand. He spread one corner of the cloth over the book and the yellow pad, then folded the blanket as neatly as it was before, completing the deception.

The clock read 21:36--9:36 p.m. Completed with four minutes to spare before his shift replacement came, precisely on time as he always did, like he surely would this night.

He stood and placed the folded blanket on top of the cabinet before returning to put the lamp back on the table and pick up the few scattered pieces of glass he missed earlier. The Scanner camera continued to monitor his movements, but he was certain the staged accident had accomplished its purpose. He fantasized how his next plan would succeed as well, and how it would be even more productive. The terror of tasting their own blood would wipe the smiles from their drug-bloated faces. Although Clarendon Street, like most other streets in the area, was empty except for a staggering man here, a bicyclist there, or an occasional official vehicle of one sort or another, Jacob felt caged, hemmed in by the omnipresence of INterface. The once-familiar streets and alleys at the heart of the great city were now pitted, barely recognizable heaps of concrete and asphalt. Boston, like other megalopolises, was among the first areas ravaged by the terrorist-looters in the chaos that followed the great disappearance, as governments were unable, at first, to deal with the crises.

Maybe the survivalists had been right all along. Jacob fiddled with the rubber strap that kept the cheese-cloth mask over his nose and adjusted the mask to keep out the pollutants. With the food supplies of the big cities so quickly depleted, the outlying business districts and suburbs then thoroughly plundered, the mass swarm of human vermin moved to the mountainous and forested areas. Many of the wooded regions were burned, making it easier for scavengers to find food and other essentials that the survivalists had horded in case such an eventuality happened when other supplies were contaminated by radiation and disrupted by the after-effects of the brief nuclear exchange and the disappearance phenomenon.

No. The survivalists had not been right, and Boston was Boston no longer, but Geoquadrant 3 of INterface. It would never be Boston again, just as surely as New York City, vaporized by a nuclear blast, was no more.

He had to stop, put the blanket on the broken pavement, then remove the mask and rethread the strap through its metal retainers on either side, which meant he had to take the goggles from his eyes—a thing not pleasant to do in the corrosive atmosphere.

Instantly, his eyes began tearing up in the heavily particled air. The inevitable hacking began, his cough-reflex center fighting to defend against the painful intrusion.

Finally managing to get the mask strap restrung, and, mercifully, the goggles back over his eyes, he picked up the blanket from the street and glanced at his watch. 9:49—just enough time to make Facility 500 before the commanded time.

But what of the blanket? The forbidden Bible, the note pad? The questions undulated through his mind while he began a slow jog up Clarendon. What difference did it make? If they made a move to examine the blanket, whoever did so would join him on a trip into the afterlife...if there were such a thing.

Across Columbus Avenue and left onto Massachusetts Turnpike, or what had once been Massachusetts Turnpike-- it did not matter when the button must be pushed. When the time came, he would be up to pushing the button. The last look at the unsuspecting faces, before their descent into hell, would be reward enough. He wished there to be a hell.

Right on Exeter—Facility 500 was in sight! His breathing was now labored and his vision darkened, as if he would faint. If so unconcerned about what the controllers might do, why the exertion to get there at the commanded time? Still, there was a chance, a possibility, there might be another purpose for the call to the headquarters. Possibly another reason...

Was it all bravado? A false sense of his self-destruct capability? Karen's face floated in his mind while he continued the jog toward Facility 500, the huge stone building that once housed the public library. There was no longer a need for such institutions. The great would-be Utopian state provided everything the citizen needed in the way of reading materials. And all the citizen needed was to know the laws of INterface. Six Ways to Law — Six Ways to Order — Six Ways to Peace. Karen's face, floating before his mind's eye.

Inside the building, dispassionate eyes dissected him, black-uniformed controllers glaring at him and the blanket he held.

This was it! They would want to examine the blanket! They would find the book, the notes! His heart thumped viciously. Perspiration, the familiar, unhealthy sweat he had known for months, beaded, then rolled over his face and body.

"Your goggles!"

"Pardon? I'm sorry... What?" Jacob said.

"Remove your goggles and step up to the IN," the fat man behind a half-circle desk said, clearly irritated.

Jacob complied, taking off the yellow-lensed eye coverings before stepping up the four inches onto the rubber-covered platform.

"Come on! Come on! You know the procedure! Face the circle and hold your head erect!"

Jacob held the folded blanket tightly, knowing that any moment the fat controller would demand it from him, discover its secrets. What would death be like? He would probably know... soon!

He did as he was told, stiffening to a rigid position of attention, his head facing the crimson circle. Behind the desk, the controller watched the INterface Response Unit's screen on the board in front of him.

Time passed agonizingly slowly for Jacob, whose face the screen in front of the controller displayed; the name "John I. Garver" popped on the screen beneath the image; a bar code symbol materialized on Jacob Zen's forehead.

Beneath the name, the decoded numbers were generated one at a time:

"BBB-IN-3- 1 88827 1" and beneath that line, the words "SUBJECT CONFIRMED — " flashed brightly in yellow characters.

"You are IN, Sector Coordinator five, five, zero," the fat man said from behind the desk. "Follow that officer."

The controller nodded in the direction of the stocky man who had stood at parade rest a few paces behind Jacob during identification.

The fluorescently lit hallway floor was of brilliant white tile, the surfaces of the walls and doors covered entirely with mirrors. Once Jacob's eyes adjusted, he was struck by the symbolism: the vast sterility of the walkway contrasting with, defiled by, the black-attired controllers who moved busily through it. The pure good; the unalloyed evil. He had been here before, but not since Boston became Geoquadrant 3. Then, the walls had been paneled and painted, the floors carpeted, and there had been warmth and books and time to dream. There had been freedom...

The controller walked with military aloofness, stopping at one of the mirror-covered doors near the center of the hallway. "Wait here for further instructions," he said, allowing Jacob to pass by him into the room. "Be seated and do not leave for any reason."

"What is this about? Can you tell me what...?" But the stern-dispositioned policeman left before the question could be completed.

Jacob moved his fingertips around the bulge at his waist, not too conspicuously, because INterface Eyes were no doubt watching. The feeling was strangely comforting, touching the ridges and bumps of the belt, knowing enough explosive charge was there to wipe out a room the size of this one. His sanity had slipped; he did have a death-wish. Maybe it was best that his mind had finally begun to fall victim to Trachetrol's brain-eroding effects, and to the Inculcation Sessions that anesthetized one to the fear of death.

And Karen was gone... there was nothing left to live for. It was fortunate that the Watchers could not read the mind, could not yet probe the thoughts of the finale he planned. But it was just a matter of time until their technologies gave them power to invade that only remaining sanctuary.

The room was battleship gray, with old, scarred tables and folding chairs. There were no windows. He considered how the library, before it became Facility 500, had been configured, how the basic structure remained the same. This had been an interior room, housing, he thought he remembered, a special section on Spanish history, or French. Maybe Italian. It was a dark, dull, totally depressing room then. It had not changed in that respect, he surmised, pulling a folding chair from beneath one of the tables and sitting.

"Sector Coordinator five, five, zero!" He stiffened in the chair, turning to look around, trying to pinpoint the deep voice coming from speakers somewhere in the room. "Termination Session will commence in 30 seconds! Face the wall behind you!"

"Termination Session?" The terminology was new.

Would even INterface, in all its twisted illogic, give its victim a propaganda speech before erasing him from its data banks? The announcement, he noted calmly, had little effect on him. He was becoming callous to the thought of dying. He did as the voice commanded, shifting the chair to face the wall.

"Do not move from the room when this session is ended. You will be instructed what to do at that time."

The room went black; the wall in front of him then became awash with faint light, and the gray paint separated, unveiling a large screen.

"Termination Session seven, seven, five," the voice announced, while the screen came alive with the translucent pyramid symbol of Interface. An elaborate production to waste on one who was about to be terminated.

A sudden explosion shook him from his lethargy! The picture on the wall-screen lurched and jerked violently before locking into a stable image of a burning, crumbling building from which 20 or more people staggered, their clothing and skin ablaze. The horror of the second scene was even more starkly presented, so diametrically did its silent tranquility contrast with the ear-shattering violence of the first. Torn bodies of women and children, internal organs exposed, brains spilling from erupted cranial cavities—captured by a slowly panning camera. And, the terrible silence...

He felt nothing, nothing at all while viewing the grisly scene. That was the thing that bothered him. And, that contradiction of thought itself—the concern that he felt badly only for his own inability to feel—troubled him, made him somehow more a part of the impersonal atrocity. The flesh spattered about the exploded room was simply organic machinery that had ceased to function. He had seen it all too many times.

"Since Interface time began," the computer voice narrated, while the death scenes continued, "the truly civilized have been victimized by sub-human filth; and, on an increasingly alarming scale. It seems the greater the effort to show mercy, to try to convince through love and understanding, the more heinous the acts by these enemies, who are led by the Jew—murderers, the scourge of mankind. The Jew is at the heart of every evil in our world today, a world that will achieve its perfection only after the Jew is eradicated!"

The same diatribe, repackaged, with new, updated horror-video. As desensitizing as the Trachetrol in its effect on an INterface-vtorn nervous system. But the next moments were designed to break the monotonous pattern of the Inculcation propaganda; it worked!

He snapped to alertness in the chair, seeing what were obviously a series of controller raids upon, not the pitiful Jews or scavenging looters as depicted in all the previous Inculcation tapes, but upon their own kind—upon Product Center Supervisors and Society Watchers. Black-uniformed men and women were dragged from their stations of duty, clubbed, then carted off in the controller vans to one precinct headquarters or another.

"Now INterface Controller Central has the capacity to cut out the individual and collective malignant cells from among the healthy, productive tissue which comprises the growing, networking organism that will soon become a perfect universal body. Those who have been mistakenly placed in positions of responsibility within INterface are being gathered, as you can see, from everywhere they infect us. They will pay for their treacheries, even a greater price than the Jew-dogs who inspired them!"

Controllers with rifle butts and shock sticks prodded a van full of prisoners from the big vehicle, forcing them through open heavy-gauge metal gates, whose tops were forged with Gothic spikes and barbed-wire, as were the 10-foot high fences that rimmed the complex of floodlit concrete buildings making up the compound.

The scene changed to the interior of one of the structures; several of the bloodied and bruised prisoners stood at attention, their eyes glazed and wide.

"These have been among the elite of INterface. They have tasted the best our magnificent society has to offer our citizens. They betrayed that trust by hiding Jews, by entertaining forbidden activities. These have taken what they wanted for themselves, without permission from the provider of us all, Master Manya, and INterface Universal. They will now, as will all who are our enemies, taste the bitterness of INterface wrath!"

The video changed again, showing a prisoner who had been stripped naked being held by two controllers. Every inch of his head and body had been shaved then covered with what looked to be a coat of clear, glistening lacquer.

"These traitors deserve the most cruel deaths that can be devised, because they have perpetrated the cruelest crimes of all—taking from their trusting brothers and sisters of INterface, while those brothers and sisters sacrifice to bring in the perfect order we all want—and because they have aided the Jewish swine in their drive to enslave the world with their Zionist, humanity-robbing ideology!"

The prisoner was thrust into a room and the door locked behind him. The narrator's voice continued.

"The Jew, in most cases, dies a quick, merciful death. INterface is not unfeeling, even for the rodents that infest us."

The room in which the man stood was illuminated by dim, red light, it soon becoming evident that the camera providing the view taped the event with an infrared lens. The prisoner could not see. He moved cautiously ahead in what was, for him, total darkness, looking in all directions, trying to pick up some glimmer of light.

"Our mercy ends where betrayal begins! This man, a Sector Coordinator, was found to have hidden at his apartment two Jewish females, with whom he sexually consorted as if they were of his own kind instead of being of the lowest order. He also read from the Talmud, which he kept hidden away along with many other pieces of trash formerly passed off by the Jews as literature."

Alone, naked, and in total darkness, knowing his death was imminent but not knowing how he would die, the man became increasingly panicked, reaching his hands to feel for obstacles. He stepped slowly, extending his feet with each step to feel for openings in the floor that might swallow him and dash him to pieces somewhere below. The infrared lights allowed the cameras to capture the terror on the man's face and each movement of his glinting body while he felt his way.

"Watch the former Sector Coordinator grope, lost in his sin, alone in his punishment, terrified in his hell," the narrator-voice said, while Jacob followed the doomed man's movements.

"There was salvation for him—salvation through INterface— through our Master Manya. This man chose darkness —death—hell!"

INterface added audio to its video presentation, urging the viewer to become even more caught up in the victim's agony. Crying could be heard, soft, guttural sobbing, when the camera's lens zoomed quickly in for a close-up of the man's face. The tears and terror on the glistening face, graphically presented to shock those who watched. Jacob was unmoved. For him it was anti-climactic, this vulgar display of INterface cruelty. They took everything from him. His personality, his vitality... Karen. Everything except his life. He would take that himself. He had lost control of his life —he would control his own death.

"This is the fate of all who betray the Cosmic Whole of INterface, of all who are disloyal to our loving Master Manya," the voice continued while the man inched his way until he made contact with one wall. He ran his hands along its surface, his unseeing eyes still trying to gather in his surroundings.

"Not knowing what is in store for him is part of this traitor's hell. But that is only a small bit of the punishment he is about to... enjoy. You see, his body has been prepared, through bioelectronics computer analysis, for the finale, for the ending to his miserable, disloyal life."

The scene before Jacob became one of a room equipped with various electronic circuitry boards.

"We shall take this former Sector Coordinator's analysis as our case in point."

The video showed the man, at an earlier time, being hooked up to the electrodes and probes that surrounded him, giving the appearance, when the process was finished, that thin, white tentacles grew from many parts of his nude body and attached to the modular machinery that almost encircled him. He showed no fear, but stared straight ahead.

"Our subject has been injected with newly developed serums that interact with his body functions and with this new technology, to which he is attached. The process provides answers to essential questions such as: Which chemical agents, when comingled with his body's bio-galvanic constituency, can produce what types of reactions when different stimuli are introduced at a later time? You will soon understand and see the answers in this traitor's case."

With two controllers standing at parade-rest behind the man, who sat strapped to a wooden chair, a young woman in a white lab coat fidgeted with several gadgets on the circuitry boards to which the prisoner was attached by the white wires. His body convulsed each time she threw a switch or manipulated a rheostat.

"This process feeds the computer the necessary information for it to assess the data and read out the answers we seek. The result, this answer, combined with further hypnotically secured data, tells us the subject's inner-most secrets. More precisely, his greatest fears. In the case of this former Sector Coordinator, we learned that his most dramatic fear is the fear of being attacked by wild animals. Rodent-type mammals, to be exact. We considered rats. They registered very high on his fear index. Ah... but bats! Bats were the answer! Therefore, this traitor shall indeed have bats!"

The scene changed back to the man in the red-hued room. He looked to be struggling, his hands still on the wall, trying to pull his palms from it. His struggle increased, became frantic in his effort, while the voice explained.

"The wall is treated with a special adhesive which when first touched, feels dry. Body heat quickly dissolves the chemical, turning it into a powerful glue, which makes the wall like flypaper for human insects. This enemy of INterface will remain in this position until he is removed after his death."

The narrator, loving his job, sounded delighted while he explained. If only the narrator could be nearby when Jacob pressed the button. If only... But the narrator was merely speech, synthesized! A computer made to enjoy its work. So sophisticated, so efficient had the Masters become with their technologies.

"Now we provide just the faintest illumination, so our friend will be able to see his companions."

The indirect lighting negated the infrared light, the camera now able to capture every movement of the glistening prisoner, who ceased his struggle and turned as far as his predicament allowed to see what was planned for him next.

"Now we tell him exactly what is in store for him. His fear will produce the chemical body agents which will combine with the compound painted on his body to create a fascinating phenomenon. Through the computer bio-psychological analysis process shown earlier, we are able to produce this lacquer-like substance, which in itself is totally harmless. However, when extreme fear is induced, the subject's unique secretions and galvanic responses—all analyzed and recorded before the lacquer was prepared for him — encourage the chemical to strip the top layers of skin from his flesh, exposing more and more nerve endings. The chemical reaction also becomes more pain-stimulating than does salt when poured in an open wound."

The stuck prisoner had resumed his struggle to free himself from the wall while the narrator-voice continued with seeming pleasure. "Let us induce fear into the matter."

The voice changed tone. "Six, six, six, four, one, five, seven, three, three."

The prisoner stopped struggling and glanced quickly around the room, looking to see from where the voice emanated.

"My, my... you have gotten yourself into a bit of a problem, haven't you?" the narrator-voice said. "We must at least make your stay more interesting. We would not want you to become bored." Jacob could see the man screaming at the speakers located in the corners the room's ceiling; he could not hear the man's words, but imagined they must be pleas for mercy.

"You are in for a most interesting time, four, one, five, seven, three, three, I assure you. Let me explain. The compound spread over your body... We won't bother you with the technical name, do you mind? Suffice it to say, the compound has the most peculiar effect on bats.

"Bats of every type--brown bats, fruit bats, vampire bats —they are drawn to it as sharks are drawn to blood. Even the huge, fruit-eating bats dive right in to whatever this compound is spread over. To them, you would appear or smell to be a giant, sweet, delicious fruit to be enjoyed. To the bloodsucking variety, the vampire bat, the scent tells them, of course, that you are a mammal, full of warm, nourishing blood to be sucked and enjoyed until they are sated. We know how much you like bats, four, one, five, seven, three, three."

The man screamed silently on the screen in front of Jacob.

"Now, now... let's not make a spectacle of ourselves," the mocking voice continued. "We have for you... bats... bats of every description! Small, gray bats with razor sharp fangs, with mouths that can suck the juices from a rabbit in a matter of minutes. Gigantic fruit bats that have unbelievably ravenous appetites for the flesh of fruits, which, of course, you will, to them, seem to be."

The man twisted to look toward the speakers, then turned and placed his bare feet on the wall in an attempt to pry his palms free. He was sobbing, begging to be delivered from his fate. He turned his head when he heard the fluttering beat of hundreds of the winged mammals as they were released into the small room, his eyes and mouth gaping wide with terror.

"Of course, what I have just told our subject is somewhat of an exaggeration," the narrator voice said while the man's struggle to free himself became more furious. "What we are doing, as I said before, is inducing fear in our friend."

Jacob analyzed the words and events of the past several seconds. If they were setting John I. Garver up for a similar

experience—the use of fear in helping with his own execution—why let him know they lied to the doomed man about
the effect the skin-glazing chemical would have on the bats?
Were they not concerned that a similar ploy would not work,
should they want to use fear as part of his own termination?
There were perhaps other, more stimulating forms of execution available to provide even greater entertainment for
those who would view John I. Garver's elimination. Could it
be that his being forced to watch this torture--being given
the reason and time to wonder what was in store for himself-
-might be the first stage of the termination experience
chosen for John I. Garver?

"Inducing fear is our main objective, not securing this
traitor's death by letting these creatures feed on his bodily
fluids. His death will come through his own terror, and, of
course, through the pain that will occur when the nerves are
sufficiently exposed to the chemical... and the bats. The bats
would eventually kill him, perhaps, because the compound is
extremely attracting to them. They will be drawn to him, and
will use his body as a place to seek refuge from their fellow
creatures. The chemical will not cause them to begin feeding,
but will, as his skin and inner-flesh are more and more
exposed, mix with his blood, causing a panic reaction in the
beasts. They will tear at each other and at his open flesh in an
attempt to defend themselves against the imaginary enemies
the chemicals and blood combination tricks their senses into
believing are trying to harm them. Probably, however, he will
die from shock and exposure, or perhaps, before that, from
heart failure brought on by fear and pain."

The room was filled with hundreds of the frenzied, fluttering animals, becoming a horror chamber for the man
adhered to the wall. His struggle had stopped, and he cringed
in a semi-fetal position against the wall, his head buried
between his arms while the grotesque creatures slammed

against his skin, which now had begun to dissolve due to the glazing compound's reaction to his body chemistry.

Jacob watched the open-mouthed scream of agony and fear he knew the man was enduring. The bloodied prisoner tried to stand but could not, because now his left side, shoulder and hip were also firmly affixed to the fly-paper wall at points where they touched during his effort to protect himself.

"See the end result of sin against the righteousness of INterface Universal." The narrator-voice was high-pitched and increased in its frenetic excitement, as did the chaos inside the room when still more bats were released. "Watch while the traitor endures the hell he has earned!"

Jacob felt a sickly perspiration begin, the beads of his own sweat-juices emerge from the pores of his forehead. If not fear, he certainly felt something, and suddenly knew the psychological punishment was working! They were telling him he would die by the most agonizing method they could devise! He ran his hand around the belt again, fingering the metal clasp that hid the button; he still controlled his own destiny. There would be no such show for the monsters to enjoy at his expense.

Blood showered from the man's serrated flesh, splattering against the wall and floor where he lay writhing in a semi-comatose state, the bats clawing and biting him and each other. Jacob looked past the gore, forcing his memory into time, where Karen was still there for him and hope was alive —though life was anything but trouble-free.

* * *

Conrad Wilson shouted to be heard above the whining thump of the big helicopter that whisked them along at 300 knots above the cobalt-blue Aegean.

"They never stop! They'll always be Cossacks! If we let it, this thing will have a disastrous effect on our timetable. And I'm sure that's a big part of this posturing." Wilson flipped through loose papers atop the briefcase on his lap while he talked.

Jacob sat in the seat next to his foster father, taking in the magnificent view afforded through the big window. "They've done this sort of thing before. Maybe not on as large a scale, but it's probably like you said, just designed to throw confusion into the unification process—to get the Western leadership's collective mind off the business at hand."

"It's an expensive bluff for them if that's the case. And if it doesn't accomplish their purpose, the top Russians will pay with their heads."

"Could we stop them, if they were to go down into Palestine?"

"Not short of using tactical nuclear weapons. Since Turkey left NATO to become closer to the Russian coalition and with Israel neutered, its army greatly reduced in order to satisfy the treaty with the Arabs, we don't have the capability to put a significant conventional force in the area. Not like during the action taken against Iraq in '91. It would take months to get enough strength there to fortify Israel," Wilson said. "If they go down at all, they'll go full force."

"Nothing on earth, short of nuclear armaments, could deal with them in that event."

"Would Israel be worth World War III to us?" Jacob queried.

"No. But those tremendous new oil finds around the Red Sea, and the fantastic amounts of mineral goodies Israel's been taking out of the Dead Sea through the new mining techniques they've developed—plus all that lush territory they've developed through their recently implemented hydrological methods—all that might make it worth defending, if there were time. Defending with nuclear force? I don't know. That's what the Russians have to think about before invading Palestine, and of course, that's primarily why they want the region. I just don't know.

"The President and all the other heads of state sent a joint note to Moscow just before we left Brussels, asking for explanations. The President told me the Russians replied that they are simply carrying out maneuvers with the coalition forces to learn more about how to defend their southern flank in case of attack," Wilson said, punctuating the revelation with a disdainful laugh.

"Defend against whom? Against Israel? The Arabs are their pals, so they can't be afraid of them."

"*Rearmed* pals, by this time, I strongly suspect," Wilson interrupted. "There's intelligence to the effect that Russia has secretly stockpiled a lot of conventional armaments in and around Damascus, as well as in Libya. And, of course, Iran—never a part of the peace agreement—has much conventional hardware, although a lot of it is somewhat antiquated."

"Then you think any attack would be a joint invasion that would include even Iran and the Arabs?"

Conrad Wilson considered the question, his forehead wrinkling above the silver-white eyebrows. "If it were to happen, all the hatreds that the Arab holds for the Jew would be instantly rekindled. The Russians would certainly welcome that joining to rid the area once and for all of Israel." Wilson's somberness changed to a lighter mood. "But that's a worst-case scenario, Jake. Not likely at all. It will all be over within a couple of days and we can finish our business and get you back to Karen." He patted Jacob's arm. "I've been so busy with this Russian build-up thing...did you talk to her?"

"I knew you were involved with that problem, so I didn't bother you with mine."

"Oh? Something wrong?"

"I don't know. She said she's found out something—that Dr. Marchek left a diary of some kind in his home. He wrote about something he apparently discovered involving the Vice President and some others in government. We were cut off before she could tell me about it. She was really upset."

"The Vice President, huh? You didn't call her back?"

"The lines were having problems. We got the urgent call to leave Brussels, and I didn't have a chance to call again."

"Don't worry, Son. She's okay." Wilson again patted Jacob's arm. "You call her again first thing after we get settled in."

Crete, the largest of the Greek Islands, lay spread beneath them. A many-colored paradise sprawling across the gateway to the Aegean, appeared from that height to be a great, partially submerged beast of the sea displaying its ridged, spiny back. To the south, the mountains of Dikta and Ida were beautiful, in full bloom now with their new crowns of snow. Jacob's mind wandered, though his eyes remained affixed on the nature-created masterpiece. He had promised Karen he would get back to her, yet here he was, headed in the direction opposite from McLean, toward a destination he didn't even know. He was discussing with Conrad Wilson things that were of apocalyptic importance to mankind, but which for him—at least in his private thoughts--took a rear seat to personal concerns. Yet he sensed a connectedness, linking these world-convulsing matters to those which were violently shaking his private life. His uneasiness was magnified by the fact that something within him caused, for some reason beyond anything he could figure, a nagging suspicion of the one person he loved as much as he loved Karen. Anything that was afoot in government could not get past Conrad Wilson.

If the stakes were high enough, if the security of the

nation was on the line, Conrad Wilson could know about the killing of Hugo Marchek--or anyone else—and look the other way. Maybe even have an active part in an assassination which he considered vital to the interest of the United States.

No! Conrad Wilson could not be a party to killing—not to killing someone he loved— not to killing Karen or Jacob Zen. The people in the tow-truck had tried to murder them. Their accomplices murdered Hugo Marchek. But were the killers of Marchek and the would-be killers agents of different political sources?

The one-time whites and blacks of viewpoint had long since turned to indistinguishable grays in national and international interrelationships. What was right depended now on the lesser of evils: on who was making the decisions, on whose interests must be served. Those who were assigned to serve at Stone Oaks could, in an instant, be called on to act as instruments of execution and kill the people they had moments before been protecting. He had urged Karen to stay put in the old mansion. By doing so, had he put her directly in the path of the very source the two of them had escaped from on the highway that night? The ones who had killed Hugo Marchek?

"Mr. Ambassador, we are approaching our destination," the helicopter's pilot said over the intercom. "Our ETA is eighteen twenty-three."

CHAPTER 7

W hen the ladder unfolded to the rocky ground, Jacob strained to see through the whirling cloud of dust kicked up by the helicopter's huge blades and was able to make out, finally, a number of human forms approaching. He still did not know where they were. Conrad Wilson didn't volunteer their destination; Jacob didn't ask. His only concerns had been, and were now, whether he would be able to call Karen, and when. Seeing the desolate terrain surrounding them, his concern grew. Was the island's communication system capable of connecting private hook-ups to the United States, to McLean? Were private calls permitted? Using email was out. Even with government safe-guards, it would be too big a risk to use the laptop.

"Mister Ambassador!" One of the men dressed in an orange jumpsuit with black trim, like those worn by the others in the greeting party, offered his right hand to Wilson.

"Hello, Harry! Nice to see you!" Wilson smiled.

"And you must be Mr. Zen." The man thrust his hand out to take Jacob's. "Yes... Jacob Zen."

"Jake, this was one of my classmates at Princeton, and probably the only man I've been able to beat at golf in 30 years. Dr. Herdrick Franke, the Unified European States' top computer genius."

"Well, I am not so sure about that," the short, balding man said with a German accent. "Let us just say I know a good deal more about computer science than I do about the game of golf."

"He beats me pretty regularly, too, if that's any consolation," Jacob said.

"It is not, my friend. He always wins our wagers. Fortunately, I am intelligent enough to carry only the old currency with me. The amounts we bet are so small as to make it too much trouble for Conrad to bother exchanging, therefore he forgives the debt," the German said happily.

"Ah! But that will soon change, eh, Harry? A universal currency will eliminate such inconvenience!" Wilson said.

"But how does one carry electronic currency units in one's trousers?"

"Perhaps, Doctor, we've uncovered a new product and its future market. A portable golf-bag computer for just such occasions as wagering and making electronic funds transfers right out there on the course! What do you think, Jake?" Wilson said, turning to his foster son.

"If there's time for such things as golf."

"It takes the serious mind of youth to bring us back to reality, Dr. Franke. From here on out, it's work, work, work... if we're to bring in our utopia!"

"Then let us begin by seeing the start we have made here in Naxos!" The pudgy scientist seized each man by an elbow and guided them toward a boulder-strewn area 50 yards from the helicopter.

"Naxos? Is that where we are?" The German smiled when

Jacob asked the question. "I am sorry for the need of all this mystery about where we are located."

"Naxos is the largest of the 24 islands in the Cyclade chain, Jake," Wilson explained while the three men, followed by the others who met them when they landed, walked toward a cliff-like appendage. "As you can see, it's pretty well fixed so far as privacy's concerned. Just a few scattered towns in the mountains and an old Frankish fort that's falling down now. It used to be a Catholic convent, but the U.E.S. has moved those people and most others on Naxos to other islands in the area."

"They are considerably better for the move," said Franke. "Here, the electricity and transportation were very limited. We have provided much better facilities for the people on the other islands. They can still grow their traditional crops of oranges, tomatoes, olives, and potatoes, as well as, still export their Citron wine. They are better off, all things considered."

Jacob failed to hear Franke's last words, his mind at work analyzing the deeper meanings of Conrad Wilson's words. His foster father was thoroughly familiar with Naxos—with its history, with its displaced population, and with the facility apparently still under construction. This man he knew so well, or thought he knew so well, had kept the secrets easily. Was he capable of more nefarious deception, in the name of national and allied security? Jake's paranoia was growing. He must stop it! Conrad Wilson was his father!

"You think our young man here could find a means of reaching a certain young lady back home, by any chance?" Wilson said, turning to the scientist.

"Of course. If we are not capable of such a simple thing here, then our cause is lost," Franke said with amusement in his voice. "You are welcome to use whatever means you choose, Jacob--cable, telephone, Satelvid, or electronic mail."

"Satelvid?"

"It is a temporary system until we can get more permanent manned space arrangements set up to provide one-hundred percent global coverage. With the equipment at Stone Oaks, you'll be able to see her, as well as talk to her. It will be just as if she were in the room with you," concluded the German scientist.

"Holography," said Wilson.

The thought that he would be able to see and talk to Karen lightened Jacob's mood, but in the next instant even that happy prospect dimmed in light of the fantastic sight before them. While they stood at the foot of the massive boulder, its sheer gray face split apart, four men in orange jumpsuits and black helmets, armed with automatic weapons, emerged and stood at order arms. The German urged the two Americans to precede him into the opening.

No one talked while the floor on which they stood descended quickly and silently. Jacob glanced up to see the light at the top of the shaft growing smaller, then looked to Conrad Wilson, who, he noticed, seemed unimpressed.

They reached the end of their downward journey, the platform slowing then coming to a smooth stop. The wall they faced appeared to be solid rock, like the cliff face above. Then, like the cliff-face, it split and gaped open, revealing a brightly lit horizontal shaft which narrowed to a vanishing point in the distance. A transparent, box-like covering slid over the men, locking with the floor to form walls and a ceiling, to which, Jacob noticed, were attached cameras—one on each of its corners. Metal handrails emerged from the platform and stopped at elbow level. Jacob grasped the rail, following the examples of Wilson and Franke.

The just-constructed room jerked slightly, then began moving, accelerating through the shaft. The lights whisked past them faster and faster, creating a stomach-churning

Gestalt illusion that the lights, rather than they, were moving.

"Most suffer motion sickness the first time in the tube," Herdrick Franke said, seeing the pallor of Jacob's face.

Jacob stared at the floor for the next two minutes and the nausea eased. The conveyance slowed with a high-pitched grinding wheeze, stopping finally in front of yet another wall of rock, which split, then parted in the same manner the other had.

"A fascinating trip, eh Jake?" Wilson looked to see his foster son's reaction.

Before Jacob could answer, four armed men, dressed in the now-familiar orange and black jumpsuits, stepped between the three men on the platform and the entranceway to what looked to be a brightly lit room--its white walls broken at various points by dark television monitors and computer keyboards. The computer display screens, below the television monitors were filled with images, but there appeared to be no one operating the equipment. One of the armed men spoke to Franke in a curt military manner.

"An Identity Scan has been prepared for the subjects. They will be escorted to C-41, where they will be established for integration."

"Yes, yes, Major," Franke said, a disgruntled look crossing his round face.

"The military, as always, must feel they have control of matter," the German said moments later while they walked in the big room, following two guards and being followed by others. "We must humor them; they have the guns!"

The truth in the scientist's facetious remark was not lost on Jacob. Studies he was privileged to see as a member of Conrad Wilson's Project Eagle team produced the conclusion that cyclical swings in governmental control—alternating between civilian authority and military authority—were historically intrinsic to cultures who managed to win for themselves a degree of liberty. True of the ancient Greeks, the Roman Empire— and all who studied such data were in agreement: the pendulum was presently swinging in favor of those who had the guns.

"Step through here, remove your clothing, and move into the Degermination Chambers," the major ordered, pointing stiffly to a small opening into a darkened room. "Leave your gear here." Jacob looked at Wilson for clarification.

"He means our briefcases," Wilson said with a chuckle.

"These men are not your troops, Major..." The scientist squinted to read the nameplate above the officer's breast pocket. "Major... Brandel. This man is a personal emissary of the President of the United States, and one of the greatest statesmen of our time. He is to be treated with respect—not as you treat your corporals!"

The officer assumed the position of parade rest with his back to the wall near the entranceway. He stared straight ahead, showing no sign he heard the scientist's scolding.

"It's okay, Harry. We have our jobs; he has his," Wilson said happily, then followed Jacob into the room, which lit up when they stepped through the doorway. Jacob surmised his body had broken an electronic beam, activating the room's illumination system.

"Remove your apparel, please, and place it in the receptacle to your right. It will be returned to you upon your departure."

The voice was computerized. Jacob looked around the enclosure to determine where it was coming from, while complying with the command.

"The machine is more polite than the soldier," Wilson joked, removing his shirt and tie and dropping them into the chute affixed to the wall.

"Why didn't you tell me you've been here before, Uncle Conrad?"

The bluntness of Jacob's tone startled Wilson, who stopped unlacing his shoes momentarily. "Need-to-know, Jacob. Besides, it's been a while since I've been here, and most of this wasn't completed when I was here last. For all practical purposes, this will be my first orientation to the complex."

Wilson's words were matter-of-fact, not apologetic; Jacob was sorry he had questioned, because it served only to create an uncharacteristic moment of unpleasant distance between them.

The computer-voice instructions continued, temporarily interrupting their conversation. "Move to the Degermination Cubicles to your left and press the red button located on the panel to the right of its door. Enter the cubicle and stand with feet on spots indicated on the floor. Please remain motionless until you are informed the decontamination process is completed."

"You know, Jake, this entire complex is primarily the brainchild of one man," Conrad Wilson said from the cubicle next to his. "Herrlich Krimhler."

He was glad his foster father considered the uncomfortable words between them a closed matter.

"At his age, his accomplishments are phenomenal, with his contribution to the Arab-Israeli Treaty, and now this fantastic complex."

"How old is he?"

"Twenty-eight."

"I didn't know he is Wilhelm Krimhler's adopted son," Jacob said, trying not to move while an apparatus passed over his body spraying its cleansing foam, "until I heard someone mention it at State the other day."

"Tragic story, really. Wilhelm Krimhler had two sons by

his first wife. Their mother died in a plane crash somewhere in the Tyrolean Alps. He married again three years later, to a woman of Middle Eastern extraction. He adopted her little boy. His own two sons, both in their late teens, disappeared while skiing in Austria. Speculation was that they got caught in an avalanche. Of course, Wilhelm's own death was unusual itself, as you know."

"Killed by a snake bite, wasn't he?"

"A sea snake of some sort, while he was diving near Corsica. They were too far out to get the antitoxin in time. And the tragedy didn't end there."

"His wife—Herrlich's mother--died, didn't she? I remember something about it."

"Yes, it's a real horror story. When the elder Krimhler died, Herrlich's mother just went crazy. It's not common knowledge, but according to people who knew the family, she went into a deep depression. To make matters worse, she blamed the boy, who was by then 10 years old. Said he caused the snake to kill her husband, said that the boy was evil--the son of the devil or some such thing. She tried to kill him with a butcher knife. I understand she's still in an asylum somewhere near Bonn."

The similarities and differences between himself and the young billionaire ran quickly through Jacob's thoughts. They were both victims of family tragedies. On the surface, the younger Krimhler had it all—riches, notoriety, genius—a future which, according to all the hyperbole the media could muster, was limited only by Krimhler and what he himself chose to do with his life. Jacob had Conrad Wilson, a man who considered him his own son. He had Karen, who loved him. He would never exchange places with Herrlich Krimhler, he decided.

Twenty-three minutes later, Wilson, Jacob and Herdrick Franke, riding aboard a sleek silver and transparent monorail train, glided noiselessly to a stop and were escorted by several uniformed men from the monorail's tube-shaft, then down seemingly endless white-marbled corridors.

"We are approximately one kilometer beneath the surface at this point," Franke said, gesturing with a sweep of his right hand. "It was not noticeable to you, I'm sure, but while being conveyed on the tube-train, we were actually descending. The depth, of course, gives this complex a relatively good survival prognosis, should the unthinkable occur."

They approached large, heavy metal doors that slid electronically apart, allowing entrance to a cavernous room that pulsed with life, both human and artificial. Men and women, mostly dressed in either the orange jumpsuits or totally in white, went about their respective jobs, apparently oblivious to the new arrivals.

"All of this equipment, the state-of-the-art in computer technology, is protected against any sort of earth shock, be it manmade or natural in origin. The computer itself formulated the blueprint for the shock-absorption system. Herr Krimhler estimates we could successfully absorb an earthquake measuring well above eight on the Richter scale, or say an almost direct hit of the largest nuclear detonation. Our biggest threat would be the Aegean's attempt to flood us. However, we have unique machinery to prevent such an occurrence. A pumping system based on internal pressure, which would handle all but the most severe breaches of the almost solid rock in which we sit."

"Sounds like the place to be nowadays," Wilson said. "Maybe we should all move in, eh, Jake?"

"In effect," said the German, "that's what the leadership of the U.E.S. has done. Not because of the nuclear threat, of course, but because Unified Europe can be run much more efficiently these days by computer communications and so forth. Very little time will be spent in the headquarters at

Brussels once this facility is fully activated. Upon its completion, governing will be distributed between the Naxos complex, Europa Rome, and New Babylon."

"What about the leadership in the other various capitals, and the royalty, such as the British royalty?" Jacob asked while they walked. "Everybody can't be brought here."

"You have hit upon the very heart of the concept," said the scientist. "Ah! But I am not a politician. Or I should say, I'm a politician only to the extent that I must do what is necessary to assure that my team has all the funds essential to accomplishing our mission — that of technological unification. I leave it up to you and Conrad, and to Herr Krimhler, to provide leadership in bringing us all together ideologically and governmentally."

"These are some of the difficult issues we face. To take centuries of cultural, political, socioeconomic and religious ties and somehow convince the people that things must change if we are to..."

"If we are to move into the age of enlightenment and truly equal freedom for all peoples."

The men turned to see the man whose words interrupted those of Conrad Wilson.

"The people will be convinced. Circumstances will make them see the wisdom of such change." The tall young man, whose dark, compelling eyes scanned the three men, took Wilson's hand, then those of Jacob and Herdrick Franke. Jacob recognized him as Herrlich Krimhler. Instantly, he sensed what others had told him—that though Krimhler was present in body when you talked with him face to face, he seemed somehow absent in spirit. The distant look from the eyes gave the feeling, nonetheless, that one was being sized up for some monumental purpose.

"Nice to see you again, Ambassador," Krimhler said before turning to Jacob. "And I am pleased to meet you, Mr. Zen."

Jacob nodded, feeling the cool flesh of the man's large, firm hand. "You are right, Ambassador: our task is difficult. But the circumstance of our time will be made to serve us. The people shall be made to understand that national sovereignty and autonomy cannot be selfishly exercised at the expense of universal liberty. Freedom for all can be assured only through strength of unity in the days ahead."

"Our President Lincoln said it well: "A house divided cannot stand," Wilson put in.

"Those words, first spoken by Jesus of Nazareth, have never been more appropriate than now, Mr. Ambassador," Krimhler agreed, walking between Wilson and Jacob. "If we cannot find common ground and come to the point of intelligent compromise, we cannot stand as civilized people. That is our purpose here—to provide the technology and the political forum where the meeting of the mind and spirit of collective Man can begin to take place."

Krimhler's English was tinged with a nondescript accent, neither German nor Middle Eastern. His words were spoken with economy of effort; the baritone voice, unabrasive to the listener's ear, at the same time had an urgent, disquieting quality that mesmerized. Recalling the articles and news stories he had read, heard, and seen about Herrlich Krimhler, Jacob thought the man's reputation as a persuader well-deserved.

"I hope your President and Congress are of similar mind, Ambassador," Krimhler said.

"We are for unification, Herr Krimhler, of course. It remains to be seen whether we are in complete agreement regarding every detail of the Unified European States' concept of how our coming together should proceed."

"As I said, that is why we are here, Mr. Ambassador. To come to a meaningful compromise, a meeting of the minds, so that we can become one in spirit."

"We would certainly agree to that, providing there is equal input by all parties involved."

"Then let us begin as soon as you have been made comfortable. There is to be a time of getting acquainted at six this evening." Krimhler turned to Jacob. "You will find our Communications Center suitable to your needs, I believe, Mr. Zen."

He motioned to a woman wearing a white smock, who stood from behind a control console table and walked to them.

"Show Mr. Zen to Satelvid Three, Ms. VanHorne, and instruct him in its use." The young German looked again at Jacob. "Enjoy your visit with Miss Mossberg."

Krimhler's knowing about his wish to talk with Karen startled Jacob. The young woman hooked her arm between his right arm and body and tugged gently for him to accompany her away from the other men.

"Come. You will find this most interesting, Mr. Zen."

"Oh, I already do, Miss VanHorne," he said lightly.

"I believe you will find Satelvid Three even more interesting," the pretty woman said with a knowing smile.

At last! A warm, good-humored person with whom to share time in this otherwise impersonal place so far from home... from Karen. "I'm Jacob," he said while they walked.

"Fredria."

"Fredria VanHorne... Dutch?"

"Yes." She continued to hold his arm captive in the crook of her escorting arm. "I was born in Amsterdam, but spent much of my life in England. My father was assigned there in various diplomatic capacities until I was eighteen. When he died, I went back to Holland to study for a while, then later returned to London to complete post-graduate work."

The name VanHorne — a diplomat in London. The correlation jogged his memory. "You're not Ambassador Robert VanHorne's daughter?"

"Yes. His younger."

He remembered the circumstances of the Dutch diplomat's death five years earlier. A victim of a terrorist bomb taped to his Mercedes. Three men and one woman killed in the blast. The woman had been this girl's mother.

"We've probably come close to meeting at some of those boring diplomatic social functions at one time or the other... maybe in London or D.C."

"Your parents were in the American diplomatic service?"

"Not my real parents. They both died when I was quite young. Conrad Wilson has been more than a parent to me."

"I remember seeing Ambassador Wilson when I was a teenager. It was at a tea or something in Paris, and my father introduced me to him. I think I fell in love with him instantly. And I notice he is still as handsome as then. However, at the time, I certainly was not aware of his handsome stepson."

"Foster son."

"Oh, of course, the last name."

"He never was allowed to adopt me because of my aunt's objection. You don't remember me, probably because there were so many other young men trying to impress you. We probably just missed each other somehow. I certainly would've remembered you." The girl smiled, letting the subject drop.

With the escalator ride at an end, they walked at a fast pace along the 8-foot wide rubber mat that sat atop the cement walkway. A monorail track, similar to the one that had conveyed Wilson and him earlier, ran parallel to the walkway along the ceiling of the long tube-train shaft that narrowed in the distance into a pinpoint of light, giving him the feeling that he was looking down the inside of a gigantic rifle barrel.

"I have just about every kind of clearance known to the western world, and I've never heard anything about this." He gestured with a sweep of his free hand. "It's incredible!"

The tube train overtook them, then came to a stop 50 feet ahead. People in uniforms, some in white coats like that worn by Fredria, some in the orange jumpsuits like he wore, either boarded the train or stepped from it.

"How long have you been working on this project?"

"Six months or so ago, Herrlich Krimhler asked that I join the project's communications section. I was not long out of graduate school and had just begun work within his laser robotics facility outside Bonn when he asked me to work here."

"Then you aren't involved in any of the political aspects?"

"Heaven forbid! Politics is the farthest matter from my interest. I know little or nothing of the ultimate purpose or grand design for this complex; only my job, which is over-seeing the development and implementation of its communications capabilities. And that is what I am about to show you now."

"You know Herrlich Krimhler. I'm puzzled about something that happened just before he introduced us. Maybe you can help me."

"I will try, of course."

"He seemed to know that the one thing on my mind was to call someone back home. He mentioned her specifically, by name. To my knowledge, no one had time to say anything to him about my wanting to contact her. He knew who she was and how important it is to me that I get in touch with her."

"I can only tell you that Herr Krimhler makes a point to know everything about everyone with whom he has dealings.

How he has this ability is a mystery many of us have questioned from time to time. Many things about him stimulate one's imagination. I have been associated with him for more than a year, working closely at his side for long periods of time, and still I am amazed at the extent of his knowledge. So it doesn't really surprise me, what you have told me."

"The classic enigma."

"A perfect description of Herrlich Krimhler," she said, reaching into a pocket of the smock and bringing out an identification card. She inserted it into a slot on the wall and a door slid open. They entered the room, Jacob's eyes taking in a fantastic array of futuristic machinery.

"Our miracle technology, Jacob," Fredria said with pride. "This is what I have spent the last six months of my life working on. Satelvid Three!"

She smiled, seeing the look of intimidated amazement on his face. "Don't worry. I will have you in contact with your young woman before you know it. She is young, isn't she? And beautiful?" Fredria cocked an eyebrow and grinned.

"No lovelier than my present company," he continued the banter.

"My... you Americans have all the right words to turn a girl's head," she said lightly, leading him toward a maroon-colored chair that faced a darkened booth-like chamber.

"I promised you an interesting experience. Here is where it begins." She placed her hand on the chair. "Sit down, and we will start." When he complied, she went to the console board to his right and manipulated a number of controls, causing the chamber in front of him to come alive with colored lights that danced in brilliant flashes. "Push the large button on the right side of the chair's arm when I tell you."

"That seems easy enough, even for me."

She ignored his joke, her attention fully on activating the

machine. When she had done so, she swiveled in her chair to explain.

"So far as I am aware, this is the first such operating system in the world. It involves holography. Are you familiar with the term?"

"Only slightly. Has something to do with three-dimensional images, doesn't it?"

"To put it in its most simple terms, yes. It is a process by which a three-dimensional image is produced using lasers and photography. There have been, of course, many successful uses of holographic techniques over the past 10 years. And, holographic television will be put into the commercial markets of the world soon. But there has never to this point been a workable holophone. That is, holography that is applied to picture phone technology, whereby one can see the three-dimensional image of the person with whom they are conversing."

"And that's what this light show is about?"

"Yes. It is still somewhat primitive as compared to what we hope it will become very shortly, but, as you will see, it is a wonderfully radical departure from conventional picture-phone technology."

She turned to the control panel and punched several buttons; the interior of the chamber took on a foggy appearance, and an undulating electronic whine began at a low pitch, and accelerated until it became a steady hum. "The system is ready now, Jacob. Do you know the number you wish to reach?" He nodded affirmatively. "Press the button on the outside of the chair arm and speak the number. If she is not near a picture phone, the holographic portion of the transmission will automatically be activated when she does plug in the picture phone."

He pushed the button. "Now follow the instructions on the marquee above the Holochamber," Fredria said. The readout displayed the input needed to make the connection to McLean, and Jacob gave it in the order requested. When he finished, the bright mist within the Holochamber formed into a solid white mass. Fredria VanHorne spoke quickly.

"They answered on a conventional phone. We will get the hologram when they switch to picture phone. Just talk as you would by telephone."

"Hello? Jacob Zen here," he said, interrupting the man on the other end of the line, who had already spoken into his receiver.

"Yes? This is Stone Oaks, residence of Ambassador Conrad J. Wilson. May I help you?" Jacob recognized the dignified voice as belonging to Andrew Cogdon, head of Wilson's domestic servant staff.

"Cog... This is Jacob. I need to speak to Karen. I'm on picture phone."

"Yes, Jacob."

They seemed to be temporarily cut off, but Jacob could hear muffled voices in the background.

Moments later, Cogdon was back on the line.

"Jacob. We shall have to get her out of her bath. Can you hold for a moment?" There were more muffled shuffling noises in the background. "She is on her way to the basement, now," Cogdon said. "How is everything with you and the Ambassador?"

"Fine... just fine," Jacob replied impatiently.

"Hello?"

It was Karen!

"Hello, Sweetie! You okay?"

"Where are you?" she asked; he saw her put her hand over her eyes, apparently trying to see his image on the picture phone's screen.

"I'm in the Aegean. Sorry, can't give you my exact whereabouts. You know... Top Secret... and all that," he said lightly.

She made no response, and he looked to Fredria. "There's something wrong with the image in the chamber."

"One of our problems, I'm afraid. It takes a few minutes to reach maximum clarity."

"Jacob, I'm told this picture phone unit has lost audio reception, and they can't fix it. They say all our phones here are having problems right now, and I can't see you clearly at all. In order to talk with you, I'll have to leave Stone Oaks, and I don't think you would want me to do that. I'm fine. Can you call me later? They tell me they'll have the problem fixed as soon as possible."

Karen's image was clear in the Holographic Chamber now — as if he could walk into it and put his arms around her and hold her. His frustration with not being able to do so was overwhelming.

"Karen! I've got to talk with you... It's okay to go find another phone! I'll give you a number where I can be reached."

Desperate, he looked at Fredria VanHorne, who shook her head negatively. "Sorry. We can't give our communications contact information until it is okayed by Herr Krimhler, and that will be when the center is fully operational. We can only call out... she can no longer hear you."

He slammed his fist against the chair arm. "You mean there's no way I can contact her? With all this technological garbage around here?!"

"Perhaps the communications can be reestablished shortly."

"Jacob, I don't know whether you're still on the line, because the picture is a blur now, but I want you to know... I love you..." Karen's image seemed to break apart... "I love you."

He looked to Fredria, who had left her seat to check something on another console panel several yards away. He started to call for her to restore the video, but changed his mind when it reassembled on its own. "...I want you to know... I love you..." Her words were repeated with the same inflection as before. The hologram broke apart once more then reassembled, seeming to slip backward several seconds in time, then repeat itself. "I want you to know... I love you..." Karen's image said again before disintegrating completely.

* * *

AT 5:58, the room with the long tables, arranged in a squared banquet configuration, was animate, with perhaps, Jacob silently estimated, 150 people. He knew none of them as far as he could tell.

Like himself, they were dressed in formal eveningwear, his tuxedo given him by one of Herdrick Franke's colleagues.

He considered, while sipping his drink, how this could be any one of the many dinners he had attended with Conrad Wilson over the past 15 years. And the Ambassador was treating it no differently than he had on those occasions, making his way along the table toward Jacob, nodding, smiling, shaking hands, bending to kiss the cheek of one woman, then another.

His face was reddened, causing his white hair, mustache and eyebrows to glow effulgently above the black tux. Wilson looked to be what the old man liked to term "in full sail"—inebriated to the point of having the best possible time, yet in control enough to protect the image he treasured —that of consummate senior statesman of the United States. Jacob worried that the red glow meant the old man's already-high blood pressure was probably elevated to a dangerous level.

The noise level in the big room increased, shrill laughter coming from the table across the open space from where

Jacob sat. A cacophonous mixture of old men's guffaws and young women's giggling, of tinkling cocktail crystal and boisterous toasts that vied to outdo those offered before, of promises that would not be remembered the next day, much less kept. He wanted, more than anything he had ever wanted before, to be with Karen.

Something about the aborted conversation bothered him. Should the stopping, restarting and slipping of transmission be a part of holographic communications? He had not seen it happen since the earliest days of the more familiar two-way telecommunications known now as picture phone. Maybe the holograph was now going through a similar ironing-out-the-bugs process. But the slipping and repeating of Karen's image, her repeated words, were not the most troubling aspect of the one-sided conversation. It was the distance that seemed to separate them during his attempt to reach her. A spiritual distance never before experienced, no matter the number of miles keeping them from each other.

Things could not have changed that much in that short space of time. She was practically frantic when he talked with her from Brussels. Now she seemed content to the point of being sedate. The whole thing was eerie, unnatural, even allowing for his first-time experience with the holographic set-up. Was he truly paranoid?

Stone Oaks, one of the best maintained residences in the world—right up there with the White House--its telephone systems, totally out of commission?! And, even Conrad Wilson seemed to find the situation not unusual, even though he had boasted on many occasions that Stone Oaks would have communications, even if most others should be disrupted.

The old mansion had priority second only to the White House, the vice presidential mansion, the secretary of state's residence and a few key congressional leaders' apartments and homes. Something was significantly amiss at McLean, and no one but him seemed to care! Was it the Russian threat? Did that crisis so totally dominate all else at the moment? Certainly not to look at the faces, everyone equal in glow to that of Conrad Wilson's.

"All alone in this crowd? One's own thoughts can sometimes be better company on such occasions, though, can't they?"

The tap on his shoulder and the soft voice startled him. "Good evening, Fredria."

She was dazzling, in a midnight blue evening dress, her honey-blonde hair drawn in a tight, piled-swirl above one of the loveliest faces he had seen. Pear-shaped diamonds, at least a carat each, dangled and danced brilliantly from either ear, reflecting light from the chandelier above them.

"I'm not going to say how great you look, because whatever I said would fail to do you justice. I hope you don't find that too corny of me," he smiled, taking her hand.

"Corny? I'm not familiar with the expression."

"It means trite... backwards... socially silly. I guess that's the definition."

"Ah! But do you mean what you said?"

"You'd better believe I mean it," he said, holding her hand more tightly.

"Then I have not, how do you Americans say it? Been handed a line?" She laughed. "No... No... don't tell me. If I have just been handed a line, my ego could not tolerate a fall from such heights as your compliment has placed it."

"The line might be a bit worn, but in your case, it's totally true," he said.

"You are kind, Sir." She tried to look teased. "Now let us see if you think me... corny. I haven't time to be subtle, because I do not know if we will be together again before this is over."

Fredria cocked her head, her voice becoming less businesslike, her pretty blue green eyes sparkling. "Would you stop by my flat this evening? Around 11? It has been a long while since I've enjoyed the company of someone I really wish to be with. Do you think it terrible of me to say so?"

"Of course not. Why should I think badly of you? I'll look forward to it."

He answered before thinking about her question, and he hated himself for sounding so formal. Too, he thought himself crazy that there was something he would rather do than be with this fabulously desirable woman. He had to try to get back to Karen.

"Marvelous! At 11, then," she said, reaching into her evening bag and pulling out a card. After handing it to him, she slipped her slender fingers beneath the sleeve cuff of his shirt and ran them seductively through the hair on his arm.

"I see you young folks are enjoying this little get-together." Conrad Wilson, having made his way along the table, gripped the girl's arm while waving and smiling to someone calling for his attention from across the room.

"You wouldn't know the world is at the brink of crisis by the looks of this group, would you?" He kissed Fredria lightly on her cheek. "One of the privileges of age. Nobody minds, because we're considered harmless." He winked at Jacob.

"Nonsense, Ambassador. It is the privilege of us girls to be granted the benefits of your experienced attentions." She stretched to return the kiss.

"You're in the wrong business, my dear. You should be in the U.E.S. Diplomatic Corps," Wilson said, smiling broadly,

"The way things have been going with our work lately, that would be a welcome occupational change. That's why you see everyone here enjoying themselves so merrily. They've earned their break from work." She looked at Jacob. "We've all earned our time of recreation."

Reading her meaning, Conrad Wilson smiled, then became serious. "There's been trouble with your work?"

"Only the rush. We've been working 12-hour shifts. I'm not complaining; I enjoy the work. But I and a few others who have been supervising the installation of the H.C.S. have been working 15 and 16 hours at a stretch in some instances. Being cooped in the complex day and night, we are verging on becoming claustrophobic!"

"H.C.S.?"

Wilson broke in to answer Jacob's question. "Hemispheric Computer System. Wildest concept you could imagine! Makes UNIVUS and UNIVER and all other communications capabilities between continents as obsolete as the telegraph made the Pony Express!"

"A very good analogy, Ambassador Wilson, but thank God it is no longer only a concept. Now it is fact, and will be operational by the end of the month. I don't know if any of us would care to go through this sort of schedule again."

"How does it differ from the international computer hookups we have now? We have instant and total Interact capabilities already, don't we?" Jacob said.

"I think only Herrlich Krimhler can answer that question satisfactorily. And I see things are about to begin, so you'll have at least some of your answers within a few minutes, perhaps. All I will say is that you can sum up the concept — as the Ambassador calls it — in a single term... commitment." I must be seated. "See you at 11?"

"At 11." Jacob held his glass in salute to Fredria, who said with her eyes, her intentions.

"I don't know what's going on, Son," Wilson whispered out of the corner of his mouth, his eyes straight ahead. He smiled and waved to a group of Japanese at the table directly across from them. "They've gotten wind of Project Eagle. I don't know how much they know, but I've been warned. We've got to be on our toes, my boy."

Wilson was not overly affected by the drinks. Only one other stimulus would turn his face so red and put his personality into overdrive — that provided by a crisis of first order. If the Europeans had learned the gist of Project Eagle, such a crisis was upon them now!

"Who let you know?"

"Doesn't matter now." Wilson quieted him with a motion of his hands, his own voice becoming an almost inaudible whisper. "You're going to have to get back to D.C. under one pretext or another and talk to the President. We can't securely communicate with him from here, and I've got to stay and pretend we have no idea that they suspect our intentions. If I leave, they'll know something is up, no matter what the excuse. After all, what back home could be more vital than dealing with the current Soviet situation and with unification?"

"If Project Eagle has been compromised, what can be done?"

"There's a small group of us who know the details of the project. The President has to be informed as soon as possible about this so that if it's being leaked by one of our group, he can cut off the leak. No one except the President and I know all the factors involved in the project, but each member knows some aspect, and their collective knowledge pretty well covers Project Eagle. We can't afford to have the mole, whoever he is, weaseling information out of somebody else, and we can't take the risk of his stealing additional information. Whoever is responsible for the leak has security clearance to do great damage. The sooner we find the culprit, the quicker we can avert that possibility."

"What can we do if we find who's responsible?"

"I'm in favor of lopping off his head. But we'll turn him

over to the right folks, who can squeeze some counterintelligence out of his hide."

"That would include opening Project Eagle to more interactives."

"Yeah, well, if we're looking for real problems... what if the spy in our midst is Director Quinton?"

He was right. If the Director of the CIA was the guilty party, that meant a number of agents were in it with him. However, the possibility of Edward Quinton being a part of such a scheme was remote; he had been adamantly against an ultra-close alliance with the Europeans since being named director seven years ago. The CIA was forced to give up much to constitutional safeguards. Quinton was not about to voluntarily subject the company to an even greater set of restrictions. Almost certainly, he was as strongly a supporter of Project Eagle as the President himself.

"We both know Quinton is one of the least likely suspects. We'll find a way to extract the information from the traitor without involving too many others in our plans."

Wilson stood from his seat behind the white linen covered banquet table to shake hands with a representative from Sweden who had walked over, and exchanged a few words with the heavy-set man.

"Watch that girl, Son," Wilson said in a whisper after being seated again, lifting his glass in silent toast to another group of dignitaries. "Remember Delilah, Salome, Mata Hari and all the rest."

He would be cautious with Fredria VanHorne. But he couldn't help pondering whether he should not be equally cautious of this old man. He had never had reason to mistrust his foster father, but his instinct told him that Wilson knew more than he was saying. All the research Jacob had done, all the facts he knew about the project, were scattered bits and pieces of information in his head. It was clear to him, though, that the aim of the project was to put the United States at the top of the unification heap, but some undercurrent ran beneath the flow toward dominance... Something beyond the leadership imperative smoldered beneath the surface facts he had been charged with researching.

"I'll tell you something, Son. We've got to get a handle on this thing, now! We're being outmaneuvered, and there's the fellow who's doing it to us!"

The noise increased when Herrlich Krimhler and several other tuxedoed men entered through a doorway at the opposite end of the room, toward which Wilson pointed. There was a rush of people, all trying to get nearer the German, who seemed from Jacob's vantage to be enjoying the attention.

"Looks like if we don't want to be conspicuous, we'd better go pay our homage to Herr Krimhler." Conrad Wilson stood, touching Jacob's shoulder. "Think I'll wait until the clamor dies down a bit."

"Well, one of us had better let him know how much America loves and appreciates him." Wilson grinned then downed the remaining liquor in his glass.

"You're just the man to represent us." Jacob lifted his own glass in salute to the old diplomat.

"Look at them! You'd think he'd solved all the problems of the world!"

Jacob watched Wilson move toward the crowd around Krimhler and sipped the drink he had been nursing for the past several minutes. Maybe Krimhler didn't have all the problems of the world solved, but there was something about the man that made people think those answers lay somewhere behind the darkly handsome face. There was no denying the charismatic magnetism, and even Conrad Wilson, who moments before facetiously praised Krimhler, was drawn to him like the others. Star-struck women, their eyes fixed on him, obsequious men, smiling, patting the young German's shoulder, vying, for his attention — each trying to out-congratulate the other.

Was he, like his foster father said, conspicuous by sitting there by himself, observing the worship? If so, he didn't care. The first flush of the alcohol's effect drenched his sensibility. If his disgust over the attention being given Herrlich Krimhler was jealousy — he also did not care.

Who was the man who already, at an age younger than his own, had eclipsed most world leaders in recognition? It was probably envy that generated his disdain for this transplanted Middle Easterner—an aberration of pettiness that would most likely transform into respect, then into admiration once he got to know the man. It was time to show himself, if no one else, that he was bigger than pettiness allowed.

He stood, somewhat unsteadily, surprised that the small amount of liquor had affected him to such an extent, then made his way to the last of the congratulators around Krimhler.

Herrlich Krimhler disengaged from those around him and slid between several people in order to take Jacob's offered hand. Perhaps it was merely his own self-estimation that caused him to think he saw an extra measure of appreciation on the young man's tanned face.

"I don't understand it at all, Herr Krimhler, but the complex and the technologies you've developed here are absolutely astounding!"

"I believe it will serve us well as we move into the dawning age. Thank you for coming this evening, Mr. Zen. You will not be disappointed."

With their grips broken by a woman of about 50 who

pulled Krimhler toward another group of people, Jacob said, "I am already glad I came, Herr Krimhler."

Although Krimhler didn't deny he was personally responsible for the complex, as Jacob credited him with being, and although the young German didn't verbally share the praise with the hundreds of scientists and others who no doubt made the massive undertaking successful, the self-centeredness by omission was not offensive. There seemed no arrogance in the act, rather acceptance of a fact, much like royalty might accept credit for being royalty. It was at the same time acknowledgment, and of no matter, by virtue of the fact, that it was what Herrlich Krimhler was born to.

When he returned to his seat beside Wilson, who was engaged in polemics with three men gathered in front of their table, the large doors at the opposite end of the room swung open and people carrying various electronic paraphernalia rushed in, snapping pictures and surrounding Krimhler with floodlights and whirring cameras. The frantic activity seemed to be a signal for the German to move to the platform to which the long banquet tables were joined.

"The press?!" Conrad Wilson looked genuinely shocked, as did the men he had been talking with. "All this is supposed to be top secret. What's the press doing here?"

The conversational buzz made it obvious the flood of reporters had taken most in the room by surprise.

"Ladies and gentlemen, if you will take your seats, please." The man behind the podium at the center of the platform was Gular Hendstrom, chairman of the E.E.S. Commission of Ten. The rumble died slowly, quieting to the shuffling and clicking sounds the press made while competing for the best angles from which to record the event.

"As everyone here knows, the world faces catastrophe at every turn." Hendstrom spoke extemporaneously, in English.

"The challenge, on a day-to-day basis, has been not to better the circumstances in which we live, but rather the challenge, since the time nuclear war became possible, has been to survive as the human race. You sit today at the heart of the technology which will, with the cooperation of all of us here, with the cooperation of all peoples everywhere, not only save mankind from that genocidal finality, but will help in ushering in a period unparalleled in human history. An age only dreamed of to this point by the great Utopian dreamers."

"We of the Commission of Ten have taken it upon ourselves, in fairness to all peoples of the world, to invite the press so the word can be spread that a New Age is upon us. Not in word only, but, if we will all do our parts, in deed, as well! My fellow citizens of the world community, I give to you the chief architect of this Earth-saving center of man's progress... Herrlich Krimhler!"

Flash units exploded in light; the men and women of the world press moved in, crowding toward the platform where Krimhler stood smiling, subdued, while nodding and giving quick, chopping waves of his right hand. All were out of their seats, applauding, their eyes on the man they came to honor.

"Got to give the devil his due." Conrad Wilson's smile was broad and approving. "Whatever it takes to be a winner, he's got it!" The old man's smile dissolved, his lips becoming a thin, solemn line when he turned to speak his confidential thoughts into Jacob's ear. "He's got to go... or we will have to go."

Had he heard correctly? If Wilson meant what Jacob thought he heard, it was out of character for the man he knew so well. It was said as if Jacob was supposed to know something Wilson knew. As if the two of them had discussed the matter before. Was he talking about assassination? Did Wilson think they had talked about it before? A senile slip, thinking of someone else who did know what Wilson thought Jacob knew?

Was Conrad Wilson, in fact, capable of condoning killing someone merely for political purposes? If so, was Wilson... was the United States government right in considering it acceptable to murder for the sake of assuring success in achieving political goals? How did such thinking differ from that of the Sino and Russian beasts? More personally to the point, was Hugo Marchek the victim of such rationale? Had he and Karen almost become victims of such philosophy on the highway that terror-filled night? Was Karen in danger now... sequestered within a nest of assassins who believed such killings were for the ultimate good?

"Just look at 'em!" Wilson said, looking around the room. "He's got them all under his thumb!"

Jacob said nothing, but agreed cerebrally that the applauding, adoring throng said with their glazed eyes that to which Wilson testified. Herrlich Krimhler, on this night at least, held captive this agglomeration of some of the free world's most influential people.

They quieted finally, and Krimhler stepped to behind the lectern; his expression changed from appreciative acceptance to concern. He waited until all noise subsided. Reporters were the last to settle, decreasing in activity until only an occasional camera shutter click could be heard.

Herrlich Krimhler's facial features were stark contrasts of darks and lights beneath the harsh, precisely directed spotlights beaming down from the high ceiling. His black hair, thick and flawlessly groomed, glistened above the black eyebrows. His eyes appeared to have no pupils, the color surrounding the pupils being nearly as dark as the pupils themselves. The eyes' mirror-like depth reflected an intelligence inexplicably discomforting to those coming under their gaze.

Even from this distance, Jacob could sense the power. He had heard of it and read the conjecture about Krimhler's well-publicized paranormality. If the mesmerizing influence on this audience could be counted as example of what was written and spoken about the man, he agreed; whether paranormal or not, the effect was real enough.

Herrlich Krimhler seemed to him at this moment not a modern man at all, but a fictionalized antediluvian prince who generated a type of excitement found only in tales of sorcery and wizards and enchanted swords.

To the others, this technological messiah standing before them was as a fresh, senses-stimulating wind, promising to cleanse their decaying world with his computer-age miracles. And, there was no turning back. The masses demanded the future. The future stood at the lectern in the person of Herrlich Krimhler, telling them what they ravenously hungered to hear.

"To those who say the free world is on the edge of societal collapse... That mankind has, through thoughtless industrialization, painted itself into a corner of ecological extinction... To those who preach that we have militarized ourselves to the brink of nuclear apocalypse... To these I say, at this time and at this place... What man has done, man has within himself the power to undo! Resolve with me, right now, that we shall begin that glorious task. That we shall take the necessary steps on the pathway to peace!"

The words were not new. Jacob had heard them, or some form of them, hundreds of times. But the electricity sparking from this unique personality, he had not felt during all his years in government. When Krimhler said it, you believed it could be done.

Jacob looked over the room, seeing the expressions of euphoria. It wasn't just him, he concluded. The ambience pulsed with a life of its own, invading, permeating the emotions of each man and woman. He, himself, was struck by diametrically opposite desires — wanting to at the same time join and resist the magnetic tug his gut-feeling told him was concentrically wrong. Wrong with the man... With the thoughts he spoke. He couldn't determine exactly why. Maybe fear of Krimhler's motive. After all, he had lived in an atmosphere of clandestine threat for some time. Maybe it was only a self-generating cynicism, paranoia... that everyone was out to destroy the few remaining things good with the world.

"The path to peace is one that will not long remain in place. We must take it soon or we will perish! I propose to you, here and now... I challenge the world at this most crucial moment in history... I propose, through EARTHSPHERE-10, Six Ways to Law... Six Ways to Order... Six Ways to Peace!"

Despite his best effort to dispel the feeling, it grew. It had something to do with the faces around him. The blazing eyes, the expressions of slavish approval. Suddenly he knew where he had seen them. They were like the expressions on the faces of the millions of Germans he had seen while watching documentary films about the Third Reich.

CHAPTER 8

Morning poured into the bedroom, spilling across the thick, rose-red carpet and bathing the end of the flower-patterned bedspread with sunlight. Holding his hand over his eyes, Jacob fought to gain consciousness. The music of the birds helped draw his senses into focus.

"We certainly didn't act like someone who so desperately misses our lady friend back home!" The cheery female voice pulled him the rest of the way from his sleep. "I must say, I certainly missed none of my friends last evening!"

Fredria VanHorne stood over him smiling, holding a cup and saucer.

Jacob looked at his wrist for his watch; not finding it, he glanced around the unfamiliar surroundings. "What time is it?"

"Eight-thirty." She handed him the coffee when he had adjusted to receive it. "How do you like my little slice of the upper world?" She sat on the bed and swept the air with a slender arm.

"These days, I don't think there's any place you can find this much sunlight on the surface. How's it done?"

"Special lighting effects, recordings and scents created by some of my scientist friends. I wake every morning this way. Well, not exactly this way — but as far as the illusion of being on the surface is concerned." Fredria smiled coquettishly, then lay beside him. "I don't suppose I could keep you as my pet? To make my little place here just perfect?"

"Right now I can't think of a more desirable life's calling." He put the cup aside and took her in his arms and kissed her. "But it's a luxury neither of us can afford. I presume Herr Krimhler will require some help in saving the world."

"You are envious." Fredria laughed and cradled his face in her hands.

"Maybe a little... yes."

"Of his wealth? Of the admiration people, particularly the ladies, have for him?" she said, still amused.

"Those two aren't mutually exclusive, are they?"

"It is my opinion that everything, with men, comes down to a matter of virility. You invariably link all accomplishments and failures to the ability to perform sexually."

"I didn't know your areas of expertise include psychology," Jacob interrupted.

"A woman doesn't have to be a psychologist to know the mind of a man. It is so obvious that you more often reason with your libido than with logic. That's not altogether bad, of course." She kissed his cheek lightly.

"And Herr Krimhler?"

"What about him?"

"How's his reasoning ability?"

"To get to the point you will eventually reach after all of this sparring, I have no idea how good a lover Herrlich Krimhler might be."

"Come now, Fredria. You've never...?"

"No. I've never!" she interrupted with playful irritation in her voice. "As a matter of fact, we girls have wondered among ourselves for quite some time why none of us have had the pleasure of his... attentions. He seems to have no interest, I am sorry to have to say. So automatically he is homosexual, right?" Her blue-green eyes flashed suspicion when she put the question.

"Did I say that?"

"Yes. With your thoughts... thinking with your libido. All things involving achievement translate into varying degrees of virility. Herrlich Krimhler has intellect, power, prestige, and limitless financial resources. He should be the great lover, but he seems to have no interest in women, therefore he must be homosexual. Do you want to know why there's the great number of homosexual males today? The problem is created by just that attitude. They are terrified they cannot live up to the standard-- so they retreat into a less competitive, less threatening sexual world."

"I give up. He must not be homosexual. You've convinced me." He shrugged submission.

"You are obstinate, Jacob Zen!" She loosened her hair from its swirled pile atop her head, letting it tumble about her shoulders to full length. "Now show me again how you think only with your libido."

Thoughts ricocheted in his head — kept pounding the same question over and over. Who was she? He closed his eyes, feeling her warmth, scenting her feminine essence, his apprehensions giving way not altogether grudgingly. Before losing control, those inner words came again, unmistakably clear. "*Watch that girl, Son. Remember Delilah, Salome, Mata Hari and all the rest...*"

He was still mulling Conrad Wilson's admonition three-and-a-half hours later while he packed a gray blazer into a clothes bag. Karen's pretty face formed a translucent backdrop against which a hundred other thoughts flashed some-where in the center of his brain. Trying to shrug off the depression as merely a feeling of guilt for having enjoyed the time spent with Fredria VanHorne, he rationalized that he and Karen had long ago made a pact. They agreed that sex with others was not wrong unless the physical union forged emotional bonds, damaging their own love for each other. The theory was okay; the practice was flawed.

A more profound rationale, one whose source he couldn't pinpoint, dissolved the barrier separating emotion from biological act. One sure thing emerged. Though he believed he had truly struggled to be the Renaissance man, a believer in the New Age Reformation, he would be hurt, even enraged, should Karen be with another man. A more deeply seated worry troubled him while he, without thinking about it, placed clothing and toiletry articles into the bag. The feeling had been with him even before arriving at Naxos, where one might expect to be watched to some extent. It was, since the encounter with Hugo Marchek, a sense of having lost all privacy, of being constantly monitored.

"Almost ready, are you?" Conrad Wilson said, then put an index finger to his lips, forewarning that unwanted eyes and ears watched and listened. Jacob, who stopped packing when Wilson entered the room, was quick to go along.

The old diplomat moved to Jacob's side by the bed. "Our message to the President can be one of optimism, Jake," Wilson said aloud, handing the younger man a leather port-folio. "I've prepared a briefing for him that pretty well sums up my feelings on the matter of tri-level participation, and what I think our part in it might evolve to."

He then crowded next to Jacob and began helping him put articles into the suitcase, a move to conceal the message he whispered. "There are mikes and cameras on us. There's no place we can meet right now where they can't watch us, so read those papers somewhere you won't be seen. You'll have to figure out where. In them, I've suggested a place we can meet just before you leave for D.C."

Wilson resumed normal volume. "Of course, you can give the President your observations, as well. Tell him how you feel about things."

"I'm sure we pretty much agree on things. But thanks. I'll add whatever observations I can, that I feel might help, of course."

"Good boy! Then I'll see you off at fourteen-thirty hours," the old man said, opening the door and turning to face him.

"See you then, Uncle Conrad."

So this was to be the system that would save humanity from itself, he thought when Wilson left him. His suspicions were not unfounded after all. He was not paranoid! Cooperation among peoples was not merely to be sought, it would be assured. Demanded! At whatever price required. Would western man now have his own KGB-style watchdogs? Even more efficient than the former Soviet terror-police because new, super-sensitive eavesdropping technologies would perform the surveillance? Would the citizen of the New Order have his own electronic Berlin Wall surrounding him, suffocating his every grope for lost liberty?

The realization waved over him in a hot flood of truth. The only difference between the Naxos cabal and the White House Project Eagle planners was the fact that the Unified European States and Herrlich Krimhler had been quicker to set up the machinery that would assure a successful grab for power. Was not a grab for power also the purpose of Project Eagle? Under either leadership, the individual would pay dearly for existence in the society to come.

For now, he must get a look into the portfolio without letting the snoops know about Wilson's note to him. He surveyed the room, hoping those watching thought he was attempting to find misplaced personal items instead of suspecting his real purpose--that of trying to locate surveillance devices. They were well hidden, probably within the vents at each corner of the room.

The closet might be the answer! Several articles of clothing remained hanging there, and that small space off the short hallway would be easy enough to give a quick check for surveillance equipment. There must be an excuse for spending time in the closet however, because removing three or four shirts and a couple of suits from the rack would take only seconds; it would take longer to read his foster father's instructions.

He snapped the suitcase shut, lifted it and the portfolio from the bed, then set both against the small closet's back wall. While he fiddled with the clothes on the rack, he let his eyes roam the ceiling, floor and walls. Nothing in the closet that looked like snooping lenses or microphones... No vents... Now to buy time to accomplish his task.

After gathering all of the hangers at once and lifting the clothing from the racks, he let them slip from his hands, causing them to cover the suitcases and portfolio. He cursed angrily, loud enough for those watching and listening to hear, then knelt, supposedly to gather the mess, but letting his hand wander beneath the clothing and onto the leather folder. After unsnapping the single latch, Jacob slipped his hidden right hand into the case, gathering all the papers he could feel. With his left hand, he continued to pretend he was trying to get the clothing together, all the while taking care to keep his back turned to the room outside the closet doorway in order to block the view of those watching. He hurriedly read the instructions Wilson had paper-clipped to the thick briefing report to the President; they were scrawled in the diplomat's handwriting on a single yellow sheet:

At 12:15, go to Core Chamber Z-391. You will be given a

package by someone who's on our team, I am assured that you won't be monitored while you are in that area, but you will, most likely, be watched up to that point. Find an excuse to go to the general area of that chamber, then get lost and stray into Z-391. You will be given instructions by our operative at that time. Also, you and I must grab a few minutes of privacy before you leave for D. C. Good luck, Son."

"Is everything okay with you, Mr. Zen?" The harsh, German-accented voice startled Jacob, who managed to quickly stuff the papers back into the case while concealing his activity from the man who tried to look over his shoulder. "May I help you?"

"No. I've about got it."

Jacob squatted over the jumble of clothing, effectively blocking the prying man's view. He snapped the case shut, draped the clothing over his forearm and hand that held the case, rose to his feet and walked to the bed where he dumped the load, taking care to see that the apparel covered the case.

Jacob could sense that the man in the orange and black jumpsuit uniform was verging on desperation, wanting to satisfy his curiosity about the portfolio. It gave him pleasure to keep the man, whom he was sure had been instructed to be subtle in his investigation, from getting his way. And, he was not about to let the invader go verbally unpunished.

"Is it standard operating procedure here to walk in on someone without being invited?"

"I was told you would require assistance with your luggage."

"I made no such request. Even if I had, does that excuse you from the common courtesy of knocking?"

"I apologize, Sir. Please forgive the intrusion." The words were insincere, practiced; the tone was as harsh as the accent. The man was sent to see what the camera could not, when Jacob had stayed in the closet longer than they felt necessary.

He was pleased he had so easily outmaneuvered them. No doubt there would be cameras and microphones put in the closets to prevent guests from pulling such stunts in the future.

By noon, he had figured his plan of action for rendezvousing at the spot designated by his foster father. It would be accomplished under the pretext of again trying to get into contact with Karen by Holophone.

According to the Naxos complex's schematic layout he had been given as part of his orientation, the two chambers — the one housing the Communications Center and the Core Chamber Z-391 — were in close enough proximity to make it possible for someone not familiar with the complex to, as Wilson had suggested in his instructional note, stray into the wrong area.

At 12:09, an orange-uniformed guard approached him while he walked with briefcase in hand along a marble-floored corridor, feigning confusion.

"May I help you... Mr. Zen?" the man asked after looking at the identification badge pinned to the breast pocket of Jacob's coveralls.

"Isn't Communications around here somewhere?" Jacob's words rang hollow in his own ears, but were apparently convincing enough for the Naxos security man.

"Down the corridor and two turns to the right, Sir," the man instructed, stepping closer to Jacob and pointing. "Z-three ninety-one will be on your right after the first turn."

The man's whispered words caused Jacob to jerk in surprise before realizing this was his contact. He hoped his expression hadn't betrayed them both.

"Thanks for your help," Jacob said out loud, then headed in the direction the man had pointed. He had done a credible job of appearing confused before opening the door marked Z-391, he tried to convince himself while ducking to keep from bumping his head against what looked like insulated piping that networked at eye-level throughout the room. The dimly lit chamber, he analyzed, was apparently a pumping station for one or more sections of the underground complex.

The thumping sound grew louder the farther he threaded his way toward the room's center, the noise finally stabilizing at a barely tolerable level.

He thought he heard something in addition to the pumping, like a clanking of metal against metal. Looking beneath the congestion of piping, he saw the guard who had stopped him in the hallway motioning to him from an opening in the wall just above the floor. Jacob squatted beneath the pipes to hear the man, who handed him a rectangular package wrapped in brown paper.

"Whatever happens, don't let this material out of your sight." The man's controlled tone told Jacob this was a career professional, most likely CIA.

"This is to be given only to the President, and only at the time he designates. You are to wait for his call at the White House, where you'll be staying until he calls for you. It's not likely you'll be personally searched, but once you leave U.E.S. Headquarters in Brussels, anything goes. Stay around people, that is, crowds, as much as possible. Do not let them isolate you. They'll want to get a look inside that case... might even kill for it... Make it look like a mugging. Don't give them the chance. The best way to prevent that is by staying public. You will be okay once you reach the White House, and our people will watch out for you once you get to Andrews."

The man's eyes were deadly calm, unblinking. It was easy for him to speak of life and death in terms of mission over human factors. "Remember, Mr. Zen, only President Farley is to receive this material. Absolutely no one else. Do you understand all of this?"

"Yes. But what if the case is snatched? I mean, I'm not a trained courier."

"You don't have to be." The man reached behind him into the wall's recess, and brought out a small canvas pouch. "Here's all you need to do the job." He handed it to Jacob. "It contains a special pair of courier cuffs you will attach to the case and to your wrist." He took the cuffs from the bag. "They look like any other set of cuffs, but they're not, I assure you." He held up the gleaming cuffs so Jacob could see them in the scant light. "They have a timer lock that can only be safely released before the preset time, by a certain combination of things, which only you and I and the President will know about. If the cuffs are forced open before that time, the timer, through remote electronics, activates a device inside the package I gave you to give the President. That device has enough explosive charge to destroy the package and anyone or anything within 10 or 15 feet of it."

"But what if someone removes the handle of the briefcase, or cuts it open?"

"In that case, when they open the package and unfasten a latch to get to the materials, the device will explode without the help of the timer in the cuffs. When the timer opens the cuffs at the preset time, there can no longer be an electronically activated detonation, but the latch on the box is still a functioning detonator."

"There's no way this thing can be safely taken off my wrist until the automatic timer unlocks it at the preset time?"

"The key," The man held up a key, then handed it to Jacob, "will unlock the cuffs. At the same time, just as when they are forced open, the cuffs activate the countdown to detonation. Snapping the cuffs together again shuts off the electronic detonator."

"How long from the time they are unlocked or pried open until the package explodes?"

"Three minutes, exactly — 180 seconds. Snapping the cuffs back together after they are opened by key automatically restores three full minutes of time until detonation. However, if the cuffs have been forced open, then for some reason snapped back together, the time will continue counting down until detonation."

"Then the countdown can't be stopped once the cuffs are forced open?"

"There's only one way this device can be disarmed, totally," the man said clinically, reaching behind him again and bringing out a blue metal rectangular box. "The materials in the package you are to give the President are inside a box identical to this one," he said, holding it in the palm of his hand. "This is the latch." He pointed with an index finger to a stainless steel mechanism near where the lid of the box over-lapped the box's deeper portion in a tight fit. "As you can see, it sticks out from the box to some extent and looks to be a latch you must pull up to open. If you pull straight up, like so..." He put his thumb under the latch and pushed up. "...there is an instantaneous explosion; it is, in effect, a manual detonator. But if you push three times inwardly..." He did so and the lid of the box sprang open, "...you do two things — disarm the explosive device and open the box. If you then re-close the lid, you rearm the device. Have you got all this straight?"

"I'd better have," Jacob joked feebly. It was all quite clever and spy-like, but why was he chosen to deliver the volatile (in more ways than one) package to the President? He supposed he should be excited over the honor; at least he should be nervous in anticipation of the hazardous mission. He was neither; probably, he pondered, the result of having too much happen to him, too recently. "Yes. I understand."

"Remember. If this box is shut again, it is automatically

rearmed. Our people in D.C. will deactivate the thing." Jacob nodded understanding.

"Good luck then, Mr. Zen."

The operative shrunk back into the opening behind him, leaving Jacob suddenly alone in the humming, semi-darkened pumping station, feeling the meeting was unfinished, wondering if he had gotten all the instructions right.

Two minutes later, he stood near the spot where Fredria had introduced him to the elaborate Naxos Communications Center. This time, however, there were no men and women in white smocks rushing frantically about their respective jobs of interacting with the unfathomable machinery that lined the walls, although the equipment seemed to be fully activated. A row of multi-colored lights blinked in what appeared to be rippling synchronization along one large wall panel above the control board Fredria VanHorne had manipulated to put him in contact with Karen.

Standing alone in the chamber produced eerie sensations of being the pawn of some Promethean mind. Symbolically, the last man standing in some future courtroom, being judged by his own ultimate, final computer-creation. The silence of the room, except for his own shuffling and heel-clicking sounds, brought home the total efficiency of this exponential intelligence, devoid of warm, familiar... mortal noises. The human was not, after all, needed. He could take his breaks for food, for conversation, for whatever, while his superior electronic progeny carried on with business — even the business of security.

He had been admitted after inserting his identifier card-badge into the slot device at the door, and now the huge room seemed to follow him with its artificial senses. He smiled, letting his eyes roam the chamber, feeling a fool for crediting the technology with so much thought power. It was machinery erected by mankind, nothing more. — So, to it!

The Holophone's chamber was dark; the chair he had sat in during his attempt to talk to Karen had to be turned to face the glass and metal enclosure. Fredria's console board to the right of the chair looked at first glance to be a jumble of every conceivable kind of toggle and button and lever. He decided, upon closer examination, that there was a pattern to the tangle. He determined to have a go at activating the Holophone, musing that any catastrophe resulting from his fiddling could be charged to the U.S. State Department. What were a few million more electronic dollars, added to a multi-trillion dollar deficit, that would soon be wiped clean with one or two strokes of the presidential pen? Each control was clearly marked in English, French and German. He pressed a green button with the designation: "Holophone Chamber Initiator." The darkened chamber filled instantly with misty light and began the remembered low humming that increased in volume and became rhythmic after several seconds.

Although uneasy over unfamiliarity with the technology, his need to reach Karen overcame his worry about angering anyone who might walk in and find him at his unauthorized activity. Too, he welcomed the chance to be alone while he made the attempt. There were questions to be answered — questions his last session at the Holophone brought up that would not go away. Why was all of Stone Oaks' communications out? Why was Karen subdued in her one-sided conversation yesterday, yet during their earlier Brussels' conversation she had been near panic? Why, just before the communication broke off, did the video and audio slip backward in time, then repeat, when it was supposed to be a live rather than recorded transmission?

Jacob sat in the big chair, hopeful his button manipulations had accomplished the same things Fredria's manipulations accomplished a day earlier. At the same time, the thought struck... he was most likely not alone. Why would they let him wander into this super-sensitive area, with its operators nowhere in sight, and not be watching through their many security cameras?

No time now for assessing everything that bothered him, such as: Conrad Wilson not letting him in on the whole truth about Project Eagle; his being under surveillance at Naxos; the ominous package he carried in the briefcase; and ultimately whether there would be survival of freedom for the people of the Western world — All must be pushed aside for now. All that mattered at the moment was talking to Karen and getting to her at McLean, once the package was delivered to the President.

He pushed the button on the right arm of the chair while facing the Holochamber, whose noise had reached a high, steady hum. He glanced up to the marquee above the chamber and read the input information on the display. When he finished the input, like before, the white mist of light in the chamber formed into a solid mass. After a few seconds, like the first time at the Holophone, someone answered on a conventional telephone. Fredria had said that the video portion of the Holophone would work once the picturephone was connected.

"Hello? This is Jacob Zen," he responded to the voice on the other end.

"Yes? This is Stone Oaks, residence of Ambassador Conrad J. Wilson. May I help you?"

It was Cogdon.

"Cog... Get me Karen on the picture-phone." He relaxed, relieved that he remembered the procedure necessary to complete the connection.

"Yes, Jacob." Cogdon's words were cut off. Jacob heard muffled voices in the background at Stone Oaks, then

Cogdon was on the line. "Jacob, we shall have to get her out of her bath. Can you hold for a moment?"

The same words as last time! He turned to look around the big room. Was someone playing an elaborate prank?

Cogdon's voice was on the line again. "She's on her way to the basement, now. How is everything with you and the Ambassador?" The words, the inflection were the same! Exactly the same!

Jacob remained silent, listening, his heart jumping near his throat.

Seconds later, Karen's voice came through the line. "Hello?" He started to answer, but didn't. "Where are you?" the voice said. Her image had formed in the chamber, and, like before, she put her right hand over her eyes, trying, apparently, to shield them from excessive brightness. He waited for her to speak, knowing it was futile to talk, himself.

"Jacob, I'm told the picture-phone unit has lost audio reception and they can't fix it. They say all our phones here are having problems right now, and I can't see you clearly at all. In order to talk with you, I'll have to leave Stone Oaks, and I don't think you would want me to do that. I'm fine. Can you call me later? They tell me they'll have the problem fixed as soon as possible."

There followed a long pause, Karen's image becoming clearly visible within the Holochamber. Finally, her image spoke again. "Jacob, I don't know whether you're still on the line, because the picture is a blur now, but I want you to know... I love you..." The image broke up, and she was gone.

He got up slowly from the chair — seeing or hearing nothing while he walked to the control board and switched off the Holographic machinery. Confusion clouded his thoughts, then slowly gave way to the realization he had come to some time before. He had been deceived at every level: by those here in the pit of Naxos; by Fredria Vanhorne;

by his own government; by Conrad Wilson. There was only one person he could trust, and she had been forced to participate in the deception. What did they do to her to get her to cooperate in betraying him? Why did they let him live, if he was such a liability that he couldn't be trusted to be a full partner in their plans? But someone had tried — on the interstate! Why not since, though? Why were they waiting?

He looked at his wrist for the watch that wasn't there, then to a digital clock inset in Fredria VanHorne's console board. 13:08. He quickly translated into civilian time — 1:08. Less than an hour and a half before he would leave for Brussels on his way to D.C..

How deeply involved was his foster father? The thought that Conrad Wilson might willingly be a part of deceiving him, of possibly hurting Karen, pained him, as much as, his fear that she had been harmed by whatever force was sucking him ever deeper into itself.

At LEVEL 2, Jacob emerged from the Degermination Center holding the briefcase in his left hand while straightening his necktie with his right. He then switched the case to his right hand and stretched his left arm, exposing his wrist. He cursed quietly, seeing the vacant spot where his watch should be.

"Jacob!"

He turned to see Fredria VanHorne trotting toward him. "Wait! I'll walk with you to the surface lift."

He did so, enjoying the movement of her feminine form beneath the snugly fitting white coveralls she wore.

"Why must you leave just now?" Her question was sincere enough. But any expert operative would have, among other talents, the ability to act. She put her arm through the crook of his and they walked slowly up the wide, red-carpeted concourse.

"Something's come up in Washington; they want me there

by tomorrow night for a meeting. I really don't know myself what it's about."

"Nothing to do with Miss... what's the name?"

"Karen."

"Yes... Miss Mossberg."

"No. Nothing to do with her. Like I said, I don't know what it's about, exactly. Maybe you can tell me."

Fredria seemed to recoil. "I? How could I possibly know why you are called to Washington?"

"Because it may have something to do with the new computer union between continents. Since Krimhler is at the center of it all, I assumed you would know something about it."

"It could be the Satelvid Interact phase we'll be instituting within the next two weeks," she said absently, apparently thinking out loud. She stopped and looked up at him. "I shouldn't have said that," she said, realizing the breach of security.

"I'll know about it by tomorrow night anyway. And I do have top clearance in most of these things."

"Oh, I know I can rely on your discretion. After all, we have shared many... secrets, have we not?"

Jacob smiled, but wanted to distance himself from Fredria and from the Naxos complex as quickly as possible. "What time do you have?"

She took her arm from his to see her watch. "Fourteen-twelve." She took his arm again while they continued up the concourse. "I am sorry about your watch, Jacob, but it will turn up somewhere within my apartment. Shall I mail it to you?"

"I'd appreciate that. It was a gift," he said, stopping in front of a large, electronically activated door marked SURFACE LIFT and turning to face her. He saw a softness in her expression he had not seen before, and she pulled him to her and kissed his lips.

"I shall not forget you, Jacob Zen. Please do not forget your Fredria." She kissed him again — a warm, lingering kiss that caused, for the moment, thoughts of deception and suspicion and clandestine betrayal to melt beneath her undeniable charm. Maybe she didn't know anything about the phony link-up to Stone Oaks. About the insidious intrigues of those she served... *about*...

He tried to force his ties to her from his emotions, recalling Conrad Wilson's warning: "*Remember Delilah, Salome, Mata Hari and all the rest...*"

Fredria VanHorne had to be aware of what was going on. Regardless, time no longer afforded the luxury of personal involvement. Whether she was innocent or guilty, he would remove her from his thoughts. For his sake and for Karen's.

He bent to give her a brief, detached kiss of goodbye. "How could I ever forget you?"

On the surface, the air hung heavy with humidity, an untimely fog obscuring all but those objects within 40 meters of them. The two men shuffled slowly away from the helicopter that soon would fly him to Brussels.

Conrad Wilson spoke quietly so not to be overheard by the contingent of Naxos guards and Unified European States officials gathered near the huge black and gold bird.

"I wish I could do this myself, Jake, but there's just no way. I've got to stick around here and try to keep the toehold we've managed to dig."

Wilson gripped Jacob's shirt sleeve between thumb and fingertips and nudged him even farther from the group of men, turning his face from their direction and talking out of the corner of his mouth secretively.

"Jake. Something catastrophic has happened to the Russians. I watched it all this morning with Krimhler and his bunch through one of their special communications set-ups.

They swarmed full-force into the Middle East, just like you and I talked about — The Russians, the Turks, and, get this, some renegade divisions of the German Army, which was something we didn't anticipate. Iran and Libya formed a pincer action from the East and South, with Egypt apparently only providing passage through their territory. I guess Israel was their objective. At least, they appeared intent on taking over the entire Palestine region."

The reason for the completely deserted Holochamber room. Fredria knew about the invasion, but didn't mention it.

"What happened? Who stopped them?" Jacob's mind went almost blank, feeling his senses darken with the rush of emotion.

"It was total blitzkrieg, Jake. Nothing could've stopped them short of nuclear weaponry. They came with every conventional thing they could bring. I still can't figure out what happened. According to the limited video we had, and the reports from people along Israel's northern borders, there were unbelievable deluges of rain, followed by falling fire and hailstones — some as big as medicine balls, they said.

"But the weirdest reports were those telling of greenish vapors escaping from wide cracks in the ground and engulfing the men and weapons. When that happened, according to the reports, the ground troops, those commanding, those driving the tanks and so forth, just went berserk! They began slaughtering each other! They say in some areas there's blood standing in five-foot deep pools. Bodies stacked five and more high for as far as the eye can see!" Conrad Wilson drifted into his own disbelief, staring downward at nothing in particular.

Jacob questioned through his shock, not realizing what he was asking until he had asked it. "Then Israel wasn't affected?"

Wilson's glazed eyes cleared when the question brought him back. "What?... No. They never got to the Golan Heights. Every plane was knocked out of the sky by the storm and by the hail. The Jews are saying God did it for them."

Both men were silent for several seconds, then Wilson straightened, as if he had searched inwardly and found new resolve. "Not only that, reports are that every site in and around Russia, where they had their ICBM bases and their reserve forces of conventional weaponry, were hit by these tremendously large hailstones or meteorites, or whatever they were. The Russian coalition's military capacity is destroyed! Do you know what that means, Jake?"

"The world has a chance for real peace for the first time in history, I should imagine."

"It means that now the war is between us and the U.E.S.. Now, more than ever, we've got to see to it that the United States gets control in what will very, very shortly emerge from all this. Whoever moves the quickest will be the future, my boy! That's got to be us, because the Europeans have made a mess of every civilization that they've developed."

Jacob started to say that Herrlich Krimhler had already put forward a plan, just the night before. That Project Eagle was only in the kindergarten stage of development, whereas Krimhler's, the Naxos group's, was on the verge of graduation, of implementation. As if it were masterfully arranged to coincide with the obliteration of the Russian war machine. But Wilson spoke first.

"There's definitely a double-cross in the making here, and I'm not sure diplomacy, or political shenanigans, or anything else we can do, can head it off. But we've got to have a go at it!"

Wilson put his hand on the younger man's back while they continued to distance themselves from the helicopter and the group gathered around it. "I can't overemphasize the critical nature of the materials contained in that briefcase, Son. I'm convinced that if we can't come up with a near-perfect strategy immediately, there's no way the North American continent is going to be able to even hold its own in this thing."

Both men stopped, Wilson's arm pressuring his foster son to turn toward the helicopter. Only a small portion of the aircraft's golden fuselage could be seen through the coagulant fog while Wilson spoke. "Now, Son, I realize it's not fair to ask you to make this trip, giving you only enough stuff on it to scare the devil right out of you, but it's got to be up to the head man to fill you in as he sees fit. To be blunt, Son... although I trust you implicitly, it wouldn't be prudent to let you have the whole plate-full right now. The less you know, the less anybody could..." The old man let his thought go unsaid, his gray eyes reflecting worry. "Everything is so critical now because of this development in the Middle East." Wilson squeezed Jacob's arm in a gesture of affection.

The rotors began turning with an accelerating whine, violently churning the green gray mist, which began to dissipate, improving their view of the aircraft.

"If there be a God," Wilson said, distantly, "we have surely seen Him at work this day, I think."

CHAPTER 9

The flight across the Atlantic aboard the old converted-for-military-passenger-service KC-135 had been rough. Periodic thoughts of what was attached to his left wrist added to Jacob's discomfort — a burning ache in the pit of his stomach that had been with him ever since the airplane first hit turbulence over the English Channel shortly after lifting off from Brussels International.

Raising the attaché case to check his watch, he mumbled an obscenity at the fact it wasn't there, then looked around the Base Operations lounge area for a wall clock or for anyone who could give him the time. A WAF Colonel, hurrying through, obliged.

"Nineteen-sixteen," she said, checking her wristwatch while backing toward an exit.

"Thanks."

Sixteen minutes past seven, he translated silently. Thirty minutes since he walked off the military jet, and still his escorts had not shown. If the materials in the case were so important as to require an explosive security device, why were they not important enough to be met promptly by the promised escorts?

Maybe the tremendous upheaval over and apprehension about the Russians being destroyed had thrown everything off schedule. Certainly, everyone with whom he'd come in contact buzzed in conversation about the Russians going down.

Then, again, he pondered through his impatience, to give too much attention to the matter of the information he carried might not be a good thing. Better, perhaps, to treat it as routine.

Not much could happen here, where Air Police security was exceptionally tight because of the diplomatic courier activity which routinely flowed through Andrews to and from the capitals of the world. And now, with the Russian disaster and the many unknowns surrounding it, security was more alert than ever to possible trouble.

Worried looks on the hurried, harried faces of the military and civilian-government people, who made hushed talk while they strode briskly through the crowded main lounge, told the story of the effect on Washington, D.C. If there had been elation here, it had faded.

Karen was less than an hour away. Karen and answers to the mysteries of their phone conversations. Stone Oaks — less than an hour away.

"Mr. Zen!" Two men approached, the taller one offering his right hand. "I'm Agent Dobson, Treasury." He nodded toward the other man, who took Jacob's hand. "He's Agent Garrett. Sorry for the delay. This Russian thing has us jammed up." Both men presented their credentials. "Our orders are to take you directly to the Oval Office."

Traffic moved slowly at first, when the navy blue Chevrolet entered the Beltway headed North, but it thinned after the transfer loop was negotiated, putting them on State

4 leading into the heart of the District of Columbia. The late evening flow of vehicles coming from the city crawled, but traffic on their side moved more quickly the closer they traveled toward the capital.

Lights from the eastbound vehicles pierced the thick night-haze, creating an aura of yellow luminescence against the darkness. Jacob wondered, of the people behind those lights across the median, how many comprehended the true circumstance of the world while they struggled to complete their daily ritual of pushing their ways home? Did even one of them know of the decisions that would be made, that were being made, while they pushed and honked and shoved? Decisions that would prick their protective bubble and change forever the way life would be lived.

Had the bubble already burst for Karen? Certainly it had for him. "They've been behind us for a mile or so."

The driver's words pulled Jacob's attention forward from his position in the back seat. His eyes meeting, in the rearview mirror, the eyes of the broad-shouldered Treasury agent. Jacob looked out the rear window to see a set of lights 200 yards back.

"Mister Zen, you better be ready to stay down and hang on in case there's trouble." The agent riding shotgun held his revolver and checked its cylinder while calmly making the suggestion.

"They've closed on us, Brett. I'll put a squeeze play on them, and we'll try the infrared."

The driver floor-boarded the accelerator and in the same instant swerved into the inside lane, then shot past a car and moved alongside a pickup. Although there was no opening, the agent nudged the nose of the sedan toward the left headlight of the pickup in the right lane next to them. The driver of the truck hit the brakes and whipped right to avoid contact, nearly hitting the guard rail, but he managed to keep control.

In a tire-screeching lurch, the agent jammed the Chevrolet between the still-swerving pickup and the van ahead.

"Can you get the scope on him?" the driver said above the blaring horn of the truck behind them.

"Not yet!"

The other man, Jacob could see, was working at the dashboard area, finally settling his face into a binocular-like instrument the way one would look through a submarine periscope.

"Nope! Can't get 'em," the man at the scope said. "We'll have to run with them."

"Okay, let's do it! Hang in there, Mr. Zen!"

The driver jerked the Chevy into the passing lane and crammed the accelerator to the floor. The helpless thought flashed: What might be the odds for living through a second chase like the one that night with Karen? Not good, he decided as the careening sedan, despite the seat belts, threw him first against the left door, then onto his right side against the seat, before he managed to brace himself in anticipation of each spastic lurch. Would the thrashing detonate the briefcase?!

"He's coming with us, Brett!"

The Chevrolet's speedometer was on 95. Their acceleration caused the vehicles in the right lane to appear motionless. The agent riding shotgun was again at the scope instrument. "Okay, Marty. Got him!"

Jacob looked out the rear window to see the chasing vehicle's headlights several hundred yards behind, but closing. He turned to see the driver's eyes, nose and forehead in the mirror. They were cool, professional eyes, assessing the next move in coordination with the man's experienced brain and hands.

Then, in a fraction of a second, the eyes in the mirror were gone! The driver vanished!

The agent disappeared! No... It must have been a blast from an unseen, unheard weapon. It had to be! Jacob struggled forward against inertia, trying to see what was happening, but was thrown backward, then slammed against the left rear door. The car was jerking violently, the steering wheel spinning unattended!

Unfastening his seat belt, he pulled himself forward again, gripping the back of the seat in front of him.

No time to puzzle over the driver's seat being empty, as the car was bearing down on a concrete drainage pipe at more than 60! He dove for the wheel and captured it with his right hand, then his left —the attaché' case making the effort a painful one. Jacob pulled himself in a slithering fashion across the seat, at the same time, turning the steering wheel right to avoid the culvert. An eternity passed during the seconds before his lower body slammed onto the front seat, the maneuver causing the handcuff to rip the flesh of his left wrist, his feet to catch on the man slumped against the right door. He pulled his feet free and flung them toward the brake pedal. A dark form came into his peripheral view and there was a grinding thud that caused the car to convulse, then tip onto its left side.

The attaché case would explode! He gripped the wheel tightly and felt it snap. The world became a dark, rolling blur, and in his mind he prayed... "Dear God... not now!"

The car was upright, with the roof on his side badly caved in. Blood was everywhere!

Where was he hurt? Only at his wrist, where the handcuff and attaché case caused it to twist and the skin to tear. He had a dull, throbbing pain in his forehead, the pounding becoming sharper as his senses regathered. He wiped his fingers across the wound. There was some blood, but not enough to cause the profusion. The agent's head and left shoulder plopped heavily against him, the man's eyes open wide, the mouth gaping. Jacob pushed the seat-belted body to an upright posture in order to help the agent; he saw the reason, then, for the volume of blood!

The tear in the left side of the neck oozed with what must be the last of the man's blood. After pushing the body against the right door, he painfully eased himself through the opening between the crumpled door and its jagged facing and looked around for help. The carnage was incredible! Everywhere, crushed and burning vehicles! People moaning, screaming, begging for help.

Siren wails coming from Andrews on the east and from Washington on the west met at the spot where Jacob stood unsteadily, then faded while making their 360 degree sweeps. The eerie horizons in both directions pulsed sanguinely with glows of gigantic fires, giving silhouetted illumination to structures between himself and the city to the west.

Nuclear attack! D.C. would be among the first struck! His heart flip-flopped in his chest, his throat constricting with fear. The world was finally doing the unthinkable: committing suicide. His consciousness faded, and he had to go to one knee. His chest felt like it would erupt with each heart pulsation. His mind and vision cleared when he lowered his face.

No —This was not consistent with the characteristics of thermonuclear holocaust as he imagined it, not like he had been led to believe it would be. There was no blinding flash, no devastating blast or firestorm, nor depletion of oxygen.

The agent had disappeared in front of him! But it couldn't be! He stood, then bent to look into the badly compressed car. The other man lay in his own coagulating blood, corpse-white, his throat still seeping the bright arterial liquid from the jagged tear in his neck. He searched the interior which was well-lighted by several burning wreckages nearby. Only the floorboard on the driver's side was darkened by shadows, and he ran his free hand over the carpet, feeling crumpled cloth. He pulled the material to eye level. A pair of slacks with a dark leather belt running through the loops — still buckled. Exploring further, he found a suitcoat, a shirt, a pair of shoes and socks--the shoes still tied, as if the driver had dissolved within his clothing! The seat belt and harness, buckled!

"Help me! For godssake, Mister! Help us!"

The woman's frantic plea while she gripped his arm yanked Jacob from total immersion in his thoughts of the phenomenon he still was not sure he had witnessed. Her features, he could tell through the spattering of blood on her face, were those of a pretty woman. He wondered why he noticed such a thing, when the world was coming apart. Perhaps because the mind involuntarily selected out whatever small bits of beauty were to be found in all this... spectral ugliness.

He allowed himself to be pulled along by his arm while they stumbled across the divider. She pleaded with him in emotion-choked words that were barely understandable. "My little girl... Help me find her! Please... I can't find Carrie!"

They reached the Toyota wagon, Jacob's still somewhat addled thoughts on the face that disappeared from the mirror — on the rolling car — the bloodless corpse — on Karen.

"My mother! Please help her, Mister!"

Without thinking about it, he checked the woman who looked to be in her fifties. She had a cut along her left jaw and blood on her hands, either from the wound or from abrasions on her hands and arms. "Where's Carrie? Is Carrie all right, Misty?"

"I can't find her, Mother. Mister, can you find her for us?" The young woman looked at him, her face, her voice strangely calm.

"Miss, I'm sorry. There's no child here," he said, checking the back seat of the wagon. He opened the back door to look around the cargo area. Just clothing. A child's dress, white leotards, patent shoes, a stuffed toy animal.

"There's some clothing back here; that's all I can find."

The woman took the dress from him and stared at it, a blank expression on her face. "It's Carrie's dress, Mother," she said unemotionally, then sat down behind the steering wheel and held the dress in her lap. "Thank you for finding it," she said without looking up at Jacob. "See, Momma... Carrie's dress."

Jacob stumbled backward, his eyes wide with realization that the little girl had disappeared like the agent, clothing ... the only evidence of her former presence!

He wandered, meandering between wreckages, ignoring cries of the injured — the dying. There were too many. Too many...

A hand reached from a window, clutching at his right bicep. He instinctively jerked free, then looked inside to see the man whose face was a mask of blood, his nose smashed from impact with the steering wheel. The man held a hand-kerchief against the head of a woman lying beside him on the seat.

"Help us! My wife... she's bleeding." His plea was offered weakly; he, himself, would soon lose consciousness from loss of blood.

"Where are the kids, Joe? Oh, Lord! Where are the kids?" The woman whimpered the question without moving.

Jacob reached for the door handle; the metal just above

his hand suddenly dented. A hole appeared in the dent's center. A sharp report cracked somewhere behind him. A large caliber handgun!

Dropping to his knees beside the truck, Jacob, in that mind-boggling instant, wondered about the man and woman in the truck. The round must have hit one or both of them. Another shot! The bullet ricocheted off the road shoulder's asphalt not 10 inches from him! Only one direction to go! The second shot had definitely come from the other side of the divider, behind where the wreckage of the government Chevrolet sat. He had to make it to beneath the pickup, if he was to have a chance! Another blast and ricochet off the asphalt, the bullet piercing a front tire of the truck.

He cast a quick look in the direction of the gunfire, seeing a broad figure kneeling, readying with both hands for another shot. Why, of all the people to survive, did it have to be one of the men who had been in the car chasing them?! He felt the sting on the calf of his left leg before he heard the report of the pistol. He was hit!

Shoving the case in front of him, he crawled on his stomach beneath the truck. The leg was still working; the sting was gone. He was now out from under the pickup on the side opposite the gunman. What good was an exploding case? He needed a more usable weapon!

He stopped to consider his position among the wreck-ages, then checked the damaged leg. If he had been hit, he couldn't tell it. No blood, no pain. But when he took his next step, it felt like the calf muscle had been slapped with a heavy gauge chain.

He tried to see the would-be killer, find the man so he could plan what he hoped would be a life-saving strategy. He saw the predator stalking about the wreckages, looking for his quarry, moving slowly with the pistol held at the ready position wanting another crack at his prey. The assassin was at the back end of the truck. Jacob ducked behind the upside-down car lying just ahead of the pickup. He had to move quietly away, eastward - back toward Andrews. While he limped in a crouched position between the stalled and mangled vehicles, he kept the man with the gun in sight, and devised his plan.

Moving more quickly, he duck-walked in great pain, occasionally stopping to look back in the direction of the stalker. He had lost the man among the wreckages and the dazed people who searched the carnage for those who needed help. He must move more quickly still... must put distance between himself and his attacker, then put his plan into action.

He searched the lane next to the grassy divider, seeing finally what he had been looking for. Perfect! An old Volkswagen! Unoccupied.

Circumstance and end justify means, he assured himself, looking inside the small car, then pulling the door open. Keys were still in the ignition. He turned the key and the motor churned, slowly, then caught. Movement in the rearview mirror! The attacker! The pistol aimed with both hands at arm's length, sighting the target! — Him! Jacob dove to his right across the gear console an instant before the rear window and windshield exploded. At the same time, he clumsily stomped the clutch, jammed the shift lever into first, whipped the steering wheel left, then floor-boarded the accelerator, causing the car to jump into the divider.

Staying bent across the gear console, except for a quick look at where the car was headed, he heard a series of shots and the rounds thumping into the VW. Now he had to chance it. He sat upright to weave his way through the west-bound traffic, which, though stalled like the east-bound traffic, was much less congested.

The windshield was fractured in spider-web design,

obscuring his view. Too late! The Volkswagen's left, front fender ripped into a wrecked car's bumper, severing the VW's fender and causing him to nearly lose control. He straightened the wheels; he had to make it to the shoulder on the far side of the road, where he could be afforded at least some protection by the vehicles that would then be between him and the man trying to stop him. If he could only survive the next volley!

Two more reports from the pistol. No damage. He was on his way!

He threaded the Volkswagen carefully between the jumble, then drove rapidly when it thinned along westbound 4 toward Washington. Thinking the man might be able to follow or radio ahead, giving someone a description of the VW, he slowed to find an empty car. There — its engine still running, the automatic transmission lever still in drive, the car apparently undamaged by its contact with the wreckage in front of it.

When Jacob started to slide beneath the steering wheel, a ripple of chill went down his spine. Clothing on the seat, shoes and socks on the floorboard! He looked around the interior and saw that each passenger position was littered with clothing, and on the floorboard there were shoes. All seat belts — fastened!

Minutes later, he eased the dark brown and tan Pontiac by a tangled heap of metal that had, less than 45 minutes earlier, been two cars about to cross the Anacosta River over the John Phillip Sousa Bridge. This part of the city was strangely quiet, he thought, picking up speed again after crossing the bridge. An absence of human activity, except for the red and blue lights rotating a mile or so up Pennsylvania Avenue. A road block, probably stopping, then checking — maybe turning away — incoming traffic. That might be the procedure for any major city during a crisis such as this, whatever this was. The nation's capital certainly would have a plan for dealing with such emergencies.

One reason for his disquieting feeling stemmed from the darkness of the inner city. The great granite and marble edifices looked like black, hulking behemoths against the glowing bronze backdrop created by fires even farther westward than he had estimated from his earlier vantage just outside Andrews. Whatever happened, it had knocked out primary power to the most vital city in the world. Back-up sources were undoubtedly now feeding essential systems. The roadblocks were part of dealing with the disaster, nothing more.

But apprehension grew and dominated his logic. Had his pursuer alerted someone among those waiting just ahead that Jacob Zen was approaching the city? The car was different, but the face — certainly well-memorized by those who so desperately wanted the materials in the case — the face on the UNIVUSCARD they would tell him to produce, remained the same face.

He had to get to the President. Because he had the credentials, those at the roadblock who were not in on the attempt to get the materials from him would see to it that he was taken to the White House. They would believe his story about losing his escorts — about the agent vanishing when the phenomenon occurred. Or would they? And, if they did believe him, which people at the roadblock could he trust?

What about the President? What of the government? Instinct, based not on panic, but on something beyond pure reasoning, warned that matters of monumental importance to humankind were forever, fundamentally altered in that millisecond when the agent's eyes disappeared from the mirror's reflective surface.

Disappearance! Something massaged his memory, creating a need to know that would grip his mind in a tightening vise until he remembered. He had heard something about a massive disappearance of people. Of course! The prophecy told him by Hugo Marchek at Marchek's home that night the old man was murdered. The night, rather the early morning, that he and Karen almost died.

How did it go? He strained to remember the eschatologist's words, but they wouldn't come. It would have to wait. Now, there were more pressing worries. But he would keep the promise he made that night when they had their discussion about good and evil, and the end of the world. He must get himself a Bible.

The radio! Why hadn't he thought of it before? He pulled to the side of Pennsylvania Avenue, stopped, and switched on the car's radio. The roadblock was coming up too quickly; he must find time to think, to plan. He twisted the dial knob, hearing nothing but static and piercing emergency tones.

The Unified Radio Operations Keeper, UROK. Yet another idiotic acronym in this town of idiotic acronyms. Number 6 on the dial. The system, intended to reassure in time of national emergency, was instituted less than two years earlier by an act of Congress. At this point, he needed reassurance, he thought, continuing to tune until the radio's lighted indicator touched the number 600.

"...theorize that a cosmic disturbance, not unlike what some scientists believe might have caused the end of the age of dinosaurs, might have recurred. And, the Russian allied disaster could have been an earlier part of what happened an hour ago. A sort of universal, astrophysical phenomenon which periodically takes place, in terms of millions of years. Somehow acting upon the subatomic structure of certain organic matter, disrupting cellular cohesion and causing that matter to literally fly apart, and, in effect, appear to vanish.

"There has been, though it is not commonly known, a

great deal of study given to such a theory over the past several decades."

The accented voice, obviously a scientist being interviewed, calmly put forward the conjecture. Jacob's attention was jerked from the radio by a huge commercial jet, which descended, as if it were making a normal landing. But, in the middle of the city!

He closed his eyes, imagining what it must be like for the person trying to put the plane down in the only relatively clear area available. The pilot, most likely gone. Vanished in the catastrophe. Other members of the flight team capable of handling the craft, too — no longer there. Someone must have taken over; tried to land the big jet. What must the person's thoughts have been, when the huge, white obelisk suddenly loomed in front of him and he knew it was his and the others' last seconds of life?

"The Vice President has things well in hand. So there is no need to worry about who is in charge of the government."

The President! Jacob turned up the volume, then tried to get rid of the static by manipulating the tuning knob.

"The last I saw of the President, he walked out of the Oval Office and into Miss Kelly's office. I'd been alone with him, sitting in a side chair by his desk. I didn't know anything was wrong."

Jacob recognized the southern drawl as belonging to Senator James Waldon Bernett of Mississippi.

"I finally walked out to Miss Kelly's office, and about that time, Len Masters, the President's appointments secretary, came bustin' in and said 'everybody was disappearing"

The President - *Gone!*

He looked down at the cuff linking him to the attaché case, remembering the words of the operative who instructed him in Core Chamber Z-391. "Give the case only to the President." But soon another man might be President.

No — He recalled the operative's exact words: "Remember, Mr. Zen, only President Farley is to receive this material. Absolutely no one else."

Now the attaché case — its contents--were solely his responsibility. He had to keep those trying to kill him from getting it. And, he must get into the material himself in order to find out what he was dealing with.

The thoughts hammered at him: Avoid the road-blocks...Stay away from people until he had time to digest the materials...Find Karen. He had to find Karen.

CHAPTER 10

Avoiding the roadblock bottleneck where Pennsylvania Avenue intersected Independence had been no problem, but finding another car was not so easy. He was practiced enough now, however, that the thievery no longer pricked his conscience, and he cerebrally separated himself from the looters who were, according to radio reports, ravaging the city. His only concern was that police or military squads might stop him and take action before he had a chance to explain his circumstance.

He wanted to, but could not, stop to help the people scattered along the Mall — smoothing the guilt-feeling with the thought that no one could have lived through the impact and fire. Still, the mind-picture would not go away. The large, intact portion of fuselage lying between the long reflecting pool, the blackened, badly-damaged Washington Monument, and Constitution Avenue. He fought to clear his mind of the grisly scene while he drove at high speed southwestward along the 120 cutoff. Taking the alternate through Franklin Park, then to McLean would, he hoped, lessen the chance of contact with those trying to maintain order — and with those intent on doing him in, who would likely be staking out the more heavily used expressways.

The Ford sedan he appropriated on Connecticut near DuPont Circle, after the long roadblock-circumventing jog/walk from where he left the Pontiac, should be unobtrusive enough to let him get close to Stone Oaks unnoticed; he appeared to be just another confused, frantic commuter trying to get home. And, there were a hundred mini-disasters to divert attention from him. His chances for slipping into McLean, then onto the grounds of the estate, seemed good. His heart pulsed more quickly with anticipation the closer he got to the old mansion and to Karen. If not to Karen, then to those at the bottom of the strange Holophone call and her inexplicable change of mood from fear when he talked with her from Brussels to total lack of concern during the one-sided Naxos call. If she had been harmed —maybe killed — he, too, was in danger. Not only from those chasing him for the materials in the attaché case, but from the ones who apparently infested Stone Oaks.

Were they one and the same? Or two opposing ideologies of equal virulence, each seeking power, probably more voracious than ever now as they rushed to fill the vacuum created by the disappearance of many leaders around the world, and by the removal of the Russian and other megalomaniacs as a force with which to contend.

No matter. If Karen was dead, he didn't want to go on. But until he knew about her, knew for sure what he faced, he would not throw off all restraints of caution. He would take time to survey his problem.

The radio told much of the story while he made his way from D.C. to McLean. Although most capitals of the West were spared their top leaderships, the United States, Great Britain and Spain were not; all suffered losses of leadership at lesser levels of government. The people, of course, were not told everything, probably not even the truth, concerning how deeply the governing institutions were affected. What was the truth? He sensed the answers lay very close.

Stone Oaks, the only home he could remember, for the first time in his life sat alien and forbidding in the blackness of the Virginia night. His wish was to drive to the guard hut and say hello to Bill Roark, who would smile and push the button that would swing open the gates, like all other times when he was a teenager coming home from a night's carousing.

Again the instinct — unsubstantiated, psyche-clutching forewarning. Bill Roark had been dead for five years. The gate hut manned since by uniformed guards from a private security company, except when Conrad Wilson was in residence, at which time they were supplemented with Treasury agents. Instinct--his most reliable innate ally —popped the drag chute of his urge to go to the gate as if nothing had changed.

Had his enemies been affected by the phenomenon? Maybe they, themselves, had fallen victims to whatever had happened. Instinct again told him differently. The old house, hulking darkly in the middle of the sprawling acreage, seemed to shout to him — like a friend caught in the sucking death of quicksand might scream — warning him to stay clear, at the same time desperately needing, wanting rescue.

There was a way into the grounds not even Conrad Wilson or the groundskeepers knew about. It was in an area not covered by electronic security contraptions, only by the dogs that patrolled on a half-hourly schedule. That is, if things remained the same. How much they had changed, there was no way of knowing. Was the effort worth the risk? Yes! And more than that, the risk was imperative.

He pulled the sedan to the curb beneath a huge oak on the front lawn of the old Georgian-style home. Years ago, it had belonged to Lester V. Framington, then Assistant Secretary of Agriculture, the father of Joey Framington, Jacob's best friend. Now the home was vacant, awaiting the next in a succession of bureaucratic families to live in it since Joey moved away. Joey... Jacob found himself smiling, remembering the ears that stood out from the face of fair, generously-freckled skin. The red hair which, even when the boy was dressed for Mass that he was regularly forced to attend, was as unruly as when the two of them waded the creeks and mudwallows of their favorite haunts.

Now Joey was gone, a victim of an undistinguished skirmish in some forgotten African war. Gone, too, those carefree times when they roamed the neighborhood and beyond. They had explored every intriguing inch, including the one way into Stone Oaks, that would now give him a chance to slip in undetected. The old Framington-Zen Subway was the answer — if it were still passable.

He moved the Ford into high weeds beneath heavy shrubbery on the alley side of Joey's house, an area still flanked by an open field. The sedan could not be seen from the street. Slipping from behind the wheel, he quietly closed the door, then moved to the back of the car and opened the trunk, taking from it a wedge-ended tire iron. As quietly as possible, he closed the trunk-lid, trying to remember the exact spot where he and Joey entered their secret passageway.

The darkness would ensure that his movements remained covert while he pried open the cast-iron cover of the manhole 20 feet west of the tall, now unmanicured hedge. He searched the unkempt ground, spreading the thigh-high, yellowed grass with his hands, feeling for the grooved cover recessed in three inches of concrete.

There! Now to use the tire iron, spade end first, as a lever between the lid and the concrete encasement. Done! He slid the heavy disc until it fell, propped against the concrete and ground, then thumbed the wheel of his cigarette lighter and held the flame inside the black cavity.

He shivered at the thought of what he might encounter along the storm drain during his blind trip beneath the street separating Joe's house from the grounds of Stone Oaks. The prospect would, in earlier times, have delighted the fearless friends, whose last names the subway was privileged to bear. Jacob wished for Joey now, while slithering through the opening, then dropping to the cement below.

He held the lighter at half-arm's length, bending his head and shoulder uncomfortably while walking crouched. The flame flickered from a sudden breeze and died. When he rolled the wheel with his thumb, there was one spark, then nothing; the flint was gone. He pulled the case from the guts of the lighter and searched the cotton with his index finger for a new flint and cursed, not finding one.

Now he would have to feel his way with his feet. Several steps farther along he tripped over something and fell to his knees, instinctively protecting the attaché case from banging against the floor and sides of the drain. His calf burned from the exertion, then the pain dulled and stopped. He felt with his fingertips to see if the skin, nicked by the ground, was bleeding again.

Scrambling, clawing noises made him forget the wound. Rats! The squealing screams grew louder. He felt the rodents bump and scratch against his hands and legs before he could get to his feet, banging his head against the top of the drain in the process. He stood stiffly with his back curved against one side of the conduit, repulsed at having had contact with the creatures. The noises grew faint and he moved farther forward toward the grounds of Stone Oaks, reminding himself of what was at stake, and what he had already gone through, which made all the rats in McLean insignificant by comparison.

His journey ended with his bumping against a solid wall of concrete. He felt with his free hand for the heavy metal grate that covered a drainage pipe one-third the circumference of the tunnel. The grating was not there, probably the victim of time. But he found the smaller pipe, and just to its left, on the ceiling of the tunnel, should be... Yes... the cast-iron manhole cover.

Situating the attaché case so that he could push upward without bumping it, he applied steady pressure to the cover, then strained harder; no use. He would have to try and jar it loose. Its edges probably sealed with the mud of a hundred rainstorms since it was last pried open. He hit the cover with the heel of his right hand, but still it would not give. Feeling around on the floor of the tunnel with a foot, he found a broken piece of wood, which, when he picked it up and examined it, felt like part of a 2" x 4". He could use it to good advantage, but would the banging be heard by anyone passing nearby?

He stood on his toes and pressed his right ear against the cover. He heard nothing, which meant nothing, the iron lid being three inches thick. He would have to chance it.

Moments later, the seal that nature had put around the cover's edge broke, and when he strained with both palms against the cover, it gave way, sliding until it dropped against the ground. Jacob carefully put the case through the hole and let it slip to a resting position. He then struggled, with as little jostling as possible, through the manhole, painfully scraping his stomach and legs before sliding his body over the concrete and onto the dirt and dried twigs beneath the ten-foot-thick hedge. Thankfully, the hedge had put the manhole beyond the convenient reach of the groundskeepers and sewer crews.

Now to sit quietly and wait until the next pass by the security men and the Dobermans. But what about the dogs?

They would sense his presence. Would scent him! If so, he would dive back into the hole and be gone before the men and the dogs could fight their way through the heavy brush beneath the hedge.

Footsteps crackled through the dried vegetation. He could hear, but not see, the guard and the animal, who began to whine and growl while they approached. The dog was obviously agitated and Jacob knew why; he edged closer to the manhole.

"What's the matter with you, Franz?" the guard asked. Jacob heard the Doberman's low, throaty whine; the animal had his scent! He threw his left leg into the hole, but hesitated to hear the handler's words.

"Come on, Franz! We don't have time to chase that rabbit tonight. Coffee's waiting!"

He imagined the guard jerking the Doberman roughly, hearing the animal give a rebellious squeal.

His nerves quieted while he listened to the guard and his charge crunch farther along the hedge. Soon they would be patrolling the far side of the estate and he would be free to make his break across the grounds and into other places only he knew about.

He had to know how often the guards made their rounds. It used to be every 25 minutes, but that could have changed-- and probably had, along with everything else. He needed to know precisely the time in order to gauge when he could safely return to the manhole when his mission was finished. The watch! Lost in some trash receptacle or being worn by someone inside Naxos. Maybe in Fredria VanHorne's purse, ready for mailing. Before he made his escape, he would find a vantage point from which to observe the guard and the Doberman while they passed by his and Joey's tunnel opening.

Peering at the old mansion through the tangle of hedge

trunks was a nightmare, like one of those slow-motion excursions through sleep-terror — so vivid at the moment of the dream that it becomes real — the natural world, the surreal. But this was no dream, because he didn't have to ask himself, as he invariably did during the dream-state, whether he was dreaming.

He gave one more quick examination of the grounds, then squirmed his way on his stomach between the widest opening he could find. Outside the hedge, he felt naked, an easy target. He fought to control his urge to bolt full-speed toward the cover offered by the heavy shrubbery immediately surrounding the mansion — with the calm rationalization that so long as the spotlights remained unused, the guards could see him no easier than he could see them. Besides, he had the advantage of knowing where, and approximately when they made their rounds, while they were unaware of his presence. The noise, however, that he would make galloping across the dry leaves and dead branches would grab their attention. Better to move slowly from one thick-trunked oak to another, staying low and quiet.

After allowing time to make sure the guard and his dog were no longer a threat, Jacob crossed the expanse as planned, then hurried on hands and knees through the bushes near the house. He scanned the grounds to see if the security people had spotted him. All clear! And, he had entered the shrubbery at exactly the point he wanted, not 20 feet from the basement's western-side cellar entrance.

There were three ways into the basement on this side of the home: a large door with steep stairs descending into the cellar; a double, metal-paneled hatchway with fewer, more shallow steps to the basement floor; and the way he and Joey always took, the way he would take now: a four-foot-square opening, covered with a hinged, metal cover over a steeply inclined chute that dropped directly into a small room.

Few people alive, if any, knew of the opening now, because the hole was safely tucked beneath the beautiful greenery that no one had disturbed for years, except to trim. The chute's function four decades earlier had been to receive coal deliveries.

Prying the covering open proved to be easier than he had thought; however, climbing in the opening beneath the low vegetation was more difficult, and he struggled to get into the hole. He remembered that once he and Joey dropped through it in less time than it now took to put a single adult leg into the opening.

Jacob had not been in this part of the old mansion since he was 12, but little had changed. He felt his way in the semi-darkness, his vision aided by a low-wattage bulb burning above a fuse box on one wall. He moved quickly through the coal bin, the area housing the no longer used coal furnace. Then he passed through several small storage rooms before reaching the steps leading to the home's first floor.

What if he had concocted the whole problem in his mind? What if Stone Oaks, the people in the mansion, were innocent of the misgivings he had about them? Was all this skulking about necessary? He was tired and growing more so because of jet-lag and hunger, which burned at the center of his stomach. The nerve-wracking ordeal he had been through combined with the body-weakening process to dilute his mistrust — to lessen his caution. He couldn't afford that. The faithful instinct assured him that to let his guard down, even briefly, might be a fatal error.

Moving quietly, Jacob edged up the stairs slowly, watching the closed door at the top. He forced his mind to re-analyze the facts that supported his need to continue considering those in Stone Oaks his enemies.

Fact 1: His call to Karen from the hotel in Brussels. The fear in her voice, afraid at first to talk. His own fear that Treasury agents, who Marchek felt might be part of a conspiracy of some sort, could be listening in on his and Karen's conversation. His, perhaps wrong, decision that they would have to take a chance and discuss what she had learned.

"I know it sounds paranoid, Jake. But that's what you thought before we were nearly killed and Dr. Marchek was... murdered," Karen had said. She had found notes of some sort in which the eschatologist had written something about a secret place where he kept what Karen said were things he told no one, not even her. Marchek died the night of that day he made the notes. "I found out the reason he was murdered," Karen had said. "...I found out that they killed Dr. Marchek because he learned that this country, that is, some people at the top, have..." They had been cut off.

Fact 2: The surveillance, the cameras, the guard at Naxos who walked in on him, obviously wanting a look at what he was concealing in the closet. Was this part of something to do with the evil in this old house? Or a separate evil?

Fact 3: The certainty, in his own mind at least, that his own government and Conrad Wilson were keeping the full truth from him.

Fact 4: The most troubling of all--his Holophone conversation with Karen had been doctored. A pre-recording that duped him the first time around, in which her voice displayed no emotion. Her demeanor having changed completely from the terrified state she was in when he talked with her from Brussels. That call had been made, supposedly, to this house. The picture phone connection made in a basement room within 20 yards of where he now stood.

A strong case for regarding those in the mansion as his collective nemesis.

And, what about the disappearance? A factor he could not even fathom. Where did the sudden disappearance of all those people fit in his nightmare? Or did it?

Looking first into the other basement area was the logical tactic. The governmental nerve-center of the old house, consisting of the latest telecomputer communications and cryptology equipment, was the place to start his search for answers — and for Karen. During the least precarious of times, that area was manned by at least three people from State. Now, with the dual cataclysms, with the certainty that martial law would be instituted, security would be stepped up. Increased activity surrounding the estate lent credence to that likelihood.

What if he were discovered? He could claim indignantly that Stone Oaks, after all, was his home. Why, then, the sneaking in? Because of the disappearance or whatever it was... Because of the Russian thing... He simply did not know what to expect, the old mansion being an unofficial international liaison point for the State Department.

Whether those excuses would work ultimately made no difference. If it came down to it, he would use the one weapon he had, the explosive in the attaché case. Unless this enemy knew about his mission to the President, and about the explosive and how it worked. The operative had said however, that only he, the operative and President Farley knew the explosive device's formula for detonation. So, he must be satisfied, for the moment, with that thought.

The immediate problem was how to get to the DNC, Conrad Wilson's pet term for the Diplomacy Nerve Center. Again childhood experience made a way for the adult to proceed with the least chance of being exposed. The sealed-off dumbwaiter was the answer. Like the sewer-tunnel, there was a question of whether it was usable after so many years. And could he get to it without drawing attention to himself, considering the noise it would be necessary to make?

Opening the door at the top of the steps, he looked through the crack in all directions. He must make it through the dark hallway, through the small, informal dining room and into the pantry just off the seldom-used kitchen, with the hope that Wilson had not ordered the antiquated elevator taken out.

Moving into the hallway, he crept along one wall and through the doorless archway into the dining area — stopping, then ducking beneath a big oak table in the center of the room when he heard voices coming from the kitchen only a few steps away. The dining room was dark, except for the light spilling beneath the kitchen's swinging doors. He would be safely out of view when they passed through — something they must do because there was no other exit from this kitchen.

The feet of two men shuffled back and forth in the line of light beneath the doors. The voices were clearly audible.

"As I see it, it's our job to present this thing in a way that will convince, or at least explain in the most convincing way possible, what's happened and why it happened."

"Yes... that it's more than just theory. It's rationally explainable."

"But that the details have to wait."

"Exactly. The details have to remain classified."

"For security reasons."

"Yes. We tell them that the details of what's happened have to remain classified for security reasons, until such time as the facts can be fully presented without danger."

"We'll talk only in terms of a natural phenomenon, then..."

"That's right. The scientists will continue to explain it as two separate events, caused by a single phenomenon. They'll say that due to the complexity of it all, they won't talk about it further, publicly, until they can give all the facts in under-standable terminology."

"So what we'll be doing for now is just expanding on what we've already given them. The cosmic disturbance story."

"Exactly."

The doors swung open and Jacob moved deeper into the darkness beneath the table. Both men stood for a moment in the doorway, silhouetted against light from the kitchen. The taller, slimmer one spoke. "Well, we've been looking for a reason strong enough to warrant the merger. This has certainly provided us a legitimate reason."

The voice — the familiar face — discernible now while its owner faced the light. Lawrence Thorton, top-rated network news anchorman. "It's all in place, and the Social Security input makes it easy to make the conversion. UNIVUS and UNIVER aren't that different from INterface, as I under-stand it," Thorton said.

"Except that INterface is a million times faster in its ability to provide detailed data on everyone who's lived since Social Security records have been kept. And its capabilities in the area of physically keeping tabs is unparalleled."

"I'm talking about the ease of converting all personal data and transactional aspects from the old system to the new... they're similar."

"Yes... they are basically the same as far as basic tech-nology is concerned. It'll just be a matter of pushing a few buttons. The satellites, lasers, fiber optics and computers will do the rest. Our main thrust is to get people to accept the concept, once and for all, of global citizenship."

"With these calamities they've witnessed, that shouldn't be a problem."

The other man moved slightly, to a position where the light struck his face. He was Martin Vestoble, President Parley's chief of staff. "Certainly not in Europe. And people here will come around once they know we've lost so much in this disappearance thing. People in this country, despite political differences, have always looked to the sitting president as leader in a crisis. With Farley gone, and the Vice President doing what he's going to do, they'll accept a more global leadership."

"He will have to institute Executive Order 16,000 to get the authority he needs to do it," Thorton said.

Executive Order 16,000! Giving the Executive control over every facet of national activity! — In effect, dictatorship!

"Farley would've never imposed 16,000. If not for his disappearance, and the Russian invasion, we would have had to go to the alternate option. Farley would've had to go," Martin Vestoble said.

So they didn't know what caused the Russian destruction or the disappearances. They simply accepted those cataclysms as fortuitous to their one-world plan. And, that plan would have been carried out, even if they had to create artificial calamities. They would have assassinated the President, if necessary, and invoked Executive Order 16,000, regardless. What about the Vice President? What could he do, once he took the oath of office, that Vestoble apparently believed would be even more dramatic than invoking the Executive Order?

"We're lucky this thing didn't happen earlier," Vestoble said, reaching into the kitchen to flick off the light. "A month ago we could've offered only promises. Now, the system's in place and ready to go."

"I'm looking forward to seeing how it's all going to fit together," Thorton said, while both men passed through the dining room, then walked down the hall, their voices becoming muffled in the distance.

His instincts had been right, drawing him clandestinely to Stone Oaks. Whatever lay at the heart of their plan to deal with the monumental changes taking place in the world could, perhaps, be learned here in the old mansion. And, maybe, whatever was at the root of his own problems.

After an estimated two minutes, Jacob moved from beneath the table and crept through the kitchen into the pantry. A large china cabinet covered the wall where the dumbwaiter was once loaded and unloaded in the transport of food, laundry and trash -- the shaft running vertically the height of the three stories. The last time he rode the manually operated lift he was 13, and probably 70 pounds lighter. Would it support his weight now?

He strained to move the old cabinet from the wall. The opening was covered by 1/8"-thick plywood, hinged at the bottom on either side and latched at the top with a throw-bolt. He pulled the bolt to the left, freeing the covering to swing down and against the wall. He wished for light to see the condition of the dumbwaiter, but had to settle for feeling the chains that were strung over pulleys and gears at various points up and down the shaft. They felt relatively clean, not rusted or corroded, but more flimsy than he remembered, and he did not relish climbing into the black shaft, or trusting the wooden floor of the lift to support his 182 pounds.

He reached into a recess inside the wall and unfolded a handle. Cranking it slowly at first, he became bolder when the sounds of the apparatus proved less noisy than he had feared. The platform came to him after 20 seconds of cranking and he ran his hands across the flat, dusty surface after locking the cranking mechanism back into place. He had to risk it.

Carefully placing one foot at a time on the carrier and pressing down to test its solidity, he continued to support the bulk of his weight on the heels of his hands until satisfied the old platform was reasonably trustworthy. It creaked and swayed, but seemed to want to hold the weight. Would the gears allow him to lower himself slowly, under control? Only one way to know.

He crouched, his full weight now on the carrier, and turned the tension knob on the brass plate beside the cranking mechanism to full tension. Holding tightly to the chain that held him suspended, he freed the crank handle. The platform jerked and fell a few inches, but the tension chain held. He tested the lift by slowly letting it ride downward; for the moment, at least, the thing was working well.

The dumbwaiter arrived at basement level with a bump against the shaft's floor. He fumbled through the right pocket of his pants for the nail clippers, silently cursing when he realized they were not in the right pocket but in the left, making it hard to retrieve them because he had to slide the handcuff and the attaché case as far up his left arm as possible, then get his left hand deeply enough into the pocket to reach the clippers.

Painfully managing the feat, he pulled open the clippers' handle and slipped it through the crack between the wall and the piece of plywood that was the door covering the dumbwaiter shaft. Would the bolt still be accessible, like when he was a boy? Would the noise alert someone? The door opened into a small room with a concrete floor, an area formerly used for dirty laundry and garbage pickups. Outside the room lay a network of hallways and larger rooms used by the State Department.

The bolt slid to the right, but not without considerable resistance, unlocking the covering, which began its swing downward. He quickly grabbed the edge of the plywood to keep it from banging against the wall below.

Now to analyze his situation. How many times he had done this — happily. A little boy's adventure, troubled only by the villains skulking about in his imagination. How different now, with real terrors to test his stealth.

With the plywood bolted back in place, he moved to the door leading to the maze of corridors and rooms. No activity in sight, but he could hear human sounds coming from somewhere several rooms away. One last childhood secret — the crawl space between the basement and the first floor, accessible only through a maintenance equipment closet just off the hallway. If the closet was not locked.

Outside the tiny room, the hallway was brightly illumi- nated with squares of fluorescent lights mounted in the ceil- ing. The off-white walls were uninterrupted by anything that might offer a hiding niche. If he could just make it 30 feet to the maintenance closet.

Made it! - Tried the door - Unlocked! Quickly, he shut the door behind him when he heard voices and footsteps. Two men! There would be only one of two places they were going -- only two doorways in this part of the corridor. The door to the room he had just come from, and the maintenance supply room, where he was now! He backed into the corner that would hide him if the door swung open, and felt around in the darkness for something, anything, that might serve as a weapon. He had not come all this way to be trapped in a janitor's closet! A pipe wrench! He could wreck at least one skull before having to deal with the other man.

The handle turned and the door opened. When the man turned on the light, Jacob would yank him inside and smash his head, then face the other man as quickly as he could. But the intruder didn't turn on the light; instead he fumbled in the semi-darkness, searching the corner directly across from where Jacob stood.

"Where's that cleanser can, Joe?"

"It's just to the right, beneath the sink."

"Yeah... here it is. I got it."

Jacob lowered the pipe wrench, weakness replacing the battle-ready muscle tenseness. Heels clicking in the distance told him the men were no longer a threat.

He would not risk turning on the light in the closet, but must be careful not to knock things over in the crowded area. The ladder was built in as part of the wall, just to the left of the sink — still there, just as he remembered. Feeling his way up the 2" x 4" strips to be sure they were still solid and that there was nothing that might fall hanging on the steps, he used his right hand to touch the plywood piece that covered the opening to the crawlspace. Unlike the coverings for the dumbwaiter shaft, this covering was removed more often, and it raised easily. The wiring and the metal ventilation tubes, as well as, the plumbing, were regularly inspected through this opening to the crawl area.

After struggling upward onto the flooring, he replaced the plywood, then crawled, feeling ahead with his free hand. Like the sewer-tunnel and the dumbwaiter, this one-time friendly play area now seemed hostile, and was more confining than when he and Joey Framington crawled these same planks to spy on the unknowing State Department men and women inhabiting the forbidden regions below. Now, the spying would be for real, the penalty for being found out, much greater.

There was hope, because despite elaborate security — though certainly not as elaborate as what now surrounds the estate — he and Joey were never caught in the act of spying.

It was a simple enough procedure: remove the ducting tape, quietly slide the square, metal duct sections apart, and peer through the grated vent. One could observe, without being seen, everything going on in the room below. Each room in this basement area had at least one duct and he would have a look at them all. The trick was to take the silver tape off slowly, carefully, so it could be replaced when the spying was finished.

His first two attempts led to darkened, empty rooms, and he replaced the ducts before moving to the third, the room he remembered as the largest in the State Department complex. Looking between the thin, slanted vent louvers, he saw four big television screens, three filled with images of human activity; the fourth appeared to be a massive computer screen displaying data and graphics. People, maybe a dozen — it was hard to tell because some were out of his line of sight — occupied chairs facing the screens. A tall man wearing a navy blue suit stood with a pointer in his hand.

The President's chief of staff and the anchorman sat in the front row. The man's clear, distinct voice was that of Grant Halifax, Vice President of the United States.

"Each of us here represents government, business or media institutions counted on to maintain order in this Geoquadrant. And it is our job to convince the people that 'The Plan,' which will soon be put forth, is the only thing that can assure peace and safety in this crisis and during the transition. It is a transition which has been coming, as you know, but which can now be put into effect with great urgency because of this... cosmic disturbance."

The words were spoken with inflection that implied foreknowledge. "Cosmic Disturbance" — obviously, that was to be the official term for it.

Halifax turned and stepped near the screen displaying the graphics, and pointed. "Of course, it's still too early to know exactly the number we've lost, but according to all indications, it will exceed 25 percent. That, in itself, doesn't sound so bad." He moved the pointer to a line on the screen. "Here are the critical statistics: We've lost 17 percent of the Senate, 13 percent of the House, 19 percent of the Executive Branch, including, of course, the President, and one member of the

Supreme Court. Of course, there's no way of knowing right now the total loss of the Judicial Branch on a national scale.

"Even all that doesn't seem so bad. However, a quirk of fate, or whatever, took people with critical knowledge of our system and how it operates. Top people, particularly in economic matters. Two examples: Ways and Means Chairman Beniton is gone; several members of the Federal Reserve Board were killed in that crash in the city a short time ago. Many others in vital positions with UNIVUS."

Grant Halifax stepped forward and slapped the pointer against his palm, his features more clearly visible to Jacob when the overhead lights struck the Vice President's thin, sallow-skinned face.

"In other words," Halifax said, smiling broadly at those sitting in front of him, "...this thing has worked out just the way he said it would! We just didn't expect it this soon." There was delight in Halifax's tone.

"We now have the facts and figures and most of all, the crisis, to back up our contention that we have no choice but to throw our lot in — totally -- with the one and only plan that will move us into the New World Order we've worked so long and hard to bring about."

Halifax's audience mumbled approval and agreement to each other; he raised his hands for quiet, his face taking on a more somber expression.

"Ladies, gentlemen... we can implement EARTHSPHERE-10 much sooner than originally anticipated. As you know, EARTHSPHERE-10 is the heart of 'The Plan' to once and for all bring all peoples together for peace.

"EARTHSPHERE-10 will consist of ten geographical regions, each region being responsible to each other and the Commissioner, who will head the Commission of Ten.

"Those regions by name are: Eurosphere, South Amerisphere, North Amerisphere, Australisphere, Afrisphere, East

Asiasphere, West Asiasphere, Atlantisphere, Pacifisphere and Medisphere.

"Just as he said it would be, the Russian opposition is gone. And, just like he predicted, now our enemies from within have been removed as opponents of the magnificent plan for a glorious planetary future!"

The Vice President was no longer the cool, calculating politician Jacob knew him to be, but impassioned — evangelical.

"We, gathered here, will serve as the nucleus for that new beginning on the North American Continent. The cosmic disturbance has made it possible to speed up our timetable. Let each of us now put our talents as government leaders, as business people and as scientists and members of a united global press, to work for INterface. For if we lead properly, the people will follow. There is no alternative. Soon he will address the world audience. Just before he does so, I will invoke Executive Order 16,000, and, as Chief Executive, declare the United States a loyal Geoquadrant of INterface Universal."

The reason for Karen's panic when he talked with her from Brussels! The cause of Marchek's death! It had to be! Hugo Marchek must have learned that this nucleus group, even if it had to manufacture a crisis and murder the President, were intent on instituting Executive Order 16,000 so the nation could die, to be reincarnated as part of the European-centered one-world system. Karen, too, must have had to die because of her knowledge — or else be changed to someone, something other than the woman he knew, and loved.

Now, even his passion to find Karen seemed of little consequence in the rush of events. He felt trapped, the crawl-space suddenly wrapping around him — a suffocating, immobilizing coffin! The old mansion, no longer the warm, protective home of his youth, but a deadly pit out of which he must hurriedly climb. His country was no longer his; its soul had been ripped out and traded by Grant Halifax and his co-conspirators for the promise of their places within the hierarchy of the European-sired computer Utopia.

Was Conrad Wilson a part of this traitorous cabal? If so, why the attaché case? Why not just let him in on it, then, if he refused to go along, simply get rid of him? No... no... Someone had tried to kill him. His foster father had warned him of the Europeans' grab for power. That was why he was to take the case and its materials to the President. Stone Oaks had been taken over in its master's absence. And what about the attaché case? Was it still vital to anyone? Probably not. The disappearance phenomenon, and the quick-acting, usurping one-worlders, likely made whatever formerly damaging information was contained in the case, of no effect.

Jacob heard Grant Halifax's words fade, while he moved as fast as he could quietly manage, gently lifting then setting the attaché case on the crawlspace floor with each knee-forward movement. Inside the closet again, he opened the door cautiously, checking both ways for sound and move-ment. Apprehensively, he moved into the hallway and quickly into the room with the dumbwaiter.

The fact that he had not yet run into anyone who might try to stop him, or at least question his presence, bothered him for some reason, but the thought passed swiftly within a torrent of other thoughts. His mind racing ahead to the several barriers he must hurdle before leaving the grounds. Back up the shaft aboard the creaking lift, one hand over the other, pulling the platform upward with the aid of the gears and pulleys — not at all the same experience as with Joey those many times before, those many years ago.

Back through the darkened kitchen, down the hall and

stairs, upward through the coal chute and into the shrubbery surrounding the old home. Still no opposition.

Lights suddenly swept along the grounds, illuminating the hedges where the manhole escape route lay! Then the beams moved slowly out of sight. Spotlights! Did they know he was on the grounds? Had they decided to wait until he tried for his exit before taking him? Now the light swept near the home where he crouched beneath the hedge, then past him. Whether to run now, staying low, taking one big oak at a time, or, to wait for the next spotlight sweep against his objective — the hedge and the manhole. Either way, the odds of being spotted were against him now. No need to suffer the pain of waiting, agonizing over the decision that must be made; regardless, the thing had to be done.

His run, bent to present as low a profile as possible, seemed forever between the bush and the first oak tree 50 yards away. He stopped to assess the lights and the sounds of guards manning them. On to the next tree, belly-flopping at its base, just as the powerful beam of light crossed six feet to his right. His heart pounded and his chest ached from the impact. Pain throbbed in his right wrist, with which he had tried to buffer contact with the ground. The distance left to reach the hedge and the manhole, would have in earlier days been nothing; however, this night it looked to be an endless expanse, as he watched the searchlights criss-crossing the grounds. Lying curled around the trunk of the gigantic oak would not get him to the tunnel and out of danger. The lights were sure to zero in on him before many more seconds passed. Up and running, trying to maintain a low silhouette, pausing for no more than three seconds, then moving swiftly again — only 70 feet to the hedge now. The light! Trained directly on him for what seemed ten seconds! They had him!

No! The blinding beam continued to move like the other beams. He could not, would not, wait for the next sweep, but rather would keep moving until he reached the hedge, bypassing the two trees remaining between him and the escape route.

Fifty... thirty... fifteen feet... The hedge! He slammed into the many-trunked vegetation with his back and shoulders, doing his best to keep the attaché case from jostling, feeling at the same time the sharp stings of the limbs, which scratched and jabbed his face and neck. His injured calf made contact with the hedge trunkage and he started to scream away the pain, but stopped himself. He continued to crawl on his elbows and knees until he was sure his entire body was hidden, then lay silent for more than a minute, waiting for men and dogs, for a hail of machine gun fire. But they would not fire on him except as a last resort. That might destroy the contents of the case.

But, whether that influenced their thinking depended on what forces were involved. The operative who gave him the attaché case said only the three of them, the agent, the President and Jacob, knew about the explosive apparatus.

The operative could have lied, could have been setting him up. But why lie? Setting him up for what?

That was not likely, or else the men who picked him up at Andrews would have killed him for the materials. Instead they tried to get away from the people who chased them just before the disappearance. The agents he was with would have joined forces with the pursuers. Besides, the Treasury agents who picked him up had to present elaborate credentials before being allowed into Andrews' VIP Base Operations section, while the would-be killers were content to wait somewhere outside Andrews.

And now, if the security people at Stone Oaks knew his whereabouts, they would hesitate to shoot only if they were afraid their bullets might riddle the contents of the case, but not because they were aware of the explosive charge which would devastate everything.

Something — the instinct again — told him it was time to remove the case from his wrist. He threw off the tendency to debate the whys of the urgings; so far his hunches had been right.

Now to remember the procedure, while there was faint light to work by before going into the tunnel. He took the key the agent had given him, inserted it into the slot of the cuff on his left wrist and turned.

"Three minutes to detonation," he whispered, placing the leather case on the dirt beside the manhole. "Unless they're snapped back together." He closed the cuff until he heard the click, then hesitatingly opened the case, exposing a blue box, like the one the agent demonstrated in the pumping station.

"Pull the latch up... and no more Jacob Zen," he whispered, placing the fingers of both hands on either side of the metal box. "Push inward on the clasp three times... and the thing is disarmed..." He pushed in on the chrome latch slowly three times, "...and the lid is opened."

He smiled nervously, relieved the task was accomplished, and pleased at the fact that possibly he, alone, knew the exact combination that had allowed it to be done.

Two leather pouches, one 1-inch box, and one 2-inch-thick box, measuring perhaps seven-inches-square, lay before him in the occasional light, which continued to sweep the hedges and grounds. No time to examine the materials; he must find a place for them.

When the explosive blue box was shut it would be rearmed. He closed it and carefully placed it back in the attaché, then opened the cuffs with the key and snapped them shut again around his left wrist. The leather pouches fit nicely into the inside pocket of his suit jacket. The two boxes were more cumbersome, impossible to stuff into the jacket's side pockets. He pulled the back of his shirt out of his pants, placed the boxes against his back, one on top of the other, then tucked the shirt back in the trousers and let the suit coat drape over them. Uncomfortable, but, with the coat left unbuttoned, it was workable.

Jacob hurried through the tunnel, stopping several times to listen for activity ahead. Nothing. Not even scurrying rats. He reached the three-rung ladder attached to the concrete wall just below the manhole. As quietly as possible, he stepped upward to have a look around the high-grassed field. Satisfied with his reconnaissance, he struggled through the opening and crawled for the first ten feet on hands and knees. He had made it!

The car was where he had hidden it. No sign anyone had discovered it, so he moved to beneath the heavy foliage and fished the keys from his pants pocket before quietly opening the door and sitting behind the wheel.

The interior light was out! It had not been out when he opened the door, before leaving the car earlier. Coincidence, too great!

"Put your hands on the wheel, Mr. Zen... Please." The facetiously polite voice from the rear seat was detached in tone. The cold, blunt muzzle of the automatic pistol against the mastoid bone behind his right ear gave the request its authority.

CHAPTER 11

So this is how it would end — his brain splashed against the windshield of a stolen car while sitting on grounds, where as a child, the only dangers he faced were rusty nails and broken glass. At least he had come home to die.

Still, instinct for survival was with him — like when it urged him to remove the materials from the attaché case before he entered the tunnel when escaping the grounds of Stone Oaks. Now, instinct forced him to remember the critical instructions of the operative who gave him the case:

"Cuffs unlocked— three minutes to detonation; Closed again — resets timer for three minutes; Box opened safely by pushing inward three times — is armed; Push upward on latch — Explosion!"

"Now, Mr. Zen, may I have the case? Slowly and carefully..."

"I'll have to get the key."

"Very carefully, please."

Jacob took the key from his pocket and unlocked the handcuff from his wrist. Whether to snap the cuff shut and deactivate the explosive, or leave it open and wait for certain death in 2 minutes and 50 seconds... "Now give it to me, please."

He snapped the cuff closed and handed the man the case. If the man opened it now... opened the blue box, they were both dead!

"Knight Seven to King's Guard Three. I have him," the man said.

"King's Guard Three. Affirmative! Confirm contents and wait there," the voice on the other end of the walkie talkie transmission ordered. "Ten-four."

The man with the gun would open the case, then the blue metal box. Either die by the gun while trying to get out the door, or die by the explosive! The man was fumbling with the case; he would be at the blue box within seconds! Time to do it, or the chance would be gone!

Jacob wrapped his left hand around the door handle — Jerk upward and hit the door hard with the shoulder — Roll to the ground, out of the man's line of sight--There was just the chance it would work! He tightened his grip on the handle.

"King's Guard Three to Knight Seven..."

The walkie-talkie!

"Give us visual signal of your location, Knight Seven."

"Roger, King's Guard Three. Complying now." The man opened the right rear door and ordered, "Get out slowly, and put your hands on the top of the car."

The man eased out of the car on the side opposite Jacob and stood with the pistol butt resting on the roof. The barrel pointing at the captive when he had done as ordered. The man signaled for several seconds with a flashlight, then put the light aside and moved cautiously to the trunk lid, on top of which he put the attaché case.

Jacob could see the man manipulating the case with both

hands, while holding the pistol on him, alternately looking down at the latches, then in his direction. This was it! If he was to get away in one piece, he had to play it perfectly. Wait until exactly the right moment when the man reached for the blue metal box!

Inside the case now, reaching for the flashlight, examining the case's interior. Putting the light on the trunk lid, reaching inside the case for the metal box. Now! Do it now!

Jacob dove toward the car's front bumper at the same instant the blast hit him in a concussion of light and super-heated wind. He contacted the heavily grassed earth with his right shoulder, then rolled end over end, somehow ending upright on one knee. Up and running, then diving in another shoulder-roll when a second blast hit him, propelling him forward with greater violence. He came to lying on his right side, facing an inferno. Flames licking upward; hot air; suffocating, barely tolerable! He was dead...in hell!

Jacob's vision focused along with his other senses; the inferno was in the shape of the burning car. He sat up, checking himself, then the materials in his suit coat pockets and the boxes stuffed in his shirt. The hard containers had cut and bruised his back, but he was able to move with minimal pain. Nothing was broken.

The signal to the walkie-talkie! He had to get out of the area now! Light thrown off by the fire would make him easy to see if he got to his feet and ran; the best tactic was to crawl, belly-down, into the heavier brush. The fire was spreading and soon that refuge would itself be ablaze.

"Clary!"

Someone shouting, feet running toward the exploded, burning car. "Clary!"

He could barely hear the shout above the roaring crackle... and the other voice.

"Come away, Mario. Nobody could live through that."

Jacob fought to control his shaking while sitting beside the man in the khaki work clothes. The convulsions began the moment he knew he was safely out of reach of the half-dozen men who had examined the flaming sedan. Their conversations indicated they believed that both men and the materials they were desperate to have were destroyed in the explosion, which, one of the examiners concluded, was likely initiated by the booby-trapped attaché case. The second blast - from the car's fuel tank igniting.

Jacob's crawl through the adjacent thicket, just ahead of the spreading fire, and his subsequent hitching a ride, was accomplished with little feeling — merely automatic response to what had to be done. But now, his hands shook and his body quivered. His state was not lost on the van's driver.

"You all right there, Mister?" The man reached to touch Jacob's left shoulder.

"Yeah... Fine."

"Hey! You don't think you're the only one shook up. I've been haulin' people to their houses all night. Never seen nothin' like it... Never!"

The fat driver spoke in a half-chuckle, alternately glancing at Jacob and at the highway ahead. It was a nervous laugh, probably masking the man's own worry. "Or taking 'em to the hospital or someplace else."

"What? I'm sorry..." Jacob looked puzzled at the driver.

"I said, seems like everybody's needing a lift some-where. What you think it is, anyhow? Most of the folks I've talked to think it's them Russians. Some kinda experiment they did, or something they thought would work when they tried to take over there in the Middle East. Probably backfired on 'em and wiped 'em out. Then, what-ever it was, almost wiped out the rest of us. You know, some kinda secret weapon or something. Disintegrated all them people. But why not everything? Why just some people?"

The driver looked at Jacob for answers, then continued talking when his passenger remained silent. "It's scary. You know? I've picked up I'll bet 40, maybe more, people tonight along the roads. You know what? Most of 'em say their kids just..." He motioned explosively with his free hand. "Poof! Vanished! Can you imagine seein' your kids just disappear right there in front of your eyes? You got kids?" Jacob nodded negatively.

"Mine are gone. I mean they're grown up. But the little ones seem to be the ones this thing..." The driver's voice sounded worried for the first time. "You know, I've got grandkids... four of 'em. I've got to get to a phone and see if they're okay. I've been haulin' everybody else around... Guess I better call the old lady. See if she's heard from the kids. You mind if we stop up here at the station?"

"No... whatever you need to do." Jacob said, thinking, "This was probably a good man who put himself last...probably would be a hero in war. Should say something to comfort the selfless man — offer him encouragement about his wife, his children, his grandkids."

But his mind turned to the boxes in his lap, to the folded leather pouches in his coat — then ahead, to Hugo Marchek's home in Rockville. He looked to his wrist, then at the driver. "What time is it?"

The fat man straightened and raised his belly to get the pocket watch from its place in his pants. "6:09."

It would be light soon, exposing him even more to anyone who might be watching for him. Why, though, should he be concerned? Had not the men who watched the car burn said that both men died in the explosion and fire? They wouldn't be looking for him now, or for the information he carried — the materials he would get a look at once he got into Marchek's home.

"Here we are. I'm gonna call the house. Can I bring you back a cup?"

"No, thanks. Hope everything's okay for you."

"Thanks, Son. I hope so, too."

He watched the heavy driver shuffle around the corner of the station fingering the UNIVUSCARD he would use in making the call. State Highway 355 looked deserted ahead. A considerable part of the landscape beyond, visible only because the eerie glow, created by the fires resulting from the catastrophe, illuminated the horizon in all directions. It was probably 6:15 by now, not quite time for the sun to begin paling the skies.

What he would give for just 30 minutes of sleep. Maybe he should have accepted the offer of coffee. His lids grew heavy beyond any heaviness he had felt; his body ached strangely, as if it had lost most of its circulation, like it was intent on falling asleep, even if his brain was ordering it not to. Time to get out of the van, walk around, stretch the body to convince it the brain was still in control, maybe get that cup of coffee.

He got out of the van after laying aside the two boxes on the seat, then thought better of it and picked them up, before walking toward the service station building, around whose corner the driver had disappeared less than two minutes earlier. He heard the man's voice when he approached the corner and stopped to listen while the driver spoke into the satellite phone. Not a cell, but one for only government usage. Not the public phone attached to the outside of the building.

"Yeah. It's him. This is the same guy I've been looking at on film and in those pictures we were given to study."

The voice was different, the accent changed from country

drawl to efficient metropolitan inflection; it displayed irritation.

"Yeah. The guy's name is Zen. Of course, he didn't tell me his name. That's what they told us the guy's name in the dossier was. It's the same guy. He's nervous as a bird about to fly. Find out what they want me to do. Yeah, yeah... I'll hang on."

Cold fear shot through Jacob's body, drowning the burning need for sleep, filling him with new alertness. He fought his urge to panic, forcing himself to stand his ground, to analyze the overheard words. How could they know where he was so quickly? They couldn't have traced him. A mutant occurrence of fate. He had been picked up by one of their agents! Probably one who was sent out to patrol the roads just in case he did somehow escape the fire.

Attack the man? Or run? There were no other vehicles nearby. His chances of hitching another ride were not good, and if he were picked up, he ran a high risk of being picked up by yet another of his enemies.

"Yeah. Gregory here. What you want me to do?" The driver paused for several seconds, listening. "Yeah. I got it. Drive two miles down the highway and pull over like something's wrong with the van. You'll have somebody there to give me a hand with him. Got it."

Jacob put the boxes on the ground. After several seconds of a frantic search for a weapon, he picked up a two-foot piece of iron pipe lying against the building's concrete foundation. Defensive maneuvering seemed to be allowing him to be drawn deeper into their whirlpool. From this moment forward he would take the offense — beginning now, with his driver friend.

The solid thud of the pipe against the fat man's head felt good. He regretted, in that instant, only that he used but one hand to deliver the blow. The man groaned, still semiconscious and Jacob drew the pipe back to strike again. He couldn't do it, conflicting urges battling to dominate his exhausted will. He threw the pipe aside; if there was to be any civilization left after this, he would remain a part of it.

Killing, even after what they had put him through, even with what he still faced, was repugnant. The pleased way he accepted the explosive horror at Stone Oaks — the almost sensual feeling when the iron pipe contacted the man's skull — he was becoming one of them — like the would-be masters of a world gone mad.

Karen's pretty face kept him going, sometimes fading into the fatigue-created brain-fog, but always returning to beckon him toward whatever would be the ultimate ending to the nightmare. He left the van along the shoulder of 355, pointed southward toward Washington, then walked back along the outside of the north-bound lane toward Rockville and Hugo Marchek's old stone-façade home.

Luck was with him, having managed to steal a van, much older than the previous one, whose driver lay in a drunken stupor after apparently having pulled to the side of the highway to sleep it off. The man probably had no idea of what had happened during the course of the past 13 hours, Jacob reflected, guiding the rattling van to a stop. Nor would the drunk know why or how he was deposited here, a block-and-a-half from the late eschatologist's house. From this vantage point, Jacob could safely watch the area for the next hour — giving his antagonists time to check out their suspicions, should they have them, that he would, for some reason, return to Marchek's home. He hoped that the pointing of the other van in the opposite direction along 355 would send them searching elsewhere.

Two things bothered him: they had pinpointed his location on the grounds across from Stone Oaks, and he had, before knocking the fat man unconscious, been headed in the direction of Rockville. The driver had probably told them by now the direction their quarry had been headed before stopping at the station. Jacob hoped the van had thrown them off the scent, but he would take no chances. He chose to sit here, with the drunk man sleeping it off in the rear of the van, and observe Marchek's block for signs his ploy had failed. An hour should be enough.

Soon, though, a burning want to know what Marchek had hidden, and the mind-image of Karen in the grasp of the likes of the men who dogged him, combined to make a more persuasive case for leaving the van. His caution made for staying put. The sun was up now, its light muted, however, by a purple-red overcast that permitted only limited view beyond 200 yards. Marchek's old rock home lay, slightly less than that, away from where he walked along the antiquated, badly cracked sidewalk which disappeared into the early mist. His imagination, heightened by his weariness, played tricks. His strained eyes seeing dark objects moving toward him from the fog, then, in the next instant, seeing nothing but the barely visible black trunks of the big trees lining the yards of the homes beyond. Movements to the right and left — between the houses — imagined eyes peering from the fog...

He carried the boxes beneath his right arm, while hurrying along the concrete walkway, forcing himself to overcome his apprehension, turning his thoughts to the interior of the house. Where to begin the search? What to look for? The thing that had so upset Karen.

The boxes he carried with him — where would their revelations lead? Certainly, they could not put him any deeper into confusion. They had to help. If the papers he carried were so important that only the President of the United States had clearance high enough to digest them, they should provide clues to his own boggling dilemma — to the Vice President's treason — clues to Karen's fate.

Karen — the thought ignited his hate-passion. Answers lay close by and he would rip away the deceptive, rotting flesh that covered the frustration-beast trying to devour him from within, and would get to those answers. The specters that had been raging in his imaginings dissolved while he drew within 20 feet of Marchek's front door. No matter what, he was committed.

He knocked on the heavy wooden door and waited for Marchek's sister to answer. She would not have moved from this old house; she was as devoted to it as she had been to her brother when he lived here with her. She might be with relatives temporarily, though. If she weren't home, he would break a window or do whatever necessary to get in.

No answer. He tried the door — locked. He walked to the side of the house along one of the 14-inch wide runners of concrete that made up the left half of the driveway leading to a separate garage. Finding the back door locked too, he removed his UNIVUSCARD from his wallet and slipped the card between the door latch and the door's facing, then manipulated it up and down until the locking device tripped and the door opened. It stopped abruptly, restrained by a security chain.

"Miss Marchek! Saryeva!"

His calls were not answered and after several seconds he stepped back and kicked hard just below the door handle, ripping the chain from its screwed-in position. Once inside, he stuck his head back through the door opening and looked outside to see if the break-in had been noticed. Satisfied, he moved quickly through the kitchen and the dining room, stopping in the foyer to see, with surprise, that the security chain on the front door was fastened, as had been the chain on the kitchen door. Probably a back way out. Yes. He remembered Marchek's study having a door to a flower garden. Saryeva Marchek probably left the house through that door.

There was a feeling about this old place, he perceived while walking down the long hallway toward the study. Not merely an empty feeling, but a totally vacant one. It was as if the house had somehow been vacuumed of all things human —just a feeling. The fatigue, probably.

The morning's dingy illumination filtered in through the double French doors that led to the garden. Across the doors, where they met, brass security devices were in the locked positions. Saryeva had not left the house through the study exit to the garden.

Then he saw evidence of the old woman's fate. In the leather chair behind Hugo Marchek's desk, lay a rumpled pile of cloth — just like in the car with the Treasury agent — like all the others!

He examined the flower-patterned print dress, finding it wrapped around underclothing. On the floor beneath Marchek's desk chair, opaque gray stockings lay crumpled over black, orthopedic lace shoes. The white slip and portions of the dress had brownish discolorations, as if the material had been scorched. She was taken by the catastrophe. The house -- like it had been vacuumed of all things human. Evidence told the story of what must have occurred. The old woman was sitting at the desk when it happened, writing on white paper, the words:

"To honor the memory of Hugo Marchek properly is to honor Jesus Christ, because Christ meant everything to Hugo Marchek."

The fountain pen had fallen on the paper, point first, as if she had dropped it. The pen's impact sending ink spattering across the paper and desk. He picked up and read a handwritten letter lying next to the writing the woman had begun. The penmanship was familiar.

"As you know, Saryeva, we will be honoring Hugo Sunday evening. We would be greatly pleased if you would say a few words about your brother at that time.

Also, Hugo told me of some information he had in his possession, which he put in his place, for safe keeping. It concerns some vital matters for PAL, which he and I discussed not long before his death. I must have them. Do you know where he might keep them?

I couldn't call you because we are under surveillance here, so I had a friend bring this note. He will be by tomorrow for the materials. Thanks for your help. Cordially, Karen M."

Karen! — There was still hope! He didn't know why, but he was certain she left a message in this note they forced her to write. Clues to where Marchek's secret papers were kept.

The first part of the message's puzzle was clear. She wrote this note under the gaze of her captors. She would not address Marchek as Hugo, rather as Dr. Marchek. She would never call Saryeva Marchek by her first name. Always it was Auntie Sarah. She loved and respected the woman as much as she did Marchek, thus she was saying, that it was not her thoughts, but theirs which she conveyed.

She ended it "Cordially, Karen M." an ending that should have been "Love, K... or, Kay." The best news in the message was that as of yesterday, Karen was alive and mentally alert enough to trick her incarcerators.

Saryeva must have picked up on the message. Rather than gathering the materials, she began writing a speech to honor her brother, as if she was complying with the first part of Karen's note, which invited her to speak. The old woman knew about her brother's work and knew that Karen was in trouble. She began writing thoughts about Hugo Marchek to make them think she had taken their message seriously. When they came to pick up the materials, her explanation would likely be that she had no idea where Marchek kept such things. She was, in fact, his close partner in work.

Now, Saryeva was gone, and Jacob was alone in his search for a way out of his torment. Alone — the cruelest part of his circumstance.

The key to the eschatologist's hidden materials had to be somewhere in Karen's note to Saryeva. The words and hand-writing were hers, but the message's tone obviously was not. Key words in her composition ~ the way she put her captors' message together — could unlock the secret of the old man's hiding place. Too, if Jacob could accurately remember the first phone conversation he and Karen had — he at Stone Oaks, she at Brussels — he might gain insight.

Thoughts moved in no particular order through his mind while he stood over the big desk, forcing open the first of the two boxes he had carried with him since leaving the island. At the same time, he glanced again at the letter, written in Karen's hand.

He remembered her words: "Oh, Jake... I found the secret place and the things he was talking about in the note. I found out the reason he was murdered! I found out they killed Dr. Marchek because he learned that this country, that is, some people at the top have..." Cut off.

He could now finish in his mind some of what she wanted to say, but could not, before they were disconnected. The traitors were about to sell their country. But the Marchek materials — the hiding place?

Karen said that night that she had found the apparently volatile information. If his and Karen's conversation was bugged, and surely it was, the people holding her should know that she was aware of where Marchek's secrets were kept. Why, then, did they continue to search? Why did they make her write the letter to Saryeva, asking the woman if she knew where the old man kept the secret materials?

Of course, the unwritten message Karen wanted to convey to Saryeva was that the people holding her did not know the whereabouts of the secret things and that Saryeva must lie in her reply, to the one sent to pick them up. Say to him, that she had not been privy to her brother's business affairs, therefore did not know where he kept such things. Almost certainly Saryeva did know where Marchek kept such things. Had she been around when Karen came to the house that day, Saryeva, too, would likely have been their prisoner, because Karen would have included the old woman's name when she talked with him when he was in Brussels.

The people who made Karen write the letter were not informed that Karen had located Hugo Marchek's materials, yet the people who bugged that Brussels call had to know. They would make her tell them.

If they were not the people who listened in on their Brussels' conversation that night, then who? The only answer: The people, originally holding Karen, were replaced by others who did not know about the phone conversation nor that Karen knew about the hiding place where Marchek kept the information.

The Naxos bunch, the Vice President, the others, they must have taken control from those who placed the interests of the United States above the interests of the Utopian dream. That Naxos group had not heard the phone conversation. They only knew that Marchek had information which might damage them.

The fact that they took over so quickly following the disappearance disaster said something about the power of the European one-world nucleus. It said something else, too; they were neither omnipotent, nor omniscient. They still did not know — at least, not as of the day before this one — where Hugo Marchek's secrets were kept.

Another question, perhaps more troubling: If their plans were already in place, if the government of the United States was already under the thumb of the Naxos group, why did they still have such a deadly interest in whatever Marchek's documentation had to say? How could they be hurt by the information?

The letter they forced Karen to write held the answer to where Marchek deposited his secrets. There had to be a message there, in the letter. He scanned the note quickly, taking in several lines at a time for a word, a phrase, something. If not what was written, perhaps, how it was penned — maybe a change in style, a grammatical inconsistency.

There! He read it aloud, accentuating the portions he thought significant. "Hugo told me of some information he had in his possession which he put in his place, for safe keeping..." Not a place; his place, for safe keeping. Jacob turned and looked at the rock-façade fireplace directly across from Marchek's desk. Could it be? Had she left him a clue? He examined the stones carefully, trying to dislodge the most likely ones first. All were solidly glued by a half-inch of mortar. He tried to lift the oak mantle; it wouldn't budge. Working his fingertips around the edge of the left side of the fireplace and finding nothing, he moved to the right side and began manipulating each rock with the fingertips of both hands, trying to force each of the rough stones to move. A bad guess.

He turned again to the letter. What might he have missed? Was there a message there at all? His excitement degenerated to depression. He had been sure the fireplace was the answer. That Karen had given clues.

"In his place, for safe keeping." She had used the phrases

in a totally uncharacteristic way. It had to mean the fireplace. But he had checked it thoroughly.

Not the hearth! Karen wrote "in his place."In!" It was raised more than a foot off the floor and was of solid stone.

He pounded the top of the hearth with the heel of his fisted hand to detect looseness. Unmovable, like all the other stones. Leaning to one side, while sitting on the long rock hearth, he reached behind the fire screen, into the fire pit, feeling first the left side of the interior, then the right, achieving nothing but blackening his hands with soot.

He adjusted his position, kneeling, then crawling forward, making his shoulders narrow by reaching forward with his hands at full arms extension toward the back wall of the fire pit. He ran his palms over the stony surface, then his fingertips around each of the large stones. There--in the center of the back wall, a different feel to the fire-blackened stone. He brushed the rock with his fingers, then with a handkerchief, until something at the stone's center appeared gleaming. A strip of metal! He pulled outward on the strip. A handle! Recessed to lie flat against the fake stone. He continued to pull until the stone facade glided on rollers from between the other rocks. A box of some sort, made of very thick metal! Upon further manipulation, the phony stone cover swung outward on hinges, revealing a metal front with a heavy brass-colored handle at its center.

His pulse quickened. It was brilliant of the old man. A fireproof box behind the fire, even the handle of the fake rock blackened by the smoke of hundreds of fires. Brilliant, too, of Karen. He found it!

The knob turned easily and the box's door fell open. Jacob pulled a long, rectangular box from the fireproof safe and removed its lid, after setting it down on the desk beside the boxes he had carried with him since Naxos. Karen's lovely face floated in translucent mind-image before the agglomeration of materials on the desk, while he spread the Marchek papers and boxes, looking for a place to begin making sense of it all.

Insurance policies in a leather portfolio, bound by a leather strap and buckle; a brown envelope, filled with photographs. Very old, probably old family pictures; letters from people with whom the old man must have shared deep friendships. Nothing that looked like the diary-type notes Karen talked about that night.

After lifting the remaining materials out of the rectangular drawer, he hurriedly sifted through them, near panic in his need to find the information. Nothing but personal financial records, more photographs, a scroll-diploma from a seminary. He swore in frustration, picking the drawer up and examining it in better light for anything that might be stuck in a corner. Nothing there.

He slammed the metal container angrily against the desktop and it bounced onto the floor near his feet, ending up leaning on its side against the desk. Its bottom had loosened by the impacts, and several items spilled onto his feet from beneath the container's newly opened secret lid.

Stunned for a moment by the new development, he picked up and examined the items and the container, determining that there was a small button on the rear portion of the box that must have been bumped when it hit the floor, springing open a false bottom. The things Karen told him about! A small, brown leather-bound notebook, and two 12" x 15" brown envelopes containing, he discovered upon opening them, a videocassette and a number of old-style computer disks. He dropped the contents from the envelopes onto the desk and spread them out to get a total perspective. Four disks, one tape.

Hugo Marchek had, like most everyone else, the government-subsidized UNIVUS computer system. It was the hybrid creation by corporate technological giants which made access to important databases and to other networkers possible for users in the United States and in Europe, where the comparable system was designated UNIVER. It would be the foundation on which to build the structure of a unified world. The ultimate outgrowth of Internet and the World-Wide Web. It was an instrument with which to begin networking toward global understanding and cooperation. It was a noble conception, but, from what he had experienced, a monstrous birth.

Hugo Marchek, Karen told Jacob on one occasion, accepted the government computer in his home only because he could better keep track of the gestating beast, and to carry on with life as it had technologically evolved, though it disgusted and disturbed him. For his PAL work, he used an old conventional personal computer, whose disks Jacob held in his hand now. The UNIVUS system, which had occupied one corner of the study when Jacob was last in this room, was gone now. Taken, no doubt, by the government upon Marchek's death. Saryeva Marchek, Karen had also told Jacob, hated the UNIVUS system and expressed to her brother often that he was sinning by allowing the satanic equipment to stay in their home. The scoldings, Karen said, amused Hugo Marchek. When he died, Saryeva probably ordered the system removed.

The old-style computer was private, unless hooked by phone to any of the few databases still available to those who continued to use personal computers. Marchek's personal computer, which was in the same corner it had occupied before his death — given the eschatologist's mistrust of those he suspected were watching him, and given his innate cleverness — would no doubt be secure through some well-devised indexing technique. The old man would have created his own code for information classification and retrieval—characters, words, or perhaps entire phrases taken from the data texts. Whatever the keys, he must find them, and quickly.

But first, he had to discover what secrets he had carried with him since leaving the Aegean island. He opened one of the leather pouches and unfolded a sheaf of 8-1/2" x 14" papers, seeing that the first was a letter, rather a memorandum, on United States State Department letterhead.

To: The President

From: C. Wilson

P.E. ill due to unanticipated growth of Germ-Diagnosis: total involvement of system. Prognosis: terminal without immediate surgery.

The accompanying page, borrowed from a Naxosfile, is part of a Top Secret document composed by Herrlich Krimhler.

Jacob turned the page and, seeing it was typewritten in German, translated it silently while he read:

"The cosmos, having been prepared for the ultimate mystery that must soon be endured by those not attuned with the New Age into which humankind must enter, the Six Ways, is equally prepared to light the path for the worthy. When the uninitiated are withdrawn into the inner worlds' subconsciousness to be ministered to and made worthy before their new-birth experience back into the physical body, post-dissolution society will bloom with unprecedented prosperity. Peace, which has been an unattainable end for mankind, through 'The Plan,' will be achieved,

'The Plan' necessitates the elimination of national entities within our body, who can never be depended upon to accept anything other than the predominant role in this new beginning. The dissolution will accomplish the excision; 'The Plan' shall prevail."

Jacob read the document again, his eyes burning, tearing because of lack of sleep. The page, apparently taken from a longer communication, was for a readership comprised of a select few people close to the great man, Krimhler.

Jacob's fatigued brain drew into focus the stabbing fact that shocked him into a new level of alertness. The German had written about the disappearance! The effect the cataclysm would have on the United States! Somehow, what should have been confusion came together into a horrible realization; he was, the world was, dealing with something beyond the explainable!

Conrad Wilson could not have anticipated that Krimhler was writing about the disappearance of millions of people. The old diplomat did see the implied threat in Krimhler's declaration:

"'The Plan' necessitates the elimination of national entities within our body, who can never be depended upon to accept anything other than the predominant role in this new beginning. The dissolution will accomplish the excision; 'The Plan' shall prevail."

That was the message. It must be. The message Wilson wanted to get to the President -- that Krimhler was proposing to eliminate the United States from contention for leadership in the new ruling structure. His foster father probably inferred that the now extremely powerful Unified European States would use its newfound economic strength to pressure America into taking a back seat to leaders chosen by Krimhler and those in the hierarchy at Naxos. Certainly, the words could not imply the threat of military force; the U.S. still wielded the nuclear bludgeon; Europe still depended on America to deter the Russian bear's lust for western European blood.

But... No! Again there was Krimhler's inexplicable foreknowledge! The Russian allied threat was no more. Gone. Nuclear leverage, how was it affected? And Conrad Wilson could not have foreseen the geopolitical changes that took place in that millisecond of cataclysm. Jacob had firsthand knowledge from time spent in the crawlspace in the basement of Stone Oaks of just how much relationships, power bases, abilities to dominate, had been altered.

That change was dramatic, and the words of Herrlich Krimhler — written a considerable time before events of the past 24 hours — testified that his was the real power, which not only controlled the Western world's present, but understood what had caused the sudden change and what that change would mean for the future world.

Conrad Wilson did not know the extent of Krimhler's power, but sensed that it was not good for the United States, and in his memorandum to the President recommended that the German be assassinated. The revelation would have been a shock, stretching believability to the breaking point, but for the more unbelievable shocks Jacob had been jolted by since shortly after his plane touched down at Andrews. And, before those events on the road to D.C., he would have been shocked at his own attitude of this moment — that assassination was indeed warranted because of the threat to America's security -- whatever that security might be worth now. No longer true.

The thought of a single life being snuffed out was dwarfed by the knowledge that millions of people faced oppressed existences beneath a regime which claimed for itself— without consideration, apparently, for the wishes of its subjects — the power to govern. The one thing those new masters failed to consider: People used to freedom of choice, of representative government, would not easily be made to bend a knee to those who claimed the right to make the choices for them. Even the people within military establishments had enjoyed basic rights and freedoms for too long; sudden chaos could not for long persuade them to back an oppressive master. The psychology was all wrong for this new order to work.

He pulled one of the videocassettes from the box and examined it to make sure it was not damaged by the beatings to which his circumstances had subjected it. No damage.

Had he misjudged his adversaries earlier, thinking that whatever they were, they were not omniscient? Herrlich Krimhler's foreknowledge, demonstrated by the document in which the German seemed to have anticipated the disappearance, appeared to refute that. And they were able to follow his movements to this point. Omniscient? No... just tricks played by his tired mind — fatigued by seeing the agent vanish, by the wreckages, the missing children, by seeing his country betrayed by its leaders.

Hugo Marchek's old videocassette recorder sat on top of an even older console television set near the computer. Jacob was not sure he could figure out the device, so different was it from the equipment he was accustomed to working with. He managed, after several seconds of study, to recall the way the machinery operated, a lesson once learned in a basic telecommunications class, then forgotten. The tape, smuggled out of Naxos and dragged with him since, slipped easily into the receptacle-slot. He pressed the rectangular button marked 'PLAY.'

Why he was taking the materials apart and digesting them in such random manner he didn't know. Maybe to spare himself the labor of thinking about a more orderly procedure. Maybe his intuitive side, or his imagined intuitive side, was guiding him through the unraveling process in the best way possible.

The video on the console's 27-inch screen flickered, then straightened. The image of Herrlich Krimhler's face, close-up, with a serious expression; he turned up the volume, hearing that Krimhler spoke in English.

"To each of you who are to lead the way while we move into the New Age of peace — strength to do what is essential, no matter what your feelings and preferences, is the attribute which makes you worthy, which made your selection to key positions necessary." Krimhler spoke fluently — authoritatively.

"Human beings yearn for strong leadership and appropriate rules by which to conduct their lives. Never before in the history of the world has adherence to these principles been so important, as they will become during the first phase of INterface. The citizen must cooperate, must obey without questioning the authority of those of you entrusted with initiating them into, and cultivating them for, the paradise that awaits the loving, obedient citizen. The citizen's only responsibility during INterphase will be that of obedience. And do not think this will be without its difficulties.

"For too long, the old order of things has nurtured the false doctrine that individuality and unbridled self-interest was freedom. If freedom, it was the virulent, malignant freedom to prevent peace by keeping the peoples of the earth apart. The freedom to invent and use weapons with which to annihilate all forms of life."

"But the great Cosmic Mind has seen fit, after eons of natural evolution, to intervene into human affairs, allowing man to partake, on a conscious level, of the wonders that are the Universal Mind-Body. This will require the removal of some and the training of all others into the oneness of love and perfect order. This is to be your part in the new world of INterface."

'ThePlan' is perfection. INterphase consists of Six Ways to Law... Six Ways to Order... Six Ways to Peace. These must be enforced with iron-willed resolve. There can be no leniency for those unwilling to cooperate. There must be reward for those who show exceptional willingness to point out the rebellious ones who pose dangers to society. All children born during INterphase must be educated to INterface society standards, from six months through year 18."

The children! All born during INterphase! The children! All disappeared! Was there something to the similarity between the children's disappearance and Krimhler's message, recorded for the ruling elite of INterface well before the occurrence? Did he know there would be no children... small children, as he seemed to know there would be a cataclysm of some sort, which he termed in the document from Naxos the "ultimate mystery that must be endured" — "the dissolution" — "the excision?"

Krimhler's dark, unblinking eyes glistened, his smooth features, youthful beneath thick, black hair, seemed to glow — not reflecting the studio's light, but from inner illumination. The baritone voice seemed older than its owner's years, and echoed the prescient assertiveness shown in the eyes.

"You, as the most vital members of the coming society, especially during INterphase, must prepare yourselves with self-motivated re-education, while at the same time seeing to it that those for whom you are responsible yield cooperatively to their own re-education. The Cosmic Mind has, through its universal wisdom, seen to it that you have the technological power to carry out 'The Plan.' The great Cosmic Force has shown the way to the higher order intended for man. Mankind has, through the eons of the ages, through the grand evolutional design, been allowed to create a means for his own salvation. Receive now that message from the Cosmos, which has chosen you to be inheritors of its wisdom — to be the administrators of its perfect justice and order. Understand the technology it has given — strive to use it to best advantage."

Krimhler's image dissolved and a colorful graphic took its

place. The voice of an unseen instructor lectured while the graphics changed with the changing text.

"INterface society during INterphase must be carefully controlled, almost, some might say, to the point of totalitarianism."

The voice sounded without gender, mechanized. Synthesized speech, probably produced by computer vocoder of some type.

"All must lose the old ways of nationalism; all must become indoctrinated citizens of INterface, the global community."

The graphic on the screen, a globe set in a background of black, at first portrayed the many nations of the world as the representative earth rotated slowly; colored lights lit them individually. The continents of North America, South America, Australia, a huge chunk of Europe, scattered sections of Africa and Asia, as well as, Japan, and many other islands, became the same brilliant color of gold; the national boundary delineations vanished. Inspirational, militaristic music played beneath the computer voice.

"When the great leap into peace comes, you will be prepared to control the masses, to guide each into becoming what the Ascended Masters intend for them to become... Individual cells within the Universal Mind-Body, each networking with another to finally attain total harmony."

The sphere within the sea of black changed to gold, and in the next instant, a crystal clear pyramid came into focus within the golden globe.

"Peace will be achieved."

The fulfillment of man's aspirations accomplished.

Six Ways to Law!

Six Ways to Order!

Six Ways to Peace!

The words as the voice spoke, popped onto the screen as

they were being spoken, bright golden letters generated on the jet-black field surrounding the pyramid symbol. Then the graphic changed again, to a chart which outlined what was obviously a chain of command. The voice lectured on each position within the structure, instructing about purposes and job functions — the computer-generated images changing, giving specific information relating to each governing position - from Continental Head at the top of the chart, to the four Quadrant Commanders on each continent, to the 666 Sector Coordinators and, finally, down to the thousands of Controllers and Block Governors represented at the bottom of the chart.

With the videotaped presentation finished, Jacob looked to his wrist for the time, then at the clock on the credenza against the wall several feet behind Marchek's desk. 10:38 - a quartz-type clock, not affected by power disruptions in the area. The introduction to the new order had cost him more than two hours, but the education was transfixing, a blue-print masterpiece for what looked to be a terrifyingly feasible authoritarian monster. "The Plan" was so complete, so encompassing, it would have no doubt dumbfounded the President, as it must have Conrad Wilson. But, when would his foster father have had opportunity to view the tape in Naxos? The constant surveillance probably made it impossible for him to do so. Most likely, Jacob, himself, was the first person, not a part of the INterface planners, to see the tape.

The thing was like it was choreographed by a master director. The only resistant force that might have had a chance to thwart INterface ambitions — the President — the United States government — had been eliminated in a single catastrophic second. However, the master-director had let one monkey wrench slip into the cogs of INterface machinery. Jacob Zen now knew what was to come to a world ripe for dictatorship. And, although he couldn't grasp what possible threat he, one human being, presented to such power, it was supremely evident they considered him more than merely an irritant.

He picked up the other Naxos videotape and weighed whether to put it into the machine, or to get into the Marchek things. He chose the second option, inserting one of the diskettes into the computer and punching the appropriate keys. The computer's display screen lit up with information, and when he punched other keys, it became evident the program was devoted to personal finances — nothing to indicate the old eschatologist had entered a hidden code. He removed the diskette then snapped in another and manipulated the keyboard. The screen displayed: "Apyr Doopo nowa"oBaTb!"

Beneath the confusing garble, the computer automatically generated the message: "Jerome, I am thirty-seven, old enough to know better! Where time sublime, they make no crime and perfect rhyme. There is no sin -- no fools rush-in."

He searched his memory for the antiquated methodology that might help solve Marchek's cryptology. He mentally ran through the computer, straining to remember technology he once struggled to put out of his mind so the new could take its place. Had Marchek used KLIC? KPIC? KWOC? A hybrid creation of his own ingenuity? Most of the indexing was smokescreen, he was certain. He would have to break through that screen to determine if Marchek left the message to unlock his secrets.

Jacob tried to shake the illogical thoughts. There was no reason to the feeling, but it was there, and he couldn't get rid of it. Marchek had left a message for him. Each time he forced his mind into a more rational frame, the almost tangible intuitive sensation struck again. Hugo Marchek's secrets could be unlocked only by Jacob Zen.

He must think back to their time together—to what he knew about the man. If the key to unlocking the indexing system rested with him, it would likely be found in his memory of the brief time the two of them were together in conversation. He felt it more strongly than ever — Marchek had left a message for him.

He wheeled from beneath the computer in the chair, rolling backward until he could consider the entire machine while studying the data glaring at him from the display screen. The key was there; he knew it!

"Jerome, I am..."

Who was Jerome? No one he and Marchek had discussed. It had to be a code word.

"Jerome, I am thirty-seven."

Nothing even remotely familiar. He looked at the line above. "Apyr Doopo nowa"oBaTbl"

Why the quotation mark in the middle of the last combination of letters? Something familiar about the effect. He read again the entire message. "Jerome, I am thirty-seven, old enough to know better! Where time sublime, they make no crime and perfect rhyme. There is no sin -- no fools rush-in."

"Rush... hyphen... in" Jacob said aloud. "That's it! It's Russian!"

Marchek had headed this message in Russian. Using English letters as best he could, the quotation mark as close to the intended Russian character as he could manage. Russian, the one language besides English that Marchek had known both he and Jacob understood.

"Apyr," the Russian masculine for "friend." The greeting, in total: "Friend, welcome!"

The old man would not have left him a code for finding the index key that did not relate to something both of them understood from their knowledge of each other. What was close to Marchek's heart? Karen, PAL, God, the Bible. That was it! Marchek had said it himself! All the answers to mankind's dilemmas were in the Bible! Even in death Hugo Marchek had something to tell him that might give insight into what more and more looked to be the biblically predicted apocalypse. Things at which Jacob would once have scoffed, but which now chased him like a predatory demon out to devour him. Searching the Scriptures was the message. Search the Scriptures!

"Jerome, I am thirty-seven." Of course! Jeremiah. The Book of Jeremiah, one of the prophets of the Old Testament, chapter 37. He looked through the desk drawers for a match and found a book, then fumbled for a cigarette from the crumpled package taken from his suit coat pocket. He lit the cigarette and jammed the book of matches into the pocket of his pants.

He searched the many volumes in the bookshelves lining the study walls, finally spotting and removing the black leather-bound Bible. He put it on the desk and quickly looked up the book and chapter. Nothing there that was familiar, he decided after five minutes of reading and re-reading. Just the prophet Jeremiah, talking with King Zedekiah about the prophet's imprisonment, being released, and trying to get the king to repent — nothing that struck a familiar note.

A false trail, so he returned to the computer and looked again at the message for several seconds.

"Jerome. I am thirty-seven."

Thirty... dash... seven. Could it be that simple? He moved from the chair to the desk and again fumbled through the pages until he found the Book of Jeremiah, chapter 30, verse 7: "Alas! for that day is great, so that none is like it: it is even the time of Jacob's trouble; but he shall be saved out of it."

Jacob's trouble! It sprang at him in all its truth! Marchek had somehow anticipated this moment — his predicament.

The Bible — the Scriptures could be the key to Jacob Zen's survival! "It is even the time of Jacob's trouble, but he shall be saved out of it."

Glass exploded from the French doors, ripping him from his euphoria. They had found him!

CHAPTER 12

The doors were giving under the violent blows. Jacob frantically pulled the suit jacket from his body and spread it on the desk. He shoveled the computer diskettes, videocassettes and Marchek's notes and Bible into the coat, then wrapped the coat around the materials. Only one direction to take — down the hallway and out either the kitchen door, or the front.

He scrambled from the study into the dark hallway, hearing the glass of the French doors shattering, and their wooden frames splintering. Escape did not seem possible, and he fleetingly wished for one of the miracles Hugo Marchek credited his God with performing. He must decide now which of the exits to try, or else turn and face those who were breaking through the stubborn doors separating the study from the garden. Too late! Now the other doors were being pounded! Soon he would be hemmed in on both sides; nowhere to go but up, down, or out one of the bedroom windows — but they would be waiting outside the windows — *There! Above him!* A way that might put off the confrontation for a few seconds more.

The chain, attached to a large, rectangular piece of wood at the center of the hallway's ceiling. It had to be. He grabbed the dangling chain and pulled. Yes! A folding stairway to the attic, something he had not seen for years. The contrivance was his lone remaining hope. But was there time?

He unfolded the ladder to the floor and, without taking time to consider its sturdiness, vaulted up its steps. At the ladder's top, kneeling on the planks of the attic floor, he leaned as far down the ladder as possible and grabbed one of the rungs to refold the steps against their plywood base.

Footsteps! Running heavily toward the hallway! They were in the house! They would be in the hall within seconds. He tugged the folded stairway toward him, and its spring mechanism guided it into place flush against the attic floor. Did they hear the spring-slap sound? Or did their own noisy rush through the house drown out the stairway's closing thump?

They were beneath him now; beneath the folded ladder. The voices of at least three men, looking for him, telling each other that their quarry could not have gotten out of the house, could not have gotten past them. If only there had been time to take the hanging chain off the plywood.

His eyes had adjusted to the darkness of the attic, and there was enough illumination to make his immediate surroundings visible. Boxes with old clothes, Christmas tree ornaments, papers. A box with tools and cans of glue, cans of paint and three one-gallon cans of paint thinner.

The paint-thinner! He pulled one of the cans from beneath the tools and other cans. It was full. Then the others — all were new cans and full!

He unscrewed the caps and sniffed to be certain. Yes! Paint-thinner. He emptied the contents of the cans into an empty bucket he found nearby.

One of the voices below him was shouting. "Here! He's in the attic! In here!"

He heard the hurried shuffling of feet as the others ran back into the hallway. There would be no more chances. It had to work, or he was finished!

He fumbled through his shirt pocket — empty! Where were they? Had he dropped them? His tormentors were pulling the chain now, lowering the ladder! He shrank back into the darkness, still searching. His pants! They were in his pants pocket!

The ladder was being unfolded and events were simultaneously shifting into slow-motion. The book of matches pulled out of the pocket — the steps unfolded — the cardboard covering of the matches flicked open — the ladder making contact with the floor -- the voices, angry, desperate to get to him! — pressure on the ladder — the disappearing stairway creaking and groaning beneath his pursuers' weight — the match struck — not lighting the first time — another try and the match disintegrated — a new match, handled with a shaking hand — Lit!

The head and shoulders of the first man, a square jaw, the black eyes not seeing Jacob yet in the darkness of the attic. Jacob hid the glow of the match by cupping his hand over it. The head ducked back down just below the attic's floor. They were hesitant, probably concerned that their quarry had a gun. Jacob wadded and twisted a piece of cardboard and held the match to it until the paper lit. Now was the time to move!

He had positioned himself at the back of the rectangular hole in the attic's floor so that the attackers' backs were to him when they ascended the steps. He moved forward on his knees in order to see them, three in all, two on the ladder and one on the hallway floor below — all with drawn handguns. He splashed the paint-thinner on them with one douse. The two men on the ladder staggered, almost losing their balance.

Jacob threw the cardboard torch at the man at the top of the steps. The attacker erupted in flames, and in his agony he triggered two rounds into the ceiling. The fire spread instantaneously to the man just below him. Both men, screaming, fell on top of the third man.

He had to break out of this attic! Others would be waiting outside, possibly, but he would quickly be overwhelmed by the smoke and fire if he stayed longer; the old home would go fast. Luck! A sledgehammer in the box of tools. But could he beat his way out of the attic through the roof? No. The ceiling was too high to reach the 1" x 8" planks of the roof with any degree of leverage. He looked at the gable vents 30 feet away, where the light poured in through the slats. The answer! He hurried toward the light, hearing the sounds of his would-be captors writhing and screaming on the hallway floor. Pressing his face against the vents, he looked out on the grounds, having a good view in all directions, and satisfied himself that no one was waiting outside.

The men had stopped screaming. Had they been overcome by the flames? Or was the fire extinguished, and their pursuit on again? No... Impossible... The fire was too engulfing, too intense. The men were unconscious, or better yet, dead.

Using a side swing, he crashed the 10-pound sledge head into the old wooden slats that made up the gable vents. Because they were brittle, their destruction was quick and complete, and he stuck his head and shoulders through the opening he had just made, to again look for potential threats. It was a long drop to the ground, with little vegetation to break his fall. He could not afford a broken ankle or leg. He had to remain mobile.

Leaning out the hole farther, he looked at the surface of the house and saw what looked to be a pipe, painted white, which apparently was a conduit for electrical wires because it ran up from an electric meter located six feet off the ground on the house's rock surface. There should be just enough space between the pipe and the stones, at various points along the pipe's length, to provide a good grip.

His first try at the pipe almost ended in disaster, but he regained his balance and, after stretching again, he finally managed to reach the pipe and get a firm grip. Then, by carefully negotiating the rock surface with his feet, he let his legs straighten beneath him until the toes of his shoes dug into the crevices between the stones on either side of the pipe. He wouldn't risk dropping the coat with the tapes and diskettes wrapped in it; he had fought, almost died, for the secrets they held. He could not chance damaging them. But the descent would be clumsy if he held the folded coat; maybe even cause a fall. The best way to carry his cargo was with his teeth, leaving his hands free for a better grip. He paused, holding the pipe with one hand while using his teeth and free hand to make sure the coat was still wrapped securely around the materials. He held the coat between clenched teeth and slid down the pipe, using his shoe soles to apply braking friction against the stones.

Already, thick, dark smoke was billowing from cracks around the window sills. Whatever he had left in the home that might be of use to him in his search for the truths he must uncover was now irretrievable. But, irretrievable to his enemies as well. The old home would be gone in minutes, and because of the calamitous events of the past hours, all available firefighters and equipment were concentrated on the major disasters. One burning house meant nothing, now. Why, then, did one man mean so much to his enemies? Why could he not, like the burning house, simply be ignored? To be allowed to come to his end in his own, natural time?

They would not stop. He knew that now. However, four of them would no longer hound him — no longer come at him on highways, in the back of cars, in attics, with blood-lust in their eyes, murder in their hearts. Like the ones that night who had driven the tow-truck, trying to run Karen and him down; but were they a part of the same group of murderers? One thing for sure, three of them were now only a stench, swirling skyward behind him. He moved cautiously from the yard, looking around to spot trouble and to get his bearings, trying to find the van he had left parked along the street.

The nauseating thought clutched at his instinctive side; they had been able to follow him since he left Naxos. What made him believe he could elude them now? There was an answer and he had to find it, if he was to survive, find Karen, and somehow, somewhere, the two of them were to wring a new beginning out of this nightmare world.

The van was just ahead, the hood to its engine pulled forward — open. Someone had been at the motor, tampering. His enemies, or just vandals? He would stay clear of the van. He had to find another vehicle and get away from Rockville -- drive until he could figure where to go to look over the materials without fear of being found again. But, was there such a place? Their agents seemed able to anticipate his every move. Probably were at every roadblock looking for him.

Fatigue was again his greatest nemesis, now that his human tormentors were temporarily off his back. Paranoia filled his head with defeat, hopelessness, terror. There must be a place to rest, somewhere. Surely there was a place to hide while he assessed his best options and analyzed his chances.

He hurried along the sidewalk, back toward the burning house, becoming aware that he was limping, feeling the skin on his right knee begin to burn. His right pants leg was torn at the knee, the result of making contact with the protruding stones on his way down the pipe. A small spot of blood had soaked through the cloth. The injured calf, too, ached, contributing to the limp.

People were gathered in the street in front of the burning house, and it was good to see them — to know there were still human beings who were not intent on attacking him. They made no effort to fight the blaze, or to enter the house to see if someone might need rescuing. They were quiet, scarcely talking to each other, as if in shock. Their eyes transfixed on the flames that streamed and flickered upward into the morning sky. They paid him no attention when he passed behind them in the middle of the street, limping toward the navy blue car parked on the side opposite Marchek's, now almost consumed, home. It was the agents' car. Plain, without decorative chrome, a government-issue vehicle. It could not belong to anyone in this crowd of onlookers, all obviously native to the neighborhood. No outsiders among the gawkers. No one looking for him, looking for associates who had gone into the Marchek house to take Jacob Zen. The blue Chevrolet was the car that had brought his would-be captors here.

He opened the door and slid behind the wheel, then scanned the crowd again. The people were oblivious to all but the flames. He looked over the interior, his eyes meeting a round screen of dark glass 13 or 14 inches in diameter. The keys were in the ignition, the agents having left them there, no doubt, in anticipation of having to chase him. During an escape attempt, they would not have to fumble for the keys, losing precious seconds.

He started the car and the scope lit up with a circular line-schematic, white on a dark blue background. Obviously tracking equipment. They were tracking him! But how? He would have to be carrying a homing device of some sort with him. The most likely place for something like that would have been the attaché case; but it detonated at McLean. The videotapes — it could be in the videotapes! If the homing sensor was in the tapes, he was still carrying it, and other tracking devices like this one were tracking him now, or soon would be. He must find the transponder and get rid of it.

He unwrapped the coat from around the materials and looked over the videotapes. Nothing but plastic cases and the videotape which the cases protected. Though he was neither expert nor totally up-to-date on the latest technological advances in mobile surveillance, he did have some knowledge of such things, and he knew of no tracking device so powerful yet small enough that it could not be seen by the naked eye. But that did not mean that new super-micro breakthroughs had not been achieved, his knowledge thus made obsolete. What if the videotape, itself — its celluloid-like composition — possessed innate qualities that provided those radar-like instruments with a homing signal? The device must be found and destroyed!

For now, though, the best thing was to keep moving until he could find where they planted the signal device. In the lining of his clothing? In his shoes? He must check at first opportunity.

Where to go in order to have time to check for the transponder — to review the materials — to rest--to figure out how to get to Karen, if she were still alive.

He could take this car belonging to his enemies, and... No... They must not know that he learned they had the tracking capability. They might then bring into play new methods, new devices. He must let them continue to track him, if they could, until he could find the homing device; then he could destroy it, or deactivate it. Somehow use it to his own advantage if, of course, he could elude them long enough. He had to leave the car as he found it, the keys in the ignition, the homing scope turned on. He had to get away. Now! The ring was tightening; he sensed its deadly noose, felt it gathering about him. He must get away from Rockville and the eschatologist's burning house.

Time — it no longer meant anything, he supposed, but he wished for his missing watch. Time was something familiar — silent — an invisible companion that linked his rationality to a world which two nights before had made sense, but in that one confounding second, vaporized when the agent's reflection disappeared from the rearview mirror. Time was still a real commodity, even though one he could not see, represented by the incremental sweep of the second hand on the watch Karen had given him. The watch was at Naxos — rather, in Naxos. Time could now be recognized, be fleetingly harnessed in his mind, only by the silent counting of the seconds, and the buildings shadows creeping traverse of the vast concrete surfaces across from the apartment, from whose window he watched the pitiful, meandering souls dazedly shuffle along the streets of Boston. Time remained a constant; time could not have changed as had everything else during the past hellish hours. The electric clock in the kitchen which he could see through the narrow, doorless opening read 11:56. But the long shadows indicated it was more like 3:00 in the afternoon.

Electrical service was disrupted for more than a day when the disaster happened, and Boston was one of the luckier of the big cities. Most were still without electricity, according to reports he monitored between naps since the quick trip to Boston and the occupation of the apartment, one of many dwellings left vacant by the disappearance.

Had the high-speed helicopter trip from the small Maryland airport — the result of a hastily-made friendship with a pilot who was trying to find missing members of his family in Boston — thrown his enemies off his trail? Did the flight break the chain binding him electronically to those who wanted him dead? He had checked clothing, shoes, everything he could think of where the transmitter might be hidden. Had it fallen from wherever it had been placed? Jostled loose, perhaps, during the latest leg of his flight from his enemies? And if not, if the device was still in place, had the distance put between himself and them broken that invisible umbilical cord which drew him into the center of their devilish surveillance screens?

The naps had helped relieve the terrible drag of fatigue, but not eliminated it. He longed for hours of sleep. Sleep free from the need to keep watch out of the eighth story window — free of his inner urgings to search for a video recorder in order to play the tapes, to locate a compatible computer, in order to go over the data on the diskettes. The compelling necessity to remain watchful. The dread, that if he left this apartment the transmitter would again put him within range of the surveillance screens, kept him from looking for the equipment he needed to plan. Soon, he must break out of this cocoon of hiding; soon, he had to open himself up to them.

His eyes burned from the strain of watching the street below and the streets surrounding the buildings across the way. Nothing of consequence, only people continuing to shuffle about in shock, searching for a corner of sanity to grasp. An occasional car moving one way or another along the streets, swerving to avoid the several wreckages strewn about. His eyes next focused on slender, colorful objects which darted in a hazy, liquid world; his mind followed, its thoughts aborted by the realization he was looking into the large aquarium atop a wooden cabinet that was layered below with shelves housing items for maintaining the fish tank.

Exotic fish darted or treaded in mid-water, their gills

opening, their O-shaped mouths puckering then dilating. Some of the larger ones, apparently less easily frightened, seeming to observe him as intently as he did them. Bubbles ascended in a steady stream from the tank's re-oxygenation system, but the water looked murky, most likely a result of the hours without electrical power to run the cleansing machinery. Should the fish be fed? The tank cleaned?

Jacob smiled, mildly surprised that such simple thoughts gave him, for a brief moment, remembrance of the formerly normal world — a small degree of relief from the bizarre present. He looked through the supplies, seeing a half-dozen boxes of different kinds of fish foods. With his index finger, he tapped what he considered a generous helping from each of the boxes and stirred the floating bits so that most sank.

"I don't know if this is how they did it for you, my friends, but eat, drink, and be merry... for tomorrow your feeder may perish," Jacob said, bending to look into the tank to watch the fish take the food, then dart swiftly from the others before returning near the surface to gobble more.

His own stomach rumbled, persuasively arguing that he had not been faithful to it since leaving Naxos, except for the meals on the plane while crossing the Atlantic, and the crackers and light snacks of cookies and chips he had munched since. He was reluctant to attack the more substantial foods in the refrigerator, not knowing how long the electricity had been off. In the kitchen, he opened the refrigerator door, the food aromas entering his nostrils, setting in motion deep cellular hunger that weakened him and burned the pit of his stomach. He decided to risk it, and ate his fill. Within minutes, the warm, satisfying waves of replenishment flooded his body with energy he had not felt in a week.

At some point, he would have to get more food. And, someone was bound to come to check this apartment sooner or later, whether relatives of its former occupants, building management or some other authority. He sipped the soft drink from the aluminum can and returned his thoughts to matters he had managed to put aside while he ate. Troubling things, but things which, with a full belly and at least some sleep, seemed less overwhelming than before.

First matter to attend to — find the VCR and the computer, then study the materials, while at the same time avoid being located by the assassins. The VCR wouldn't be hard to scrounge, but the computer could prove difficult to find. The particular type he needed had been made obsolete by the UNIVUS equipment. Most people had turned in their old home computers as token payment for the new.

The Federal government had supposedly sold, but actually had given, the antiquated computers to Third World countries. This was, of course, after making substantial modifications, to make the computers compatible with telecommunication systems throughout Europe, the United States and Japan. Odds were against his finding one of the old computers without putting himself in jeopardy, because he would probably have to range far from the apartment. Regardless, it had to be done.

Throughout his time spent in the apartment, he had listened and watched with an eye and an ear tuned to the 40-inch TV screen set into one wall, while keeping the other eye and ear alert to things happening on the streets below. Since the disappearance, all networks had periodically given way to the Emergency Broadcast System, which continued to drone only official government speculations about what had happened. A government, he reminded himself, which had proven to be his enemy. And, he was convinced that government was the puppet, or at least the client, of those in the man-made caverns of Naxos. He was equally convinced that their intentions were to persuade all people of the world that they, those elite few in Naxos, should direct the course of world affairs from here forward.

The officially sanctioned theory had evolved and remained unchanged--that a sudden cosmic illness, one like which must have devastated the dinosaurs, had occurred. It was a non-stop assault aimed at quelling panic, and all the major networks lent their top anchor people, as well as, lesser journalists to the effort. Now that the networks had been given back the airwaves, they continued the concerted attempt to put the public at ease.

Gone now from those networks was the formerly innate skepticism, the antagonism to the questionable intents of governments and politicians. On all issues involving the great disappearance--and that was the only thing being pondered by them--the line remained the same: it must have been a cyclical cosmic disturbance like the one that made the dinosaurs extinct. They added to the supposition: Now scientists were quite certain that such a phenomenon had erased from paleontological record all traces of the missing-link anthropoid/homosapien beings of evolutional theory. Emergence evolution was thus made unnecessary to the explanation of man's beginnings.

But he knew that the words were lies--that the government, like everyone else, had no idea what really happened. He knew from the things he learned while listening to and watching the Vice President that night while in the crawl-space at Stone Oaks. It was all a sham, and they would mold and herd the people through their deception into some sort of computerized, one-world society unless somebody made people aware of "The Plan."

And that, if for no other reason, was why they wanted him dead or alive. If he were going to die anyway for the data contained in the tapes and diskettes--or worse--live a life of such confining, agonizing existence as to make it not worthwhile, good sense as much as enraged ego dictated that he pursue that knowledge and claim it for his own.

The inner voice, that same instinct or whatever it was, told him that the volatile materials had locked within them directions for survival— escape for himself, maybe for humanity, and for Karen, if she were still alive. She had to be among the living; that hope, he felt to his marrow, was the source that kept the inner beacon lit, his energy fires kindled.

He knew the truth of their conniving. Once he had viewed the tapes and the information on the diskettes, he would know the extent of their deceit and their ambition. He was doomed for certain if he merely sat and did nothing. They would find him and kill him, or else the system would gradually absorb him along with every other pitiful creature under its dominion and snuff out all personal liberty. One man alone could do little to assuage them or to stop implementation of their plans for their victims. But to sit and do nothing was slow, excruciating self-execution. Worse. As one man who possessed information that could damage the monster, to sit and watch those terrible jaws tighten without using that weapon as best he could would be genocide through omission. But one man—one man, alone.

Suddenly, he heard a clicking, rattling sound at the apartment's front door. The brass knob turned quickly, one way, then the other! Had they found him again? How many would there be this time? What route would he take to escape? Eight stories...no fire escape from the apartment's balcony. *Nowhere to go to get away!*

He must face them, surprise them! Bash their insidious brains out before they killed him. The stricken thoughts caromed in his mind while he hurried as noiselessly as he could to the door, tightly gripping a pewter statue of an American Revolutionary War soldier he took from a lamp stand. He stood beside the door with his back to the wall, which met a plaster and wood door-facing that protruded 12 inches into the room, providing him a recess that could hide him for a few valuable seconds when they came through the door.

If they were his would-be killers, why were they trying to open the door with a key? They had surely scoped the situation, knowing that he could not escape this time, except by climbing on the facade of the building or jumping from the iron railing to another balcony. Why did they not burst in like they did at Marchek's home? But, then, they did not need to burst in. They would take their time; there was no place for him to run.

The door would open any second. It would move open, away from him, giving him a free swing at the first one in. The first through the doorway would pay admission with his skull!

Drawing back the pewter soldier, he glanced first at the area of the opening where the man's head should appear, then looked downward where the feet would take their first steps into the apartment. He caught a glimpse of the toe of a black, patent-leather shoe and he blinked, his panicked reasoning ability thrown out of sync by the shoe's appearance. It was a woman's shoe! And it pushed the door open to its fullest extension before disappearing momentarily from view. A woman! Could they have sent a woman to do their work?

Papers crackled in the hallway. The sound of paper sacks or bags being gathered from the hallway floor. She was picking up something made of paper. Not the premeditative actions of someone intent on rousting out her prey. *Keep the weapon poised,* he thought. *Do not be caught by surprise.*

Jacob pressed his back flat against the niche, holding the soldier high, ready to strike.

A hand came into view and pushed against the door,

which had swung fully open, then rebounded to a nearly shut position. Oval, perfectly manicured nails of crimson, tipped the ends of the slender fingers. Smooth skin — a young woman's hand.

She struggled through the opening, trying to handle a large paper sack full of grocery items, and at the same time her purse and keys. When she closed the door, he stepped from the wall.

Her piercing shriek startled him, even though he thought he was prepared for it. She was unable to speak, her complexion going chalk-white, her face frozen in a look of terror. The sack and purse had exploded against the floor, sending its contents askew. She started to fall, her knees buckling. Jacob lunged and caught her, then carried her to the long sofa, put her on it, and knelt beside her.

"I'm sorry... I won't hurt you." He held her hand and patted it, wondering why people always patted the hand when someone fainted, or the cheek, which he then patted gently, trying to revive her. "I'm not going to hurt you."

Her eyes fluttered sleepily, then opened to their normal width before gaping in panic. She looked at Jacob, who put his hand over her mouth and pinned her gently against the sofa cushions, feeling her stiffen beneath his grip.

"I'm not going to hurt you. Believe me... I... will... not... hurt... you. I'm going to let you go, now. Please don't scream... Please."

Relaxing his grip and taking his hand slowly from her mouth, he backed away a couple of feet, still kneeling on the floor on one knee, his hands, palms up in the air for her to see. "See... I won't hurt you."

The young woman lay still for a moment, then sat up quickly and withdrew into the corner of the sofa. "Who are you?"

"My name is Jacob Zen. I didn't think anybody still lived

in this apartment. I've been here for three days. Please believe me... I won't harm you... Okay?"

She silently considered his words, but did not relax her stiff posture against the arm of the sofa.

"Look." He took his wallet from his back pocket. "See. My name is Jacob Zen. I'm a liaison officer with the United States State Department. Take it... See for yourself."

He offered the wallet and she cautiously accepted it and examined the card, her pretty eyes glancing fearfully at the photograph then at his face. "What are you doing here? What do you want?" Her tone betrayed the fact she was near tears, and he moved slowly farther away from her, hoping to put her more at ease so he could begin winning her trust. She tossed the wallet timidly in his direction and he leaned to retrieve it from the carpet.

"Like I told you. My name's Jacob Zen. May I have your name?"

"What are you doing here?"

"As I said, I'm liaison officer with the State Department. You know what's happened... All these people vanishing... These crazy things that've been going on. I thought whoever lived here disappeared like the rest." His explanation met icy silence.

"Look. This is classified," he lied, "...but I was sent here to do some work that requires staying out of sight. I felt I could do that by picking a place like this, rather than checking into a hotel under a phony name. When I checked this apartment out, I found evidence that whoever lived here hadn't been around for quite some time. The fish tank hadn't been cleaned after the power was off for so long — there was spoiled food on the counter top ~ things like that. I thought it would be a good place to do my work."

The woman eyed him warily, but with a bit less suspicion, he thought.

"Look, I really am sorry I frightened you. I thought the place was okay to use — that no one would return. I'll just get my stuff together and get out."

"I haven't been able to get back..." the woman said, ignoring his offer to leave, her voice quietly soft. "I was in Maine when... it happened... at my mother's home. She just..." Her tears came. "She was gone." The girl looked at him, her eyes liquid with her grief. "Mother was there, having coffee, eating, laughing... then she vanished. She just wasn't there anymore."

He wanted to take her in his arms, to comfort her, to give the human compassion he, himself, wanted — needed. Such an action would be misunderstood. Best simply to commiserate from the safe distance separating them across the carpet. "We've all lost someone close to us." The words were not acknowledged; she wiped away the tears with her fingertips.

"I've been trying to get back home since then," she said, able finally to choke back her emotions. "Everyone's gone crazy. The whole world is insane."

"I know. I've been out in the middle of it. But everything will get back to normal. Things will be better soon."

Without realizing it, he had moved across the carpet and put a hand on her shoulder, and she had made no move to get away from him, her fear apparently lessened. He was glad. He, too, needed the contact, and they silently spent the moment locked in each other's arms.

"You know my name. What's yours?" he said in his most gentle tone, looking into her eyes, brushing her tears with his fingers. "Melissa Jantzen."

He took her hand and cupped it in his hands. "I'm very happy to meet you, Melissa. We'll work our way out of this thing together. Don't worry." He lifted her chin with a crooked finger and offered a reassuring smile, which was returned shyly. She nodded understanding agreement. When he released her and stood, he bent to pick up the grocery items and the purse. He put her things back into the purse except an open package of cigarettes and her gold cigarette lighter.

"Do you mind if I have one?" He showed her the package and she nodded. "Are you from Maine?" he asked, then savored a deep inhalation.

"From Boothbay Harbor."

"Yeah? Where's that near?"

"We like to think other places are near Boothbay," she said. "It's not far from Brunswick and Lewiston... just north of Portland."

"I lived, as a very young boy, in a little bay town in New York. Didn't stay there long, though. My father died and Mother and I moved to the Washington D.C. area when I was six or so. I haven't spent much time in really small towns. McLean isn't all that big, but with the D.C., Virginia, Maryland region being so heavily populated, you don't get the feeling of living in a small town. Like most of the northeast, it's all become megaplex."

"What took you and your mother to Washington?" Her tone sounded of genuine interest, and he was glad she had relaxed to the point she apparently felt she could trust him.

"Mother was a looker at 25 and caught the eye and heart of a diplomat, who whisked us off to his home at McLean, Virginia. And, except for Mother's death, I lived happily ever after. Well... until recently, anyway."

A stupid mistake—bringing her thoughts back to their dilemma. Her eyes filled with tears again. "What has happened? What is this all about?"

He cradled her head against his chest. "Everything's going to be okay, Melissa. We're in it together and we'll work it out, together." He hated the trite clichés, even while he spoke them, and the words rang hollow in the room while the two of them sat clinging to each other. It ran quickly through his mind that their plight was symbolic of that of humanity. Confused and huddled, awaiting their fate. Together, yet solitary in their second-by-second journey into the uncertain future.

CHAPTER 13

The hot tea chased the chill from Jacob's body while he sat sipping above the long glass-top coffee table. Melissa Jantzen huddled close, looking to see over his right arm.

The electricity had been off for more than 10 hours this time, after sporadic restorations of no more than 20 minutes at a stretch. The only illumination was that oozing through the balcony's glass doors, sunlight diffused by thick clouds and smog so that it looked to be early evening. Melissa's quartz clock displayed 11:01 in the morning. Gone with the electric lights was the central heat. They endured the cumbersome matching wool sweaters Melissa said were to be presents for friends, but which, Jacob suspected, belonged to her and her male apartment mate. His suspicion arose when, two days after she arrived, he came across a man's clothing and a man's initialed cigarette lighter while searching through a bureau drawer for a flint for his own lighter. She had entered the room at that moment, and, becoming embarrassed, had directed him away from the chest of drawers by quickly getting what he needed. He did not mention it, but knew she was aware he found the clothes. Neither did he question the gray turtleneck she gave him to wear.

It was easy to understand how one could form a special feeling for this girl, who was at the same time strongly self-protective and vulnerable. Too, it was good to have someone to remind him that human warmth did still grace the earth's cold, troubled surface. They had not and did not share the same bed, but somehow for the past four days, they had shared something inexplicably more intimate. A feeling, a sense of belonging together. Not in the same way lovers belonged together — although sexual desire for her had crossed his mind — but in the sense that people working together in a common heroic cause belonged together.

From the beginning, when she learned that she could trust him, knew that surviving their mutual ordeal could be best accomplished by helping him, he was consummately charmed by her and made aware of her resourcefulness. She had directed him to two apartments in the building where acquaintances had lived before the disaster. In the first, they found a computer of the old type, compatible with the diskettes, and in the second apartment, a video-cassette recorder.

Power had been disrupted to the point it was impossible to begin making use of the machinery, but Melissa had been able to brew the tea without electricity using an ancient, oil-burning samovar. With it, she was also able to heat canned beans and potted meats. If not ideal domestic life, it was, he reckoned while downing the last of his tea, as nearly so as anyone during this maddening time was likely to manage.

She propped an elbow on his shoulder and rested her chin on top of her wrist, watching him move the materials about on the coffee table. Her presence was good, bringing thoughts of Karen and what she might think if she saw this pretty girl so near him. Although he and Karen had pacted not to begrudge each other occasional outside relationships, he suspected she would be angered. Although on Melissa's part, he was fairly certain the feeling of closeness was innocent. Under circumstances like these — the world disintegrating, seeming to have a hostile will of its own toward its inhabitants — he hoped he would not deny Karen such companionship. Of course, he would begrudge her; he knew that as well as he knew he would not be able to keep from stepping over the fragile barrier of fidelity should this desirable girl invite him across. Melissa's sweet, feminine essence was an inhalation of cool, pure oxygen in a world choking with malice.

"What do you expect to find in all this?" she said after several seconds of watching him arrange, then rearrange, the items.

"I've already had a look at one of the programs and some of the papers. But without the computer and the VCR to look at this other stuff, I've only been able to confuse myself. I hope these other things will shed light on what I've already found out, or think I've found out."

"What's that?"

He looked at her, contemplating whether to burden her with suspicions that might frighten her senseless, or make her think he was a lunatic. But, then, she knew about the disappearance of her mother and millions of others. She knew about the things being reported by the one-minded news establishment. He had explained to her his own dilemma, although the explanation was a lie. Now, he needed her — to share the truth with him, to maybe give him insights from new perspectives. He must tell her everything he knew — all that he suspected.

"I told you I'm with the State Department. I'm afraid that's about the only thing I've told you that's the truth, Melissa."

He got to his feet and walked to the sliding glass door to the balcony, then stared blankly into the overcast morning sky.

"I am a liaison officer with State, like I said... That is, I was with the State Department. I'm not so sure there is a State Department, or any other governmental institution as we're used to thinking of them." He turned to face her. "Can I have some more of that tea?"

She brought his cup to him, along with the pot, and poured while he held the cup for her. Her expression was one of puzzlement.

"I know what I'm going to say, what I'm going to tell you, might scare you. But it's the truth as I understand it. I told you we were in this together, all the way. That was the truth too. We have no choice. What's happening is happening to everybody, everywhere — at least to everyone in what we call the West. And, you deserve to know the facts. Maybe, just maybe, somehow, we can get the truth to others, once we ourselves fully understand. If not, God help us all. I don't know how the truth will ever come to light — at least, not until it's too late."

He again stared out the glass, past the balcony, seeing, yet not paying attention, to the light rain that had begun to fall from the depressing sky. He turned his head when he felt her hand against his shoulder, then turned farther to accept her face against his chest, wrapping his arms around her. She said nothing, her warmth and closeness conveying her thoughts, telling her everything would be all right. Her hair felt soft against his cheek and smelled clean and good when he kissed it lightly.

"They're after me because I have these things." He gestured toward the materials spread on the coffee table. "I've been to an island in the Aegean. A place called Naxos. It's an insignificant little island in the Cyclade chain. I went there with my foster father, who is also my boss, Conrad Wilson."

She looked surprised; he knew she would. "Yes. The same Conrad Wilson," he said. "I was raised by him after my mother died. We went on behalf of the President, and that little piece of rock sticking up out of the water turned out to be somewhat more than what it appeared. It's an incredibly sophisticated governmental center, full of the latest technologies. It's a series of chambers and tunnels more than a mile beneath the surface, from where they intend to rule the world," he said in a dazed voice, as if he meant to say it to no one in particular. Then, he looked at her. "They might have the ability to do it, too."

"Rule the world? Who?"

"I'm not really sure. I don't think all the people involved in the Naxos project themselves know the members of the inner circle — the real power. I know it sounds like a fanatical raving. I sometimes feel like I'm living somebody else's life — that it's all a delusion. Only I keep waking up morning after morning to the same realization. That they've tried to kill me — on three occasions. That they've done something to hurt someone special to me."

"A girl." Melissa's words were emphatic, knowing. Not a question at all. "I'm sorry, Jacob."

The compassion he sensed when she embraced him in that moment, cemented the already special feeling between them. She seemed to understand when she felt him quiver involuntarily against her, that his crying did not make him less a man, but more human.

With his back turned to her, he watched the rain splatter off the iron furniture and the railings of the balcony. "Uncle Conrad sent me back with a package to give the President. I never got to deliver it, because I and the secret service agents who were taking me to the White House were followed by agents of the people of Naxos, who didn't want the materials in the hands of our government. It's a power thing. Them wanting the U.S. to take a back seat. At least it was a power struggle. Now, I just don't know. There's something weird in it. I know you'll think I'm nuts, but there's something almost supernatural about it."

He turned to face her, in control again. "While they were chasing us... and they fully intended to kill us... to take the materials I had with me. While they were behind us, I was looking into the rearview mirror from where I was sitting in the back seat, and the guy, the secret service agent who was driving — he disappeared from the mirror. He was watching in the mirror, looking at the car following, and his face — it vanished."

"How can you be afraid I'll think you're crazy? I saw my mother disappear."

"It's not just people vanishing. Other things, too. These people in Naxos, at least an elite few of them, apparently knew beforehand that this was going to happen. That a catastrophe of this sort would take place and that it would give them an opportunity to institute what they call INterface. It's some kind of computer government to eventually control everyone — everything on the planet."

"But how could a small group of people possibly hope to do that? How could they ever get the remaining communist countries to go along?"

"That's the really weird part. They seemed to know the Russians would be out of the way when it came time to put what they called the 'Six Ways to Peace Plan' into effect. The top man in the thing seems to be Herrlich Krimhler."

"The German? The one who's always in the news?"

"The same." Jacob paced while he talked. "Krimhler as much as predicted something like this disappearance phenomenon would take place. He called it something else —

'a withdrawal into the inner world's consciousness.' He said the uninitiated would be drawn into this inner world, where they would be made worthy to re-enter the real world. Krimhler called it a 'new birth experience back into the physical body.' Said something about a dissolution so that New Age society could enjoy unprecedented prosperity — that all nationalism would have to be done away with."

"This 'Six Ways' thing is supposed to do that?"

"The 'Six Ways to Peace Plan'... Yes. Krimhler said the dissolution would accomplish the excision, meaning, I take it, the cutting out of undesirables, and that the 'Six Ways to Peace Plan' would bring in Utopia."

"You learned all that when you were in this Naxos place?"

"No. After that. It's all in this pile of material. In a couple of pages from a speech made to those in the Naxos project. I didn't read it until I reached the United States. The whole package was given to me by a U.S. operative working under the directive of my foster father. I was to bring it to the President in an attaché case. The package of materials in the case was rigged with explosives to detonate in the event I was assaulted."

"Explosives! Why?"

"That's how critical these things are to the security of this country — to freedom. That explosive charge turned out to be a friend, believe me."

During the next hour he told her everything. His suspicions and his fears. His escapes on the road from Andrews and from Stone Oaks after the overheard conversations in the old mansion's basement complex. The explosion that killed the agent who had held the gun on him from the back seat. He went on to tell her about going to Marchek's home in Rockville after the encounter with the fat driver of the van, and about viewing the speech by Krimhler on the VCR in which the German outlined the planned ruling structure of INterface. His recent experiences continued to flow from his mouth as he described in detail the agents finding him again — as they mysteriously were always able to — and about his escape through the attic, the fire, the helicopter trip to Boston. His telling of it all was cathartic and he felt lighter, free for the moment of the weight which had grown heavier since the U.S. agent handed him the package in the pumping room.

She seemed glad to share the portentous revelations, rather than reacting the way he had feared. Although her words were not trivial, the lightness of her tone made him wonder whether she understood the full implications of what he told her. "It's as if we're both caught in the same horrible dream — one of those you have when you're drifting off to sleep. You're falling and you wake with a start just before you hit bottom. Or you're running away from something or someone, only your legs are so heavy you can barely move and everything is in slow-motion, and you wake up just before whatever's chasing you can grab you."

"That monster has almost caught me three times now. So if it's a dream, I wish I had boogie men with less bloodhound in them."

Her expression became more somber and he thought he saw a trace of fear return to her pretty face; but she deserved the truth.

"I've searched every inch of the stuff I brought with me from the island and haven't found anything they might be able to home in on. The only thing I can think of is that the chemical composition of these tapes or papers might have some properties that allow them to get a fix. I've never heard of anything like that, but with what I've seen lately, I wouldn't be surprised at anything. I've got to see what these tapes and things have on them. That's more important right now than worrying about them finding me again."

Her eyes told him she was grateful for his shared thoughts.

"Look, Melissa," he said in a tone that tried to appeal to her reason while holding her hand. "Maybe it's best to find you some other place for awhile. I would leave, myself, and let you keep this apartment, set up shop somewhere else. But if they've been able to get a fix on my position again, they'll come here first, no matter where else I move to. It would be safer for you to find another apartment in some other building."

She shook her head, cutting him short. "Like you said, we're in this together. I don't want to be separated from you, even for a minute."

The bulbs in the lamps flickered with light, then stayed illuminated, and Jacob walked to the balcony.

"The traffic lights are working again. They're on again as far as I can see toward downtown. I think this time they might stay on." He put his cup and saucer on an end-table where one of the lighted lamps sat, and went back to the coffee table, where he began readying the videocassettes and computer disks.

Like before, he had no particular plan in mind about where to begin dissecting the materials. While the Marchek videotape and computer diskettes were important, the tapes from Naxos were critical; he would digest their information first.

After inserting the cassette, the first scene his gaze met made him think, for a moment, it was the tape he viewed at Marchek's home. A sea of black, globe at the center, then the familiar sparkling crystal pyramid came into focus within the globe. Picking up the other videocassette, he examined it, deciding quickly that he had not made a mistake in his selection.

Martial music played, softly at first, then grew in volume

and inspiration. The disembodied voice spoke when the music subsided.

"What follows is a detailed operational video manual for the position within INterface government to be known as Sector Coordinator. This presentation details all aspects, minor and major, first of the Sector Coordinator's responsibilities to INterface Council, and second to INterface citizenry. Next, the responsibilities of the citizenry, individual and collective, to the Sector Coordinator, to all other instrumentalities within INterface government, and to each other."

Bright gold characters were generated over film of hundreds of pedestrians walking the sidewalks of a large city during a business day. Film that had to have been shot, Jacob decided, within the last two years. Seeing the people dressed in their business attire, and at the time of the film's shooting, so terribly rushed, he wondered how many of those men and women now moved about within Herrlich Krimhler's inner world...having disappeared in the "dissolution."

"They're not kidding about this, are they?" Melissa asked.

Jacob put his hand up for quiet, squinting in concentration at the activity on the screen, which continued to present changing scenes.

"In addition to the specific duties and responsibilities of Sector Coordinator detailed in this inculcation session, there will be outlined the technologies which will assist you, the Coordinator, in the governing of entities within your Sector."

"We're no longer considered people, I guess," Jacob said, thinking out loud. "Now we're entities. A quick demotion from citizens."

Scenes of sophisticated communications equipment flashed and faded in and out on the screen, along with people operating it. Some of the technology was familiar to him from his time in the Naxos complex, some was not.

All the while, the music played on, although more softly

than before. The video seemed to flash and change in time with the percussional beat while the voice continued.

"It is no longer practical to transact business using currency in the traditional, historical sense, although INterface Response Unity will utilize currency of a modified electronic type — somewhat like that which has been used since the inception of computer banking. Naturally, as an outgrowth of this evolution in computer currency, it will also no longer be feasible to use names in everyday business activity. Each citizen-entity of INterface society will be assigned an INterface Number to make INterface Response Unity work."

"Naturally," Jacob agreed sarcastically.

"A cashless, checkless system," continued the computer instructor, "designed to eventually eliminate altogether and forever the debilitating scourge of paper and coinage which has slowed economic progress.

"The founders of INterface thus have directed and supervised the development of this identification and verification machinery, which will make interaction within our world-saving monetary system immune from the thievery and graft that have plagued every socioeconomic system in history. This marvelous technology assures that everyone it serves remains unimpeachably honest.

"What follows is a demonstration of what will be referred to, henceforth, as the INterface Response Unit. 'I.N.R.U' will be the acronym for the computer unit which will be used in conducting all business matters, as you will understand when this session is completed."

Bright yellow letters popped on the screen one at a time:

I...

N...

R...

U...

"The verbal command which will be used to confirm User Identification and will clear the way for transacting business within the system is the statement: 'IN ARE YOU.'"

The words for the acronym above them popped one at a time onto the screen, bright yellow letters on a brilliantly blue background.

IN...

ARE...

YOU...

Jacob and Melissa watched for the next 10 minutes the intricate home-to-business, business-to-government, continent-to-continent, individual-to-individual interconnectedness, displayed through colorful computer graphics spiraling and networking in mesmerizing demonstration of the system in its conceptual totality.

"Now to demonstrate how you, the Sector Coordinator, physically and psychologically fit within the framework of INterface Response Unity," the voice said when the networking display was completed.

The video changed to a man sitting in a chair-computer console — a sleek combined modular unit with sharp, angular features and made of black on gold fiberglass and stainless steel. The chair was thickly padded and covered with red velour material. A video screen, in the center of its own oval-molded shell, sat atop a keyboard unit at the end of the chair's right armrest. The keyboard curved in school-desk fashion in front of the man. The operator was dressed in an orange jumpsuit of the type Jacob remembered wearing in Naxos.

"This is the INterface Response Unit. It will become as much a part of you as your brain and arms and hands are parts of your body. The INRU makes you a vital link in the Universal Mind Order. As healthy, effective neurons and synapses provide linkage within the brain to make a conceptual-level-of-functioning biological unit, so the Sector Coordinator will serve the Universal Mind. Helping link one cluster of cells to other clusters of cells, making INterface Response Unity function as an effective whole, for the good of all."

The man sitting in the console chair began manipulating the keyboard. The camera made a slow sweep, giving perspectives from behind and above the operator. The computerized voice continued instructing how the Sector Coordinator fit within the networking, governing process, and how the INterface Response Unit functioned for the good of all who were part of INterface Response Unity.

After several minutes, the presentation ended with the same graphic demonstration of the total system's interconnectedness shown at the beginning. Jacob sat forward on the sofa, his interest piqued when the voice and the video produced new revelations.

"Of course, the position of Sector Coordinator, as do all positions of authority within INterface, carries with it great responsibilities. And with that authority and responsibility, must be included accountability."

When the man in the chair manipulated the controls, his screen displayed:

FELIX SMITH

lN-3-010101010

SECTOR COORDINATOR DO 1

"This Sector Coordinator," the computer voice said, "at this point hears and responds to the following command."

A different mechanized voice, one less human-like issued the order: "You are instructed to read the following pledge, zero-zero-one."

The man watched his screen and complied by reading the electronic copy it displayed.

"I, three, zero, one, zero, one. zero, one. zero, am one with

INterface, as are all within Sector zero, zero, one. We swear this before Almighty God."

The voice emanating from the console speakers continued: "Prepare for Print Ident. Seize Print Plate."

The Coordinator reached forward with his right hand to the end of the right armrest; at the same time, the camera zoomed in, bringing the viewer a close-up shot of the man's right hand and the dark glass plate, upon which he placed his right index finger and thumb.

The video became a still frame while the voice explained: "Accountability of the Sector Coordinator is achieved through use of the Ident Print Plate, which also assures that the information cannot be subverted. That only this individual has access during INRU accounting and allegiance periods. The Print Plate feeds INterface the Sector Coordinator's thumb and fingerprint simultaneously, plus reads his temperature, which must be close to the normal range of 98.6. Any significant variance from this temperature will automatically set in motion an investigation into the matter. Of course, duplicating the fingerprint and thumbprint would be highly difficult. However, there are safeguards which will be used in conjunction with the Sector Coordinator's fingerprint and thumbprint, to eliminate possibility of forged access, for example, retinal scan."

The video was in motion again, the camera pulling back slightly to include the man's right arm and most of the chair's right armrest. A metallic tubular device swung upward electronically from somewhere beneath the right armrest and covered the man's hand and wrist.

Jacob heard the same words the Sector Coordinator heard, and watched while the man's console screen displayed the words:

AFFIRM: FELIX SMITH
SECTOR 001

CDDRDINATDR IIM-3-O 1 D 1 O 1 D

Interface accepts. IN ARE YOU

"INterface accepts," the voice from the console announced. "IN ARE YOU!"

"You have just witnessed INterface, during which this Sector Coordinator — fully aware of activity within his assigned portion of INterface society — assured Central INterface Terminal Coordinator that order is maintained and the peace is secure within Sector zero, zero, one.

"The INterface Terminal Coordinator, who is responsible for a much larger segment of INterface Unity, known as an Octadrant, affirmed that this Sector Coordinator's Print Ident and IN Scan proved he was IN — that he had legitimate access to the INterface Response Unity computer system, and therefore, the Sector Coordinator's claim that all was well within his sphere of responsibility, was acceptable to INterface Response Unity.

"All Sector Coordinators report to all Octadrant INterface Terminal Coordinators, who then report to the INterface Response Unity Center. Thus, completing the chain of command and assuring that all are One within INterface Response Unity. By INterfacing -- law is maintained, order achieved, the peace secured."

The graphics on Jacob's screen displayed a line chart illustrating the chain of command outlined by the mechanized voice. Ten seconds elapsed, then the now-familiar crystal pyramid symbol took the place of the graphic. Moments later, the tape was finished.

"Can you believe it?! It's like something out of Orwell or Huxley!"

"I can believe it. I have the bruises to show they're serious about it," Jacob said, beginning again to shuffle the materials in front of them on the coffee table. There was so much to look through to understand. So much...

His first inclination was to put the second Naxos tape, the one he had not yet viewed, into the recorder. Thoughts ran through his head of Krimhler's videotaped speech he watched at Marchek's home before they broke in on him. Herrlich Krimhler — surely the architect of what was intended to become INterface Unity. That earlier videotape had revealed a much more sinister, more concentrated intent. Thoughts of something the tape and the papers he brought with him from Naxos termed "The Plan." The blueprint that would lead mankind into his finest hour: Utopia achieved! Would the cassette he held now in his hand provide answers to what this grand design for heaven on earth might entail?

A face behind wire-rimmed glasses, a balding head — its imprint stamped over Jacob's thoughts of Herrlich Krimhler and Naxos. "Listen to the inner voice," Hugo Marchek was saying to him from the grave, from somewhere... "When all else fails, listen, heed your innermost urgings; be guided by them."

The actual words the eschatologist had once given him in counsel seemed the derivative paraphrasing of the words he imagined now—the imagined advice, the actual. A cold shiver rippled along his spine and he convulsed in the moment of eerie sensation.

"Anything wrong?" Melissa touched his arm in concern.

"No. What is it they say when you shiver? A mouse running over your grave, or something?"

"I never heard that. It's the devil sticking you with his pitchfork, I've always believed."

Jacob smiled, but his thoughts were already turning back to Marchek and the materials on the coffee table's top. His gut feeling was that there was at the moment more to be learned from the old man than from the propaganda of Naxos. He dropped the Naxos cassette onto the coffee table and picked up the video taken from Marchek's fireplace, then fed it into the recorder.

"What are we watching?" Melissa, who had left the room for a moment, returned and sat beside him on the sofa after placing a bowl of soup on the table near him.

"A tape I got from an old friend." It felt good to say it for the first time.

Hugo Marchek was a good friend, although fate had allowed them only a brief time together. And, while it felt good to finally verbalize his feelings for the old man, there came at the same time a sadness he had not sensed before about Marchek's loss. In a strange dichotomy, the bitterness toward those responsible for Marchek's murder relieved his nerve-taut emotions, freeing him to proceed with clearer vision of purpose.

He ate the soup, his eyes cut upward at the screen. Lively music sounded while the screen displayed a huge curtain of sparkling gold color, emblazoned across with bright red script-written letters:

"THE RANCE JORGENSON SHOW"

A voice, rising in volume and flourish, announced, "Make welcome Dr. Hugo Marchek, Professor of Eschatology for the Institute of Christian Studies at Rockville, Maryland — who is also President and Founder of PAL, Preservers of American Liberty."

Light applause greeted the guest, who walked through the part in the curtains. A slightly built man of about 70, who although obviously younger than when Jacob knew him, was instantly recognizable. The new guest walked to the booth where the show's host sat and reached to shake the host's hand. He then moved beside the booth and shook hands with Lauren Winchester, Rance Jorgenson's previously inter-viewed guest.

"Glad you could join us, Dr. Marchek. Did I pronounce

the name right?"

"Whatever you wish to call me, Mr. Jorgenson. It is your show," Marchek responded in his thick Polish accent. He patted the host's arm lightly, taking the seat next to Jorgenson, the seat just vacated by Lauren Winchester.

"I think I like you already, Doctor. Most of my guests don't give me the respect I deserve," Jorgenson said pseudo-indignantly.

The sounds from the audience, in feigned sympathy for the host's self-described plight, brought a look of disdain from Jorgenson.

"Who let these people in here tonight, anyway?" said the host, looking somewhere in the direction of off-stage. "They're obviously not members of my family, who I got tickets for--at 10 percent off regular price," he added.

From off-stage, the voice of the program's booth announcer enjoined, "Those tickets were given to you free, Rance. You mean you sold them to your own family?"

The studio erupted in laughter, causing the host to look sheepishly about the stage for support that could not be found. "See you at contract time, Morton," he said with feigned irritation. "I finally get one who shows some respect, some regard for me, and what do you do?"

Turning serious after the laughter subsided, Jorgenson questioned the guest. "What, exactly, is an eschatologist, Dr. Marchek?"

"One whose work is in the field of eschatology," Marchek said.

Jorgenson was silent for a moment, a blank expression on his face, the expression changing then to resignation. "See what I mean?" he said while the studio audience laughed. "I finally get one who shows some respect and you win him over to your side."

The old man was finally able to speak above the laughter.

"The field of eschatology deals with the study of the ultimate destiny and purpose of man. The branch of theological eschatology, to which I have devoted myself for the past 38 years, is the apocalyptic prophecies. It is the road map that God has provided through His Word, the Holy Bible. The road map points to events leading to the end-of-the-world system as we now know it."

There were snickers and scattered hoots throughout the studio.

"You mean the end is coming... and you can tell us when?" Jorgenson questioned smugly.

"I can definitely answer 'yes' to your first question with some qualification, Mr. Jorgenson. The end of this present Earth Age is definitely coming, but it is not the end of the world. And in answer to your second question, I must tell you 'No.' I cannot tell you when. But I know who does know the precise time it will happen."

"Who's that?"

"God, of course."

"Oh? Whose god? Yours? The Muslims'? The Hindus'? Mine?" The host's facetious prodding delighted the audience, which broke into applause.

"There is but one God, Mr. Jorgenson. The Lord God Jehovah."

"So, if your God is the only God there is, why won't He tell you when doomsday will come? I mean, I can understand why He won't let me, a devout libertine, in on it. But you obviously don't have those sins pulling you down; you're in good with the big man upstairs. Why won't He tell you? I mean, for gosh sakes, you're the one who's trying so hard to understand. Right?"

"To answer your question," Marchek spoke slowly, deliberately. "I will not use my words alone, but the words of the One who has all the answers. From His Holy Word..." Scattered shouts from the studio audience cut the air sarcastically.

"No!... No!... No sermons, preacher! Preacher go home!"

Jorgenson raised his hands for silence, a smile of patient understanding on his face, his eyelids heavy with tolerance. "Now, children, we invited the good professor to play. So we've got to let him have his say. Am I right, Lauren?" Jorgenson looked past the old man to appeal to the young woman, who smiled, then gesticulated with a whatever-you-say gesture.

"Sorry, Dr. Marchek. They're bad kids, sometimes," the host apologized. "Go ahead and tell us what the man upstairs has to say."

Marchek patiently mustered his thoughts, unfazed by his tormentors, then spoke. "A moment ago, I said only God knows the answer to when the present dispensation, that is, the church age, will come to a close, and the tribulation of the earth will begin in preparation for the coming millennial kingdom."

"Forgive me for interrupting, Doctor, but you'll have to fill us in. At least fill me in, on what you mean by the church age."

"The church age, Mr. Jorgenson, is the period of history from the time following Jesus Christ's resurrection, when the Holy Spirit descended upon believers at Pentecost, as told us in the book of Acts, to the time He returns in the air for all born-again believers. When that happens, the present dispensation, or 'church age,' will come to its conclusion."

"And that's the end of the world?" Jorgenson said amidst groans from the audience.

"Oh, no. As I said. We believe the world in its present form, that is, its physical composition, will not be destroyed for at least seven years after this event occurs. And then, not totally destroyed for a thousand years."

"Seven years? Why seven years? What will happen during those seven years?"

"In order to answer your questions, I would prefer to start with events taking place now, even at this moment in history. Can you spare a few minutes? I shall try to be brief."

"I might have to call time-out for a commercial, but go ahead; I'll stop you when we need to break."

"The best way to begin is with the words of the Lord Jesus Christ himself, spoken to His disciples one day on the Mount of Olives just outside the city of Jerusalem." Marchek held up a black covered book. It was a Bible--the same Bible Jacob had taken from the study of the old man's Rockville home. Jacob picked it up from the coffee table and examined it while Marchek held it during the videotape run through the recorder.

"You are aware you can't read from Scriptures on the air, aren't you, Dr. Marchek?" Lauren Winchester prompted from Marchek's right.

"Oh, yes, Ms. Winchester. I am up on the latest Supreme Court rulings concerning public readings of written Scripture belonging to any religion that does not recognize that all religions and faiths are one under God. Did I paraphrase the ruling fairly accurately?" The eschatologist looked to Lauren Winchester, who sat sullenly.

"I will not read from my Bible. I simply like to have it along when I can, like an old friend. The ruling of our wise justices on the nation's highest court has not been interpreted to prohibit the quotation of Scripture from memory, however. So I will quote from this book."

He offered the Bible to the woman, who refused to take it. "You may follow along, to make certain I am quoting accurately, if you like. Or you, Mr. Jorgenson." He offered the book to the host.

"I'll take your quotations as accurate," Jorgenson said good-naturedly.

"The Lord Jesus Christ is on the Mount of Olives at Jerusalem — I shall quote from Matthew the 24th chapter, beginning with verse 3."

Hugo Marchek quoted swiftly and selectively from portions of the Scriptures, giving Christ's many prophetic predictions for a future time full of human misery, ending with the words,"...Heaven and earth shall pass away, but my words shall not pass away."

Interrupting his quotation of Scripture, Hugo Marchek raised his index finger, looked to the host, then into the camera's eye. "And listen very carefully to this.

"But of that day and hour knoweth no man, no, not the angels of heaven, but my Father only. But as the days of Noah were, so shall also the coming of the Son of man be. For as in the days that were before the flood they were eating and drinking, marrying and giving in marriage, until the day that Noah entered into the ark, And knew not until the flood came, and took them all away; so shall also the coming of the Son of man be."

Marchek pulled the thick-lensed glasses from his nose. The silence lingered in the studio, but was broken, finally, by the host.

"A very impressive piece of memory work, Doctor, I really must say."

"But, Mr. Jorgenson, let us forget my ability to retain biblical prose. The thing that matters, the only thing that matters, is the truth contained within the text I just quoted. Therein lies the answer to most aspects of the question you posed a few moments ago."

"That's what you say, anyway, Doctor," interrupted Jorgenson, with sincerity in his voice. "Jesus was obviously a great prophet. At least, most all religions of the world will admit that. But I'm not personally sure He had authority from the perspective of a deity, in making His predictions. Besides, all of His teachings, like those of other prophets, were given in such metaphorical illustrations and symbolisms and such nebulous terms. I mean, why should this one man, this solitary human being, have the one answer to all of man's future history?" Jorgenson's rhetoric became bolder with the urgings of his audience, which applauded.

Marchek listened, then smiled and spoke in a strong, yet gentle voice. "Yes. You are right. Jesus is considered a great prophet by major religions of the world. And, no doubt, by you, too."

"Well, a great man who influenced millions of people for good, at least. I'm not sure I'm committed to a belief in prophecies and religious, supernatural phenomena," the host said.

"But you do concede that Jesus of Nazareth was a great religious Man with moral principles and philosophies, and that He was a teacher who encouraged the doing of good? A man who told truths as He saw them?"

"Sure. Of course. I'll concede that."

"But how could He be such a person? How could this Jesus be the honest, good teacher of principles you describe? How could He be the great prophet for the great whomever?" Marchek smiled again, a trace of humor in his tone.

"I'm afraid I don't follow you, Doctor."

"Jesus said that He is the Son of God. That He is the one sent to die for the sins of mankind. Therefore, He is who He says He is, that is, the Son of God--or He was the greatest liar who ever lived. How could such a liar be a great prophet of good and truth as the religion of Islam says, or the great teacher of moral principles you say He is?"

The talk show host was silenced for the moment by the logic in Marchek's words.

"But I believe we're all sons of God," Jorgenson said, finally.

"But Jesus did not say He is *a* son of God. He claimed to be the *only* begotten Son of God!"

"Then I guess I must rethink my belief about Jesus was... what He was," said Jorgenson, mild irritation infiltrating his tone.

"And that, Mr. Show Host, is the great question of all time. What will you do with this Jesus? What is your belief about who He is? On the answer to that question rests the fate of the soul of each and every individual who has lived since the church age began, since Jesus Christ died and arose from the grave two millennia ago.

"You see, Mr. Jorgenson, this is the question which you, which I, which every human being, must answer for himself or herself. 'What shall I do with Jesus?' How we answer that question determines where our immortal souls will spend eternity."

There were scattered jeers from the audience; it quieted when Jorgenson spoke.

"In your belief, this is what's called being 'born again' or 'saved,' isn't it?"

"Yes."

"Well, how can I, for example, be born again?"

"Believe in the Lord Jesus Christ and you shall be saved," Marchek said. "This is God's prescription, His only prescription, for redemption."

Jacob lit a cigarette when Jorgenson interrupted Marchek for the commercial break, thinking of the ludicrous contrast between the two priorities — the eternal destiny of the soul and the all-important commercial, which Marchek had not edited out of the videotape.

The screen blared a message about birth control and how it could now be a pleasure for both partners through the use of STW 66 Serum, and how Unitrex International Industries guaranteed the preventative for a full two years. "Now, enjoy the greatest pleasure of life, without the worries of creating problems, no matter where you are, or what the tune of day or night. Safe, quick, and guaranteed effective for two years!" said the announcer enthusiastically while the video displayed a woman and man locked together sexually within a thatch of yellow-green grass, with quick cuts from different camera angles showing explicit close-ups of their naked bodies.

"My favorite commercial," Rance Jorgenson said when the commercial ended, his quip eliciting laughter from his audience. The host reached to place his hand on Marchek's arm. "You'll just have to forgive me for that, Doctor."

"It is not I who forgives such things, Mr. Jorgenson."

"Oh... That's right. Only God can forgive sins."

"See. You have learned something tonight," Marchek said, smiling.

"You don't approve of such commercials, I'll wager."

"Whether I approve or disapprove makes no difference. What matters is that it is but one more indication of the fulfillment of prophecy for the end-times. We have witnessed great degeneration of morals in this nation. From the Flapper era, which, I believe, the United States partially paid for with the Great Depression of the 1930's, through the post-World War II era of so-called national self-fulfillment, with its increased promiscuity and unparalleled level of entertainment at the expense of godly principles. I believe we are still paying for it today with unprecedented, untreatable venereal and other diseases which always end in death. We are still paying with worldwide economic chaos, and, by these scientifically unexplainable natural — or should I call them 'supernatural' — catastrophes. We have brought about the fulfillment of those prophecies ourselves. There's no one else we can blame."

The studio crowd voiced its disagreement with the old man's assessment through whistles and jeers.

"Excuse me, Rance, but I just can't sit back any longer," Lauren Winchester said from her seat on the sofa to Marchek's right. "Dr. Marchek, for someone who says it isn't his place to forgive or to judge, you're doing a pretty thorough job of playing God here."

The audience erupted in applause and cheering.

"I, for one, want to go on record as saying that what I have listened to for the last 15 minutes is a crock."

Again those sitting in the studio went wild in agreement with the pretty actress' scathing words. "And, quite frankly, sir, I really don't care whether you or your kind forgive me or not."

The host looked at the woman, at Marchek, then to the studio audience, a feigned look of loss of control on his face. He grinned, then. "Geez, Doctor. You know what they say... I think you've stirred the proverbial wrath of the woman's scorn."

"And I have not yet even addressed the homosexual issue, Mr. Jorgenson," Marchek said with good-humor in his voice.

Jacob Zen, pulling easily on the cigarette, squinted to focus better on the old man's face. There was genuine calm there, an eloquent serenity that exuded confidence. The audience had turned hostile, stirred by Lauren Winchester's searing attack. Marchek was undeterred.

"What about the homosexual issue, Doctor?" The woman pressed boldly. "What words of divine wisdom do you have for us in that area?"

"In the Book of Genesis, the 19th chapter, the Bible tells us of the previous sin of homosexuality, which, among other sins, brought on the destruction of the ancient cities of Sodom and Gomorrah. Cities which not too many years ago, as you know, were claimed by archaeologists and others to be figments of the biblical fundamentalists' imagination. But, the remnants of these places have been found in areas near the Dead Sea. And, I might add, according to secular scientists, that area seems to have been subjected to nuclear-type devastation.

"The Bible record shows that the Lord God, true to His promises, caused complete destruction of the area. Genesis 19, verses 24 and 25, tells us, 'Then the Lord rained upon Sodom and upon Gomorrah brimstone and fire from the Lord out of heaven; And he overthrew those cities, and all the plain, and all the inhabitants of the cities, and that which grew upon the ground.'

"And the same conditions have recurred throughout man's history, my friends," Marchek said, turning first to Jorgenson, then to Lauren Winchester. "It happened in Noah's time; it happened in Lot's time. There was a significant infestation of homosexuality, to the point that finally, homosexual rather than the heterosexual relationships were considered the norm.

"Coming down in history, it happened to Pompeii to the greatest culture perhaps of all time, ancient Greece, and to Rome. And, it has been happening to the United States for many years now. The results of that repeated offense against God Almighty has always been the destruction of the affected, or perhaps I should say, the infected society."

Lauren Winchester stiffened, her face reddened with anger. "That's hate speech! There are laws against that sort of hate-mongering, Doctor."

Hugo Marchek's gray eyes narrowed, his face taking on a grave expression. "But it is this generation, Ms. Winchester, who is speaking hate against the Creator of all things by engaging in such terrible activities. His judgment is inevitable when there is no repentance."

"You religious paranoiacs always relate your doomsday

predictions to periods of supposed history for which there are few, if any, records," Lauren Winchester said angrily. "And as for Rome and Greece, they fell under the weight of their own bureaucracies and colonial over-reaches — not as a result of homosexuality. To attribute the fall of those societies to homosexuality is crazy!"

"And yet, Ms. Winchester, what was the most prevalent sexual activity of the times, according to our secular historians?"

"Of course, the Roman orgy is what we hear about most, but that, too, is overblown."

"Is it?" The old man said quizzically. "And the most noted type of sexual activity, again, according to secular historical records, pertaining to those orgies? Was it not homosexuality?"

The woman made no verbal response, but turned her face from Marchek, shaking her head and grimacing.

"But you say homosexuality was not the cause, either directly or indirectly, of the fall of the Greek and Roman Empires?"

"That's right, Doctor. That's exactly what I'm saying. Those civilizations collapsed from many governmental and societal strains, over an extended period of time."

"I agree with you, Ms. Winchester. They did collapse as you have described. But I maintain they were judged and fell, primarily, from the state of decadence that was reached in the latter years of their existence as empires. And the most marked societal and cultural distinction of those times was the tremendous proliferation of hedonistic activity, in general — and of homosexuality, in particular."

"The moral conditions of those times had little or nothing to do with the fall of those civilizations. The collapse was due to an erosion of economic and military stability. And if you are trying to get me to admit that the United States is following in their footsteps, as you super-informed clergy of the radical right always claim, I can tell you I agree completely.

"This nation is in a state of collapse at present. But not because of moral conditions, or sin. It is because of government mismanagement and consumer and governmental deficit spending. And I believe we will be able to do something about those problems long before the final stages of collapse are reached. We are capable of controlling our own destinies. And I believe we will."

Loud applause almost drowned the woman's last predictive words.

"That, Ms. Winchester," the old man said when the applause subsided, "is exactly the same ploy Satan has been using since the creation of man."

His words brought angry jeers from the studio audience.

"The devil, Lucifer, told the woman, Eve, the same thing. That man could control his own destiny. That God did not want her and Adam to eat from the fruit of the tree of the knowledge of good and evil, because if they did so they would become as wise as God, himself — and God would not like that.

"The philosophy, the theology, really, of humanism is telling our generation the same thing, my friends. And Satan, the superdeceiver, the author of humanism, is telling us that we do not need God or His wisdom, or His moral influence and restrictiveness. That we are self-sufficient. This is the same thing Satan told the Babylonians and the Greeks, and they fell because they took a bite, figuratively speaking, from the fruit of the tree of the knowledge of good and evil, when they told God they did not need Him. We are doing the same thing today in America, and throughout the world. The result will be the same for this generation as it was for those of the past.

"There are not many things we can depend upon in this world. But upon this one thing you can depend, my friends. God will remain true to His promise of mercy for those who repent, and true to His promise of judgment for those who do not."

From the sofa in front of the television set, Jacob and Melissa Jantzen sat in silence, as did Rance Jorgenson and his audience in the studio.

Finally, the host broke the disturbing quiet. "Ooo...kay, Dr. Marchek, I appreciate your being here, I guess." Jorgenson said lightly, looking uneasily into the camera, then to his subdued audience. "I can't say I agree, but I respect your right to say it."

"That, too, will soon come to an end," the eschatologist interrupted.

"What will come to an end?"

"The right for a person, like me, to say the truths I have just expressed to you."

"Oh?... How so?"

"There is coming, Mr. Jorgenson... Ms. Winchester, the world's last great dictator. A man who will completely subject the world. He will be the son of the devil himself. The time of the great Antichrist is near. A time, as the Lord Jesus said, such as the world has not known since the beginning of time, and shall never know again. The time of the great tribulation. Then, all peoples will express, in their actions and words, only what this demon-possessed leader and his devilish one-world system allows. He will be, my friends, the final fuhrer, the beast of Revelation 13, who will make Adolf Hitler seem like a Boy Scout leader by comparison."

"And you think this..." Rance Jorgenson paused, searching for the right words, "...gentleman, is near at hand?"

"I do indeed, sir."

"If this final great leader is near at hand, Rance, she will be a woman," Lauren Winchester said solemn-faced, bringing laughter and applause. "Most likely, a lesbian, who is also a mother," she added, to the delight of the audience in the studio.

"But I assure you, Ms. Winchester... Mr. Jorgenson, the matter will not be one of merriment for long. The time will come, and I believe in the very near future, when this leader will arise out of the revived Roman Empire — out of the European Economic Community of nations, as prophesied in Daniel, the 12th chapter. He is, I am convinced, even now awaiting his time in man's history. And he will give those who do not leave this planet little to laugh about when he comes into his full power."

"Leave the planet?! You mean some of us will leave?" The actress questioned in an incredulous tone.

"Yes. The rapture to which I referred earlier. God will take His people — those who are saved through faith in Jesus Christ — will remove them from this planet, to meet with Jesus in the air. Just as God took Noah to safety on the ark before the flood, just as He took Lot from Sodom before He destroyed that city, they will vanish in the blink of an eye. And I believe when that happens, that is, when God's people — righteous in His eyes because of their acceptance of His Son, Jesus Christ — are raptured from this earth, God will also remove for a time His restraining influence on mankind, the Holy Spirit."

"Oh! Here we go with ghosts and spirits and the like," Lauren Winchester interrupted. "I thought you fundamentalists didn't believe in the occult!"

"The only supernatural ghost I do believe in, Ms. Winchester, is the Holy Ghost. And when God's Spirit, the third member of the Trinity, the Godhead, is removed for a time from this planet, then you shall see the greatest period of hellishness ever in man's history. The great tribulation. The last seven years of earth's existence, as we now know it."

"This... Antichrist... Will he be known, or come to power before this rapture thing? Or after?" the host said.

"I believe he has a certain amount of power already within the European Parliament, or one of its consultative bodies. But he shall receive his full satanic powers to control all the world, after the restraining godly influence of the Holy Spirit is removed. The Antichrist and the unholy satanic spirit will move in to fill the vacuum left."

The audience grumbled its disapproval, and Rance Jorgenson held both hands up asking for silence.

"Just vanish into thin air, huh?" Jorgenson said whimsically, lowering his forehead into his hands and shaking his head in disbelieving amusement. "Well, Dr. Marchek, we did invite you here tonight, albeit to discuss Preservers of American Liberty — P.A.L. — Boy! How did we get off on this weird track? Well, I thank you at least for the entertainment value of your visit." Jorgenson rose and extended his right hand to Marchek as he spoke while the studio audience shattered the air with verbal displays of their agreement with the host's facetious remarks.

"I would invite you to stay, Doctor, but I'm afraid you'd find it hard to love Ms. Luv, even though I know your kind loves everybody."

Hugo Marchek smiled, looking into the host's eyes, causing Jorgenson to break his fun-poking grin and look sheepishly away.

"Thank you for allowing me to be with you here tonight, Mr. Jorgenson. I sincerely wish you could be with us in the air, when our Savior comes for us."

When Marchek had broken the handshake with the host and had shaken hands with Lauren Winchester, he smiled and waved to the audience and departed in a slow shuffle, amidst hoots and shouts mixed with whistles of disdain.

"Another cup?"

"What?... Yes, thanks." Jacob held his cup for Melissa to pour the tea. He watched Marchek slowly walk the distance from Rance Jorgenson and Lauren Winchester to the huge draperies that filled the television screen.

He empathized with the old man. Yet, the same look of self-assuredness, he saw in the eschatologist's eyes when the two of them had talked together, was there as strongly as that night they met. Despite his age, which caused Marchek to move slowly, there was the distinct look of one who knew he had done the job he came to do the night the show was taped.

Jacob did not really hear nor see the naked woman who led the animal onto the stage to rhythmic strains of music.

He couldn't shake the thought that raked his mind. Everything was happening the way Hugo Marchek said it would. His friend who left him the message of hope in the computer — "the time of Jacob's trouble; but he shall be saved out of it"--left him his Bible.

Stronger than ever was his need to understand more about what, exactly, all of it meant. Stronger, too, his intention to try and stop his own slide into oblivion.

CHAPTER 14

"I can't see where this thing will cripple our ability to think and plan our way out. A very significant factor to think about, I believe, is that the Russians are out of the way now. So there are great and good things that can come out of all this chaos -- that have already come out of it, for that matter."

Henry Laxton's normally solemn demeanor was upbeat, and he looked and sounded like a caricature of himself while he spoke to Lawrence Thorton in the Washington studio.

"Like practically eliminating the nuclear threat, for example?" Thorton said.

"That's right. It's probably the greatest thing to happen, in diplomatic terms, in history. Everybody's been looking for, praying for, a way to get all sides to the negotiating tables on that one most crucial issue. We have been trying for decades to find a common ground where we can put away self-interests, and, together, find our way out of the nuclear nightmare."

"This phenomenon has, if nothing else, drawn into focus

exactly how closely knit the family of man is, and how essential it is that a joint effort be made."

"And you know, Larry, one of the most amazing aspects of the phenomenon is the fact that many, many of those who opposed our New Age marvels, and opposed those visionary technologies that offer so much hope, were taken in the cosmic disturbance. I don't mean to sound cruel or like an occultist or religionist, but by fate, or whatever, the road that can lead us to a peaceful, productive future has been cleared of much of its congestion."

"Thank you, Mr. Secretary," the journalist said, turning to face the camera. "And that, we are told, is basically what the telecast from Brussels is to be about. That broadcast coming up in..." He looked to a clock on one wall of the studio then back into the camera's lens, "...about five minutes from now."

Out of habit, Jacob started to glance at his left wrist, but remembering the missing watch, looked at Melissa Jantzen's table clock. 7:01. Six minutes faster than Thorton's clock; the broadcast was scheduled for 7:00.

Fingering the Naxos videotape he had not yet viewed, his mind zagged between wanting to have a look at it and wondering what would be forthcoming from Brussels. He got up from the sofa and walked into the bedroom.

"Melissa..." He shook the girl gently and spoke quietly. "It's time."

She lurched upward at his touch, her face open-mouthed with fright.

"It's okay... It's okay," he said. Her expression softened and she relaxed. "You wanted me to wake you at seven."

"I must've been dreaming something awful. I can't remember what," she said sleepily, pressing against his chest and wrapping her arms around him while he sat on the bed beside her. He wanted to cradle her, to reassure her. Nothing lustful in his motive, just a momentary feeling. But when she pulled his face downward, forcing his lips to hers, he felt the embrace meant more to her.

"They won't hold up the broadcast for us, I'm sorry to say." He broke their kiss, but bent to again brush her lips lightly with his, saying with his eyes he did not disapprove of the invitation, only its timing.

From the living room, the voice of Lawrence Thorton announced that the U.S. networks were joining Euronetwork in a live broadcast from Brussels. Melissa followed Jacob to the sofa, from which they watched hundreds of men and women mill about in the huge Parliament chamber of the U.E.S. headquarters building.

At first, the camera swept the delegates, then drew back to frame the entire chamber. Far away, a colorfully attired figure walked slowly toward the lectern on the vast podium. The camera zoomed in on the figure until only he filled the television screen in Melissa Jantzen's apartment.

A man in religious robes of white, red, gold and purple, with medallions, shaped-like crosses and unfamiliar symbols, suspended against his breast by gold chains. A tall, gleaming headdress sat atop his head, while he moved to the ornate lectern and held aloft a scepter, which glinted in the beams of brilliant light radiating from the ceiling.

As if the raising of the scepter was a signal, the people stood and applauded, while the television cameras captured their ecstatic expressions from many angles. The religious man's face and diadem filled the screen in a ghost image over the mass of people. Still cameras flashed and strobe-like lights illuminated the ecclesiastical figure and the men and women of the audience while the applause increased, along with shouts of approving exultation.

"Is that the Pope?" Melisa said, not taking her eyes from the scene.

"Him, too?" Jacob said, concluding with disappointment that

even this man, probably the best loved pontiff in history, had been taken in by the Naxos lot. Maybe not. Perhaps His Holiness would now make the announcement that the plot had been uncovered — that the murderous, would-be rulers, of what was left of the world, had been forced out of their Naxos burrow, and the rest of humanity could now safely come out into light again. This earthy, humble, though brilliant man, whom he had personally met at the Vatican, who had made him feel genuinely loved, could not be a part of the monster. Not unless the pontiff thought the monster to be something other than what it was.

Still, the religious man stood receiving the accolades, the scepter held aloft in his right hand, holding the other hand above his head in a symbolic gesture of humble acceptance and gratitude.

"His Holiness looks to be enjoying his first public appearance since succeeding his predecessor," Lawrence Thorton said from the D.C. studio while the applause continued.

Of course! Jacob thought. So much attention had been given to the calamities caused by the disappearance phenomenon there was no time for hoopla about the changes at the Vatican! This was not the same Pope, the man he knew.

"There is gathered in that great hall probably the largest, most diverse cross-section of the world's nationalities ever assembled anywhere at any time. Even the United Nations has never seen anything like it. From just about every known country, representatives have come, at the request of this new Pope. Every religion, including Christian, Buddhist, Muslim, Hindu, and the many sects and denominations within those great religions, as well as many reclusive, little known cults, have come at the request of His Holiness."

Thorton was silent for 20 seconds, letting the video and the noise of the adoring throng within the great hall of the

U.E.S. put across to the viewer the exultation of this historic moment. Finally the crowd began to quiet.

"We don't know what language His Holiness will use, or whether he will speak more than one language; he is a master of many. Whichever he chooses, those in attendance at Brussels, and we here, will have the benefit of instantaneous translation, thanks to the recent breakthroughs in computer-language vocoder technology, which can almost exactly duplicate the speaker's own voice tone after translating the meanings of his words."

"Greetings!" the holy man said in mildly accented English, smiling when the mass of people before him responded with a tumultuous, synchronized shout. "It is past time that we come together as one!" Again, a single shout of response. "Now... Let us begin anew!" The people were on their feet before the pontiff could finish his sentence. A sustained, frenzied show of acceptance. The screen in Melissa's apartment was imaging the Brussels' camerawork that combined a series of quick-cuts, dissolves and super-over impositions, which captured the spirit of oneness raging within the chamber. The man drew his hands into a palms-together position, holding the scepter erect between them, and bowed toward the representatives while maintaining the prayerful pose. The exuberance was infectious, drawing one into its excitement. The talk of oneness; of the brotherhood of man; of beginning anew. All deceptions of the most insidious kind, promising a bright future — all problems solved — perfection.

Maybe this religious man really did believe, but Jacob knew the price for the proffered paradise. He had experienced the utopian bill collectors. The memory of their painful tactics made it easy to churn his own hatred back to the surface while the eager, accepting faces beamed glowingly toward the pontiff, who now stood with his hands clasped before his bowed face.

Jacob watched the faces, those bright faces, effulgent in the television lights while the cameras panned up and down the aisles. They differed in expressions from all the faces he had seen since that night the secret service agent's face vanished from the car's rearview mirror. Absent was the fear, the apprehensions. As if they knew something other faces of the world did not know. And somehow, in an instant of fleeting foreknowledge, Jacob, too, knew what those faces at Brussels held secreted away behind their glowing, jubilant facades. This religious man who stood before them had the map that would, they thought, lead them out of the greatest world crisis ever. He was about to introduce them to the system, the person, who had the answers.

"How could the Pope be mixed up in government that would be cruel to people? They wouldn't have selected a man who wasn't concerned about people, about human rights. He couldn't be a part of a dictatorship, could he?"

"Not if he knew the things I know. Not, and be the kind of man everybody thinks he is."

Jacob's confusion was no less than Melissa's. Popes were regarded as the world's great champions of social justice, constantly putting forward the principle that man is responsible for taking care of man, and that the individual's rights must not suffer at the hands of any collective will. That society must serve the individual, not the other way around. Yet this man had apparently thrown his lot in with those who spit on that principle.

"Maybe he's decided the Naxos idea is the lesser of evils. That what they're offering is better than the chaos we have now," Jacob said, thinking that the real answer was that this Pope had been fooled by the promise that once things were under control a more humane rule could be instituted. One that served rather than oppressed. His Holiness had not experienced the real character of the Naxos assassins.

It ran through his mind that Melissa might be questioning his own truthfulness. "Are they after him because he is the one actually at fault? Is he the real liar in all this?" He imagined her asking herself. It was easy enough to understand how she could be entertaining such suspicions from the glorious appeal gushing from the Brussels meeting.

He looked at her profile in the brightness projecting from the screen. No. There was no easy acceptance of what was going on in the U.E.S. Council Chamber. Unlike the faces at Brussels, there was still apprehension on hers. With him, she was in the presence of flesh and blood. One whom she could touch, receive comfort from. Despite the broadcast's appeal, it was an unembraceable appeal that could not solve her hurts.

"We have come to a most crucial time in man's history," the holy man said when the noise quieted. "A most terrible time. And yet, a most opportune time. For we hold in our hands the ability to destruct our world in a moment of nuclear insanity, or to destroy it through years of slow deterioration. At the same time, we have the capability to build heaven on earth. Does it not make better sense, human, common sense, to choose the course of life, rather than make the choice of extinction for the human race?"

Again, the great hall at Brussels erupted in deafening applause and shouts of agreement, while the video presented the faces of the hundreds of world representatives.

"There is, I am convinced with all my heart, one sent from God to lead us upon that sensible path that will take us into the prophesied millennium. And, this servant, I am equally convinced, has been given 'The Plan' drawn directly by God's hand. A plan as divinely appointed as the Ten Commandments and all the great truths God has given mankind throughout the ages. Give your ears and your hearts to this, God's servant."

The Pope put his palms together and addressed his deity, face raised toward the ceiling.

"Oh great Father, the Light of the universe. Grant your Son the power to lead in this hour of trouble. Grant, too, the understanding of us all and give us the will to accept what thou hast for us through Thy divine hand upon this your chosen one, whom you have borne into this world to lead the way into Thy eternal kingdom. In the name of the Father, the Son, and the Holy Spirit. Amen."

The prayer concluded, the pontiff waited for the audience to settle, his robed arms stretched forward, his white hands gripping the edges of the lectern's top.

"My friends, my children... God's man for this critical hour!"

Spotlights near the stage swung their beams from the pontiff and crisscrossed, their large circles of light congruently fixing on a human figure approaching the lectern from the darkened area behind the platform. A striking masculine form in a dark suit, whose quick, graceful stride was of youth. He smoothed the suit coat near the hips while he walked, reaching then to take the hand of the Pope, who met him enthusiastically.

There seemed an unnatural stillness in the chamber while the men held hands briefly in the circle of light, then broke their grasp. The holy man issued the other toward the lectern with a gesture of his right hand. The camera zoomed in for a close-up, and, as Jacob expected, the young man was Herrlich Krimhler, a somber expression on his handsome face.

The Pope was smiling broadly and saying something to Krimhler the microphones could not pick up. The audience responded at first with a few scattered handclaps, then, more sure of what their response should be, released their feelings in a frenzy of cheering and applause.

Krimhler stood behind the lectern, acknowledging with generous, though controlled, smiles and slight nods of his head to his right, his left, and to those directly in front of the lectern. He began in the familiar, slightly accented baritone that charismatically commanded the attention of all whose ears the famous voice fell upon.

"We have indeed reached, as His Holiness said, 'a terrible moment in man's history.' Yet it is a moment of magnificent opportunity--a time which, I assure, will never again be ours. For in the words once spoken by a great leader, 'Man holds in his mortal hands the power to abolish all forms of human poverty, and all forms of human life.' And, as John Kennedy also said, 'Asking His blessings, and His help, but knowing that here on earth, God's work must truly be our own.'

"That is the message I bring to you, my friends of the global community. This is the hope that rests within our own God-given capabilities. To be... To really be... or not to be." Krimhler held an index finger aloft and paused, looking about the vast chamber at the many faces held in the grip of his words. "Ahhh...That is truly the question of our precarious time, my brothers and sisters of the world-family. What shall it be? The joining of hands and hearts and minds to eradicate poverty, disease, crime, hunger, natural catastrophes, and war? Or will we begin again to take the same path mankind has taken for so long? That of self-serving nationalism? Thus, all of the scourges that such a course brings with it, ending in nuclear holocaust. And, as His Holiness said, 'extinction as a species' — the end of the greatest drama God has allowed mankind to act out. Only we can write the next chapter. Only we can begin writing the most glorious chapter of all!"

No wavering on the part of this man who would be

savior, who inspired certainty that he could deliver what the Pope promised--leadership out of the calamitous mess in which the world found itself. That inspiration showed in reflected belief from the faces at Brussels. Krimhler was in the process of activating the germ of noble aspiration, which all people who were sane harbored dormant in their core beings. The German was able, Jacob knew now, to cause those coming under his influence to ignite others in a chain reaction that would ultimately link all together in the promised global familyhood. But, it would be a linkage in the form of manacles, because in order for that global design to succeed, stumbling blocks had to be removed--of which Jacob Zen was one.

"My fellow passengers on spaceship earth, is it not time we put aside the prejudices and biases separating the family of man one from the other... a separation which would soon bring us to that Armageddon so long predicted by the myopic doomsdayers? Instead, should we not concentrate on the things common to all? The good, productive things... The human things which are the inherent right of every citizen of our world community to enjoy?

"Make no mistake, if we do not take action beginning here, beginning now--and there is no one else to take action for us--we will be forever lost. The ultimatum is this: Build a great and glorious world in which there are none of the plagues humanity has endured since the moment man stood erect and began recording human events... or else disintegrate in the future fireballs of our own creative folly, and be consumed in the blackness of nuclear winter. There is no turning back. The Great Universal Mind, who issues the ultimatum, has also provided the technology and intellectual capability through which man can solve his potentially fatal dilemmas.

"Do not worry for now about what has happened... about

why millions have vanished. Be assured that the great giver of all knowledge will put into each and every mind, individually, the acceptance of what has happened, as each becomes individually able to comprehend. I will say, for now, only that for some who are gone from our midst, it is a great evolutionary reward, while for others it is, sadly, punishment for false teaching of things about the Father of all. Most crucially, we must understand that although this phenomenon seems a tragedy, it is in fact God's gift to His creation, offering a new beginning, a purified pathway to a higher evolutionary order."

The German's piercing eyes, like when Jacob viewed the Naxos tapes, caused the feeling they were x-raying one's brain. That those black, intelligent orbs were invading, unveiling the soul. Krimhler stood with almost arrogant posture, surveying the silent, intensely attentive representatives, then turned his eyes again to the camera encased within its mobile, mechanized scaffolding just above the center aisle.

"I must tell you also, although the end result of the course the Great Universal Mind has prescribed will be glorious beyond imagination... that course will require many sacrifices from everyone. Those who refuse to live within lawful boundaries must be dealt with and shall be treated as not worthy of our love, of God's love. Let us begin by understanding this precept, yet... with the prayer in our hearts that there will be none among us who will be so unloving and so foolish as to test our resolve as we begin our march into the glorious New Age of, ultimately... perfection."

A gigantic reflective screen descended from the ceiling at mid-stage while Krimhler spoke. Its expanse covered the blackness that previously had framed the German and the lectern. Projected light streamed from above and behind the audience, lighting the screen with a graphic presentation which highlighted what Krimhler was saying.

The Plan

"The blueprint for perfecting mankind in a less sudden and less dramatic way than the great leap into perfection in which our now ascended brothers and sisters participated... 'The Plan' to make God's creation what he intended... I now give the world... Interface!"

The screen above and behind the young German reflected the word: "Interface."

"INterface... the joining together of human to human... linking, through our self-created miracles, each to the other... Oneness!"

The screen above the platform was alive with brilliant visual effects. Krimhler's eyes seemed ablaze while the lights and colors burst, disturbing the general darkness of the chamber.

INterphase

"And INterphase, the period of learning to live together as true children of God's Universal Family. The final evolutional period that will lead each to the godhood locked within the inner-self. INterphase... to consist of the Six Ways.

1. Terrorism and crime will dissolve into exemplary citizenship through joint effort and innovative discipline.

2. Poverty and economic chaos will be eliminated by working together to share abundance equally through computer disbursal ingenuity.

3. Hunger, like poverty, will be forever done away with through distribution of the wealth left by those who were taken in the great dissolution and evolutionary leap, plus,

through sharing of the plenty. No more will there be Third-World nations.

4. Ecological disaster caused by floods, earthquakes, wind and fire, can and shall ultimately be overcome through human determination and divine help within our technologies.

5. Disease will be eradicated through intensive, concerted efforts of the world medical community.

6. Peace shall replace war as man learns to give rather than only to take.

This is the Six Ways design I give to you, my fellow citizens of the world."

With the six points outlined in huge letters upon the screen, Herrlich Krimhler gestured with a motion of his right hand toward the projected image, then turned to again grip the lectern and address his global audience.

"Every nation, every people is represented in this chamber. I appeal to each representative, on behalf of your people. Join in this effort... I implore you in the name of God. Endorse and embrace this gift of love, this gift of life and a future free from the threat of nuclear annihilation and all other of the horrible scourges outlined. It is mankind's last chance. Your only chance, my friends... My brothers and sisters." The graphic changed while Krimhler paused; he spoke again, his tone now grave, yet inspirational while his appeal rose to authoritative finality.

"Join with me. Together let us create the world God meant for you to have.

Six Ways to Law!

Six Ways to Order!

Six Ways to Peace!

6! 6! 6!"

Jacob felt what he knew those at Brussels must be feeling, what everyone who heard the dynamic young German's words must be feeling at this moment. A coursing of excitement, causing eruptions of goose bumps. He, like they, wanted to believe, to accept what Krimhler was saying. So desperate was the plight of every human being who prayed for something to give them hope. But even now, with the goodwill gushing from the many representatives in the Brussels chamber, he knew better. Knew at the most primitive gut level that the price Krimhler was asking for Utopia was too great ~ more than anyone should have to pay. Herrlich Krimhler walked toward the blackness, the screen having ascended into the ceiling, and paused to shake the hand of the Pope before departing the platform. A noise, indecipherable at first but becoming clearer, the volume increasing. A chant by the representatives, who were on their feet now and clapping hands while they gave the incantation in English.

"Six Ways to Law!! Six Ways to Order!! Six Ways to Peace!! Six!! Six!! Six!!"

The audio and video from the television set in front of Jacob and Melissa was that emanating from Brussels. The image remained for several seconds, before Lawrence Thorton again took control in the Washington D. C. studio, his image superimposed through chromakey over the scene at Brussels.

"A most stirring and profound message," the newsman said, turning from watching a monitor to face the camera. "It would seem that the billions of people, represented by these national and religious leaders in attendance at U.E.S. Headquarters, will not have to pressure their leaderships into going along with this magnificent plan put forward by Herr Krimhler. I have never in my years of journalism seen such complete agreement or enthusiasm by such a diverse group of government officials as we are now witnessing. It seems also that Herr Krimhler has inadvertently created what it looks like might become the battle-cry for 'ThePlan' he tells us comes directly from God. As you can hear in the background, they are chanting, 'Six Ways to Law! Six Ways to Order! Six Ways to Peace!' and capping off the appeal with the words, 'Six, Six, Six.' Herrlich Krimhler's message comes as a welcome harbinger of hope at a time when we all need above all else, hope."

Jacob saw on Melissa's face the expression that asked if the journalist's words, if Krimhler's plan, could be a true effort at solving the world's great problems. It was the same question he fleetingly asked himself.

No! It could not! More than that, it was a lie! A wicked lie of the most cruel sort. A deception that dangled in front of a chaotic, terrified world, hope for a solution, while the deceivers were even now tightening their deadly coil around their billions of victims. How appropriate, he considered while lighting a cigarette and looking to the screen that displayed the almost gleeful face of Lawrence Thorton, that he should compare the Naxos group to a snake coiling around its victim, snuffing out freedom. Man was first deceived and enslaved by a serpent, according to the legend. Yes... Hugo Marchek would have appreciated the analogy.

"To the message given by the Pontiff, and by Herrlich Krimhler... I, on behalf of my fellow journalists throughout the world, say... 'Amen.' We will do our parts to disseminate that word of promise offered by the Six Ways Plan.

"INterface should become a part of our daily lives now. The Six Ways to Peace, our motto. One gets the feeling that we are indeed marching into a New Age, which will see the end of these six great scourges of man... Crime, poverty, hunger, ecological disaster, disease, and finally, war. Most of all, peace will replace war."

The network newsman looked to be in deep concentration; his tone was reasoning. "And the simple elegance of one part of 'The Plan' at which Herr Krimhler allowed us a brief look--that all wealth left behind by those gone in the dissolution will be distributed to the least of our brothers and sisters--demonstrates 'The Plan's' brilliance. It is a beautiful picture. A biblical picture, really, of the commandment to 'love thy neighbor as thyself.' Let us make that principle a part of our daily lives. 'Do unto others, as we would have them do unto us.' Only give even more... always more than we receive."

"Now we will go to the East Room at the White House, and the swearing-in ceremony for Grant Horton Halifax as President of the United States."

Thorton turned again to the monitor. The ceremony was already underway, the Chief Justice holding the large Bible on which the right hand of Halifax rested.

"...faithfully swear to execute the duties of the office of the President of the United States, so help me God," said Halifax, who smiled and took the hand first of the Chief Justice, then, in turn, the hands of each of the men and women gathered nearby him in the East Room. The new President made his way to a cluster of microphones, faced the cameras and smoothed white pages of paper on the top of the small lectern. He waited for the rustle of the guests and reporters to quiet down before he began reading in the polished New England brogue.

"This is a bittersweet time for me. My wonderful friend, my President... is gone." There were tears in his eyes; he paused to regain control. "Herrlich Krimhler, another of my very dear friends and colleagues, has told us that many of those who have departed from us were taken to a grand cosmic reward, as was the destiny of those people at this dramatic juncture in universal history. Raymond Parley is surely in his heaven... the first to arrive... Smiling down on us and telling us to follow the dictates of the great cosmoginal mind... To heed the admonitions of God's man, Herrlich

Krimhler. So I shall not mourn long for Raymond Parley's loss; rather, I shall celebrate his gain... and our opportunity to attain the same elevated state he now enjoys. That said, let us proceed. Let us, as Herrlich Krimhler said, and as John F. Kennedy before him said, 'make God's work here on earth truly our own.'"

The tears in Halifax's eyes dried as quickly as they came, and Jacob smiled inwardly, admiring the new President's ability to carry the act through with such obvious feeling; at the same time, he hated Halifax for what he knew the man was about to do.

"We, my fellow Americans, have the opportunity to invoke God's blessings by sharing in a way no other people on this planet can. We possess the technology to help assure each of our global brothers and sisters an equal right to life, liberty and the pursuit of happiness."

Jacob's face tingled, his anger and exasperation constricting his blood vessels, forcing the blood painfully into his eyes and forehead. The birthright of every American was about to be wiped out with a few spoken words. The Constitution of the greatest nation in the history of the world was about to be dissolved by this Judas. While the tears filled his own eyes, he tried to calm himself with the thought that the disappearance calamity had probably already done both things anyway.

"The good intentions of the great people of America shall no longer be doubted, because we will lead the way, take the first step, form the first link in the chain. Not a chain of bondage, but one of strength, which will assure true freedom by putting all our resources at the disposal of INterface. So, as President of the United States of America, I hereby invoke Executive Order 16,000 on behalf of the people of America for that purpose, and voluntarily offer this great nation to INterface Governing Council, within which I shall be Chief

Deputy to Herrlich Krimhler, who has today been chosen INterface Chancellor. This does not abrogate any treaties between what was formerly the United States of America and any of her treaty partners; rather, it strengthens those treaties by bringing them under an umbrella of all nations who choose to link with the INterface network. Trade agreements will be treated likewise, that is, they will be considered part of INterface Commerce, assuring each trading family member equitable treatment, based on gross national productivity, under terms stipulated by INterface Governing Council."

Halifax shifted his tone and demeanor, obviously wanting to become more personal with his viewing audience. "And now, my fellow citizens of the United States... and I must begin using the terms 'brothers and sisters' because we can no longer afford the divisiveness of nationalism. So, my brothers and sisters of INterface, we will begin distributing, at no charge to you, the interpersonal computer equipment known as the INterface Response Unit, also referred to as 'INRU.'"

Halifax watched men in white coveralls wheel in the example device on a flat dolly, and park it beside the lectern so that the television camera could give the viewer a good look.

"Because the great numbers of people who have the UNTIVUS can network with INterface to some extent, we will first concentrate on installing the INRU equipment in the homes and businesses which have only the obsolete computer units, as they are inadequate to interact on the level that will be required. In a short time, the old UNIVUS will be replaced by INterface Response Units in all remaining households and businesses, just as the European UNIVER systems will be replaced in Europe."

The new President, who would shortly abolish that office

to become Herrlich Krimhler's Chief Deputy, spoke in a tone that pleaded for understanding and cooperation.

"Unlike when we instituted the UNIVUS, a system which during its time proved its usefulness a thousand times over, acceptance of this new system will be mandatory. If it were not so, if even a small portion refused to accept it, the networking effort would be harmed irreparably."

Jacob heard no more of Halifax's words. His thoughts, instead, were on the hatred he felt for this man who had sold his country for personal gain. He considered calmly, premeditatively what he might do to oppose the dictatorship that was growing exponentially.

"It's all happening too fast for me," Melissa said, jarring him from his thoughts of righteous treachery. "But it's just like you said. It all seemed so fantastic when you first told me about what was happening."

"When people are panicked and desperate, it's easy to get them to accept a rope. Even one that has a noose on it. They're beginning to get hungry. They'll grab on to anything to keep from going under. This thing has been in the works for a long time. It took more than a day to build that complex at Naxos, that's for sure. If this so-called dissolution hadn't happened, they would've manufactured something, some crisis, in order to get what they wanted. I'm not sure whether they manufactured the disappearance. I don't know how they could've... but it came with perfect timing, didn't it?"

"The whole thing is crazy."

"More than crazy. And there's more to it than a magician's trickery, more than merely sleight of hand. It's as if they really didn't have control over what happened, but were fully prepared to take advantage of the situation when it did happen. I know it doesn't make sense, but they are taking full advantage of the disappearance and the destruction of the Russian military alliance."

Thirty minutes later, with the broadcasts from Washington and Brussels finished, and the soon-to-be Deputy Chancellor of INterface Governing Council having promised to tell more at a future time about the new way of doing things, Jacob set the videocassette recorder for the Naxos tape he had not yet viewed. His head throbbed violently, like it had off and on since the rush of events began following the car crash when the agent vanished. Melissa rubbed the back of his neck while he fidgeted with the recorder, then walked toward a bedroom.

"I'll get some aspirin," she said; he pushed the play button and sat on the sofa.

He was not prepared for what he saw, and his vision darkened, his headache becoming lost in the emotionally dimming realization of what he was witnessing.

On the screen, close up and in stunning color, he and Fredria VanHorne were in the throes of passion. Their naked bodies were writhing on Fredria's bed, slamming against each other at frenzied pace! Why had they taped them that night?! Blackmail? The clinical dissection went through his thought processes before the shock wore off, and his embarrassment and rage surfaced.

"Porno flick?" Melissa's question was put with amusement. "You....!?" Her declaration was not.

He got up and turned the machine off, his face reddening as much from anger as from embarrassment. "Look. You don't want to see this. I don't know what it means or why they did this, but I've got to see if it leads somewhere."

"Oh, I'm sure it will. Let's watch together. Maybe I'll learn something, too."

"Suit yourself." He restarted the recorder, recounting silently their sexual activity that early morning in the Naxos apartment. Watching the almost unnaturally white bodies, whose undulations he, strangely, did not remember experiencing. He was relieved when after another 30 seconds the video cut to him and the girl sitting up in the bed sipping from glasses, which, he remembered, had contained screwdrivers. He was relieved further that there was no audio while he and Melissa watched the mouths of the man and woman move in conversation between sips.

"Who is she? Karen?"

"A girl I met at Naxos. Fredria VanHorne. A scientist in the project."

"I can see you met her. What was she researching at the time? I can see *who* she was researching."

He held up his hand for quiet, fixing his concentration on the scene to which the video had just changed--Fredria standing naked over his own nude body.

He was asleep now, and she turned to face the camera after checking his eyes, and gave a signal that beckoned. Momentarily, two men wearing orange jumpsuits entered the room, walked to the bed and turned his body onto its stomach. The camera's angle changed from the one which had given view of the whole bed to one more mobile, obviously involving someone with a hand-held camera, whose operator moved to shoot from different positions while Fredria VanHorne and the men worked over the body.

"What's going on? What are they doing to you?" Melissa questioned.

"I'm not sure, but I think I know." He again held up his hand for quiet, sitting forward to watch the uniformed men help the woman.

One of the men handed Fredria a small, square box, which she opened and from it removed a gleaming vial. Both men held the body still to prevent reflexive jerking, while Fredria VanHorne inserted a hypodermic needle into the vial and drew its contents into the syringe. When she injected the left arm, the video faded to black before resuming a new scene.

People in pastel green surgical garb worked beneath bright lights, their faces and mouths covered with surgical caps and face masks. An unseen narrator spoke in English, but with a German accent.

"The subject will be implanted with the most advanced biochip, which, as you know, consists of living cell properties being married to the chip, in this case, to form the most sophisticated biosensor yet devised. Our subject, a highly placed member of the American diplomatic community, will be monitored as to his location, as well as his biological functioning, that is, his respiration, et cetera, et cetera, so long as the chip is active. The device is activated by galvanic stimulation... electronic impulses from the subject's surrounding tissues. The sensor's internal battery is stirred to life and will remain activated for many years. Because the element is small and extremely resilient against damage, it will even survive the subject, should he come to his end violently through electric shock, fire, impact trauma, or any of a thousand ways. Its only limitation is that its signals weaken considerably from distances greater than 100 kilometers. It can still be tracked, and eventually found, for distances of thousands of kilometers, but it is as yet a very slow process. At such distances, it takes considerably longer to zero in on our chip."

On the screen were the surgically gloved hands of two people, one holding the subject's head in a face-down position, the other one wielding a scalpel. The hand with the knife made an almost imperceptible cut on the scalp beneath the dark hair on the back of the head.

"The procedure takes only a moment, and is being done with such caution in this instance because this is our first major testing of the device. It must be conducted with utmost care, to assure its best chance for success. In this case, we must maintain the best possible controls to test our postulate."

The narrator paused for several seconds while the operation proceeded, then the animated voice continued. "Later, we can do the procedures on a run-them-in and run-them-out basis. As you can see, the wound is so tiny that the subject will think it no more than perhaps a scratch or insect bite. Being so finely done with surgical expertise, this person will most likely not know the procedure has been done at all. And, the biosensor you see here..." A gloved hand held the minuscule chip between index finger and thumb. "...is flexible and especially medicated, thus making it innocuous and unnoticeable to the bearer."

Tweezers, holding between their metal pinchers the glinting biosensor, probed the tiny slit in the skin at the base of the hair follicles, then inserted the chip. "See how the tiny wound closes behind the sensor, which, incidentally, we call the 'Allegiant' and... the procedure is completed!"

The scene changed again to electronic equipment encased in dark plastic, trimmed in chrome and adorned with scopes and colored lights and controls which Jacob recognized as equipment not unlike that he had seen at Naxos, near the Holophone Chamber.

"All of these things you see here..." The camera drew back to include the narrator, a small man in his late fifties with a black patch over one eye, standing in front of the gadgetry. Jacob had not seen him before, "...are responses to the Allegiant, which has now been activated by the galvanic activity within our subject's body."

A video dissolve on the television screen brought the viewers back to Fredria VanHorne's bedroom, the artificial sunlight streaming through the window that opened to a special-effects area just off the apartment. Fredria stood over

Jacob, a cup and saucer in her hand, her mouth moving without making sounds, while she talked and smiled.

"Our subject will not know he is being monitored, but will think only that, other than the headache, he had a very good time last evening."

Jacob watched himself having a good time, Fredria having joined him in bed, and remembered the words of Conrad Wilson: "Watch out for that girl, Son. Remember Salome, Delilah, Mata Hari and all the rest..."

He was glad the tape ended. Not because of embarrassment he felt while Melissa sat beside him watching, but because what he had thought at the time was sweet and good and something at least stronger than overnight affection was but another rape of his individuality. He was no longer angry; rather, he wanted to vomit, so physically sick did the thought of being with Fredria VanHorne make him.

"You okay?" Melissa put her arms around him, seeing that he looked like he might topple.

"No... But I will be."

He straightened and managed a deep breath. "You have any ammonia?"

"I think so. Why?" She was already on her way to the kitchen when she asked.

He didn't answer because he could not. Feeling the sickness crawl up his throat, he leaned forward, resting his elbows on his knees and cradling his forehead in his palms. He sniffed, trying not to be overwhelmed by the odor when she had handed him the open bottle.

"Thanks." He handed the bottle back to her.

"What's wrong?"

"Sick stomach. Ammonia sometimes helps."

The nausea subsided and he began probing for the device, using his fingertips to examine the flesh of his neck just below his skull.

"I've got to get it out," he said calmly, although feeling anything but calm. "See if you can tell where they put it."

She knelt on one knee over him when he turned sideways on the sofa and parted his hair methodically.

"Here. I think I've found it. It's a small, reddened spot. Looks almost like a tiny mole." She pinpointed the spot with a fingernail.

"You're going to have to take it out. I can't stand the thought of it being there," he said, a slight tremble in his voice. He convulsed in her arms, shivering.

Melissa kissed the back of his head. "Yes... Yes. We will get it out."

"There's no time. It's got to be done now. They'll be getting a fix on it. Do you have any kind of razor blades?"

"Just the injector kind, I think."

"Get them, and some alcohol, tweezers, adhesive tape, if you've got it, and some ice cubes to freeze the area."

When she returned with the items, he hurriedly wrapped the white adhesive tape around one end of one of the blades taken from the injector cartridge. The thought of what he had in mind apparently hitting her, Melissa turned pale.

"Oh, no!... I can't do it, Jacob!"

"Look, I can't reach it. You want to help, don't you?"

She nodded, looking wide-eyed at the wrapped blade. "I just can't do it. I'll hurt you."

"It hurts me now knowing the thing's in there! Take this blade and do what I tell you. They'll kill me for sure, if you don't get it out of there. They'll kill us both!"

She hesitatingly took the blade and held it with both hands while he held the ice cube against the area for more than a minute.

"Find the red mark again and cut it...," he said, "...just deeply enough to get to the thing. Be careful not to cut into the sensor. I don't want it damaged." He sat forward, like before, trying to help hold back the hair on the back of his neck and head so she could better see the spot.

"The light's not good enough. I can't see it well enough to do this. Let's move to the balcony door."

They did so and Jacob applied the ice again, then stepped onto the balcony, retrieved a patio chair and placed it just inside the open door.

"Are you sure you feel up to this right now?"

"I don't feel up to having this thing in my head one more second than I have to. Start cutting, but don't cut into the chip."

Sitting in the chair, the stench of the suffocating dampness assaulting his nostrils, the sounds of what seemed a thousand television sets blasted the stagnant air with a single incantation. "Six Ways to Law! Six Ways to Order! Six Ways to Peace! Six! Six! Six!!"

CHAPTER 15

Tragedy hung in the early morning darkness like death's decay-sweet odor. The sense of euphoria at Brussels, which had briefly touched Boston, was not evident now, while Jacob drove Melissa's small station wagon toward Cambridge. Downcast men and women milled about or shuffled along the streets. Some were the victims of the human predators who roamed, others were still dazed from the sudden loss of people they loved. Herrlich Krimhler's message of hope had made, then lost, its impact upon these pathetic souls, who, when Jacob moved past them, looked at him, then at the car, as if it might be a source of help out of their torment. Realizing they would not awake from their nightmares, their glazed, stuporous looks returned, their minds once again in their private hells.

The sense of hopelessness was once more upon him, as well. The manic-depressive pendulum of emotion had swung from the high optimism he had felt when Melissa removed the Allegiant from his scalp (at that time thinking that now he could operate free of the chains binding him to Naxos) to this depth of knowing the odds he faced.

Why not give up? Appeal to them? Tell them he had not understood the good intentions of the Naxos planners, but now, after hearing Krimhler, his outlook was changed. After all, he was not without talents to offer them. He could fight them better from inside their ranks, maybe win others to his point of view. Surely there were others who, like him, saw beyond their promises of Utopian bliss -- saw the megalo-mania of their design.

If he gave himself up, convinced them he now saw the light, the error of his ways. No! He had proven he knew what they were up to and that he was death-pledged against them. He proved, too, that he could think independently, and to have members of the glorious new order who could think in such a way would be unacceptable. "He is incorrigible," they would say when they sentenced him to whatever death method was prescribed for the enemies of INterface.

They would be right, of course. They could not change him, and so if they intended to eliminate him, they would have to find him. He had the capability of throwing them off his trail by using the biosensor, which was no longer their tool, but his. But, how to use it? The ploy must be developed — and quickly, because they could home in on the device as easily with it wrapped in a handkerchief and tucked away in the overnight bag as they could if it remained in his flesh.

His mind, now refreshed and clearer, and at an even higher emotional peak than it had been in days, formed an embryo of stratagem. Far-fetched as the hope of putting them off his scent while at the same time getting inside INterface machinery seemed, things even more bizarre had come to pass in an unbelievably short time. Things unthink-able. The selling of the United States to a European oligarchy headed by a computer genius. The disappearance of hundreds of millions of people, as if on cue by some master director. The astounding swiftness with which the Naxos

Utopians consolidated power and put INterface networking into place following the unexplained devastation of the Russian federation's war machine. The zeal shown by the representatives at Brussels, most, ideologically incompatible with each other. The dramatic ideas put forward by the young German ecumenically hailed by hardened veterans of the world's diplomatic community.

"Watch out!"

Jacob jammed the brake pedal when Melissa screamed, but the face seemed already in the car with them. Huge, fear-bulging eyes that smashed into the windshield, breaking the glass into a million crystalline fractures and smearing it crimson. The rolling, thumping of the body seemed to go on forever after the man's head-first crunch into the station wagon's front end. Jacob had swerved, but too late! He eased the wagon to a stop along the curb.

Melissa was bent forward holding her face between her hands, sobbing; she stiffened when he touched her.

"We've got to keep ourselves together," he heard himself say coldly, thinking of the probability of being caught because of the attention drawn by the accident. Thinking, too, that he felt like slapping the girl to make her act contrary to her natural instinct. "Did you hear me? We cannot do anything about that man, but if we don't handle this right, we might be worse off than him. Do you understand, Melissa?!"

He shook her violently but managed to restrain himself from striking. She nodded, trying to stifle her sobs.

"I'll take care of it. All you have to do is sit here. Try to compose yourself." Forcing himself to use a more soothing tone, Jacob analyzed their situation, looking around at the men and women who gawked through the windows. Faces, distorted...more zombie-like than human with their silent, dispassionate stares.

When he stepped to the pavement, a vehicle, its blue

lights flashing, converged on them. Now he would have to produce identification, go to a police station, and have his life searched by computers. Computers almost certainly linked by now to those of the Naxos system. These officers would not be directly a part of the hunt for him, but would they have an APB out? Or a high-priority missing persons report? If so, and the policemen discovered that they had found the subject of such a search, he would take the first chance to bolt. Melissa would have to be left behind. But she knew a great deal of what he knew. He was stupid to have shared so much with her. She didn't know everything, however. Not about his plans.

"Are you the driver of this vehicle, sir?" The big policeman said, approaching from behind the station wagon.

"Yes." Must stop shaking. Maintain control! "Give me your UNIVUSCARD, please." How long before they would run down the fact that he was being sought? Should he lie? Tell them he had lost his wallet? No. That would prompt a computer check for certain. The uniformed officer who asked the question looked past Jacob to a short, thick man in a sport coat and tie. The approaching man had just stepped out of a black car that had pulled to a stop behind the police cruiser.

"I'll take care of it," the plainclothes officer said, taking the UNIVUSCARD from the uniformed man and glancing at it, then handing it to Jacob. There seemed a glimmer of recognition in the man's eyes. Probably just a policeman's naturally suspicious way.

"Mr. Zen. You look like a sober, law-abiding guy. A guy who wouldn't hit anybody intentionally." The stocky man's tone was facetious, but not maliciously so.

"To be honest with you, this is your lucky night, because we don't have time to spend on this sort of thing right now, what with the more pressing problems we're having to contend with. If we take you in, it'll tie you up, it'll tie us up. And, what's one more body more or less these days? The guy felt it just wasn't worth it any more, so he chose you to end all his problems for him. That's how I see it. Why should we be penalized for his lunacy? It wouldn't cramp you too much if you just wash your car, straighten your dents, and we forget that it ever happened, would it?"

"No, sir." Jacob tried to hold the smile, wanting to keep from the policeman his nervousness and relief.

"Clear the area!" the plainclothes officer shouted gruffly, causing the onlookers, their faces still devoid of expression, to wander aimlessly down the streets as they had been doing before they were attracted to the death scene.

"You'd better move along now, Mr. Zen, before my chief calls for me and I have to tell him about this. He might cause us both problems we don't have time for."

"Uh... yes... I will," Jacob stammered, feeling as dull-witted as the people who had surrounded them, the numbing effects caused by the rush of events having returned in greater measure.

"Is the man dead?" Melissa said when he slid into the driver's seat. He turned into the traffic lane and edged by the policemen, who knelt over the the blood-soaked corpse.

"Yeah. He's dead."

Suddenly he felt conflicting emotions: relief, almost joy, over being freed from what could have ended in capture, and profound sadness, seeing in the incident the deterioration of humanity. The people, not concerned that a man had been killed, merely curious; the officers, who wanted only to get it over with by discarding the carcass, like one would discard a dog, dead in the street.

"We've got to get settled so I can figure it all out," he said, partially to change the subject within his own mind to force the guilt over his own insensitivity from his thoughts.

Jacob's head burned where the sensor had been removed, as did the muscles of his mid-back, and his hip and thigh on the right side. It was a vicious consequence of nerve tautness that could be relieved only by time free from the constant pressure of having to avoid contact with his pursuers.

It was, at the same time, foolish and logical that he came back to the place of his first time away from home, when at 18 he had left the safe womb of Stone Oaks to enter Harvard. Foolish, because if they had a comprehensive dossier on him, and surely they must, they knew that McLean and Stone Oaks, Boston, and Cambridge were the places he felt closest to and therefore might expect him to return. Logical, because it was home, and here he could find friends he could depend on for help, like Francis Lodierman. His tormentors' biographical file marked "Jacob Zen" might not go back so far as to include Francis, he convinced himself while trying to find the old brownstone home among the newer, unfamiliar structures near Kendall Square.

His inverse logic in coming here was that, they knew he was aware that they expected him to come to the Boston-Cambridge area and so, he would not; therefore he did. It just might work to thwart their own devious plottings. Still, they might scan the area for the limited-range biosensor just in case.

His reverse psychology might work on normal minds, in normal times; however, he was faced with the abnormal in both cases. No. His pursuers would kick over any and all rocks where their prey might hide.

"Francis was fun, not demanding, like the people I was used to," Jacob said without being prompted by Melissa, who, like he instructed, looked over the building-cluttered block for the house he had described.

"She always listened when you had a problem. Gave you the right answers and made you believe it was the easiest way out of whatever mess you'd gotten yourself into, whether it was or not. I met her my second year at Harvard. She was 35 and married to a man 15 years older who died not long after I met her. He was in bed with some guy. Died of a heart attack. I was living in a dorm on campus, but talked Uncle Conrad into letting me move to the house Francis' husband left her. She was the first woman I'd been around to any extent since my mother died. Uncle Conrad gave his permission to move off campus, but was too busy to supervise my selection of an apartment. When he finally did find out I'd moved not just into the house, but into Francis' apartment with her, he really raised the devil, I can tell you. But, you know when he met Francis, within 10 minutes he was loving her as much as I did. She's like that. Something about her you love the second you meet her.

"A 19-year-old boy or a world-acclaimed diplomat, it made no difference. She never changed her way of treating people. There was never anything intimate between us. Never. Something as good, though. Maybe better, more fulfilling. I became a man during those two school years spent with Francis. I learned that people aren't merely things you use to achieve your profits in life, but are to hold, and comfort, and to take comfort from. I needed that learning time with her."

"When did you last see her?" Melissa saw softness in his eyes for the first time since she had removed the biosensor, and heard gentleness in his voice.

"More than five years ago, I'm sorry to say. And it's my loss."

"Is that the house?"

He stopped the wagon in the middle of the deserted street and they both strained to see through the darkness. While lights could be seen as nearby as MIT to the west and the buildings between First Street and Commercial Avenue to the east, the immediate area surrounding Francis Lodier-man's home was apparently without power. A yellow glow, created by the lights of downtown Boston to the south, gave meager and diffractive illumination to the old house.

The time it took to drive the remaining yards of broken concrete leading up to the house brought quite different thoughts. A closer look presented a badly deteriorating structure, which seemed in a death struggle with its own disrepair to stand straight and strong like it once did when life pulsed and flowed in abundance through its many living places. What about Francis? The house so grossly neglected, not at all like the woman who was Victorian in devotion to appearance. "Looks like it's vacant, Jacob."

Had the cataclysm claimed her, too? Not Francis, too.

A faint light shone in the distance where the hallway reached its narrowest point in perspective. It was probably emerging from the room he remembered as being the dining area. There was no sign of life while he stood with his face close to the tiny rectangles of thick, beveled glass in the door. When he knocked for the third time with the tarnished corrosion-pitted knocker, the light spilling into the hallway brightened and someone appeared from the opening in the wall where the dining room should be. It was a thin female figure in a floor-length robe or gown, carrying a lamp whose flame silhouetted rather than fully illuminated the woman moving slowly toward them. She hesitated before opening the door only a few inches, peering at them through the crack with pale gray eyes, their irises an unhealthy yellow in the flickering light. She said nothing.

"We're looking for a lady who lives here, or who once lived here. Her name is..."

The face! Gaunt and wrinkled. Jaundiced, like the eyes. Her hair more gray than brown, and brittle. It was! "Francis?!"

"What do you want here?" The voice gravelly, like one that had spent a lifetime enduring cigarette smoke, or was the victim of a severe hormonal change that had robbed it of its youthfulness. Her words were slurred and issued in a tone that evidenced extreme fatigue.

"I'm Jacob, Francis."

"Jacob?... Jake?!" The skin of the woman's forehead wrinkled in puzzlement, the lines running across its yellowed expanse becoming deep creases. "Is that you, Jake?" Her eyes filled with tears that refused to spill from their bottom lids.

"Oh, Francis... What in the name of..." Unable to complete his expression of saddened disbelief, he embraced her; she spoke in a sing-song, child-like way.

"I'm supposed to tell them you are here. They will stop hurting me if I tell them you are here."

He felt her going limp and snatched the oil lamp from her hand, at the same time supporting her weight. Melissa took the lamp from him and he scooped Francis up and carried her to a sofa just off the foyer.

"She's in bad shape," he said, running his fingers caringly over her face, not knowing what else to do. "She's only 46 or 47... I can't believe she's aged like this!" He felt Francis stiffen.

"Jacob... My dearest Jake..." The words were nearly inaudible; she reached feebly to take his hand, then pulled it to her withered lips and kissed it. She began crying in a convulsive, high-pitched whine like a distraught child might make.

"Shssh... I'm here, Francis. I'm here. Don't talk just yet."

Straining to speak, despite his admonishment, her eyes grew large; she shook her head vigorously, indicating no. "I must! I must! They want me to tell them when you come to me... or they said they would..."

"Who? Who wants you to tell them?"

She again shook her head negatively, her deeply creased lips moving but saying nothing. Her eyes seemed to clear when she regained a degree of sensibility; the words came more easily to her. "You must leave... Now!" She squeezed his arm.

"They think they've taken over my will. They think I will help them find you."

"What have they done to you?"

"All kinds of machinery... Makes me do things I don't want to do," she whispered, her eyes bugging wildly, her head and shoulders rising involuntarily then relaxing. "Oh, Jake!... Can't let them do this to you... to..."

"She's fainted again, Jacob. I've seen this kind of seizure before. It might be drug-induced," Melissa said, holding back the woman's eyelids to check her pupils.

"I've got to get her out of here. They'll be coming for her again. You think it's okay to move her?"

"She was walking, and still recognized you. She'll be better off than she would if she stayed here, that's for sure."

Such was his conclusion already, and his mind raced ahead to other matters. He nodded approval although not really hearing Melissa's words.

"I'll find some of her things as quickly as I can, and bring a wet towel for her face."

Dawn was breaking while he guided the station wagon down State 28, the route he chose because there was less traffic on the road at this entrance point than on State 24 a mile farther west. That he had been so careful in the selection of this road, and yet so stupid as to not get rid of the biosensor by planting it in a vehicle heading in some other direction, was the paradox pre-eminently stabbing his mind. That, and the question: Why had he chosen Brockton to, he hoped, find a place where he could plan how to best use the biosensor against his enemy — which, he decided silently, explained the paradox.

Now that he was certain his pursuers were in the Boston

area, it was imperative to do something with the device. The thing to be done was clear; but how to do it, when time to learn so much that must be learned, and time to make crucial decisions that must be made, was so limited. It remained as murky as the red-orange haze that hung angrily between the wagon and the rising sun on their left. Through the mind-fog of how it was to be done, the thought of what to do remained clear: Put them off the scent and, at the same time, infiltrate.

"I think she's sick, Jacob. Can't we stop and let her get some air?"

He looked in the rearview mirror, seeing the chalky-white face of the woman whose head bobbed about with the bumping of the station wagon on the poorly maintained road. "Did she tell you she's sick?"

"She hasn't said anything. Nothing that's coherent. But stopping might help her. I think she might have motion sickness."

He guided the car onto the narrow shoulder and brought it to a stop. "You think she can stand for a minute?"

"I believe so, but she's awfully weak."

"Let's get her out." He half-lifted, half-dragged the limp woman from the rear of the wagon, then supported her while encouraging her to stand. Francis seemed to grow stronger.

"Take a deep breath, sweetheart. Try to stand on your own and walk a bit. Can you do that?"

Francis nodded affirmatively and her eyes shown with increased coherence. Jacob's attention snapped to the eastern sky, hearing the faint thump of what could only be a heli-copter's engine. Its landing lights came on almost in the same instant he recognized the sound. The chopper swooped quickly to within 100 feet of them and sat down easily in the yellow-brown grass. Its engine calming and its blades slowing to idling speed.

His inclination was to push Francis into the back of the station wagon and try to get away from the machine, which sat glaringly--a gigantic bird of prey waiting for its intended victim to flush.

"They've found us, Jacob! What can we do?" Melissa stood between him and the helicopter's beam, looking to him for the answer. But the terrain afforded no chance of escape from the predator squatting in the heavy grass, staring at them with its three painfully brilliant eyes and growling, its cold breath whipping about their legs.

"There's nothing we can do! It will be okay!" Jacob shouted above the growl.

Through the whirlwind of debris, a man, holding his cap to his head with one hand, hurried toward them. No guns. Only one man. Reason for hope.

"Need some help?" the man said when he reached them, looking quickly at each face. His expression brightened at the same moment his eyes met Jacob's. "Is that you, Jake?... Jacob Zen!"

"Kerry?"

"The same!" The tall man grabbed Jacob's hand and pumped it vigorously.

"What are you doing out here?"

"Headed for Brockton. My friend here got sick, so we stopped. How about you? You find your family? Are they okay?"

The pilot said nothing, his eyes taking on a far-away look.

After introducing Melissa, Jacob left her with Francis and walked with the man until the helicopter's noise no longer hampered their conversation.

"I haven't rested since I let you off... Been looking all over New England. All the relatives... they're gone... Like the rest, I guess." Kerry Vinchey's moist eyes had a look that only inconsolable inner pain could elicit. Jacob put a hand on Vinchey's shoulder.

"Kerry, there's nothing I can say, I know. Like I told you on the way from D.C., I've been crazy with worry about Karen."

For some reason he felt it right to let his new friend in on what his own life had been like since the disaster. Maybe that would help Kerry Vinchey cope; perhaps sharing with another man would generate new energy within himself to carry on. Nothing he could divulge would make things worse. Even in the event that Vinchey was somehow tied to the Naxos enemy — and that was a possibility, because twice this man with the helicopter had crossed his path at a crucial juncture — a release from his nightmare existence might ultimately be preferable to his agonizing struggle through it.

"The only good thing in this mess is the FAA can't control flying. I've been able to go just about anywhere I want to without filing flight plans. The Feds have too many other things going on right now to worry with one lousy helicopter. That won't last long, though. They're moving fast on this 'Executive Order' thing. We're in a state of martial law."

His friend had changed the subject, probably to keep from breaking down in front of Jacob. But the subject the pilot chose to extricate himself would have seemed, if Jacob believed in such things, supernaturally predestined to enter their conversation at this moment. Jacob's simmering plan suddenly gelled when the pilot, himself floundering without direction, was added to the ingredients, and the helicopter.

"You asked what I'm doing here, Kerry. Once I tell you, I think we might be able to help each other."

"Sure."

"Do you have access to fuel for the copter?"

"There are deserted stations, and some small airports

that've been abandoned, from here all the way to the coast. And it's probably like that all over the country. Only problem is, the radios have been abandoned, too. But I have some charts that can help me locate quite a few places, and I can set the chopper down just about anywhere. I do most of my own maintenance. Getting parts is a problem, though."

Vinchey appeared to know instinctively that the things Jacob was talking about went much deeper than their casual conversational tone suggested. Despite the pilot's calm words, it was obvious he very much wanted the help a mutual effort might bring. Still, Jacob's cautious side kept prodding his thoughts. The pilot's fortuitous crossing of his path at critical junctures. A Naxos ploy?

Yet the very fact that the coincidences were so improbable made it unlikely. Vinchey could be a part of any Naxos deception. And, there was no reason, at least no reason he could fathom, why the Naxos group would string him along, when they could capture him and wring out of him anything they wished, at any moment they chose, if the pilot was their agent. Something in Kerry Vinchey's eyes, reflections of Jacob's own hurting, of pain, the depths to which only a father's love for his missing children could descend. Little to lose by trusting this man.

"Give me a chance to finish before you decide I'm out of my mind. Or maybe I am... But hear me anyway."

The pilot's expression did not change while he was told all that Jacob knew, all he suspected. Like when he emptied his emotions on Melissa's ears, retelling it now soothed his own nerves. The burden shared, its weight redistributed across yet another set of shoulders. Even if Vinchey did not accept Jacob's fears as credible, the telling of them felt good while they stood near the helicopter, watching the occasional traffic move along the highway.

The sun was fully up now, and despite the haze, they

could make out the structures across the field. "You really believe the disappearance thing has something to do with that preacher's idea about Biblical prophecy?" Vinchey's tone said he wanted to accept Jacob's view. Said the pilot had struggled with his own rationalizations, but after bumping into many dead-ends, he was ready to explore the less rational.

"Is the biblical prophecy angle any more unbelievable than the fact that it happened, than the garbage they're trying to feed everybody? An evolutionary leap into some higher cosmic realm for the worthy. A punishment for others. All determined by some Great Universal Mind..."

"There are other theories about what caused it."

"And the official explanation is as unbelievable as any of them. I've got to get inside, Kerry, and find out what's going on. I'm limited now, but your helicopter can give me, give us, the ability to put distance between them and us, quickly. That's important to the first part of my plan."

"But why single you out? Look, I believe you when you tell me somebody tried to kill you. That they've taken Karen. But why you?"

"It's all tied up somehow with Hugo Marchek and the prophecies. At first, I thought it was because of my ties to Conrad Wilson and the government, their need to do away with all nationalism, and to get control of our nuclear forces. But they've got all that. When the President disappeared and the fabric of society in the United States disintegrated, the European States — this Naxos group, usurped, absorbed this country's essence with the blessings of Grant Halifax. And they still want me. What can I, one person, possibly do to threaten them? They wouldn't go to all the trouble they've gone to just to get revenge."

Vinchey toed the pebbles on the barren spot where the men stood, then knelt to pick up a few of the stones while deeply in thought. "What about that tracking device? They'll be able to follow you as long as you have it. And why haven't they already been drawn to it, if it's still operating?"

"When I flew with you, we took the thing out of their range so quickly, they lost contact. For some reason, they have trouble relocating its signal when it moves rapidly. That's one reason your copter can be of use... to move out of their range quickly. It forces them to guess, rather than know in advance where I'm going next. You saw what they did to Francis. That was one of their guesses.

"Like I said, their wanting me is tied somehow to these unexplainable happenings. I've got to find the connection, and that's why I've kept the biosensor. If I use it the way I plan, I think I can get inside their operation and at the same time get them off my back. I just need time to think it all out."

While kneeling, Vinchey considered Jacob's words, tossing the small stones one at a time into the high grass.

"There's this little island place I get away to sometimes out in Hingham Bay. I don't think we'd be bothered out there, unless your friends pick up on that gadget's signal again."

Jacob took Vinchey's hand. "Thanks, Kerry. It means a lot to me that you believe me. That I've got another friend to share this with."

"I don't have anything else to do," Vinchey said, smiling weakly. He saw the pilot's eyes become liquid, and understood.

* * *

MORE THAN A WEEK had passed since they arrived at the rocky point of land, whose beige sand dunes, topped by silky yellow-brown grass, contrasted starkly with the blue-green Atlantic waters of Hingham Bay. It was small, like its namesake had described, and one of the farthest of the islands from the land mass that was Boston.

Vinchey Island was more than promised, with its two gasoline-powered generators providing for all electrical necessities and for most conveniences. Both men scanned the white protrusion of land in the distance, Vinchey with binoculars and Jacob with a telescope permanently mounted on a tripod set in a slab of concrete. It was easy to see why Kerry Vinchey brought his family here most summers during those happier, more sane times, and why the pilot was sick at heart now recounting days spent with those he loved most.

"Kirk loved spotting boats and ships from here, so I bought that scope and mounted it for him. He got pretty good at it... recording class, tonnage and all that... for a 10-year-old boy."

The urge was strong to say: "He must be quite a boy," the desire to encourage with: "He'll be here before you know it, spotting boats again." Best to say nothing. To simply keep looking along the island that lay eight miles across the stretch of water. To offer hope when they both knew there was little would be wrong; to do so with conviction would be impossible. Just continue scanning the bone-white dunes for the enemy who took Karen from him; who somehow had a hand in banishing those better times to an irretrievable past. Maybe, just maybe, there was to come a better day than now. Not the same as before, perhaps, but a better time, to be forged from the beastly realities of the present. A future where little boys and fathers could again, at their leisure, watch passing boats across untroubled waters.

"It's been six days since we put the sensor on that island. Surely they'd have found it by now if they were still trying to get at you." Kerry Vinchey removed the binoculars from his eyes. "With the smog almost cleared up these past three days, we couldn't have missed any activity over there, Jacob."

"Maybe they have given up. Maybe they figure I can't hurt them. But it just doesn't feel right to me. You think I'm paranoid?"

"Of course not, but I still think six days is plenty to give them. They must've given up on you. They would've found that thing by now, otherwise."

"Let's give it another day. Make it a full week. We'll pick it up Friday morning."

"Jacob!"

Both men watched the woman struggle toward them up the dune, her gray-streaked hair whipping in the cold wind. She held her long, once elegant fingers together over her eyes to shade against the brightness, made more intense by the high, thin haze. Francis Lodierman caught her breath after reaching the concrete plateau, then spoke.

"Jake!... You've got to see it. It's just terrible!" She clutched his shirt, gasping for air.

"You shouldn't be out here, Francis." He steadied her, studying her weak eyes. "Now calm down."

She tugged at his jacket sleeve, pulling him down the sandy incline toward Vinchey's gray-with-white-trim frame house, which stood in the dark grass of another plateau 150 feet from the observation point. "Hurry!"

Melissa met them on the porch steps, her face ashen, her eyes glistening with fear verging on panic.

"It happened about 10 minutes ago," she said, preceding them into the rectangular room at the center of the house where the television set blared.

"Arab and Israeli governments are to be more than congratulated for their wisdom in concluding this, one of the most important peace pacts in man's history. They deserve the praise and the gratitude of all peoples."

Herrlich Krimhler sat between the Israeli Prime Minister and the King of Saudi Arabia, the collective Arab nations'

representative for the occasion. Each man looked to the
young speaker, whose tanned hands were interlocked and
resting on the brilliantly polished conference table top, his
eyes fixed on the camera directly in front of him.

"Peace shall grow from this moment, as mankind marches
into the New Age of INterface, in which all citizens will be
linked one to another, each the brother, the sister of the
other. This was God's intention from the beginning."

Krimhler took a small stack of white, printed pages from
someone standing behind, and placed the sheets on the table
in front of him.

"So, they're going to officially sign the peace pact between
the Arabs and Israelis. We knew that, Melissa. Why did you
call us down here for that?" Jacob said.

"No... this is taped. It happened a few minutes
ago... Watch."

Herrlich Krimhler slid the papers to his right, to in front
of the burnoosed Saudi king, who signed the peace document and returned it to Krimhler. The German passed it
then to the white-haired Israeli Prime Minister, who signed,
then looked up from the task, a solemn expression on
his face.

The scene changed quickly to a large number of people
gathered behind and in front of a small lectern, to which
Herrlich Krimhler walked and stood behind.

The television narrator explained. "After the signing by
the Israeli Prime Minister and the Saudi King, Mr.
Krimhler moved to the main conference room, where he
was to add his signature to the treaty, after a brief
statement."

"Peace has come at last to the Arab and the Jew. Let us
make this conciliation the example for what can, what must
come to be between all peoples of this fragile planet."

Krimhler's black eyes glared into the camera, taking

possession of the viewer's concentration even through the time-buffering effect of the videotape.

"The terrorists who detonated the atomic devices in Cairo and in Damascus two days ago, as despicable as such barbarism is, performed a service those anarchists could not foresee. The act proved that mankind must join hands, together in a chain of sanity through INterface networking, and must serve notice to all such diabolists that now, from this point forward, there is no place to hide from the 'Six Way Plan,' which will deal with their murderous treacheries!"

Krimhler paused while those in front of and behind him applauded with enthusiasm; he spoke again, then. "Let this pact for peace between two peoples, who have been at bloody odds longer than any other... giving the Palestinian a permanent homeland, assuring the Israeli protection under INterface law, and the right to establish a temple on Mount Moriah in Jerusalem... serve notice to all who would perpetuate hostilities that making war will no longer be tolerated!"

Applause again exploded in the room, then settled to a conversational drone. The young German opened his mouth to speak again.

Deja vu pulsed through Jacob, yet distinctively different than the sensations of the other times. He was witnessing a momentous instant of history, but something more profoundly affecting. History transcending war and, peace and diplomatic nuance; a rending instant in the ebb and flow of eternal events, when time-past and time-future is inexplicably predestined by some great eclectic agglomerate force to merge, then fuse in a millisecond, altering the direction and velocity and, therefore, forever, the destiny of humankind.

A dime-sized spot of black materialized an inch-and-a-half above the left eyebrow. The dark hair lifted as if disturbed by a sudden wind. Blood spurted from the frontal hole, and at the same instant, blood and brain tissue erupted from the rear of the exploded skull and sprayed the dignitaries behind the lectern in a fan of pink profusion.

Assassination! Replaying for the shocked eyes of the world familiar, grotesque, sudden death. Cameras gone mad, their lenses capturing wild, lurching images of people fighting to reach cover. Panic-stricken faces, eyes widened in fear, searching for medical help for the leader, who lay crumpled and unmoving, face-down on the blood-soaked carpet beneath the security men and diplomats hovering over his body.

Jacob's enemy, the leader of his enemies, lying wounded! No one could survive such a thing! Not a head shot like that!

Thoughts of what it meant flooded his brain. Now, would they concentrate on more pressing matters? Now that their leader was dead? Would they lose interest in so petty a matter as Jacob Zen, and get on with the grander design of enslaving a world? Did the death of Herrlich Krimhler mean all that Interface and "The Plan" envisioned had changed in that instant when the German's head exploded?

From subliminal mind-strata involuntarily searched, one thought emerged; the "Six Way Plan" was not altered by the death of its architect; INterface was not made impotent. Krimhler's assassination was part of, a gigantic part of "The Plan." "The Plan" was not obliterated when the leader's cranium flew apart. It was instead, in some way, he could not analytically determine, but intrinsically knew, galvanized and set in motion by the spectacle. The inner voice that told him so was Hugo Marchek's.

"So, yet another assassination. An assassination of unrivaled proportions, as far as the importance of the victim to the world is concerned. The man who seemed so much more than just that... a mere man... Herrlich Krimhler, Chief Designer and Chancellor of the INterface system, the man who had single-handedly, just moments before his death, brought together the Arabs and Israelis in an unprecedented pact of peace, although he died before he, himself, could sign it. Dead at the hands of an assassin."

Lawrence Thorton narrated in his familiar baritone voice, a stony expression on his face.

"Since the time the shooting took place, about eighteen minutes ago, there has been, as might be expected, an intensive search of the area. I understand they may now know who is responsible for this, certainly one of the most reprehensible acts in the history of the world."

Thorton turned to face the big monitor on the wall behind the broadcast desk. "John Farber has with him Maurice Clary, Chief of Security for interface. John, is this report accurate? That security might have a line on who did this?"

The thin journalist, at first could not hear because of the noise in the room, but turned to the Frenchman when a technician repeated the question through the headset Farber wore.

"Yes, Larry. It is true. Mr. Clary, can you tell us about the evidence you've uncovered about the assassin?"

While Clary answered in his native tongue, the speech synthesizer translated in the many languages of those watching the telecast.

"Irrefutable proof has been found. We have located the weapon and identified the assassin's fingerprints. Along with this evidence, we found his wristwatch, which he apparently pulled from his wrist and laid it aside to keep it from being damaged while ne rested his arm against the floor for steadying his aim. He left the wristwatch in his haste to get away after firing the shot."

"Then you know for certain the identity of the assassin.

Can you give us the name, or will we have to wait until your investigation is concluded?"

"We can tell you now. Our investigation of this..." The Chief of Security stammered, his eyes growing moist with emotion; the translation voice hesitated then continued. "I will tell you, because so far as we are concerned, the murderer has been positively identified. Also, because he is an enemy who has eluded us. A terrorist. We earnestly ask the assistance of all citizens of INterface in the apprehension of this assassin. He must not escape the peoples' justice."

The Frenchman held up a large photograph of a man's face, and the camera framed it in close-up for the global television audience.

"He is a former member of the United States diplomatic service. His name is Jacob Zen."

CHAPTER 16

E ach being of the human kind must in times of acute personal crisis — be it physical crisis that threatens life, or moral crisis that promises personal gain at the price of one's own decency — every person must at a crucial, pivotal moment, set a course that is in most instances irreversible, once selected and begun. In the face of totalitarianism, both types of crises merge at once to confront the resistant victim, and so, too, the decision to be made. Whether to walk the broad road of submission, almost certainly to destruction, because: 1) if one does nothing, simply hides away from those who seek his life, the seekers will sooner or later accomplish their purpose, or 2) if one joins the system surreptitiously, quietly acting the obedient subject of the evil rule (a thing nearly impossible because the innate, irrepressible will of the true resistor against such evil cannot long allow the pretense), he will be found out. Or, whether to walk the narrow path of aggressively combating the evil, no matter the cost to one's fellow beings, thereby, at the very minimum, delaying one's own demise (life is the greatest personal gain of all) while discharging one's pent-up hatred into the enslaving system.

Jacob already knew the course he had no choice but to follow. His philosophical ponderings were as much to salve his conscience with the idea that he had made his choice after long, rational deliberation, as it was to think through his plan to become a part of INterface.

He sucked the smoke into his mouth and inhaled deeply, letting it escape slowly from his lungs through clenched teeth before snuffing out the cigarette. It was the latest of 10 he had smoked since being left alone four hours earlier by the others, who now slept in the various rooms of Kerry Vinchey's island house.

He had killed before; why did the pricking inner-voice not realize that fact and leave him alone? Before, with the attaché case, then again at Marchek's home, the killings were self-defensive. The act he contemplated now would be one of premeditation, dredged out of the black recesses of the mind-realm from which the moral being must remain aloof, must constantly wage war with. But wasn't being falsely branded a murderer, an assassin, being made a hated, hunted creature marked for eradication, like a plague-carrying rodent, justification for doing whatever it took to fight them? Wouldn't a planned murder be a preferable, even moral action against a monstrous system that would soon be blood-purging itself of all dissenters?

Jacob stood from the kitchen table chair and stretched his aching body. He picked up the Bible and adjusted his position to read in the light of the single bulb above the table.

Common sense told him all things that had happened were either products of natural laws broken by men, or by-products of the actions of men trying to bring things back under man's control.

The disappearance of millions of people. The swift ascent

to power by the European Confederation, led by Herrlich Krimhler. Human sensibility, said these things, and those written thousands of years ago by biblical prophets, as related to each other, could be no more, than coincidence. But, if they were true --these prophecies Hugo Marchek believed as strongly as anyone ever believed anything — nothing could be more important than this old book, to himself, to the world.

Jacob picked up the videocassette and pondered its significance, weighing it balance-fashion in his right hand against the Bible in his left, while walking into the small den. He fed the cassette into Vinchey's recorder and used the search mode to locate the point at which he wanted to begin.

Through neither desire nor fault of his own, he had been driven into the tangle, beginning when he met the eschatologist and continuing until now. Krimhler was dead; he, himself, stood accused of the murder before the world. If it were all a part of biblical prophecy, and if Hugo Marchek was right about the Bible having the answers, surely Krimhler's death was recorded somewhere, maybe even his own involvement in the death.

He shook his head, smiling, almost laughing out loud. It was all too fantastic! Hunted, hated by the newly restructured world for murdering its savior. Framed like a hapless protagonist in some inconsequential detective novel. Jacob Zen, smack at the center of it all!

"...the Antichrist will be revealed in his time."

Hugo Marchek's voice jolted Jacob from his thoughts. He watched the give-and-take between Marchek, Rance Jorgenson and Lauren Winchester, sensing again power in the old man's calmness.

The eschatologist spoke after several seconds of reflection. "Paul wrote in his second epistle to the Thessalonians regarding the matter of the last great dictator of the world, beginning in chapter two, the first verse."

Jacob heard for the second time Marchek's phenomenal recollection of the Scriptures; his own sense of concentration heightened when the old man quoted:

"...And now ye know what restraineth that he might be revealed in his time. For the mystery of iniquity doth already work; only he who now hindereth will continue to hinder until he be taken out of the way. And then shall that wicked one be revealed, whom the Lord shall consume with the spirit of his mouth, and shall destroy with the brightness of his coming."

Moments later, Marchek, departing from quoting Scripture, said: "When God's restraining hand is withdrawn, the time of tribulation shall fall on mankind. Society will degenerate, become vile, so horrible, that it will make Hitler's Germany look like a picnic. And, like the Germans of Hitler's time and Americans during the early 1930's, the people of the United States and Western Europe will be willing to give total authority to anyone who can convince them that he has the answers to their dilemmas. This son of perdition, this Antichrist, receiving his deceptive powers of signs and lying wonders from Satan, will be able to delude everyone into believing he is the long-awaited Messiah."

The tape continued to roll, Jacob mulling Marchek's words; the analysis short-circuited when Marchek's taped image continued to speak.

"I believe when the restraining influence of God Almighty is withdrawn, these things will bring on immediate and total collapse of civilization. What specific sign will issue in this withdrawing of God's hand? I am certain it will be the rapture of all who have accepted Jesus Christ as their Lord and Savior."

Jacob stopped the tape and paced while lighting a cigarette, many thoughts playing within his brain. Past time, seeming an eon ago, became liquid, flooding back into his memory; he was again in Marchek's study hearing the old man's words.

The words became more real than they were that night Marchek framed his beliefs, and Jacob suddenly made sense of them, whereas, in the actuality of that past time, the words had been weird, unacceptable, theological, mumbo-jumbo.

Then, he could not understand, much less accept, Marchek's preachments, but condescended to listen to Karen's friend. Now, he was desperate to have the words, the thoughts. He wanted to understand the beliefs, in order to make sense of his own maddening present.

Common, human reasoning less and less made sense; Marchek's explanation of his unwavering belief in the prophetic writings more and more testified truth. Jacob's world had deceived and betrayed him, was intent on killing him. The prophetical world spoken of by Hugo Marchek became increasingly lucid, became history unfolding.

Their discussion had covered much that night, Marchek presenting many things to Jacob's uninitiated ears. How could he hope to recall it now? Yet the memory was etched, for the gist, if not for the precise, order and sequence of language, and replayed as clearly in his mind as had the videotape moments earlier.

Ironically, Marchek had expressed the foundational reason for his own murder that night when he answered the question put to him by his guest: "You believe that it's you, personally, they're after? Not the ideology you represent? Not the resistance you throw in their way?" (Jacob spoke of the PAL organization.)

Marchek had answered: "It is me they want eliminated, because I am one among a very few who have insight into their master plan for bringing their kingdom into being."

"You're talking about some conspiracy to establish dictatorship?" Jacob remembered asking.

"...It will be supernaturally accomplished. It will be a one-world hell on earth, presided over by the devil himself in the form of a superhuman dictator," continued Marchek.

But, if Herrlich Krimhler was the Antichrist, and certainly the German had fit the characteristics described by Marchek, why was Krimhler dead? His skull was ripped apart by the assassin's bullet! Herrlich Krimhler was dead.

Hugo Marchek said something that night. If only he could remember. Something about the eschatologist's purpose in fighting the establishment of the hellish order. Jacob stared out the window into the blue-blackness of the early morning, straining to recall Marchek's words about postponing the coming order's rise to power.

"To answer your question, how will it be done?" the old man had said. "How shall we accomplish the postponement of Satan establishing his Antichrist government? I am not at all certain it can be done. Notice I said postponement of, not stop, its establishment. I only know I must try to do my part to hold it off as long as possible."

Was this all part of postponing the coming to power of an Antichrist? An Antichrist other than Herrlich Krimhler? Did Hugo Marchek's people assassinate the German and, he, Jacob Zen, just happened to be the convenient target for Krimhler's security people to blame?

But Marchek's followers must have been taken in the rapture, or dissolution, or whatever, if, like the old man said, only true believers in Jesus Christ would disappear when it happened. Some of Marchek's people, however, like Karen, were believers in Marchek, not believers in Jesus Christ. And therefore, might have been determined to get Krimhler, whom they considered the head of the organization that murdered the gentle old man.

The wristwatch; the fanatical attempts on his own life; the Allegiant tracking device they planted against his skull. No. The Naxos group had Jacob Zen picked as the mark to focus the hatred of the world upon from the time Fredria VanHorne seduced and drugged him. No doubt the blueprint for the framing was drawn well before that. All of it tied in some way to Conrad Wilson, to Karen Mossberg, and to Hugo Marchek, whose voice he heard again now, seeing with his imagination the thin, wrinkled face superimposed over the dark Atlantic sky.

And, in Jacob's mind's eye, Marchek held the old Bible in his hand while he spoke. "I assure you these facts can be learned by anyone who cares to carefully read this book... It is all here. The answers from beginning to end."

Jacob heard again Marchek's words, whose meaning now seemed clear. "God uses human agents to carry out his work, sometimes willingly on their part, sometimes without them knowing it. And, since you might very well be carrying out a mission for the Supreme, I suggest you study His written orders..."

The eschatologist held up the Bible in Jacob's memory. "I pray that you read this book... When the great disappearance of humanity occurs, Jacob, depend on this old book to guide you. Follow your burning need to get to the bottom of the great dictatorship."

He sat in a chair near the window and clicked on the table lamp at its side. All other avenues took him to dead ends. Time now to follow Marchek's advice, given that night. Time to see if the worn old volume really was the road map.

And, if it could answer his most pressing questions: Why, if Herrlich Krimhler was the Antichrist Marchek spoke of, was Krimhler now dead, unable to fulfill his prophetical role as the world's last, most despotic tyrant? Would that role now fall to another of the devil's chosen? Had the end-time dictatorship been postponed through the actions of the Almighty's human agents, if they had assassinated Krimhler? And, a larger, more personally affecting question: If the Naxos people did set up Jacob Zen from some earlier point, and pinning the blame on him for Krimhler's murder, why would they then continue to try to kill him on the highway, at Marchek's home, before the assassination took place? Probably, he pondered, because the men trying to kill him did not know of the greater design to assassinate Krimhler. Or, they planned to capture him and hold him until after the assassination, then bring him out before the public as the killer. Or, hold his dead body until after Krimhler's murder, and tell the world Jacob Zen had been killed upon discovery that he was the assassin. And, they wanted the materials he carried in the attaché case.

Where to look in the book? Where to begin? So much of it, maybe all of it, symbolic. How could he, who had rarely glimpsed into the Christian Bible, or for that matter, into any other religion's holy writings, possibly hope to learn much from his study? Nowhere else to turn. All other roads to understanding, blocked. So many books of prophecy to choose from. Which to read first?

Logically, all important end-time predictions should be wrapped up in the last part of the book. Such was the way with works authored by mortal writers. Why not with the one volume touted by Christians to be written through direct inspiration of the one, true Deity?

Turning to the back of Marchek's Bible, Jacob searched quickly through the heavily underlined, notation-filled pages for any references he might find about a final world ruler.

The Revelation. The last book

Author: John the Apostle

Theme: Consummation, Verse 9:

"I, John, who also am your brother, and companion in tribula-

tion, and in the kingdom and patience of Jesus Christ, was in the isle that is called Patmos..."

Patmos! Separated from Naxos by only a few miles of pored Aegean waters! He poured quickly over succeeding verses.

"I was in the Spirit on the Lord's day, and heard behind me a great voice, as of a trumpet, Saying, I am Alpha and Omega, the first and the last; and, What thou seest, write in a book...

"Write the things which thou hast seen, and the things which are, and the things which shall be hereafter."

John, a disciple of the Christian Messiah, received his vision of the end-time within miles of Naxos, where he, Jacob, it more and more appeared, fell heir to fate's commission to follow this nightmare to its conclusion, or to his own end. The fact now seemed more than eerie coincidence, his own juxtaposition to Marchek, to the prophetical text. There must be much written about the coming dictator, at least some reference to the Naxos complex. Of course, Marchek had quoted verses about the Antichrist during the taping of the show. Were they from The Revelation?

He smiled inwardly. How could he actually believe all the things bounding through his mind, the things printed on these ancient pages? For sure, things happening to his world were real; his shredded nerves gave witness with every pump of his heart that his existence was something more than delusion. This Bible should be no harder to accept than the things he had seen and felt since leaving that Clyclade pit. His eyes moved more swiftly through chapters 9,10, 11, and 12, stopping as if by programmed impulse when they met the small, italicized heading just above the bold number 13: "And I stood upon the sand of the sea, and saw a beast rise up out of the sea..."

John saw it from Patmos! The old prophet had seen across the stretch of water separating the two tiny islands, across the centuries, the whole Naxos mystery! Those mysteries written of 2,000 years before, churned now in Jacob's mind, crystallizing, focusing the vision's message. John, the Apostle of Christ, the prophet, saw the last great dictator appear to rise from the sea, from the bowels of the island of Naxos! The revelation, fantastic though it was, diminished in the light of yet another, when he reached verse 3. *"...And I saw one of his heads as though it were wounded to death; and his deadly wound was healed, and all the world wondered after the beast"*

It had to be! The prophecy of the assassination! A deadly wound -- but one that would be healed! Krimhler, if he were the beast of Revelation, would somehow come back to life according to this passage! He read on ravenously digesting the words.

"...And it was given unto him to make war with the saints, and to overcome them; and power was given him over all kindreds, and tongues, and nations. And all that dwell upon the earth shall worship him, whose names are not written in the book of life of the Lamb slain from the foundation of the world..." "...And I beheld another beast coming up out of the earth; and he had two horns like a lamb, and he spoke like a dragon. And he exerciseth all the power of the first beast before him, and causeth the earth and them who dwell on it to worship the first beast, whose deadly wound was healed."

If the words were more than mere symbolism, or the rantings of a nearly starved old man banished to die on his tiny, desolate island-prison, John was describing the ruthless subjugation of a future world. The first true world dictatorship. The horror-existence predicted by Hugo Marchek, not the Utopian paradise promised by the INterface propagandists. Either system of spirit enslavement would be unacceptable to freedom-loving men and women; the systems would differ only in degree of physical atrocity. Either evil--

the one detailed in the biblical prophecies that predicted quick bloom into a state of abominable horrors, or that phased-in growth apparently intended by the Naxos criminals, now in its first stages — either evil would, finally, metamorphose into soul-rending monstrosity.

Should he change his plan in the face of things he learned from his readings? Revenge remained a factor in his will to carry through; the remote hope, too, that Karen might be alive. And, somewhere in the back of his brain a new ember of incentive burned. To, as best he could, help carry out Hugo Marchek's obsession in life — to hinder, to postpone, the inevitable dominion by the Naxos power grabbers, whether they were or were not of the Antichrist order like his friend had believed. He would not turn his back now that his objectives were more clearly focused in his thinking. His commitment, if it were altered, was altered toward greater determination to get to the heart of the beast and tear at it for whatever time was left to him on the planet.

He walked into the dark room where Kerry Vinchey slept and snapped on the lamp beside the bed, causing the pilot to stir. He shook Vinchey, who turned from the light and settled again for sleep. "It's time to get started, Kerry."

Watching the helicopter strain to break free from the high grass between the thickly forested surroundings brought back the nauseating sensation of total aloneness he felt in those dark hours following the moment the Treasury agent's face disappeared from the rearview mirror. The chopper's final jerk skyward, before beginning its smooth ascent eastward, seemed the action that broke his tie with all that was civilized. Now began the trek through both a literal and symbolic jungle, toward an enemy that both terrified and drew him with irresistible fascination. Forcing himself to gather his wits, to consolidate his thoughts of what had been, with those of what was to come, dispelled the loneliness while he moved as quietly through the heavy under-brush as the dry forest floor would allow.

Hours of videotapes that he had watched, pages of documents given him by Conrad Wilson's operative during their clandestine meeting before he departed Naxos that he had digested while at Melissa's apartment, then again at Vinchey's island house, along with chapters of biblical prophecies he had read, formed an amalgam, swirling nucleus in his mind, from which a clear path of action emerged.

Assaulting this remote INterface substation, if his analysis of the video profile on the Sector Coordinator was reliable, should not be too hard to do. Not the physical part of the assault, at any rate. The highly secretive nature of INterface's controlling structure meant that the tape he viewed was intended for the eyes of but a few. There was no need for elaborate security around these secluded computer centers; no one, other than each person chosen to be Sector Coordinator, knew where his own little concrete block building was located. One person could manage the machinery, so the INterface masters apparently reasoned.

Still, the things he saw and studied on the tapes and documents, detailed though they were, were only theoretical, basic envisionings of the INterface planners about how the Sector Coordinator should interact with the total system. Had the documents being stolen forced them to change their blueprint? If he ran into more than one person in the block-house, he would have his answer, because their plan called for one Sector Coordinator to act as caretaker of the ultra-sophisticated computer machinery, which was designed to operate itself. The Sector Coordinator was meant to perform only accountability functions, and to troubleshoot when things broke down. Each Coordinator was known personally by only one man in INterface government, according to the videotape and the papers he had studied. The arrangement was no doubt designed to isolate the individual from other Coordinators, thereby lessening the chances for collusion which might manipulate INterface machinery contrary to the Naxos group's intentions.

He gained confidence from the thoughts. The INterface blueprint was too intricate, too brilliant for them to take back to the drawing board. Ultimately, if the thief was not caught, the immensity, the complexity of it all would absorb him, neutralizing the thief's ability to put his knowledge to use. They would not change the blueprint because of such minor annoyances.

But his confidence had a double edge. His task was immense; he remembered the hours spent studying the Sector Coordinator's responsibilities to INterface, and the many and varied controls placed upon the Coordinator. Parts of his own plan worried him deeply. The identification process, when the Sector Coordinator was required to respond to Central Computer Command — Would his be the right solution? The Allegiant he carried in the backpack, could he make them swallow the deception? Could he make it all work together — his plan to penetrate INterface? Would there be enough time?

Much of his hope rested in how well Kerry Vinchey carried out his part. Having to depend on someone else went against his best judgment, weakened his effort. But, to put his own plan into action, itself an elaborate one, meant having to trust the pilot to use his skills as a flyer.

The air became harder to breathe because of the increased humidity, the closer he came to his objective. A light mist thickened to become fog in the distance, beyond the immediate density of bush and high grass in which he knelt, using binoculars to pierce the boiling haze. The stench was like that of the cities he left behind; not the normal smells of a forest shrouded with fog, or even of odors given off by the decaying dampness of marshland. The scents reeked of gasoline engine fumes. Smog, even here, 100 kilometers from the nearest town of more than 500 in population.

The blockhouse! Less than 75 meters in the distance, materializing, then seeming to disappear again within the maze that curled between it and him. A large satellite disc atop the flat roof pointed northeastward, aimed in the general direction of the orbits of the several satellites which followed each other's traverse above the continent. No windows. No apparent electronic security devices to alert the Sector Coordinator to approaching visitors. Such devices would be distracting to the man or woman, whose job it was to assure that the controlling machinery was cared for. Windows would tempt one to break the monotony by looking out them; security devices would be constantly tripped by wildlife, distracting to the man or woman. What if the Coordinator were a woman? What then? But, they would not put a woman in so remote a post as this one... surely.

Jacob crouched in the last of the high grass 15 feet from the foliage through which he had just passed and 40 yards from the blockhouse, which sat half-hidden within a copse across the small clearing. He pulled the backpack from his shoulders and checked through it, finding a liquid-filled bottle, chloroform, and a thick roll of gauze.

If he were wrong; if there were security contrivances... No time to be concerned now. He crouched lower and struggled with the backpack, slipping it over his arms and into place over his shoulders and back.

He crawled infiltration-course style, staying as flat as possible and moving across the wet, decomposing vegetation. Its stench took his breath. The humidity caused his face flesh to drip sweat, which trickled into and burned his eyes when he raised his head to see how far he had come and how far he had to go. Another 20 meters or so. Most of it, up a slight incline from the depression where he now must slither through several meters of mud.

Quick movement near his head! A hissing noise, like air escaping, only in short, uneven bursts. A snake! Three-and-a-half feet directly in front of his venerable face! A gray-brown snake, thick as a man's wrist, its white mouth wide, its fangs curved daggers poised to deliver its venom!

His heart thumped wildly while he calculated whether the moccasin could reach his head from that distance. This type had an unusually long strike capability compared to other snakes. Must remain still, watch the nervous reptile. Back away out of range slowly... very slowly.

The snake broke its tight coil and swiftly undulated from Jacob's path, disappearing into the matted marsh-grass. Sweat ran into his eyes while he scanned the grass for the snake, for others that might lie nearby.

His senses brought to a new level of alertness by the encounter with the snake, he crouched moments later, beside the blockhouse and again pulled the backpack from his shoulders and checked its contents — Kerry Vinchey's .45 Army Colt, the chloroform, the British commando knife, the Allegiant device, wrapped in foil — all in order. He glanced at the watch borrowed from the pilot, almost time for the diversion.

He squatted against the building, strapped the knife and its holster to his right calf, and waited.

Seven minutes passed, then 12. There! The thumping whir of the engine! Within seconds the black machine appeared just above the trees. Approaching slowly, then hovering over the block building, its motor noise vibrating the air about his ears, causing the building and ground to quake as he made his way to the corner where the side and front of the building met. Would it work? Or would the man inside alert his superiors before checking the disturbance?

The metal door opened, slightly at first, then swung fully open. A man in a bright orange jumpsuit stepped into the smog-diffused light with one hand shielding his eyes from the brightness while he looked upward at the helicopter intruder. Jacob noticed a dark object in the man's right hand. A pistol! No! An automatic assault rifle! Raised now, taking aim at the aircraft. He had to move now! The weapon could bring the copter down in a single burst!

Would the INterface agent turn the fire upon him when he rushed? The helicopter's engine was deafening, the sound held close to the ground by the heavy, wet atmospheric conditions. The gunman would not see him until it was too late...maybe.

The thoughts raced, as did his legs, toward the man who now held the weapon with both hands, trying to zero in on the helicopter. He turned to meet Jacob as Jacob left his feet, knocking the Naxos agent to the ground with a body block. Both men scrambled for the rifle, which flew from the man's hand at the impact. The man was too powerful for Jacob, easily throwing him aside and crawling frantically toward the gun. Jacob was quicker, diving from several feet away and landing on the man's back, wrapping his right arm around the throat jerking upward with all his strength. The man reared up, straightening to throw his rider, but Jacob straightened with him and rode out the man's effort, ending up in a kneeling position behind the Sector Coordinator.

The bigger, stronger man got to one knee, his face scarlet and contorted; the jugular and heavy veins bulged while Jacob jerked and squeezed with all his strength. Suddenly, the man spasmed to his feet, but in a squatting position. He used all his leg power on one tremendous recoil backward, landing on Jacob's chest and stomach, forcing the air from his attacker's lungs.

The Sector Coordinator was on the smaller man, tearing at his face and throat with powerful hands, slamming his right fist against the side of Jacob's head. Jacob desperately searched his right leg with his fingertips while the man pressed his elbow against Jacob's Adam's apple. Lower-inching, crawling his fingers lower. The hard, horizontally ribbed handle! The black, deadly commando knife, free of its holster.

His vision becoming blurry, dark; if not now, it would be too late! In a heaving burst of effort, he arched upward with his back, buttocks and heels, at the same time turning abruptly onto his left side. The sudden change of position threw the heavier man off balance. Jacob thrust the 8-inch blade into the Coordinator's chest beneath the sternum. Blood gushed from where the knife blade remained lodged, drenching Jacob's right hand and forearm. The warm liquid's cupreous odor singed his nostrils while it saturated his clothing. He stared into the man's eyes, only inches from his own. They were bulging, straining to burst from their sockets. The mouth opened, dripping saliva, the swollen, blue lips quivering as if trying to form a word. A slow, gurgling whine escaped from between the man's clenched teeth. An unspoken appeal for help to the one who had taken his life, before the cold eyes turned upward until only their whites shown, reflecting the dingy yellow sky. A final, violent convulsion, expelling air, blood and expectorate from the agony-twisted mouth, then total surrender to death.

Still holding the handle of the knife, his gaze transfixed upon the lifeless eyes that glared back unseeingly. Jacob's hand seemed welded to the killing instrument locked through the dead man's breastbone by the blade's serrated upper edge. He did not see or hear someone running from the opening where the helicopter had moments before sat down.

"Jacob!" Vinchey said nothing more for several seconds, seeing the crimson gore. He pulled his friend free from the body, having to force Jacob's fingers from the knife handle. "Come on, Jake. You had no choice. He would've killed us both."

Standing in the doorway several minutes later, the men glanced apprehensively at the ashen-faced corpse they had just finished clothing in jeans and a blue denim shirt. Jacob knelt and covered the body with an Army blanket.

Vinchey put a hand on Jacob's shoulder. "He had to die. If not now, then when I got him to Putnamville."

"It's not the same. I've never killed like this... Not like this."

"You saved my life, Jake. You had no choice. He'd have brought us both down with that Uzi. We have too much to do to stand here flogging ourselves for something that had to be done. You said yourself, it's a war we're fighting. The man was our enemy. It's not wrong to defend yourself against an enemy who's trying to put you and the people you love in chains."

The rationalization and the image of Karen, painfully etched in his conscience, did much to relieve the guilt feeling. Vinchey was right. No time to mourn this agent of the Naxos devils. Too much to be done.

"Let's get on with it, then," he said, reaching into the backpack. "Heat the paraffin; I'll implant the transponder."

Each went about his task quickly, Vinchey melting the wax substance over the portable burner, Jacob placing the tiny metallic Allegiant, needle point first, against the back of the corpse's neck just below the occipital bone, gently, carefully inserting it into the death-cooling skin. Vinchey poured the now liquid wax into the mold Jacob prepared days before. With Jacob's help, he placed the dead man's right index finger and thumb into the molten paraffin and held the hand immobile while Jacob discharged C02 around the mold from the fire extinguisher taken from the helicopter.

"Now the latex," said Jacob after several minutes of cooling the wax. He carefully pulled the corpse's finger and thumb from the paraffin.

Vinchey melted the rubber-like substance, then poured it into another mold, this one consisting of three pieces — two solid metal finger-sized molds, both of which fit into the third containing the just-poured latex. Jacob cooled the mold apparatus with C02 until the latex compound was in a gelatinous state, at which time he pulled the two finger-like molds from the latex-filled mold, each finger now thick with the coagulating rubber substance. He then forced them downward into the mold of hardened paraffin where the dead man's finger and thumb had been moments before. Jacob held the mold assembly immobile while the pilot applied C02.

"Let's hope this works as well as it did when I was a kid using this stuff to make models of my hands and feet," Jacob said, glancing at the pilot and nodding that the molds had cooled long enough.

He carefully, slowly peeled the paraffin away from the now cooled rubber-covered molds, examining them to see that the removal had not damaged the latex stretched over the metal fingers.

Jacob touched the latex, then pulled the material and let it snap against the molds. "Good. It's set, now."

After rolling the rubber coverings down the molds until they came loose from the tips of the metal fingers, he placed one covering over his right index finger, the other over his right thumb, then rolled them carefully down each digit.

"Make the prints," he instructed Vinchey, who pressed the

tips of the dead man's right index finger and right thumb onto an ink pad, then onto a sheet of paper.

Jacob pressed his own latex-covered thumb and index finger against the ink pad then onto the paper below the dead man's prints. "Perfect!... Absolutely perfect, Jacob!"

Vinchey examined the two sets of prints with a magnifying glass, comparing first the thumb prints, then the index fingerprints. Jacob scrutinized them when the pilot finished and handed him the glass.

"They look perfect, but we don't know how precisely the computer analyzes the print impressions. They do look good though, don't they?"

"A human eye couldn't tell the difference."

"There's only one way to determine if the computer's eye can. There won't be but one chance to test it, if it's not good enough.

"You know what has to be done, Kerry." The men stood beneath the drooping blades of the helicopter, Vinchey pulling the parachute over his shoulders, then jumping it into place on his back. He reached to take Jacob's extended hand when he finished with the chute.

"You have any questions?" Jacob asked.

"No questions. My job will be simple compared to yours. I don't envy you."

"Yeah. I think I've prepared right for it. I've studied those tapes and papers until, now, I have to force them out of my mind. I've looked the equipment over and it's just about like I pictured it."

"You think the transponder will withstand the crash?" Vinchey nodded toward the Sector Coordinator's body, which sat strapped in the helicopter's right seat.

"It's supposed to survive just about anything, according to the tapes. The main thing we have to make sure of is that the body doesn't survive in an identifiable form."

"I'll find the deepest gorge in the area and drop it from 2,000 or so. It'll have full tanks, so there should be some kind of explosion when it hits. Shouldn't be enough left to give them any clue to how many people were in the bird."

"Can you get out safely?"

"There's some risk, of course. I don't look forward to it, but if I didn't think I'd make it, I wouldn't do it."

"You're sure it will burn?"

"I guarantee it. I've put an incendiary charge with an impact detonator on one of the tanks."

"That's going to add to your risk."

"If I'm going to lose the chopper, I'm going to make sure it counts for something. It'll be okay. Just have to make sure I don't run into any trees on the way up."

"I'm sorry about your helicopter, Kerry."

"I'll borrow another one somewhere. Don't worry about it. I just hope they pick up on the signal sent by that thing."

"The crash will be well within their range. They'll pick up on it." Jacob shook Vinchey's hand again, then pulled the pilot to himself for a brief embrace. "Take care, Kerry. I can't afford to lose any more friends. And take care of those ladies. They've meant a lot to me."

His own tone and the emotion evident in the pilot's eyes summed up their feelings. They were, unless some unbelieved-in force who determined fate willed otherwise, seeing each other for the last time.

CHAPTER 17

Brilliant light flashed then faded; a tremendous blast sounded then diminished to rumbling. Jacob's attention was yanked to the glowing cloud that climbed to the top of the screen and spread, forming a boiling mushroom head.

"This is the barbarous act of the Jewish slime who infect INterface... who stand between humanity and peace!"

He straightened in the folding chair, his mind sorting the present from remembrance. The explosion! Was it the helicopter, carrying the Sector Coordinator's body and the Allegiant tracking device, blowing in its fiery consummation at the bottom of some New England gorge?

Confusion cleared, his eyes giving his brain the necessary view of the room around him, of the giant viewing screen where the nuclear cloud continued its spreading ascension. Facility 500, its own ambience of terror surrounding his senses, bringing him back to the reality of the present!

He ran his fingers along the belt of explosives, feeling the metal ridges and bumps that made up the detonator. Strange, the comfort his power to devastate gave at this moment. The choice of whether to live or die was not his to make; the power to choose how and when to die, was.

"Egypt is a wasteland, thanks to the Jew. How many more areas of our once pristine planet must suffer before these Jews are brought to an accounting for their plagues?!"

The narrator's voice put the question while the video changed from the mushroom cloud to black-uniformed controllers holding perhaps 50 people at bay with automatic rifles and dogs.

Hundreds of bystanders surrounded the controllers and the frightened prisoners, who were forced to back against a high brick barrier and pack closely together until their total mass resembled, from the camera's vantage well above them, a swarm of wasps milling about their symmetrical nest. Prisoners who tried to escape the pack were bludgeoned back into the swarm, or set upon by several of the big dogs. Spectators threw objects into the mass, more than once striking one or the other of the prisoners and knocking them unconscious. A small child squirted free of the pack, but was picked up by one of the controllers and flung into the center of the mass, which appeared to absorb the child. "Witness now the fate of subhuman enemies who pervert and destroy that which TRINITY has given the citizens of the earth's first soon-to-be perfect society!"

The voice, no longer calm, rose to threatening volume. A truck moved between the taunting spectators and the people against the barricade. Several orange-uniformed people, wearing helmets which completely covered their heads and draped over part of their upper bodies, spilled from the truck. One of the helmeted men shouted and motioned for the spectators to move back in order to clear a larger space between themselves and the people, who appeared doomed to a fate Jacob could not resist watching.

Hoses were unrolled from the rear of the truck's large,

square tank. The helmeted men and women, wearing what looked to be heavy, insulated gloves that extended to their elbows, pointed the nozzles at the terrified people against the brick wall and, upon verbal order, one of the operators released liquid, which shot in a yellow-orange, high-pressure stream, soaking the prisoners.

Their shrieks tore at his ears, and he wanted to turn his eyes from the ghastly video, but could not. Acid? Were the poor devils being hosed with some highly caustic liquid? No... No smoke from dissolving clothing and flesh. Not acid. What then?

His answer was quick in coming. The truck operator, who had turned the valves releasing the liquid, now held a black nozzle pointed at the soaked victims, some of whom tried to run from the mass but were beaten back. Pathetic souls. Men, women, tiny children, now gawking silently, submissively at the helmeted men and women standing with the instruments of death pointed at them. Pitiable forms, suddenly resembling stark black and white photographic images of war-torn captives in some long ago conflict. Their eyes no longer wide with fear, just weary of the struggle, and resigned to what must come next.

Flame gushed from the nozzle into the people. In an instant, they became a collective boiling, rolling ball of yellow and red flame, black shoots of oily smoke streaming upward. Gasoline!

Burning, flailing forms ran spastically, or jumped wildly, or crawled, then crumbled into dying heaps, soon becoming individual smoldering cinders. Most died and turned to charcoal in the middle of the huddle against the brick wall, unable to break free of the prison of searing, melting flesh that surrounded them. All movement stopped in less than two minutes and the flames went out, finally, leaving a mound of black, smoking corpses.

"Such will be the end of all illegal Jews from this moment on, who are caught outside the impounds. Jewry must be quarantined, isolated from human beings, lest mankind continues to be infected by their cancerous sub-race!"

To be alone with the narrator in this room --his gaping, brutish mouth spewing insane hatred, would make his own death worthwhile. To see the look on the narrator's face when Jacob exposed the belt of explosives and made the man know he was about to push the detonator, would make dying almost joyous. Instead, depression that the fantasy could not be realized.

"Like in all of nature, there is a place for scavengers, for parasites, for bacteria... under, of course, the right controls." The video changed from incinerated corpses to shabbily dressed, underweight people digging and scraping sludge from various surfaces which were impossible to identify because of the brevity of the quick cut, close-up shots. Only the looks on the thin faces remained consistent. Hollow, life-less eyes and drooping mouths, while the people went about their exhausting work under the watchful glares of black-uniformed controllers and the huge police dogs. No ques-tion. They knew — knew that he was Jacob Zen. That he was a Jew. Eyes peering at him from unseen cameras mounted in the walls, in the ceiling, behind the screen. They had known for... how long?

"Even as the processes of natural order depend upon the rodents, the vultures, the parasitic bacteria to clean the excretory by-products of life, so the Jew shall be utilized to remove the wastes from INterface. The Universal Mind has not randomly placed life, but rather intends all life to work in its own appointed way to serve the Universal Body. The Jew's natural function was meant to be that of the scaveng-ing, cleansing parasite, proving that the great Universal Organism, of which we, individually, are cells, can use even the lowliest, most repugnant creatures for the good. TRINITY decrees that those individual Jews who choose to serve their predestined purposes will live until their destinies are fulfilled on behalf of INterface. If not, they must join their kindred in burnt sacrifice to the well-being of the Universal Body."

The series of video quick-cuts continued, while the narrator's voice became less caustic.

"Those you see here were relatives of those Jew criminals who went underground, after detonating the nuclear devices which destroyed Damascus and Cairo, and long before that, New York."

The narrator's tone again became hateful. "More of their relatives will be rounded up and burned, until those responsible are caught or come forward to accept responsibility for their heinous crimes against civilized man!"

The screen darkened and the room was in total silence for several seconds. Jacob's heart pounded in his ears, and in his throat; perspiration soaked through his shirt at the chest and underarms, and ran uncomfortably down his belly and sides. What next? Was their teasing torture finished?

The screen lighted slowly, becoming an expanse of dark and darker shadows, interspersed with varying intensities of light. Momentarily the scene became distinguishable; the figure of a man sat in a huge, high-backed chair, dominating the screen. The face could not be discerned, although the totality of the figure, which drew closer, was somehow familiar. When the camera zoomed in on the sitting figure's head, which was cloaked in harsh shadows, the image spoke.

"You are not here, at this place, at this time, without purpose. Your destiny is tied, unalterably, to the Jew. You cannot escape your responsibility. The time is now to pay the debt owed."

The deep voice, vaguely familiar yet alien, reverberated as

if in a metal drum; the lower part of the face became illuminated enough to see the pale lips move. Shivers of chill shot upward into the back of Jacob's neck and spread throughout the nerves running ovaled over his scalp. A voice of demons, directly from the hell of Naxos, informing the condemned that INterface, that TRINITY, that the controllers, were on to his deception. Aware that he was a Jew, that he was not John I. Carver, but Jacob Zen, murderer of history's most beloved product, Herrlich Krimhler. Telling him they had known all along that Jacob Zen did not die in the helicopter explosion and fire, known all along that Sector Coordinator 550 had been replaced by the number one enemy of INterface.

But why wait so long to close the jaws of the trap? Why now? Here? What price would they exact from him for his treachery? But they could not. He, Jacob Zen, controlled his own time and method of dying. Again, like before when his nerves began to fray, the thought calmed him.

"You cannot escape notice of TRINITY. Your every activity is known and felt by the great Cosmic Mind, whether for the good of INterface, or to the detriment."

Sliding doors parted on both sides of the screen, and one Controller walked from each opening in military fashion. Jacob's hand went involuntarily to the thick detonator on the belt of explosives. His index finger gingerly feeling for the button that would obliterate himself and the INterface policemen.

"You will stand and submit to the officers, who will discharge their duty."

The controllers advanced and stood beside the chair where he sat, cold sweat drenching his body. An uncontrollable twitch began in his left cheek, drawing that side of his face, he imagined, into an easily observable mask of fear. He was afraid, the will to survive fighting its way to the forefront of his emotions. But not terrified, still in control, still capable of pushing the button. It would all be over in an instant. A quick burst of pain, then oblivion. His fingertip rested firmly against the button.

His nerves settled while he stood from the chair still facing the screen, not allowing his eyes to turn in the direction of the controllers, but able to see them with his peripheral vision. When they moved toward him, tried to touch him, he would do it! If only the dark figure on the screen could be there to feel his lethal hatred!

"You have proven through your actions to be worthy of the reward you will now receive, Sector Coordinator Five, Five, Zero."

Sector Coordinator! Why would INterface address him as Sector Coordinator? If they knew, would they not call the name, Jacob Zen? Maybe they didn't know that he was Zen. Maybe they simply had observed him in his secret Bible readings, in his clandestine note taking. Perhaps he talked in his Trachetrol-troubled sleep. Maybe...

"Shortly, you will be brought for initiation into INterface Council, where you shall be installed as Quadrant Overseer."

Feeling drained from his body; his knees started to buckle. A hot flood of realization that he had escaped the hand of the INterface executioners filled him with emotion. Something akin to gratitude replaced hatred. He had not been sentenced to death, but was being rewarded for performing well on behalf of INterface!

"Well done, good and faithful servant. Welcome into the kingdom," the voice said tenderly, before the image of the robed man faded from the screen, which then went black.

"I'm Controller Six, Six, Six, Seven, Zero, Two, sir. We're here to help you prepare for the initiation. We will assist in getting your affairs in order here, before your move."

Jacob looked blankly into the black-uniformed officer's

eyes, able after what seemed to him an eternity to answer. "Thank you."

He sat in the chair again, weak from the sudden change the direction of his emotions had taken.

"If you will get together your personal items as soon as possible, sir. You have been replaced at your Sector Coordinator post. You will leave at twenty-four hundred hours for Jerusalem."

The city had changed little since he was first here as a boy of 13. The one large exception being that the Mosque of Omar, sitting atop Mount Moriah with its golden dome glinting under an unusually bright sky, now shared the plot of holy real estate with an even more beautiful structure. The new Davidic temple. The building of limestone and granite, ornately scrolled and guarded at its front by traditional columnar statuary, was a part of the first peace settlement.

The Arabs had agreed to officially recognize Israel's right to exist and let the nation live in peace and security, guaranteed by NATO's armed might. In exchange, Israel, unbelievably, in the eyes of most geopolitical experts, disbanded its military complex and agreed to co-exist with the Palestinian state created for the Arabs of the region. The crown jewel of the peace agreement, as the Israeli Prime Minister said at the time, was the Muslim acquiescence on the question of Jewish access to the holy sites of Mount Moriah. The Arab agreement to allow the temple's construction brought about great pressure to make peace, so that even the hard-line anti-Arab elements within Israel saw the wisdom and the desirability of putting aside their hatreds.

For reasons no one could pinpoint, new troubles for the Jews began shortly after the signing of that peace accord. Not from the Arabs, but from anti-Semitic factions within the Unified European States. Rumblings which grew into U.E.S. policy, first insisting that all people of Jewish descent register so that the U.E.S. could keep track of their movements (for the purpose of assuring the Jews' safety, they said).

The troubles grew until there were instituted huge impounds where Jews were kept, for their own good, of course. Accused of being militants "warring against a peaceful Earth," by one member of U.E.S. Council, persecutions increased, becoming full-blown genocide, now, under INterface rule. Righteous genocide, in the name of God and His blueprint for the salvation of the planet. References to Adolf Hitler, to the Third Reich, to Auschwitz, Dachau, Belsen, The Final Solution, were expunged from historical records through computer ingenuity, when all books not sanctioned by INterface were eliminated, and the accepted books were re-filed in the INRU system after careful editing. A new birth had taken place; all else had died with the Great Dissolution when millions of disbelievers were ejected from the New Age earth preparing to quickly evolve into its originally intended perfection. This magnificent temple had become, instead of a blessing to the Jew, a curse almost beyond believability. All edicts, the decisions and theories of the masters relating to all matters religious and racial, came from here. The Jew was the epicenter of all that was evil. That evil symbolically emanated from this building, therefore, the cleansing must begin here.

Jacob's stomach crawled with contempt while he walked the cavernous, echoing corridors of the temple, recalling how the INterface shock-troops had stormed into this once holy place, slaughtering the rabbis and others while they were offering the daily sacrifice to their God. How INterface Response Units throughout the system had displayed the gore, while the blood of the Jewish priesthood flowed across altars meant for animal blood: *"When ye, therefore, shall see the abomination of desolation, spoken of by Daniel the prophet, stand in the holy place...*

"... Who opposeth and exalteth himself above all that is called God, or that is worshiped, so that he, as God, sitteth in the temple of God, showing himself that he is God...

"...And woe unto those who are with child, and to those who nurse children in those days...

"...For then shall be great tribulation, such as was not since the beginning of the world to this time, no, nor ever shall be..."

The words from Marchek's old Bible coursed through his mind. He did not remember the exact verses and chapters, only the words that seemed to fit together, although disparate when he had read them. Jacob's mind filled with dread while sounds of footsteps thundered off the polished granite walls. The gratitude of Master Manya, of INterface. A reward for a job well done. *"When ye, therefore, shall see the abomination of desolation... stand in the holy place..."*

The huge temple, a shadowy mausoleum, devoid of life; dank and suffocating. Like a visit to one's own tomb before death, contrasted with sunny, glorious remembrances of a youth they could not program out. The controllers and Jacob stopped before two large, brass doors, studded in sculptured-relief with gold, silver and various precious stones. The doors, each more than 15 feet tall, opened noiselessly, wide enough for the three men to walk between them. Lights radiating from prism-design sculptures within the vast chamber dazzled the eye with beautiful flashes of colors, while music, religious in presentation, dominated the senses, setting in motion, simultaneously, feelings of euphoria and apprehension. The urge to shout ecstatically, triumphantly — to weep dismally for what was a personal victory that could not be claimed. He stood at the heart of the monster which had gobbled up all he had ever, could ever, hold dear.

Suddenly alone, he turned 360 degrees where he stood at the center of the black marble-floored room, surveying the glistening walls of jewels, made fantastically effulgent by the light given off by the prism-sculptures. His body lurched slightly through no movement of his own, and to keep from falling he instinctively corrected his stance on the floor, which, he now realized, was descending slowly. A circular platform, carrying him to a silent stop on the floor of the room below.

Lighting was poor in this chamber — that there was any light at all becoming apparent only after several seconds of letting his eyes adjust. Again he turned slowly where he stood, taking in his new surroundings while his heartbeat accelerated with the passing seconds. A sense of nakedness, of impending judgment, crashed with each pulse against his cranium. Had he removed the belt of explosives prematurely?

Shadows ranging from light gray to black hugged the distant sides of the room at points 10 feet apart, disrupting the plane of the dark purple walls. Robed figures, their heads covered with hoods. Motionless specters, their faces black, beckoning holes of judgment. Stone monuments lifelessly witnessing yet another victory for INterface.

Blinding light! Everything washed out before his eyes! Then he could see again when the radiance dimmed to a level slightly greater than when he entered the chamber. Before him stood a platform, its outline gleaming in the still scant illumination. A pyramid, which looked to have been chiseled from a single, gargantuan crystal. At its apex sat a human form, which, like the gray stone figures against the purple walls, was shadowy and cloaked in a hooded robe. Master Manya! INterface personified!

The hooded head moved. Shifted its faceless hole within the hood downward toward him. Again the feeling of naked-ness, of having been stripped of his ability to keep his thoughts constrained within his own skull. "Sector Coordi-nator Five, Five, Zero..."

The voice was the same as that on the INRU, computerized in tone, and staccato in delivery. It seemed to come directly from within the facial void. "Yours is a most glorious opportunity..."

The voice grew in volume; the room seemed to move, closing toward Jacob. The hooded figures! They had come to life and were moving toward him from where they had stood along the walls! They closed until they formed a tight circle around him and the crystal pyramid.

"To serve INterface is to serve your brothers and sisters. To serve TRINITY is to serve God. You have done both with devotion, Five, Five, Zero. And so you shall be rewarded."

Moaning sounds, the sounds of human beings in extreme discomfort, filled the darkened room, rising in volume until the room seemed an echo chamber, as if the cries came from within a gigantic metal barrel. Simultaneously, the crystal throne filled with light, dim at first, becoming brighter while the volume of the moanings increased until the radiance forced Jacob to look away.

"Your reward shall include the honor of helping rid us of our enemies."

The light dimmed, the center of the pyramid beneath the figure becoming an indistinguishable blur, which slowly focused into a holographic image of perhaps 50 people huddled together, on their faces expressions of barely controlled terror. Any moment their collective calm would melt before INterface justice; they would erupt into mass panic, and the violence would begin. The small children would eject from the mob; the weaker adults would be trampled in the vicious churning of the death-trap.

"At the same time, it will serve as your initiation into INterface Overseer Council..."

The holographic image was more three-dimensional, more life-like than any he had seen. Like he, himself, could step into the crowd of doomed people, whose sickly eyes, sunken deeply within dark sockets, glistened with fear. Mouths gaping, some with fear-paralysis, others from pain caused by the crush of bodies.

"...an act that few citizens have had, or shall ever have the opportunity to perform on behalf of INterface Universal!"

The voice rose in pitch. For the first time, it sounded of emotion that was fanatically prideful. The hooded figures surrounding Jacob and the pyramid emitted soft chanting words he could not understand, while the faces of the holographic image became clearer. Each face was now a real person rather than mere blurs of human flesh, presented vividly at little more than arm's length from Jacob's own shocked gaze.

"Your voice signal will order these despicable enemies of INterface eradicated. They shall be purged from our midst with the righteous flame of INterface Universal's indignation!"

Jacob felt the heated rush of blood bathe his brain and cause his face skin to tingle, then burn. He felt the descending liquids' warmth wash the length of his body, each portion of his flesh enduring the sting in its turn. The first time he had felt really alive since he gouged life from the Sector Coordinator. But the living was only for the pain, not for life; he was, in his tormented spirit, within the hologram — doomed. He knew in that excruciating instant that he would do the unthinkable. He would give the order to murder these innocents. He would do it for the sake of staying alive, himself. To live so he could fight the beast from within its diseased brain. So a by-gone world might return. So humankind might work and play and love again.

No!! Self took over somewhere between Facility 500 and his arrival at the temple. Probably upon removal of the belt of explosives, when he lost the right to select the time and method of his death. Burning these pitiful creatures, choosing to stay alive, drawing precious breath for as long as the masters allowed.

Dark eyes from the holographic hell--eyes with helpless looks, like the many thousands of expressions he had seen since INterface justice was instituted, drew him, told him through their wordless hopelessness that this was the future. His own end, eventually, ultimately. Eyes tugging at his humanity. Familiar eyes, setting off feelings he thought seared over by his burning hatred for INterface.

He knew those eyes, reaching to him from the image within the pyramid, and he wept bitterly. Karen's eyes!

CHAPTER 18

All flesh blurred except that of Karen's lovely face, its olive smooth, unalloyed beauty within the holographic horror at the center of the pyramid. He could reach in, take her hand and draw her to himself. They could walk away together into another place, another time. With Karen... at last!

"Eliminator Three stands ready to receive your order. INterface awaits your command to bring retribution upon our enemies!"

Her expression, fearful but not panicked. Calmly prepared for INterface's decision about her fate. For his decision. The marvelous brown eyes he had so often looked into during their most intimate times trusting, loving him.

"Sector Coordinator Five, Five, Zero, Eliminator Three is standing by for your command," the voice said with more force from beneath the hood.

The hologram began to weaken, obscuring Karen's features, then causing the image to degenerate into an indistinguishable, pink-hued blob within the crystal pyramid. Although he felt chilled, sweat rolled from his hairline downward over his gaunt face. Was it Karen he had seen moments earlier? Really Karen? Were the monsters forcing him to snuff out the only light there was for him? The hope of seeing Karen again. Or was it some perverse synapse to neuron short-circuiting malfunction of his Trachetrol-damaged brain, cruelly tricking him into believing the face had been Karen's?

Refusing to give the order would not save this stranger, who happened to look like Karen somewhat. To refuse would make no difference to the poor people in that pre-death huddle. To refuse would mean his fight against the masters was ended. This woman his unreliable vision gathered for his drug-soaked thought processes was not Karen Mossberg. Even if she were Karen, she could not be helped by his refusal to do what they demanded. If he said "no," someone else would do it; he would, himself, die with them, or by some other even more grisly method.

"INterface Universal must be avenged, Five, Five, Zero. Give the command to incinerate this garbage heap!"

The hologram focused into a sharp image; instantaneously, his eyes found those of the woman. She seemed to see him also, their spirits meshing in that moment, even though the hologram separated one from another. Karen! No...The face was too thin, the features too sharp, the hair too dry in appearance. Too old. It was not her. She was gone from him forever.

"Speak the word 'terminate'—It shall be done," the voice instructed.

Their times together flooded his memory with sadly sweet reflections of what they had been to each other. The girl in the hologram, her dark, beautiful eyes haunting, magnetically pulling him. Her eyes. Karen's eyes. All thoughts converged in a reddish wash of pain; cranial pressure expanded, threatening to explode his head!

"Terminate!" Jacob's own voice startled him when he commanded the murder. It sounded as if the word issued from a part of him he did not know. Shutting his eyes, thereby not seeing the fruit of his act of self-preservation, was one way to relieve the inner torment, at least for the moment.

But the lids refused to close. His eyes stubbornly fixed instead on the image. His concentration on that one face, whose look of resignation more compelled his attention the harder he tried to tear away. Her expression reflected pity for him, that he had chosen his own pathetic continued existence over her life. Reflected forgiveness for what he had done.

When would the gasoline be released? Then ignited by the flame throwers, making his command to burn her irreversible. Any second, an inferno. The beautiful face would erupt in flames.

"To mark this personal honor for you, Five, Five, Zero, we have decided to exterminate this pack of scum one by one. For your pleasure and ours."

When the voice atop the throne had spoken, the hooded figures encircling Jacob parted to form two lines, one on either side of him, stretching from the pyramid's base to the walls. A noise behind him prompted him to turn from the throne to face another wall.

"A very special execution, Five, Five, Zero..."

The wall lifted from the floor and disappeared into the high ceiling, revealing a woman being held by her arms in the grip of black-uniformed controllers who stood in rigid posture on either side of her. Behind them sat a platform several feet tall, with steps leading to its surface, which had at its center a device resembling an ancient stock, with holes for hands and head.

"A young female Jew, who has eluded INterface security

for the final time. An enemy who is responsible for countless deaths of 'IN' brothers and sisters. Now we shall be entertained by her death."

The hooded figure atop the pyramid throne became mockingly compassionate.

"However, our mercy is great. We do not inflict lingering pain, even upon those who would do us harm."

Like fly-papered to walls, and psychologically and physically tortured and prodded and probed with their own deepest fears. Like setting babies on fire. Jacob's thoughts ran swiftly, calculating the INterface inhumanity he had witnessed, wondering what they intended to do to the helpless young woman who looked so frail beside the big controllers.

"This Jewess shall die quickly for her sins against INterface Universal." Machinery emerged from the platform and automatically made its attachments to the stock device while the hooded figure continued to speak. "Each of these Jews will be executed individually rather than collectively as is usual extermination procedure. This liquidation will be recorded for future transmission through INterface Response Unity, to serve as example for those who work against the magnificent design for perfecting our world. Approach the Termination area, Five, Five, Zero. Enjoy with us the liquidation of this enemy."

Some of the robed figures behind him walked forward, nudging him toward the girl and her executioners. Her head was down, her dark hair concealing her facial features. While he approached, she seemed to compose herself, erecting, then shaking her head so that her hair shook free from her face. Karen!

From behind and from both sides of him, the hooded ones began chanting a low, humming mantra. They moved closer until they formed a tightly-wedged half circle around him. Their chants grew louder.

Jacob's emotions filled with the haplessness and finality of his predicament. The sickening truth was that Karen would be butchered. He could do nothing to save her. But, that was not the truth either. The sickness in the pit of his stomach and the paralysis was cowardice-generated. She must die because to try to stop them would mean that he, too, would die. "Keep quiet and live," the inner voice kept saying.

"Because of your sins against the Universal Mind and for your crimes against INterface, go to your death, Jews!"

They knew! The monsters knew! That he was not John I. Carver. That she was Karen Mossberg, Jacob Zen's greatest love. In some presciently incredible way, they knew everything, and worked their plan masterfully, bringing it to this moment of supreme cruelty! It was, in its way, crueler than the death they contrived for the victim fly-papered to the wall, whose own phobia-demons caused the bats to ravage his body. Perfect revenge for Jacob Zen's sins against INterface.

His love knelt before the gleaming stock, forced to her knees by one of the controllers, who stood behind her while the other INterface policeman, standing in front of the stock, gripped her hair and pulled it toward himself, forcing her throat against the bottom notch. The top half of the stock clanked against the lower, trapping her head. Another device arose electronically from the platform and swung into position high above her head, automatically attaching itself to the top of two stainless steel poles. The Decap Unit was ready to do its deadly work.

They had manipulated him to this moment, like they shaped all things wicked. Karen's lovely face must tumble into the chrome box to provide them their sadistic pleasure. Droning, mechanized descent of the glinting blade, its edge touching the velvet neck his lips touched during those times of sweetness their love created in the nights of that long ago age. Her beautiful head in the gory ugliness of that metal basket. The blood gushing with each beat of the heart he had felt pulsing while pressed against her while she warmed him, insulating him against a world that was cold and cruel even then. Darkness descending with that terrible blade. Vomit rising from a point just beneath the Adam's apple. His legs, their strength draining. Consciousness fading... "Jacob Zen!"

The voice, miles from him, behind him, bringing light again, retrieving conscious thought. "Jacob Zen!"

His arms in the grip of strong hands, bracing him while strength came again into his legs.

"Lift your eyes, Jacob Zen! Behold the goodness and mercy that is INterface Universal!"

His brain processed a kaleidoscope of reds, yellows and blues in designs that swirled out of control behind eyes that would not focus. He, out of reflexive obedience, lifted his head to look at the execution platform. An apparition, formless, blurry, moved within the kaleidoscopic vortex, taking on shape and substance. Three figures standing between him and the platform of death. The two controllers, hulking and dark, one on either side of a small human form. Jacob blinked to clear his vision, tried to restore reason. Was this death? Had he died? "Jacob, it's me. It's Karen." Straightening, squinting, the forms became clear.

"Karen?"

"Yes, my love. It's really me."

"Karen!"

Tears came while he sobbed the name, drenching the flame of hatred for INterface, flooding his emotions with love for the one who meant everything to him; beautiful Karen, her arms outstretched to him... Alive!

Their embrace, experiencing again her soft warmth, her

fragrance, brought convulsions of joy. She returned his love, yet maintained control of her own feelings while they stood locked in reunion. When he looked, finally, into her eyes, seeing they were filled not with tears but with patient tolerance, his sense of propriety took control. He suddenly felt sheepish standing in the middle of the circle of their robed companions.

"You see, Jacob. You must not be independent of TRIN-ITY, who loves us so much," Karen said, smiling, gently urging him to turn toward the pyramid of crystal. "I was wrong. Wrong about everything. Dr. Marchek was wrong. You have been wrong, my darling Jacob." Her worshipful gaze was upon the hooded one sitting at the top of the dazzling throne.

"Approach, Jacob Zen." The words issued from the blackness within the hood. The tone was benign, unlike when it ordered the feigned execution.

They moved together to the base of the throne, Karen's touch assuring there was nothing to fear.

"You have been the prodigal, Jacob Zen. But you are home, now. Welcome, Son, to the kingdom you shall share with our brothers and sisters of INterface."

Jacob was in shock from the past minutes of deception and revelation, and from holding Karen again after reconciling himself to her death — all of which served to short-circuit his hatred for INterface. The shock, however, began to wear off.

Questions blazed to life again in his reeling brain. Chief among them: Why was he chosen? He had killed INterface agents and dealt the Naxos-centered state misery, proving his incorrigible animosity toward them. Why had they set him up for blame in the killing of Herrlich Krimhler? The drugging in Fredria VanHorne's Naxos bedroom and implantation of the Allegiant. Why did they hold him up before the world as assassin of the beloved leader? Make him the most hated, hunted man in history, then deceive him by forcing him to supposedly order the beheading of the person dearest to him, only to hold him to their breast as the prodigal returned? And, the most mind-scalding question of all, why would Karen, whose thought processes, actions and reactions he knew nearly as well as he knew his own, why would she take part in such a sham, knowing the danger he was in, knowing the agonies he had endured in the past few emotion-rending minutes?

Standing at the base of the pyramid throne, he alone looked upward to the figure. The face, though still not distinguishable because of the stark shadows created by the hood, had sharp, dramatic features which caught small fragments of light that dimly outlined the brow, nose and chin. The black area, where the mouth should be, appeared not to move. The robed, hooded figures and Karen stood with heads bowed, while the voice spoke in a tone displaying displeasure.

"Thou hast sinned against INterface, Jacob Zen. Against your brothers and sisters, who want only to be free to create the world of goodness and plenty they deserve. That world can be constructed only by the Six Ways to Peace given by Herrlich Krimhler. For your disruptive treacheries against that great design, you deserve everlasting punishment." The voice softened again. "However, because the chief building block that will bring heaven to earth is love, you are forgiven your trespasses and accepted into this Circle of Order, never to break its continuity, while we reach for perfection through the Six Ways to Peace."

"Six Ways to Law," the robed figures around Jacob chanted softly when the voice from atop the pyramid paused.

"TRINITY speaks! It shall be done!" the voice said from the throne.

"Six Ways to Order," the encircling voices chanted in unison.

"Six! Six! Six!" the voice said from the throne's apex.

"Six Ways to Peace! Six! Six! Six!" the group surrounding Jacob chanted rhythmically.

"Go now, and sin no more. Greet your family. INterface Body awaits, with great love and goodness and peace!" Feeling the crush of those closing around him, Jacob turned, catching glimpses of faces within the hoods. Hands touching, pulling him. Bodies pushing against Karen and him, forcing them together. The aggressors' incantational fervor growing, quickening in cadence, then, suddenly stopping. "Welcome home, Jacob."

The voice, impossible to forget! From a life-long father-son relationship of love. The one who spoke removed the crimson hood. "Uncle Conrad!"

His own joyous hug met with a comforting embrace by Wilson, who held him then at arm's-length, gripping his foster son's shoulders.

"We were so wrong, Jacob... so mistaken. Fighting those who love us is the greatest wrong we can do. America's goodness, her humanity, is not sacrificed. She is enhanced and magnified, my boy. Her beauty and grace, her essence, is here within INterface Body. The unproductive and nonproductive, the callous disregard for humanism, for civil and human rights, the evils, have been purged by TRINITY, with the loving guidance of Master Manya. Pure love, free of contamination."

All others in the circle removed their hoods and Jacob glanced around the innermost ring surrounding him, Karen and Conrad Wilson.

Their features came into focus slowly through vision blurred with tears. Melissa Jensen and Fredria VanHorne, both looking at him with weak, uninterpretable smiles on their colorless lips. Kerry Vinchey, too, with the same dispassionate expression that would not translate into meaning. Silent, grinning mouths beneath stuporous, mannequin stares.

"Your friends have been with you through your rebellion, while you found your way home," the voice from the shining throne said. "INterface Body shall never forsake our own."

Pink diffused into lavender and lavender into purples of darkening hues, which mingled with and became lost within the deepening blue of the Jerusalem twilight. Never had the western sky appeared so beautiful. A horizon worthy of the one who walked at his side, her soft hair lifting gently and brushing against his shoulder when the uncharacteristically fresh, cooling wind caught it and moved its loveliness. Her delicate scent filled his nostrils, almost succeeding for the moment in wiping from his thoughts the altered realities of their changed world.

Karen's physical presence was enough for now, the fire of her will seemingly quenched, leaving the impression of caricature. But she was here. Whether real or imitation, this Karen was here, and he would, for the moment, savor her on whatever terms, in whatever condition the masters allowed.

They walked along the roofs ornate edge, his arm around her, her pretty face reflecting the colors of the day's final rays.

"What happened after we talked on the phone that night I was in Brussels?"

"We mustn't dwell on things that are in times before INterface. We gain nothing by looking into the flawed past, only by looking toward a perfect future," she said without hesitation, as if her response required no time for thinking. "I am well, aren't I? I haven't been harmed in any way. Why concern yourself with what was? We must go forward... into perfection. It is what was meant for us from the beginning."

"Perfection? You really believe that this will lead to perfection?"

"Yes I do, and you will too, after tonight, when you've heard Master Manya explain things. Only he can explain perfection. Master Manya is the singular, unchangeable example of love, my darling Jacob."

"So I've heard. But what about the people they're killing? What about the babies I've seen slaughtered by this... TRINITY, who is leading us into perfection?"

"Harmful organisms within Universal Body must be excised, Jacob, so we, as one, can evolve to the highest ascended order."

"And what is the selection process? Why are some of us privileged to evolve while others are butchered or forced into slavery? Just like every totalitarian state that has ever existed? What about this genocide, Karen? The Jews. And where do we fit in? They know you and I are Jews."

She stopped walking, and pulled away from him, a stern expression on her face. "You must never speak of the Jews, or of the past. Only of perfection, of the future perfecting of man by man."

"Why didn't they kill me? I fought them. I'm still fighting them in my thoughts."

"TRINITY will explain all tonight," she said, calming. "Patience, my darling, is a virtue second only to divine love for our Master Manya. He will explain why your rebellion has been allowed for the good of INterface Body. All things work together for the good to those who love TRINITY."

A stranger walked at his side. Totally different from the Karen who had cared for him like no other. Not the same girl who was terrified that night they did with her whatever was done — changed her, like they changed, for the worse, everything they touched. They took her from him as surely as if they had taken her life. Killed Karen, like they were murdering so many others every second that ticked.

"We're together again, Sweetie. Isn't that all that matters? We are together. One with TRINITY, through INterface Body. There is no higher purpose or condition in our present evolutionary state than to be joined one to another."

She parroted, with identical inflection to the hooded one atop the pyramid, automatically saying words that preempted her own conceptual will.

"Master Manya will give all answers it is good for us to know. He only wants the best for us. He will tell us why you are forgiven your transgressions against the great Universal Mind-Father."

"You mean God?"

"The only God, who was and is. Who has overcome the counterfeit who thought he could usurp the Great Cosmogonal Throne. He is the Most High. The Great Universal Mind-Father of evolved humanity. But it is not yet time for talk of these things. All will be revealed during the Convocation, when Master Manya speaks."

To try reason with her or to question further would be futile. Her dark, beautiful eyes glistened, staring unblinkingly at the robed, hooded forms silhouetted blackly against the glow toward which he and Karen walked. Remain silent. Become a part of it all. The best course, for now. The hooded disciples closed around them and together they moved into the massive elevator before the door whirred shut, sealing them in an unsettling silence.

Less than five minutes later, the robed apostles, including Jacob and Karen, stood motionless and quiet. Conrad Wilson, dressed in a gray business suit, sat with nine similarly attired men and two women at a semi-circular table that faced the crystal pyramid. From his position, Jacob saw that the group, diametrically unlike the one of which he was a part, was animated, excited apparently over what was about to happen. They chatted freely, gesturing and smiling under the unaffected watch of the robed holy man sitting at the sparkling pyramid's tip.

Beyond the pyramid which everyone in the room faced, with Jacob's group standing 14 feet behind the seated men and women, the rounded walls slid apart in ten places, revealing ten gigantic viewing screens. They were dark for only a moment before simultaneously snapping to life, displaying video from the capitols of the newly created EARTHSPHERE-10. Jacob's mind reeled. His thoughts filled with remembered Scripture. The voice echoing in his head was that of Hugo Marchek.

"And the ten horns which thou sawest are ten kings, who have received no kingdom as yet; but receive power as kings one hour with the beast These have one mind, and shall give their power and strength unto the beast."

Two figures within his group silently, but firmly, urged Jacob to put on one of the burgundy-colored robes. Holding the garment open for him, one of them then tied the yellow rope around his waist while the other pulled the hood over Jacob's head.

He was one of them now, feeling less conspicuous, but at the same time more uneasy. Why had they not indoctrinated him, or brain-washed him? Why had they not done to him whatever they had done to Karen and the others? Why had they not filled him with the controlling, senses-dulling serums of INterface? Still, he managed to maintain self-control without their help. Despite the fact that heavy dosages of Trachetrol II, taken over many months, had minimal effect, his body had built resistances. Outwardly at least, he was able to remain calm; thanks, no doubt, to the drug's residual influence.

Boiling slowly beneath that tranquility, however, was

suspicion that his state of being, different from that of the others who surrounded him, was that way for reasons only the masters knew. Worry bubbled in his thoughts, and broke into his consciousness, while the video from the ten cities moved upon the screens, forewarning that he stood alone. The single outsider in what was otherwise orchestrated cohesion. Yet in his separateness, he felt a distinct part of all that was and was to soon be.

A sense that it had all happened before slashed across his perception of everything going on around him, in that instant bringing into confluence all his fears, the paranoiac certainties he had lived with since shortly after meeting Hugo Marchek. That he, Jacob Zen, was hopelessly intertwined with events sweeping humankind into the eternal abyss.

The vortex sucked at him now. The screens' chaos increased the churning velocity of his mind-whirlpool. The only sounds in the vast chamber were muted conversations among the 12 seated in front of the pyramid, and a faint though distinct throb, as if the event that everyone seemed to anticipate with reverential expectation was organic in nature. Its heart beating slowly, awaiting its moment of entrance with the calm foreknowledge that its destiny was preordained to be the centerpiece of all that would happen next.

The hooded mass moved forward, forcing him to jostle against Karen, who willingly pressed toward the gleaming throne, her eyes, like the eyes of all others in the room, fixed upon the holy man. Jacob managed a quick scan of the room, seeing above and behind the advancing disciples, several cameras, their large lenses aimed at the crystal pyramid and Master Manya. Other large panels separated, unveiling cameras above each large screen around the circular room, all pointing to the chamber's center.

Master Manya stood when the disciples halted and arranged themselves behind the 12 people seated at the semi-circular table. He lifted and stretched his arms outward in the direction of the disciples, who, after kneeling, bowed their heads and brought their hands together into a prayerful posture beneath their chins. The men and women at the table went to their knees before the holy man, who stood rigidly, high above the gathering.

The thumping sound became louder and faster; the screens, Jacob noticed, were filled with video of the religious man atop the pyramid, portraying his eerie image from constantly changing camera angles. Abruptly, the heartbeat stopped.

Official INterface music ruptured the silence. Its militaristic strains prompting all in the chamber to assume a position on one knee and draw clenched right fist to chest.

"To Caesar that which is Caesar's, and to God that which is God's. TRINITY speaks!"

The computer voice reverberated throughout the room, while everyone maintained the head-bowed position of allegiance.

"Interface Response Unity is the New Earth. You are either IN or you are lost. INterface is salvation. TRINITY loves you."

Each subject, Jacob, too, lifted his face to see on the screens the single image, its angular designs joined with its interwoven circular lines to form the stylized countenance of INterface Man, symbolic of TRINITY.

"TRINITY forever!
Six Ways to Law!
Six Ways to Order!
Six Ways to Peace!
Six! Six! Six!"

The martial music ceased and the heartbeat resumed at

pace and volume equal to before. All in the chamber got to their feet except the 12, who reseated themselves around the curved table. Jacob's companions stared upward at the hooded Manya, whose arms-interlocked pose they emulated. On their faces were expressions beyond adoration, tears streaming over their pallid cheeks. They, too, were meant for such heights. The disciples genuinely believed. Karen's brown eyes, never more effulgent, never more lovely than now, while she worshiped the enigmatic representation of all that was holy to her — to him, all that was blasphemous.

The tip of the pyramid upon which Master Manya stood began to turn slowly, causing the holy man to rotate. His straight-ahead gaze met each of the 10 screens in its turn. Again the 10 cities were being scanned by the cameras at those locations, capturing the throngs of enraptured INter-face subjects, who were themselves, at the same time, given view of the goings-on in the temple chamber and all other cities being shown. Master Manya's words were received by all INterface Response Units and translated instantaneously into the many languages.

"Brothers... Sisters... of INterface Body." Manya spoke softly while his robed body continued to rotate slowly upon the tip of the pyramid. "You are one with each other, although separated through limitations imposed by physical laws. One in the Body of INterface Universal."

The throbbing sound grew in volume and quickened, Master Manya's drawn, white face in close-up on the screens of INterface, the small, deeply creased mouth issuing the words ecclesiastically.

"Certain ones who were among us, but who are no longer among us, have reached evolutionary planes of ascension where they are now most intimately one with the Universal Father. Others, never truly part of us, are gone. Taken in the great cosmic excision so the Body Universal can function free of the malignancy of the before time, allowing us to progress more rapidly toward humanity's ultimate place with the Ascended Ones."

Manya's voice became harder, his expression within the hood's stark shadows changing to match the intonation.

"Before we can begin that ascension in earnest, global understanding, world unity, earthly peace, must be achieved."

His voice filled with controlled rage; his corpse-pale hands clenched into fists with which he pounded his points in short, hammering motions. "Ancient, deceiving forces and their agents have worked ceaselessly to prevent the unity we must have."

"These agents are Jews! They spew forth hatred, in order to destroy love. LOVE! The only thing which can bring universal peace, and mankind's millennium of perfection."

Manya appeared to sink deeper into the crimson hood, and seemed to withdraw momentarily to remarshal his energies before continuing.

"A great man gave his life in reaching out to these Jews. Single-handedly, he brought Arab and Jew together in rapprochement unequaled in history through the inspired Six Ways Plan, under which INterface shall march to the ultimate evolutionary plane!"

"But the Zionist devils would not accept the pact of love agreed to by those among them who saw the wisdom in adopting peace, rather than continuing the conflict which will bring about their end as a race. Claiming to be the chosen people of God, they murdered the one man who would have made their continued existence acceptable. It was a Jew who assassinated Herrlich Krimhler!"

The INterface prelate paused, as if reflecting on his words, or on the depth of loss felt for Krimhler. Jacob's mind lurched back to the night spent with Fredria VanHorne. His memory, for some reason he tried to shake but could not, dwelling on the most intense moments when their flesh moved together toward passion's emptying rush to ennui. Thoughts, then, of the watch taken from him during his drug-induced sleep, and his next seeing it when it was presented as evidence that he was Krimhler's assassin.

The Jewish race, blamed for the earth-shocking crime of which the INterface masters falsely accused him, after setting him up for the deception. Mental images of the German's head exploding while he, Jacob Zen, watched thousands of miles from the death scene. A quick flash of Christ on a blood-drenched cross, transforming into a golden crucifix attached to the chain draped between Fredria VanHorne's breasts, while he drank from the glass she handed him in the bed that night in subterranean Naxos. Christ and Herrlich Krimhler, merging into a single image within his mind. No! Not imagined! The transformation was taking place before his eyes! Now!

The crystal pyramid-throne had parted during the seconds it took his brain to work through its delusions. A figure in a robe of dazzling white stood before a golden cross within the opening, arms outstretched as if affixed to the cross in crucifixion fashion. The face, its dark eyes penetrating even the hardened crust created by months of systemic-callousing INterface existence. The face of Herrlich Krimhler!

Each of the screens displayed the face in close-up, death-white, yet alive, glowing in the light emanating from within the crystal.

"Behold the One who takes away the sins of the world with his death, burial and resurrection!" Master Manya shouted, extending his arms toward the ceiling. "Behold your salvation!"

Krimhler, like a man once crippled, now trying his legs for the first time since becoming so, took one careful step, then another. He walked from the opened pyramid, stopping and lifting his arms outward toward the robed gathering, his hands in a beckoning posture. Suddenly Jacob was being moved by those around him, toward the base of the pyramid throne, and he saw, through dizzy, reeling senses, the 12 seated people rise and turn to face him, while the mob pressed him forward. The curved table parted, allowing the robed people to move Jacob between the table halves. A whirling, spinning, falling sensation, then regaining balance with the aid of the many hands upon him. Suddenly, then, he was alone, all who had borne him along having retreated to their former places.

Alone at the base of the crystal pyramid. Naked before the world, beneath the gaze of Master Manya. In the living presence of the man the world believed he had murdered!

Jacob glanced quickly, nervously, at the screens, all showing his shocked, frightened face in close-up. His legs deserted him and he fell to his knees, his stomach turning with nausea, his mind spasming while he struggled to stand.

"Symbolic of the salvation offered to all who will accept," Master Manya said, "...consider this Jew, the very Jew who took the life of the one who brings peace to the world. This Jew, Jacob Zen, stands condemned before INterface. Behold, the supreme act of mercy... of love!"

Jacob, on one knee, felt a strong hand take his right hand and felt himself being pulled to a standing position. His thoughts cleared to some extent, while the grip of the person who helped him stand, now steadied him. His eyes met those of Herrlich Krimhler; the screens of INterface displayed Krimhler embracing him.

"I forgive you, for you knew not what you did. Your sins are washed clean in the blood of your God and Savior," Herrlich Krimhler said softly, looking into Jacob's eyes with what seemed genuine compassion, causing a strange sensation of lightness to pass through his body.

"But I... I didn't do it," Jacob stammered in a whisper. Krimhler had already turned from him without acknowledging that he heard, and began ascending the steps of the pyramid.

"There is but one God. The Universal Father of all humanity. Behold him in reincarnate form. Behold him as the resurrected Son, in whom He is well pleased! The Universal Mind-Father... Pure, undefiled, changeless love, whom death could not bind... The Prince of Peace!"

Manya's words echoed in Jacob's ears. All screens displayed Herrlich Krimhler's slow ascension to the pyramid's apex, where the holy man stood, still with his arms raised. Everyone within the chamber stood in the posture of praise, looks of adoring acceptance on their faces, their cheeks streaming tears of hypnotic ecstasy. They followed the lead of Master Manya, who dropped to his knees when the resurrected leader reached the top of the pyramid throne.

The 10 screens showed Krimhler and Master Manya surrounded, through split-imaging, by the millions of worshipers gathered before INterface cameras at the ten cities, all on their knees like the people in the Jerusalem temple. Although the scenes surrounding the two central figures continued to change through dissolves and quick-cuts and zooms, two things remained constant, the reverential chanting and the tear-glazed expressions on the faces. True worship of the one they accepted as their returned messiah.

Gone were the drawn, listless looks of defeat, of hopelessness. Herrlich Krimhler, the Messiah!

Was his mind telling him, truthfully, that he had, like Karen and his foster father said, been wrong? Or was his brain succumbing to the infectious surreality of INterface-orchestrated emotionalism? Even as the thoughts bounced about within his skull, another confronted them and drove them from his mind. Words from the Bible he could never have consciously recalled.

"And then shall that wicked one be revealed, whom the Lord shall consume with the spirit of his mouth, and shall destroy with the brightness of his coming, Even him whose coming is after the working of Satan with all power and signs and lying wonders, And with all deceivableness of unrighteousness in them that perish, because they received not the love of the truth, that they might be saved. And for this cause God shall send them strong delusion, that they should believe the lie..."

And it was at least partly lie. That much was certain. He had not self-concocted, in his drug-riddled brain, the fact of whether Krimhler had actually been shot through the head, or whether it was a hoax, he didn't know. That he, Jacob Zen, had not done the shooting, he was sure. Of the stolen watch, used to frame him, to implicate the Jewish Race... Lies! The looks on the faces, whatever the truth or the lies, they believed. Totally! Absolutely! He, alone, seemed at odds with Krimhler, making Jacob Zen, in the view of INterface Body, at odds with God. Worse, they had manipulated him into helping them with their deluding scheme. He, in the eyes of the world, had murdered the now resurrected Krimhler, and had become the object of and example for the savior's forgiveness, which demonstrated divine love. The charge was lie, the forgiveness unnecessary; therefore, the savior and his love for all, including the penitent Jews, false.

If not a savior, what then? A politician given power by other politicians, who had dementedly, though honestly, concluded that the only way to lasting peace was through purging that which lay at the core of the corruption, and concluded, wrongly, that was the Jew? Was it merely National Socialism reborn on a global scale, finally reaching the level of acceptance to which Hitler aspired? Or Hugo Marchek's Antichrist regime?

The faces, thousands collectively in close-ups, surrounding the Savior and Master Manya. Faces individually, enraptured, adoring the man who was once dead but now stood before them... Alive! The Supreme Master of INterface. Their Messiah!

"And for this cause God shall send them strong delusion, that they should believe the lie..."

Rage suddenly expanded within him, separating fear from courage, caution from boldness, and the schism brought back strength suppressed since he removed the belt of explosives. INterface must be exposed while the eyes and ears of its subjects were seeing and listening — while the live coronation of the resurrected messiah presented perhaps the only opportunity to reach them, to warn them!

He would turn INterface deception to his own advantage. Blurt the truth over the INterface Response Unity conduit, which was totally open at this moment, to establish their lies. Now, while all was quiet, the microphones and cameras ready to capture Herrlich Krimhler's message from the tip of the crystal pyramid.

They could not stop his rush up the steps nor keep him from stabbing truth into the heart of Interface! Not before he had disrupted the unholy coronation. They could not stop him in time to keep him from using their forum against them, like they had used him as a bludgeon against his own race!

There was too much distance between the controller security people and himself; between himself and the robed mob and the 12 people sitting at the curved table. The technicians at the control boards would not be able to react quickly enough to stop his exclamation of truth! Shouting to the bedazzled victims that what stood before them was not their savior, but a monster who spewed lies more toxic than venom from the deadliest snake, because the poison went exponentially further than destroying the flesh. They murdered hope for eternal freedom from servitude--slaughtered, through slow, agonizing strangulation, the very soul.

His rekindled strength would propel him up the crystal steps to Krimhler and the kneeling Master Manya, where he would accomplish through words what he would have accomplished on a more limited scale through use of the explosives, had he been confronted in Facility 500. He would strike, through the power of the masters' own machinery, a blow against the spell cast by the INterface fuehrer.

His vision darkened, his pulse pounding heatedly in his neck and temples. He sprinted in a burst of energy to the pyramid's first step and sprang quickly upward. He would not be stopped... Would not!

From high above him, Herrlich Krimhler turned to look downward, their eyes meeting in a collision of wills in which the mortal must yield. His legs refused his conscious urgings to continue the rush toward the crystal throne's tip, like in all the nightmares when he was pursued by one dream-monster or the other. His legs, leaden, each step taken in an intangible quagmire! Now he pursued the monster, and the nightmare turned real while the monster's sinister glare from the pyramid's apex made more coagulant, the invisible quicksand through which he struggled until his legs could no longer move!

The black, bottomless eyes held his in their grip while he tried to scream the words which would not come, as if they, too, were held captive in that unspeakable ambience.

"Do not believe his lies!" he tried to scream but could not. "He is not your savior! INterface is not Utopia! It is Hell on Earth!... It is all lies!... All lies!"

CHAPTER 19

Hugo Marchek's sister in the crumpled heap. Fiery trial through which passing was impossible. Clothing catching fire, burning. Saryeva Marchek's dress, taken from the chair and placed on top of her brother's desk, the material then smoothed in order to get a better look. Scorched by the flames engulfing the room. Gradations of browns permeating the light-colored print material, the burned areas outlining the form of a young woman. The image of a crucified man burned into the long, ancient linen shroud, which became harder and harder to see because it fled quickly, a white, shrinking rectangle against a black void.

Why was movement so inhibited? Why were his shoulders, arms, legs and head so terribly heavy? Herrlich Krimhler, here, now! To save the lost who were vanquished to this cold, inescapable blackness. Why the piles of empty, scorched clothing strewn along this path of saving grace — this shaft of light? Light and life again achieved!

Black eyes from the pyramid's top. Restraining him to the point of paralysis. Leaden legs. His body transformed into one of the huge, hewn blocks of stone, of which the pyramid should be constructed but was not. Rather was made of crystalline substance, unknown, filled with power emanating from somewhere within.

Darkness, and a single white cube shrinking while tumbling silently to nothingness, before returning to illuminate and make visible and audible the world.

"But if this is him, why is he here? They forgave him. Took him into the fold."

"He's Jacob Zen. Thinner and older than in those pictures of him. But it's him, all right."

Throbbing temples -- Must have Trachetrol. Each pump a burst of pain in the chest, the head. Hazy forms, checkered, crisscrossed, human forms, edged with spreading, velvet fringe that made them appear at first glance to be corpulent old men in silhouette against the squares of brightness behind and above them.

"He's almost awake," one of the two guards said. Both men left, then, through a doorway, whose door sounded of metal and great weight when it slammed behind them.

Focusing... not easy. He caught a glimpse of other human forms, like the previous ones, blurred at first, but, with effort, becoming somewhat clearer. They stood behind a barrier of checkerboard design, wearing gray, robe-like clothing. "Welcome, Jacob Zen," one of the men said.

The checkerboard. Mesh bars. A cage of some kind.

"Where am I?" Pain surged in his head when he spoke, forcing him to lie flat on his back again. "A compound near the city, Washington."

"D.C.? How did I get here?"

"Three men brought you here."

"You have been sleeping for quite some time," the other man said in an accent he could not place.

"What day is it?"

"Tuesday. The seventh of the month."

"Did they say anything when they brought me?"

"Nothing of importance," the older man said.

"Why are you in here?"

"We are of the house of Israel. That is crime enough for them."

Jacob smiled bitterly through his pain. These were extremely orthodox Jews, who would not change to placate INterface. Amazing they had survived this long, while preserving their honor; he had arrived at exactly the same place and time, having more than once soiled his.

"You were pardoned by them. We witnessed it from Jerusalem. Do you understand why you are now here, in this place?"

"Haven't you learned yet that they say and do whatever suits their purposes? Surely you know their ways by now," Jacob said with mild irritation.

"We know their ways," the younger man said. "Our brothers and sisters continue the fight against the evil now upon the world. But now, it must be waged with very different methods because of the most recent edict. Those who accept their mark can be monitored constantly."

Jacob leaned on one elbow and looked at the man. "What mark?"

"That which Herrlich Krimhler demanded three nights ago in the Temple at Jerusalem. The mark he ordered all peoples to accept in order to prove their loyalty to him."

"I didn't know. I passed out, I guess, or was drugged, or something. I don't remember anything after I tried to get to the top of the..."

"What did you hope to accomplish?"

"To call them liars. To destroy Krimhler's credibility by showing the world the hypocrisy of his claims. But that's not important now. Tell me about this mark."

"Herrlich Krimhler declared himself to be God. He commanded everyone to receive the mark acknowledging their acceptance that he is the one and only Deity. Refusal means death by decapitation without benefit of trial, if INterface wishes to execute those refusing. An even worse fate awaits those who are not executed. Those without the mark cannot interact within INterface Response Unity. Either their code is taken out of the system or their electronic funds are deleted. Their logic, to justify this punishment, is: if one does not receive the Allegiant mark, he chooses not to be a part of the system. To live without the mark, one must steal. Therefore he is not only disloyal to Krimhler, but a thief, deserving of death. The Six Ways to Peace is violated by those who break laws."

Jacob, through his headache, felt a jab of guilt, remembering his part in cutting innocents out of the world-saving system before worshiping the resurrected messiah was required.

The younger man spoke. "At the time the mark is given, a transponder is implanted, either in the top of the right hand, or in the forehead. This assures that the person can be constantly monitored, the transponder being linked by a series of satellites circling the earth, to surveillance stations many times more sophisticated than were the Sector Coordinator monitoring posts."

Unusual men! Unlikely to know such things. Almost like they were divulging their knowledge to forge an understanding of some sort with him. "How do you know all of this?"

"The 666 mark worn visibly on the forehead brings special recognition and services to those displaying it," the older man said, ignoring Jacob's question.

"666?"

"In honor of Herrlich Krimhler and his Six Ways to Peace.

The Roman Numeral for the number 666, within the pyramid design."

Jacob lay back and tried to rub the pain from his eyes. His mind researching for the single neurological impulse that would trigger the recollection process and summon the words he had heard before, or read, or both. Something about a mark. A prophetical mark.

Of course! It replayed within his brain. Hugo Marchek's unforgettable voice quoting the Scripture. *"And he causeth all, both small and great, rich and poor, free and enslaved, to receive a mark in their right hand, or in their foreheads. And that no man might buy or sell, except he that had the mark, or the name of the beast, or the number of his name. Here is wisdom. Let him that hath understanding count the number of the beast; for it is the number of a man; and his number is six hundred three-score and six."*

Without conscious prompting, his memory, or flashback delusion caused by the Trachetrol, brought remembered things to the surface. INterface doctrines his unconscious mind stored that night at Jerusalem. He heard, in his mind's ear, Krimhler's pronouncements. His lies, about what he called the Cosmic Evolutionary Purge that occurred every eon or so. That was what accounted for the sudden elimination of the dinosaurs, and of Atlantis. It affected humankind differently than other forms because the human was the highest plane before reaching the metaphysical levels of soul-mindedness, at which point one became god-like. Jews remained Jews because they were not the sons of the Great Cosmic Mind, merely a by-product of its creation. Jews, as a race, turned to the side of evil. Lucifer had been on the side of what was good and right since the beginning. Jews were the offspring of Michael, while all others were the children of Lucifer. Herrlich Krimhler gave that night, Jacob somehow knew through the subconscious remembrance, his version of the creation and all that had happened since.

Lucifer had not been chased from Heaven for leading a rebellion against God. There was no such entity as the biblical Jehovah. The war that raged was between Lucifer and Michael, the angel created by Lucifer, the true Mind-Father of the Cosmos. Michael was the one in rebellion, having persuaded most of humanity to believe that Lucifer was responsible for the world's problems. Michael, the true Satan, introduced his false messiah, Jesus of Nazareth, into the world through the Jewish seed. He, Herrlich Krimhler, was the true Messiah, the son of Lucifer, and at the same time, he was Lucifer.

Even with the great evils the Jewish race had perpetrated, if the Jews would accept the mark, symbolic of Herrlich Krimhler, in what Krimhler called the Luciferian Initiation, the Jews could receive forgiveness and obtain salvation. It was possible to offer this grace to the Jew because, as a religion, Judaism traditionally rejected Michael's false Christ, Jesus of Nazareth.

"Are Jews taking this mark?" Jacob said from the hard cot, while he continued to massage his temples.

"Some," the younger man said from the cell across the concrete corridor from Jacob's cell. "Most Jews in Palestine are well-versed in the prophecies and have taken shelter. The controllers are trying to learn where they have hidden, because Herrlich Krimhler is in an insane rage, wanting to find them and destroy them."

"Where could that many people go? Do you know?"

"We are here to be executed, because we will not tell them where Israel hides."

"Executed?"

"We have learned from our guards that the executions,

yours and ours, are to be shown throughout INterface. They are to be by decapitation. Krimhler, himself, ordered it."

Decapitation! Krimhler, he remembered, informed the world that night from Jerusalem that the severing of the head from the body symbolized the cutting off of any hope for redemption. The sentence to Hell. Which Hell, depended on the sin-condition. For some, it was simply ceasing to be. For others, it meant being reborn, reincarnated in a life form lower than before, and with each subsequent death, being reborn to ever descending levels, de-evolving to the most basic elements of matter. Reincarnation in reverse. Backward, ever backward in time and space.

Karen rubbed the back of his neck and kissed his eyes, her soft hair brushing his face. She sat, then lay beside him and their lips met. Spring lay just outside the windows, bright morning light full of pollens rising and swirling and making the colors beyond the neatly groomed garden appear to co-mingle into a pleasant mist.

One does not dream in color, it was said or written somewhere. But this was vividly colorful, looking out the window between the time of parting and fusing again with her velvet lips. More so than reality. But this was reality. She was loving him, while the unfamiliar but unforgettable fragrances came in through the open windows, her fingers long and cool and gentle, soothing the taut muscles, forcing the aching from his skull. More real than any reality. Real. Reality like he had not known. Not a dream... Not a dream. Real!

She was his, not some glazed-eyed addict. His to love, to hold, to share his passions with, to give to and take pleasure from.

He sat up, his vision at first dark, slowly gathering in his surroundings and making his other senses aware, a dream! She was not really here; they were not in each others' arms, together in an indescribably beautiful garden-place, loving, being human again.

Still night, the light outside the small, square windows causing shadows where it hit against and curved around the metal bars, creating crisscrossed patterns on the gray floor beyond the bunk.

The pain was gone from his neck and the back of his head. The dream, a God-sent physical relief, though while consciousness became more focused, the remembered beauty of the dream caused greater pain of the soul. The two men slept in their respective cells across the small corridor, the bars in their windows making similarly checkered patterns on their bunks and floors. Somewhere in the smog-filled early morning, far distant, a large dog barked, causing others to sound. Soon all was quiet again.

What would it be like to have one's head cleaved from the body? A moment of pain? An eternity? Instant unconsciousness? Or a second of flip-flopping, through dying eyes, seeing the last of the world in a violently twirling moment before thudding against the bottom of the container?

Could the brain, did the brain, stay alive for the minute or two or however many it took for the oxygen to deplete? Most likely, there was instant unconsciousness. Most likely, but who could testify to it?

To die in such a way, helplessly, unheroically. Just on one's knees, then a plop, one's blood squirting shamefully, like that of a slaughtered animal. Better to go out gloriously — An explosion or gunned down while yourself killing the enemy. But to just kneel and die, your head tumbling into a metal box before the entertained, wicked world. Better to die proudly, like a man. An explosion, gunfire. But death was death. Cessation of breathing, of blood flow, of conscious thought. A long, meaningless sleep, where dreams have no place.

Karen. Lovely, soft, yet firm to the touch, Karen. She comes again and caresses and strokes and kisses. Her skin cool in the rainbow mist surrounding them both while they love.

Her touch is different, somehow, as it changes. Hard and cold and she pulls away, or is pulled away. Her face an emotionless mask while she backs away into the mist, which itself has transformed into gray, murky haze. In slow motion, he pursues her fading form through the smog, unable to match her speed. She is not moving under her own power, but is dragged, still without expression or protest, and she disappears into the dark cloud.

The cloud dissipates and he sees her on her hands and knees, naked and white against the backdrop of absolute black, her long hair falling toward the floor, touching the floor and hiding her face from him. But it is Karen.

He tries to run to her but cannot move. He looks at his feet; they are affixed to the black marble floor by something unseen and he looks to Karen again, who seems glued on hands and knees.

From somewhere behind her, he cannot determine from where, a large, dark form emerges. A satyr-being, whose features are obscured by facial hair and hideous bumps, and whose two cloven hooves clop sharply upon the marble floor as the man-goat approaches her.

Jacob screams as Karen screams. He can move now, and will grab the thing and choke the life from it! But doors of iron bars slam between him and them, and he cannot move the crisscrossed metal, but can only grip the bars tightly and stand, helpless.

She raises her face while the thing ravages her. He shrieks obscenities but to no effect. Karen's face is turning toward him now, sweat beaded on her forehead and around her mouth.

Her eyes open, showing pain at first, but changes, while she looks into his, to an expression of sensual ecstasy. Her face is alive with passion. Not pain, not fear, but is lost in the throes of heightening pleasure. She looks at Jacob and laughs, a hideous cackle that distorts her pretty face into a face of changing features. It is first Fredria VanHorne's face, then Melissa Jantzen's. His own mother's face. Each face in its turn has "666" imprinted upon the forehead. The satyr, too, changes, to the form of a man. His face is the grinning, mocking face of Herrlich Krimhler, upon whose forehead is stamped "DCLXVI!"

"On your feet!"

Loud banging on metal brought him from the nightmare, jarring him. He stood unsteadily on the concrete floor, trying to regain full awareness, to make sense of the barking commands shouted by the man in the black uniform, who glared at him and at the other prisoners.

Time for execution! He had slept away his last minutes of life. He had been prepared for death before. Why did he inwardly now fight against resignation to the inevitable?

"Kneel before the Son," one of the controllers ordered when the steel door opened, issuing in three men, who were not recognizable because they were silhouetted blackly against the bright light just outside the cellblock. The man in the center was tall and walked with uncommon grace. His heavier, thicker companions carried Uzi-type weapons at the ready. "Kneel!" one of the controllers said angrily.

"Leave us," the tall man said in a voice unmistakably that of Herrlich Krimhler. The guards left the cellblock and Krimhler turned his eyes upon Jacob, who stood by the bunk, struck momentarily mute by the fact that he stood face to face with the man the world had seen Jacob Zen murder. Herrlich Krimhler, the master of the New Age, the resurrected Savior.

"Why do you stare, Jacob? Do you yet not believe I am who I say I am?"

The other prisoners, Jacob noticed, moved to their bars, where they listened.

"So that you might believe..." Krimhler stepped to the bars of Jacob's cell and in the same instant stood within the cell, his dark features half-obscured in the sparse light. He had passed through the metal! Walked through it! The other men, like Jacob, gawked in astonishment while Krimhler continued to speak.

"Why do you deny me? I am the Christ, the Messiah yearned for by humanity. Why do you persecute me, Jacob Zen? Why do you refuse the Lord and Savior of mankind his rightful worship? Why do you refuse the mark of adoration and salvation?"

Jacob backed away from Krimhler, who put the questions softly. He bumped against the bunk and nearly fell backward, but caught himself.

"No! You are not the Messiah. He came over 2,000 years ago." He felt his voice tremble while speaking the words weakly.

"False Christs have come and gone. I am the true Christ, the Son of God. I am God."

"No! God is everything good. You are all that is evil!"

"You are deceived, Jacob. I am come because of the evils in the world. Look at the scars of crucifixion, Jacob." Krimhler stepped into the light that streamed in the window over Jacob's shoulder. A faint, circular spot of light rested upon the bronzed forehead. Krimhler held his hand out, palms up.

"See the nailprints, symbolic of the crucifixion I suffered for mankind." The shadows seemed to again engulf the face, putting Krimhler in obscuring darkness.

"But why? I didn't fire the shot. I wasn't in Jerusalem. I

was on the other side of the world," Jacob said, thinking that if Krimhler was God, he would know that already. Wondering why he bothered bringing up the fact. Knowing at the same time that the subject came from his lips involuntarily.

"It matters not what individual pulled the trigger. You, Jacob Zen, are made a symbol of the Jews' prehistoric perpetration of absolute evil upon my creation. You were made the example of absolute evil. You were given the opportunity, on behalf of every Jew, to accept forgiveness for yourself and for them. You rejected salvation. A decision made not only for you, an individual sinner, but for all Jews of all times."

"Why tell me this?" Jacob said, caustically.

"God is absolute good. Could God do less than lovingly explain why it must be as it must, to the one Jew chosen to symbolize the race which is the agent of pure evil?"

"Lucifer is the pure evil."

"Satan is the pure evil... the devil," Krimhler corrected softly.

"But Lucifer is Satan... the devil."

"The supreme lie of the supremely evil being, thrust upon mankind by the false Christ and his book of delusions."

"The Bible?"

"The Christian Bible," Krimhler said. "If the God of the Christian Bible be God, then He is a flawed God indeed. How can a perfect God create a world of imperfection, where there is disease and famine and nuclear weapons and murder... all the evils mankind has experienced? Why could not God create perfection, if He is truly God? How can a loving God, as the God of the Christian Bible and of the Talmud declares himself to be, allow these evils to continue? How can such a loving God send a soul to a literal, burning, eternal fire, knowing in godly omniscience that soul is innocently born into a world of God's own making? Is that perfect justice?"

"Who created the world, then? You?"

"The Universal Mind Father and I are one. I and my Father and Lucifer. The so-called God-Jehovah is in reality Michael, our creation who has tainted perfection with absolute evil.

"Placed in charge of this tiny portion of our infinite creation, Michael infected Lucifer's progeny by using his own innate, though limited, creative capability to form the genetically impure Jewish seed. All evil has grown through this contamination. It now must be changed through a rebirth into salvation, or it must be purged so that creation can be cleansed. Made perfect.

"Through one Jew-deceiver, the supremely evil deception was given, the one called Jesus of Nazareth. Through another Jew-deceiver the deception is made manifest before the world, and the genetic contamination shall be cleansed from the New Age earth by his death. You, Jacob Zen, are to be that sacrifice, to satisfy the judgment of the Universal Mind Father.

Cold sweat soaked his body, his energy draining from him through his pores. Hugo Marchek's face, the wire-rimmed glasses resting upon the thin nose, eyes closed in eternal sleep. In his coffin, being lowered into the damp-smelling concrete crypt vault. Marchek's sister's neatly smoothed clothing, scorched by the fire. No! By something other. Before the fire that held the screams of the men who tried to end his flight from the entity stalking him. The shroud, stained by the brownish discoloration, the heat-created negative image of a crucified man.

"Jacob...Jacob Zen."

He awoke and quickly looked around the cell. Empty! Another nightmare.

"You are safe now," one of the prisoners assured him from the cell across the corridor.

Despite the hour, the sky was a dark hue of copper and stank of the pollutants that made it so. His last breath would fill his nostrils with the stench. His lungs with the choking abrasiveness that not even Trachetrol could smooth over, were it available, and if he were not about to face his ten-hundred hours appointment with the blade atop the Decap platform looming 40 meters away.

INterface cameras mounted on the high, thick stucco walls and on individual platforms at the same level as the Decap platform trained on Jacob and the four controllers escorting him across the expanse of concrete that separated the cell block from the platform of execution. Strangely, he experienced a surge of strength rather than the weak-kneed fear and panic he had expected. Denying them the performance they so much wanted to present to the world of those who bent the knee filled him with a kind of pride he had not known. To refuse to beg for life, which at any rate held nothing further from him, was the one act still within his power that promised the greatest damage to the INterface propagandists. Somewhere in that watching horde was someone, maybe several, maybe many, who, seeing his act of honor, would transform into spirits kindred with his own. Even in death, he could strike a blow by galvanizing fragments of hatred for the masters into a mighty resistance, thereby living on to fight with ever-increasing strength born of his death. Never had the martyr wish been a part of his psyche. Now, drawing nearer the gleaming instrument that would cleave him from the living gave him understanding of what might have gone through the mind of Christ, had Christ been merely human, when contemplating Golgotha. To die passively when the purpose was served by such death -- unlike when the millions died unresistingly during Hitler's

Holocaust, with no one to know, to care--made the dying something approaching desirable.

Iron gates on the wall to his left were opened by uniformed men. People filed through the opening and walked quickly along the wall to the Decap platform, where they encircled it. They turned toward Jacob and his guards, strangely silent, watching the five figures who now stood at the steps of the platform.

Other black-uniformed controllers ordered the people to designated areas from which they would watch the execution and at the same time add effect for the INterface broadcast. He looked at the drawn, drugged, compromised faces, each mirroring the other in sickly sameness. There could be no hatred for these pathetic onlookers, each as much a victim as himself. Even more so because they had yielded long ago without struggle, and would go on yielding until they were inevitably chewed up and digested by INterface justice. He felt only pity for them, and regret that his own physical struggle on their behalf must end. He was sure he saw in the sad, tired eyes below the triangle-shaped symbol tattooed upon the foreheads not desire to be entertained, or joy over seeing INterface justice done. They were looks that tried, in their silence, to convey helpless sympathy for a fellow crea-ture in an unalterable hell, which they realized they, like he, helped to create through their inaction during that earlier time when liberty had been alive.

INterface Response Unity cameras were active, the red lights on their tops going off and on in turn when their cameramen manipulated the levers and knobs and buttons in a nearby control center. The cameras' huge black lenses seemed to have life of their own while they trained on Jacob, who struggled with his natural inclination to look directly into them, afraid doing so might disrupt his fidelity to passive martyrdom.

Up the stainless steel steps and onto the chrome-like platform. The air became harder to breath, causing pressure in his lungs, like when scuba diving with Conrad Wilson in the Atlantic on the rare occasions the diplomat took time out from his government work.

It was impossible to think of Conrad Wilson kneeling to them. To United States' purposes and goals -- yes. Maybe even to international cooperative designs. But, to one-world megalomania? No. Yet his foster father had knelt, yielded like all the empty-eyed creatures standing around the platform beneath him. Conrad Wilson's servitude was worse! Accepting, approving, and implementing their kingdom of misery. For what? A position of dominance during the scant years left to him? Was that it? Fear of death? Certainly it was not for ideals shared with Herrlich Krimhler and his kind. Or was it the drugs? Or psychological alteration in other ways? Or...

Members of the crowd behind the rope constraints began to mumble, then quieted when one of the guards who accompanied him from the cellblock forced Jacob to kneel by pushing downward on his shoulders from behind. Another guard stood by the panel that operated the Decap Unit.

"This Jew has refused salvation through TRINITY and INterface Universal!" The voice from the loudspeakers blared at the same instant the words were broadcast to INterface Response Units throughout INterface.

"By refusing, he denies the one, true God, Herrlich Krimhler, and allies himself with the Jewish disease that continues to infect our world. He now deservedly precedes them in the fate they must all ultimately meet... ignominious extermination befitting betrayers!"

Powerful hands seized him and forced his head forward until he felt the cold steel rim of the guillotine's lower notch against his Adam's apple. The upper steel plate, with its half-circle notch descended and clanked over the back of his neck, trapped his head within the metallic circle. He stared into the bottom of the glistening steel box which would momentarily receive his head and his blood.

Tales of life's passing before one's eyes — it was not happening. Maybe that would come once the actual process of dying began. Maybe then, while the world tumbled and whirled before his head bounced against the bottom of the container. Would there be pain when the head hit bottom? When the neck was sliced through?

Before, when death seemed near, the flashbacks began to come; why was it that all he thought of now was mashed potatoes with gravy, and a smiling, happy child playing with his puppy? A child whose mother called him to dinner, the puppy following through an opened screen door that slammed behind them when they had entered the house.

Another dream? Was he still in the cell, sleeping a sleep from which he would awaken? Or was he dead? Is this the beginning of eternity? Was Hugo Marchek right, the world wrong? Would he forever be in Hell because he had refused to accept Jesus Christ as Savior? Had he accepted Marchek's Christ without knowing it? But Marchek said it was a conscious thing. It must be done volitionally, just as refusing Christ was done willfully. Was it too late for him to accept that Jesus of two millennia ago? If Jesus was Christ, if He was God, was He not, still? Was He not ageless, changeless? Could He not forgive as long as there was physical life surrounding the soul, which, the old eschatologist said, lives eternally or dies eternally, depending on the volitional acceptance or willful rejection of Jesus Christ?

The old black, worn Bible. The words, "*Who do you say that I am?*" came in an inner voice not recognizable. Was it the Holy Spirit Marchek talked about? "*Who do you say I am?*" The question asked Peter the Apostle by Jesus of Nazareth.

Peter, a fisherman who gave up his nets to follow Christ. "*Who do you say I am?*" The question put to him, Jacob Zen, now, in the same voice that Peter might have heard. "*Who do you say that I am?*" From the Bible, Peter's answer; "*Thou art the Christ, the Son of the Living God.*" Was it too late? Had God not run out of patience? Was it true, or a mind trick during the time of dying?

"*Who do you say that I am?*"

Bible verses! Why not memories of life's passing like in stories he had heard of vision-like replays while final breaths were taken? Bible verses instead! Clearly and swiftly going through his mind... .

"*Who do you say that I am?*"

"*For God so loved the world that he gave his only begotten Son that whosoever believeth in him should not perish but have everlasting life.*"

"*It is appointed unto a man once to die, and after death, the judgment.*"

"*There is but one God and one mediator between God and men, the man, Christ Jesus.*"

"God is not willing that any should perish but that they should come to repentance."

"*I am the Way, the Truth, and the Life, no man cometh to the Father but by me.*"

"*Then shall the wicked one be revealed, the man of sin.*"

"*It is the number of a man and the number is six hundred, threescore and six.*"

"*And he causeth all, both rich and poor, free and slave, to receive a mark in their right hand or forehead and none could buy or sell except he that had the mark of the beast or the number of his name.*"

"*And I saw the saints of God, who were beheaded for witness of*

Jesus, standing arrayed in white garments before the throne of God."

"*Whosoever believeth on him should not perish but have everlasting life."*

"*Who do you say that I am?"*

"You are the Christ, the Son of the living God," Jacob said aloud.

Violent vibrations and blasting, thumping noises interrupted his meditation. The crowd began to disperse. He strained to see what was happening around him, but his view was restricted by the limited movement allowed by the stock.

The roaring and vibration increased, the pulsating given off by the powerful engine of a large helicopter whose massive blades kicked up dust and debris, peppering his captive head. The wind seemed to move the remaining people backward until they cringed in a huddle against the high wall directly in front of where he knelt.

Was it INterface dignitaries, who had come to witness in person the killing of a single Jew? Was it Herrlich Krimhler, himself, come to smirk while the Decap blade pinched off his enemy's head?

Gunfire! Men and women were screaming. One of the controllers blasted from the platform, landing on the ground near the frightened people. His dark uniform drenched with his own blood, a portion of his skull flapping in the wind generated by the helicopter blades. More gunfire, then just the idling motor, decreasing wind, and feet clanking against the metal steps of the execution platform.

The upper half of the stock lifted, freeing his head. Strong arms lifted him roughly and rushed him from the platform. The men held him in their grasps and kept him from stumbling because he could not maintain proper balance with his hands still manacled behind his back. The ski-masked men at his right side released him to turn and pour a volley of Uzi fire into a Controller who had sprung from a doorway aiming his automatic weapon at the escaping men. An explosion to their left sent debris high into the air and caused them to nearly fall from the concussion. His left calf suddenly was on fire in one spot just below the knee joint. Hit — again! Like on the road from Andrews. The pain worsened and spread, causing loss of control of the leg.

His rescuers dragged him quickly toward the chopper, whose heavy blades drooped although they continued rotating — kept moving for a hasty departure from the prison yard. He felt himself being jerked into the helicopter's small doorway by someone inside while being pushed upward from behind by the men in the ski masks, then rushed, though gently, into a net hammock. Someone began cutting his left pant leg, then ripped the material to the groin.

"Doesn't look too bad," a deep-voiced man said, mopping the calf with gauze, tossing the material to the floor, then applying pressure to the wound with a fresh gauze pad.

"It's okay, Mr. Zen. You'll be okay," the man shouted above the almost deafening slamming of the engine, while it strained then jumped the big helicopter from the ground and swept it skyward and to the left at full power.

"Who are you people?"

"Hello, Son."

"Uncle Conrad?" Jacob said, trying to rise from the netting, but failing. The face, smiling and at the same time frowning with concern, dissolved to blackness.

CHAPTER 20

The glories of our blood and state
Are shadows, not substantial things,
There is no armor against fate,
Death lays his icy hand on kings.
My life did and does smack sweet.
Was your youth of pleasure wasteful?
Mine I saved and hold complete.
Do your joys with age diminish?
When mine fail me, I'll complain,
Must in death your daylight finish?
My sun sets to rise again.

"Jacob!" The bright light hurt his eyes, deluging his mind's ascension on to consciousness and making it difficult to recognize the form bending near him to touch his forehead with a cool cloth. The voice was concerned.

. . .

"Sweetheart."

Karen! Not a dream... Her arm felt warm and soft against his hand. Her lovely face was surrounded by the dark hair she brushed back to keep it from touching his face, which she lovingly wiped with the damp cloth. Her eyes--the eyes he knew better than he knew his own. Not the drugged, glazed eyes of when they walked the temple's roof. Her lips, soft, hot against his lips, against his forehead, against his cheeks. Her slender hands, cool against his burning skin while caressing him.

"Karen..."

"I'm here. I won't leave you, darling."

"Well!... How's our boy?" Conrad Wilson stood above him and behind Karen, smiling. He moved the lamp that had partially blinded Jacob, making his seeing more comfortable. Conrad Wilson appeared much older than those years before, but lively, happy.

"They gave you something to make you sleep for a while. The bullet passed by the artery and bone. I know it doesn't feel like it, but it hit nothing of consequence. Just a bit of muscle and fatty tissue, they tell us. You'll be up and around before the day is out."

"What?" Jacob's dryness of throat choked off the questions.

"Much to tell you, my boy. Much!" Conrad Wilson turned toward a nearby doorway and nodded to a man, who went into the adjoining room.

"I want you to eat something while we try to straighten all this out for you."

The man returned and set before Jacob a tray that held bacon, eggs and juice.

"Eat, Jake!" Wilson said. "That stuff is hard to come by these days."

"I'm not hungry. I just want to know what's happening."

His voice choked. "Why are you a part of them?" He looked to Wilson, then to Karen.

"Oh, Jake!" Karen cried, pressing her face against his chest while she clung to him. Her body quivered in his arms, and his anger dissolved when her tears soaked his chest, and he clutched her tightly and kissed her.

Wilson's voice, too, betrayed emotional upheaval. He spoke softly while not letting control slip. "I have never... and could never be a party to this... monstrous thing, Son. Not from the time they thought they had recruited me to right this second."

Wilson patted Karen's shoulder while Jacob held her. "She was drugged and programmed. Brainwashed through new, devilish technologies even I had never heard of. Even so, she fought them. Held on to enough of herself to be of great help to us in getting you free from them."

"I had to act as if I were devoted that night, Jake," Karen said, lifting her face from his chest. "Conrad and the others had already deprogrammed me, but I pretended to be a part of them in order to keep you alive long enough for us to break you free. It was almost unbearable... to not be able to hold you... to love you... knowing you were feeling so alone."

"Never doubt this girl's love, Son. Only a special sort could survive what she's been through." The diplomat paced the small room's floor while he talked. "From the time they took her at Stone Oaks and implanted the transponder in you, they worked their plan almost to perfection. And, incidentally, we took out the Sector Coordinator Allegiant while you were out. Anyway, their major flaw has always been their remarkable inability to take into consideration human will, especially the will of people who've been born into liberty and are determined to remain free, or at least relatively free, from oppressive controls."

"They operate on the assumption, like the Soviet system

always did, that bribery, intimidation, brainwashing, black-mail, or brute force will get them anything they want. What they failed to calculate, in my case, was that I've been dealing with just such methodology for decades. The only difference was that where the Russians and Chinese and the others were across the table from me, with no real personal holds on me, the Naxos bunch had me over the barrel. Rather than fight them, I became enthusiastically dedicated to their cause... turned totally against you. To have done less would have betrayed my ultimate objective before their quite observant eyes and ears."

Wilson's voice had sadness in it. "Of course, I pulled it off at the cost of, probably, thousands of lives." His eyes glistened. "I had to become one of them... Like you did, Jacob. Totally ruthless in the administration of their earth-saving justice. My argument with myself was and is that if this dictatorship is to be somehow converted to something better, it is justifiable to sacrifice those who must die to achieve the goal."

"If there's a chance for humanity to struggle out from under this, it has to begin with a nucleus group of people who hate injustice and inhumanity as deeply as Krimhler despises justice and freedom and human rights. In spite of their constant watching and listening, there are many of us who have never stopped fighting them. And, there are thousands of others who'll join us once they know we are organized and have growing strength. The millions who worship at Krimhler's feet will keep on worshipping, of course. But they're not fighters. They won't come to his defense in a military confrontation. They're all like zombies with their out-of-body meditation, drugs... Their total lack of sexual or moral restraints, except those the INterface imposes. They will all sit down, bleary-eyed, and not knowing what to do next, once their Interface-governed lives are disrupted."

"Our people are as determined as Herrlich Krimhler's elite, and probably almost as great in number. That is, as great as the number who will actively fight to the death for him. But the time for military is not yet. There's still a lot of organizing, much planning to be done."

Jacob sat upright on the edge of the cot, his senses going dark before they cleared when his blood flow adjusted to the changed posture. "Why did they let me live, if they knew I killed that Sector Coordinator and was planning to work against them? It makes no sense."

"It makes perfect sense. At least most of it does. Once they set you up for Krimhler's assassination, stealing your watch and planting it as evidence by the murder weapon, they had me in a position that I had to cooperate with them or else be accused of being a party to the assassination. Both Karen and I had to disavow any ties to you. The two people closest to you, testifying before INterface that you were guilty. A very convincing case!

"They didn't anticipate you would be quite so good at eluding them. Killing off their crack agents with that exploding attaché case, and later, the fire at Marchek's home... How did you do that?" Wilson paused, smiling and shaking his head with amusement in his eyes, not really wanting an answer.

"Of course they could track you, and did... until you found the Allegiant transponder and took it out. Very clever, putting it into the body and planning the fire with the helicopter to destroy their ability to identify all but the tracking device. I always thought I should've gotten you into CIA work." Wilson chuckled, continuing to pace and talk, stopping periodically to make his points to his peculiar fashion of gesticulation.

"When you removed the Allegiant, They decided to let you go on feeling your way through your confusion. Decided not to pick you up and hold you, out of sight, until the assassination was accomplished."

"Why?"

"They wanted you free to let you help them build a case they could use in a couple of ways. You became the No. 1 enemy around which all citizens could rally. That hatred for you helped take their minds off their own miserable plight. And, they used that time you were on the loose as Herrlich Krimhler's assassin to stir emotions, making him the most loved and adored martyr in history. Thus, the Six Ways Plan, as Krimhler's legacy to them, was quickly and completely embraced by all."

"What about the tracking device when it got out of their range? How could they keep up with my movements?"

"Melissa Jantzen," Wilson said, stopping his pacing.

"Melissa?"

"Real name's Moravia Krill."

"One of them from the start?"

"Yes. Sent to the abandoned apartment because they knew you would eventually find out about the implantation once you viewed the stolen tapes. A helpless female, they reasoned, could do what the other agents couldn't."

"And she did her job well! You raised an idiot!"

"No, Son. You couldn't have known those things... Not in your state of mind during that time."

"What about Kerry Vinchey?"

"They got me when I left with the body of the Coordinator." Kerry Vinchey stood in the doorway, smiling. He came to Jacob and took his hand, then hugged him. "They forced me down and would have killed me or run me through one of their torture palaces, I imagine, if not for Conrad."

"I convinced them to let me have a crack at Kerry... to learn all I could about your plans as he understood them. I, after all, knew your mind better than anyone. I convinced them after a time that Kerry would be invaluable to the cause. Made him my personal pilot. He flew you out of D.C."

Vinchey and Jacob embraced again, Jacob's throat swelling with emotion so that he had to fight the need to cry. "And what about Francis?" he said, finally getting control.

Wilson said nothing for a moment, his facial expression confirming the worst, before the words came. "I'm sorry, Son. I was away attending a meeting at Bonn. She was executed before I could stop it."

"Why her? Why did they have to kill Francis? She wasn't a threat. She couldn't have hurt them."

"She was sick and meant nothing to INterface but an unwanted effort to keep her alive. Time and personnel they could better use on other things. She was an enemy of INterface, tied to you, and could serve as an example to others who might think about resistance. They delight in demonstrating that they're not beyond butchering children or women to reinforce their demands."

Jacob sat silent, contemplating into a mind-void which filled with hatred suppressed since his rage on the steps of the crystal pyramid throne in the Jerusalem temple.

"INterface allowed your Sector Coordinator deception to go on until the time they considered appropriate because they knew they had you under their thumb at all times. They knew about the Bible, of your explosive belt contraption. Nothing escapes them," Wilson said, raising his silver eyebrows in puzzlement. "I don't know. Maybe Krimhler is, like his worshipers believe, some sort of supernatural being, some alien from out there somewhere." He gestured toward the cosmos.

"His exact reason or reasons for keeping you on the hook, I don't know. But I suspect, much of it has to do with his innate cruelty to see a man go through all that struggle, thinking he's getting somewhere, then devastating him by showing him that the world is against him and would rather believe lies than truth... Showing him, by putting him on exhibition for all to watch him kneel at the guillotine. I suspect this is one way he gets his greatest enjoyment.

"But why you, Jacob Zen... to accuse you of being the assassin so he can miraculously rise from the dead in some crazy, symbolic similarity to the way Jesus Christ was supposed to have arisen? I just don't know, Jake. I don't know. But just as I'm sure Krimhler's miraculous resurrection was a hoax, I'm equally certain all this has a natural explanation, and this dictatorship, a natural solution."

"No!... No, No, No! There's nothing natural in this! It's all too much like what's written in the Scriptures to be coincidence," Jacob said, his tone viciously argumentative.

Surprised at the sudden agitation, Wilson studied Jacob silently, then spoke, attempting to bring his foster son back to reality. "Surely you can't mean you believe that stuff. Man, not some higher power, created this hell. Certainly we shouldn't blame a Judeo Christian God! If we accept that sort of thing, we're all goners no matter what we do! Man did it to himself and only man... real flesh and blood, can change things."

"Like we've changed things to this point? Like going from clean air to this stench; from gun powder to nuclear weapons? From democracy to a degree of dictatorship the Third Reich didn't even approach achieving? Man really knows how to build a better world! He had the chance to create something good but instead created something that can obliterate everything on the planet!"

"Coincidence. It could've gone either way. To the good, or to the bad."

"But it went to the bad. It always goes, in the long run, to the bad, doesn't it? Just like the Scriptures say."

"Fallen man?... Original sin?" Wilson still in puzzlement of Jacob's stand.

"You have a better explanation for our ways?"

"Man is an ambitious animal; I certainly can't deny that. The more ambitious ones among us always seem to agree. But that's all been explained by Darwin."

"It was explained by Scriptures. The love of money is the root of all evil. Money is power; power is control. The greater the control, the greater the degree of subservience, and, ultimately, slavery... even worship."

"The Judeo Christian God demands worship," Karen interjected, still massaging Jacob's neck. He stopped her and stood from the cot.

"God doesn't demand in the sense Herrlich Krimhler demands. With God, there is free-will choice. Man chooses. With the Krimhlers of history you either worship or are tortured or killed, or both."

Jacob pulled his shirt on with Karen's help, his mind turning to Hugo Marchek.

"You shouldn't move around for a while, Son. You'll cause more bleeding," Conrad Wilson said, steadying him.

"What do you think you're doing, Jacob?" Karen said, seeing the determination on his face she had seen many times before.

"I'm going to prove that it's all part of the prophecies. That this will all end only when the prophecies have been fulfilled. We can't change any of it, but we've got to try to understand it."

"What are you talking about?" Karen questioned, more with concern for him than with irritation.

"Dr. Marchek said there would be a mass disappearance of people just before the end of what he called the 'dispensation of grace.' That is the period between Christ's crucifixion and the rapture of His church, which is what he said the mass disappearance would be."

"Which church is that? The Catholic? The Episcopal? The Baptist, Methodist? What?" Conrad Wilson asked, his voice tinged with sarcasm.

"The Church, according to Marchek, is, was, made up of all who truly accepted Jesus Christ as their Savior... trusted His sacrifice on the cross at Calvary to atone for their sins... trusted that act to serve as the only sacrifice acceptable to God the Father. Since the rapture, salvation can come only through what Dr. Marchek described as 'enduring to the end.' If necessary, one must die for faith in Christ as the only Son of God, the only Redeemer. The disappearance caused the instantaneous changing of human, mortal flesh into immortal matter designed for eternal existence. At that point, the Church Age ended and the tribulation period, which includes the rise and dictatorial world-rule of Antichrist, began."

"A short time later, apparently having something to do with Israel making a security covenant with Krimhler and the U.E.S., the era of the apocalypse was initiated."

"Come now, my boy! That's too fantastic for a logical mind such as yours to swallow," Wilson said, holding Jacob's shoulders, speaking as if he could reason the madness out of his foster son.

"It all fits." Jacob pulled away from Wilson, then limped to the doorway where Kerry Vinchey stood listening to the debate. Jacob turned to Wilson and Karen. "Clothing remained wherever the people were before they vanished. All the infants and young children, not old enough to be accountable for their souls, were taken."

"There are children," Karen said.

"Infants -- children born since the thing happened, yes,

and some in their teens. But have you seen any between those ages?"

Karen thought a moment, a look of puzzled agreement coming on her face; she did not answer.

"I haven't analyzed it, but if I had, I'll wager all who disappeared would fit very similar theological profiles. I think we'd find they believed about Jesus Christ in the same way. I'm certain of it."

"You spoke of proof. Present it if you have it, so we can all believe this... prophecy stuff," Wilson said lightly. No matter that Wilson's tone and expression said, the old diplomat wouldn't be convinced regardless of evidence produced. Jacob must know for himself whether his gut-felt suspicion, or spiritually-discerned revelation, or whatever it was urging him onward, was right, and whether it would lead him to the truth.

"I wish I didn't have to ask you to risk your neck after everything you've been through for me, Kerry," he said, turning to his friend. "But I can't fly that thing, so it looks like you're my only hope... again."

"Just say where to and when," Vinchey said, grinning and taking Jacob's arm to help him from the room.

They left at dusk, which, because of pollution, no longer differed significantly from earlier times of day. The helicopter's nose tipped slightly downward while Vinchey throttled its engine to optimum speed. Reaching Rockville would take 20 minutes, allowing time to ponder what they might find when they got there, if indeed they could carry out the search for answers without being shot from the sky or picked up once they landed.

"What's this about, Jacob?" Karen interrupted his thoughts, pressing against his shoulders for the closeness she had missed. "You really should've let that leg rest."

"There's no time. They're looking for us, and I've learned

that they find what they look for. I'm hoping they won't expect us to be moving around so freely. That they'll be looking for us to hole up somewhere. When they've exhausted their search in the hidden places, they'll start looking for us to be moving among them openly. We've got to get this done now, before they begin checking everything that moves."

"Why Rockville?"

"To prove to myself, I guess, that we're up against something more than just another attempt at world conquest."

"What difference does it make what kind of dictatorship it is? We're all on the same side. We all want to destroy it. It doesn't matter if you're right or if Conrad is right."

"The difference is important because if Uncle Conrad is wrong, and if Hugo Marchek was right, we can't fight against them... against Krimhler, the way dictatorships and dictators have historically been opposed."

"You really do believe Dr. Marchek was right, don't you? That INterface is prophecy being fulfilled."

"Of course he doesn't really believe it, my dear," Conrad Wilson said from the seat in front of them. "He would never go to such lengths to convince himself, otherwise. And I wouldn't come along, if I were not equally determined to watch him prove the fallacy of Marchek's contention."

"He believed it with his whole heart," Karen said. "He was a wonderful man, and one who would never deliberately lie."

"Of course he was a fine person," Wilson said, reaching behind him to pat Karen's hand. "My question to Jacob is: How can Marchek prove his theology to us now that he's dead, when he couldn't prove it while he was alive? It's the old thing of trying to prove the existence of God scientifically. It cannot be done."

"Maybe now it can," Jacob said with some irritation.

"How can you find anything at Rockville? There's nothing left. Dr. Marchek's home is gone," Karen said.

"There's something of him still there. Or maybe there isn't; we'll see shortly."

"I'll say this, the two fellows we took with us when we broke you out of D.C. believe the prophecy angle," Wilson said. "What?"

"Those two Orthodox Jewish prisoners. But, of course, you couldn't know. We emptied the cellblock when we stormed the place."

"And you took those two men with you? The ones who were in with me?"

"Yes."

"Where are they now?"

"Back at the compound we just left. They said something about some exodus from the INterface Pharaoh, but wouldn't be more specific."

"They said something about that to me," Jacob said. "You say they talked about prophecy?"

"I heard one of them say something about a place prepared by God to hide his people during a time of persecution. The other one quoted Scripture... from Isaiah, I think he said it was," Karen said.

"There's a place I can put down just ahead, Jake. Some pretty good cover from the trees, looks like," Kerry Vinchey shouted from the pilot's seat.

"How far from the cemetery?" Jacob shouted, leaning forward to hear the pilot's answer.

"According to the chart, it's no more than one, one-and-a-half kilometers due north."

"Good! Let's do it!"

Vinchey swung the big copter around, then nestled it gently into the open area of high weeds surrounded by trees, whose leaves struggled to achieve natural colors but could not because of the caustic atmospheric inversions that frequently squatted at ground level. Although the season should produce moist, hearty foliage that clung to its sources of nourishment, the dried vegetation flew about in the fury whipped by the helicopter blades. Jacob scanned the area through the small porthole, looking through the dust and debris for signs they might have been detected.

"You think they monitored us?" he said to Vinchey when the engine became silent.

"They wouldn't expect anyone to be so open about it. I think you're right about that. If they had suspected anything other than it being a routine shuttle or surveillance, they'd have confronted us in the air and tried to force us down in a place of their choosing... or just shot us down, period. But just in case I'm wrong..." He lifted the lid of a heavy metal box near the pilot's seat, took out an automatic rifle and tossed it back to Jacob. "They won't put us on display while we lose our heads." He took out another rifle and handed it to Conrad Wilson, then retrieved yet another from the box for himself. He pulled back the bolt and let it snap shut, feeding a round into the chamber.

"What about me?" Karen said. The pilot handed her a rifle and she followed his example, pulling back the bolt then releasing it.

Jacob watched her handle the weapon while Vinchey instructed her in its use, then took her hand and kissed it. "I wish you had stayed back there."

"Why? If anything happens, why should I be there, with no hope of being with you again? If it's to end here, then let it end for both of us. That couldn't be as bad as being alone, waiting for them to find me again."

He could not argue with the truth in her logic. Now, to wait for the blackness the thick, abrasive smog would assure, before attempting the, perhaps, dangerously foolish research into what he was driven to know.

The old backhoe had not been used for some time. It's starter and choke, as well as the controls, were stiff and stubborn from the corrosion which came with the disuse and lack of maintenance. There was plenty of gasoline in the tank, and he hoped there would not be condensation to the extent it would make the fuel burn improperly, or not at all. Jacob replaced the cap to the fuel tank, looking over the cemetery, using the flashlight's powerful beam. Conrad Wilson and Kerry Vinchey tried to see beyond the stone fences, weapons poised and alert to any movement.

"No one has attended this place in months," Karen said quietly, walking among headstones, occasionally brushing high grass away from one or the other of the markers to read the names. "The crypt is in this area, I think. It's been so long, and it all looks so different. Shine your light on this one," she said, walking toward the dingy gray crypt building centered in Jacob's light. She ripped and stomped weeds to get to the iron-barred doors of the small mausoleum, then read the words etched in the once white facade.

"This is it!" she said excitedly, wiping away caked dirt and cobwebs from the engraved word, "MARCHEK."

It was all so completely different from that day they had put the old man's body in the crypt, which looked so small now in the overgrown graveyard. A thing that should be left a part of undisturbed antiquity, and death.

That stormy day, as gloomy in its way as this black night, came back to Jacob while he joined Karen at the barred gate. Conversations and accusations of conspiracy, of cold, depressing rain, of Karen's tears, and the beginning of involvement in what Wilson called a natural development of history, but what Marchek had assured him was the fulfilling of prophecies. Prophecies that could be finished only when the supernatural had run its course as written in the old Bible Marchek once offered him. Would be consummated when the Prince of Peace returned in power and glory to bind and banish the world's last great dictator, and war from the earth. A process that would first become evident when millions of people vanished before the astonished eyes of their fellow humans. When, like Christ at the resurrection, they were in an instant, "in the twinkling of an eye," as Marchek had put it, transformed from mortal flesh into immortal beings. Like Jesus Christ, the shroud. Like Saryeva Marchek, the scorched dress.

"How are you going to get in? They won't budge," Karen said, watching him test the iron gates.

"The backhoe... if it will still run."

Moments later, he pulled the choke free from its oxidation-stuck position and worked it in and out several times. The battery should be okay if its energy was not depleted at the time the grave diggers stopped using it. It was a self-sealed battery, which had been well sheltered from the elements. But would it be strong enough to awaken the engine from its months of idleness?

He pushed the starter button and the engine turned but refused to start. Twice more and it caught. Two cylinders at first, then revved to power, its straight-up exhaust pipe cracking sharply and dispelling black smoke.

"If that doesn't bring 'em here," Vinchey shouted to Conrad Wilson above the popping engine, "They're not in the area!"

Wilson nodded agreement, both men continuing their vigilance. Jacob intent on his singular objective, steered the machine to the front of the building and rammed the comb-edge of the trenching scoop, attached to the front of the backhoe's crooked arm, into the barred gate-door. He throttled up the engine and the backhoe lurched, causing the crypt's door to creak and pop, but did not break the gate free from its moorings. He put the machine into reverse and backed, pulling the iron gate with the shovel, whose comb-like steel projections had become lodged between the bars. The gate groaned, tearing loose with a loud, scraping crunch.

He maneuvered the backhoe to directly in front of the opening so that the lights of the machine lit the burial chamber's interior, then hopped from the operator's seat, forgetting in his excitement the wound in his leg. Contact with the ground sent a stab of pain up his calf and into his back, causing both legs to buckle. Karen and Wilson hurried to help him keep from collapsing.

"I'm okay. Give me the flashlight," he said, taking the light from Karen then limping into the crypt, fighting his way through cobwebs while he directed the beam at the several cement and marble vaults lining the walls. He quickly found the one inscribed with Hugo Marchek's name and brushed away the thick layer of dust to read what was carved in the vault covering.

"To be absent from the body is to be present with the Lord."

"Hold this." Jacob handed her the flashlight. "Give me a hand with this." Vinchey and Wilson positioned themselves around the thick marble slab and in unison, jerked upward. It would not move.

"Try sliding it," Jacob said, pushing then adjusting to try to pull the covering to one side then the other.

"It's no doubt sealed," Wilson said, looking around for something with which to pry. Jacob went outside and retrieved a rusting crowbar he remembered kicking out of his way when he sat in the operator's seat before starting the backhoe.

Within seconds, the heavy marble piece was leveraged to

one side, uncovering a chamber containing a bronze colored coffin.

Jacob's heart raced. Suddenly his actions seemed in slow-motion, like much of his existence had been while under domination of Trachetrol II. He looked into Karen's eyes and saw a mixture of apprehension and anticipation at seeing the body of the old man she had worked so closely with — had loved so much. "Give me the light," he said, taking the flash-light and holding the beam on the smaller lid of the split-top casket. With his free hand, he lifted the lid, Karen looking over his shoulder. "He's not there!"

"*Why seek ye the living among the dead? He is not here, but is risen!*" The words Jacob had read in Marchek's Bible shook his mind when Karen spoke the fact, which, despite his deepest suspicions, he was not prepared to accept.

"The clothes! Look! The suit they buried him in, Jacob. They look like they've collapsed on his body. Or where his body was! It couldn't have decomposed that way. Not skeleton and all! Could it?"

Jacob said nothing while opening the larger lid of the coffin. He shined the light first along the gray suit, with its jacket still buttoned, then along the lining of the coffin's lids.

"Looks like it's been burned... Like it's been scorched," Kerry Vinchey said, adding the beam from his flashlight to that of Jacob's.

"Just like his sister," Jacob said beneath his breath.

"Curious way for the body to deteriorate," Wilson said, peering into the casket. "This terrible pollution, no doubt, can have effects we don't understand yet."

"On a body, sealed air-tight? Sealed up before atmos-pheric conditions got so bad?" Jacob's question was put with mild anger. "And what about this scorched material?"

Wilson made no response, but shined his own light along the collapsed material of Marchek's burial suit.

Jacob unbuttoned the suit coat and carefully removed each flap to uncover the shirt.

"The shirt's burned too!" Karen said.

The white shirt's front was scorched brown, from the buttoned collar beneath the tied necktie, to where it was covered by the waistline of the trousers.

Jacob directed his flashlight beam to the opened casket lids and slowly moved the circle of light down the satin lining.

"Put your lights on the lining," he said; the other men added their beams to Jacob's, illuminating the entire length of the once-white material. "Just like the shroud," Jacob said.

The discoloration, in varying gradations of brown, formed the negative image of a man's naked body, its hands folded neatly upon its chest.

"It... It's Dr. Marchek!" Karen said in a whisper.

Preparations for the move were underway by the time Vinchey set the helicopter down near the small, rectangular building. The twirling red lights on the bird's belly, and the bright landing lights, reflected off the yellowed, nearly-bare trees, making them appear from the passengers' view to be grotesque monsters with bony, reaching fingers, grasping to pull their victims into themselves. Several men carrying machine guns greeted them at the helicopter's door after Vinchey cut the engine.

"Everything is ready to move, Sir," one of the men said to Wilson, who looked over the compound, watching the darkly dressed men and women throwing the final contents from the buildings into the canvas-covered back of the old truck marked with white stars and the words "U.S. ARMY".

"Where are the two men? The two prisoners you brought with me from D.C.?" Jacob asked, getting the attention of one of the men, who looked to Conrad Wilson for approval before answering.

"I believe they're helping get things ready in that area," the man said, pointing, after Wilson nodded affirmatively.

"I need to know about the hiding place they've mentioned. Maybe they'll tell me now that they know we're not their enemy."

"Why? What good will it do?" Karen asked.

"There's nowhere to go to get away from him. I'm sure, now, that Krimhler is the one written about in the prophecies of Daniel and the Revelation. He will devour the entire planet, according to the Scriptures, except the Jewish remnant. They'll be protected. If we're to survive, it will be with them, in the place prepared for them by God," Jacob said while they walked into one of the buildings. He went into the room where he had been placed after his rescue, the room with his belongings. Karen, Wilson and Vinchey followed.

He went through his things and picked from them Marchek's Bible. "I remember the verse being in Isaiah." He thumbed to the prophetical book and found the boldly underlined passage. "Here it is... Isaiah the 26th chapter, verse 20."

"*Come, my people, enter thou into thy chambers, and shut thy doors about thee: hide thyself as it were for a little moment, until the indignation is past.*"

"Here are the men you wanted, Mr. Zen." The man who spoke moved out of the doorway to let the two strangely-robed men pass.

"How is your leg wound, Jacob?" the taller man said.

"It's nothing," Jacob said, anxious to pursue the more vital matters. "Sir, can you answer my question? In the Scripture... Isaiah 26, verse 20. That's the verse about when God will hide his people, Israel during the rule of the Beast, the Antichrist, isn't it?"

"Yes," the man's eyes flashed acknowledgment; he was obviously pleased Jacob had made the discovery.

"Do you trust me? Trust us?" Jacob gestured toward the others in the room.

"Enough to tell us where this place of hiding is? It's our only hope now. You know that Krimhler will not be stopped. He will gobble us up, eventually, just like everything else."

The robed man spoke softly. "You yet do not understand, although you believe."

"What do you mean?"

"About Jesus of Nazareth... That He is the Christ."

"I believe it. There are no other explanations. I know these prophecies have come to pass and that the others will also come to pass. What do you mean, I don't understand?"

"That there is nothing you or anyone else can do to stop the Antichrist. It will be done as written. If one is sealed within Jehovah's shelter, he is there for the duration. It is not a military headquarters. The battle is between the ultimate Good and the ultimate evil, and the Lord shall fight it. God has already won, because the prophecies will conclude exactly as given in His Holy Word. If you want to fight Herrlich Krimhler, futile though that effort would be, you must do it from beyond the safe haven prepared by the Lord of Hosts."

The words were true. Jacob knew it! The only way to survive, to endure to the end. And in that moment it became clear in his soul. The way to live, the way to salvation was, had always been, the way of the Cross, the shelter provided by Christ!

"Where? Will you tell us? Where is this place of hiding?"

"You will find it in Maan Muhafuzah, in a place known as Wadi-Sik."

"Jordan?" Conrad Wilson said with surprise. "Can you show us exactly where to find it?"

The man looked at Jacob, ignoring Wilson's anxiously put question.

"Go to the place of the Rock... to Petra. There you shall find the House of Chambers and safety."

Jacob looked to Vinchey, who was stuffing articles of clothing into a duffle bag, while sitting on a cot. "Think we can get there?"

"I'd hate to risk flying a chopper, even a transcontinental class, over that much water, although it could be done with extra fuel tanks. Couldn't take but a few people. If we did make it to the coast, there would be no parts for her if she broke down. After a flight like that, the bird would need major maintenance."

"I still have some people I can depend on to help," Conrad Wilson said. "Good people, who have access to aircraft and who will do what I ask, so long as we can make it look as if the aircraft was stolen."

"What about a pilot?" Jacob said.

"We'll get whatever Kerry's checked out on. Probably, it would be best to appropriate something with hover-landing capability so we won't need a long strip to set down on. You're checked out on that sort of thing, aren't you, Kerry?"

"A few planes," Vinchey said. "But I can handle whatever it is, as long as it's not too big."

"How soon can you arrange this... appropriation?" Jacob said.

"It will take a few days at least. We can take the helicopter to the prearranged spot. I'll have my contacts meet us there."

"How will you be able to get in touch with them without tipping off the wrong people?" Karen said.

"Old-fashioned telephone, my dear. And by using a code, which they won't have enough time to break before the deed is done. The fools don't think that anything can be carried on in such an obvious way any more. Witness our trip to Rockville. They're so heavily into secretive, high-tech stuff, they rarely monitor the good old telephone."

"We'll need fuel enough to reach..."

Wilson cut Vinchey short. "How about one that will take us straight through?"

"You can get an H-9?"

"Can you fly it?"

"Love to!"

"Then it will be available, my friend. I told you I have people who haven't forgotten this old broken-down diplomat!"

"I get the impression you don't want to go with us," Jacob said, turning to his former fellow prisoners. The men were gone.

He opened the door and looked into the darkness. "When did they leave?" he said, looking back to the others, who were equally puzzled. "I didn't hear them leave," Karen said, coming to the doorway to look out.

"A couple of strange ones. Are you sure you want to go to the Middle East on their information, Jake?" She said.

"We have to," Wilson put in. "There's really no alternative. I, of course, still can't accept all this nonsense about the Church Age ending and bodies being transformed into heavenly beings and that sort of thing. But I believe those fellows know where there's a safe place to sequester ourselves for awhile. INterface has been going berserk trying to find where all those Jews are disappearing to. If we can get that many people fighting with us, and if their hiding out place can provide adequate time for us to plan and build our forces, maybe we can put up formidable opposition to Herr Krimhler and his lot."

"They didn't leave through this door," Jacob said. "The door was bolted on the inside just now, before I opened it."

"One of us must've locked it and not noticed the men were gone," Karen said. "They probably stepped out while we were talking. One of us unthinkingly locked the door after them, and when they couldn't get back in, they probably went back to their quarters."

They watched the rain begin to fall, rain which burned the skin where it touched the body if allowed to remain for more than several seconds. Rain that caused a sickly greenish halo to form around each of the telephone pole night-lamps surrounding the compound.

CHAPTER 21

The wait had done its jangling work on the nerves of everyone since they arrived from their former refuge. But Conrad Wilson's smile said he had now accomplished what he promised three days ago, before they left for this abandoned military storage bunker.

"It's set!" He slapped Jacob's shoulder. "At twenty-two thirty hours, they'll have the aircraft in the pasture just beyond those trees." He pointed to a stand of tall, partially-leaved trees 200 yards to the north of the ground-level opening where they stood. "Where's Kerry?"

"He's still on the phone with them. They're checking him out on the aircraft as best they can on the phone. It'll save time when the plane gets here. He wanted to brush up on the Harrier system and so forth. He'll be along."

"Jacob! They've got them!" Karen rushed up the steps leading underground; her face was pale. "Who's got whom?"

"Those two men who disappeared from the compound... The prisoners who were with you."

"Where are they?" Wilson asked.

"Jerusalem. They're going to execute them! They're showing it now!"

They hurried down the steps and along several short, narrow corridors, then into a small room crowded with several people and an INterface Response Unit, whose screen displayed the pyramid symbol of INterface. When the symbol faded, Herrlich Krimhler, wearing a dazzling white jumpsuit, glared from the screen while sitting atop the crystal pyramid throne. Behind him loomed a gigantic golden cross, with a human form affixed to it, the face angelic and glowing while looking toward heaven — Herrlich Krimhler's face.

"These deceivers have preached the soul-murdering lies to the brothers and sisters of INterface Universal. Now they come to recompense for their wickedness. So that all may know these Jews are mortal hate-mongers and not prophets of some non-existent god. Behold their deaths! Let it serve notice to all who believe the false promises which, with the killing of these dogs, will be forever eradicated from the minds of humanity! No longer shall there be in our midst the barbaric practice of worshiping the false idol who was called Jesus of Nazareth!"

The scene changed to the streets of Jerusalem, to one part or the other of the oldest section, Jacob surmised. Hundreds of taunting, sneering men, women, and juveniles surrounded two men dressed in robes. One of the cameras zoomed in on the faces of the besieged men at the center of the circle of people. "It is them!" Jacob said. "They've apparently been preaching in the area for a couple of days, according to what they've been saying. INterface has been trying to catch them because they've been converting a lot of people," one of Conrad Wilson's men said.

"These wicked ones do not deserve a quick, merciful

death. Let them die as the harlots and infidels of ancient days... because they have tried to take worship from he who alone deserves worship, and have tried to direct worship to the false Christ! Let them be stoned!"

While Krimhler spewed his vehemence, the INRU screen presented a four-video split, one part showing the two men in close-up, one split displaying Krimhler sitting upon the crystal pyramid, another displaying the angry people surrounding the condemned men, and yet another showing a huge dump truck while it rolled to a stop behind the mob and dumped its load of baseball-size stones.

The people rushed to take the rocks, each grabbing as many as they could hold, then again took positions around the two men. For the moment, they were constrained by Krimhler's words from the loudspeakers and by a number of controllers, who stood in a circle between the mob and the intended victims.

"Death to the deceivers! To the deceiver, Jesus of Nazareth, whose bones lie buried somewhere nearby. Whose soul dwells in eternal nothingness for the deluding claims He made!"

The video changed again and continued changing rapidly, capturing the excited faces of the crowd while Krimhler shouted his dictate. All became silent when the taller of the two robed men raised his hands toward the sky, then slowly lowered his right hand and, pointing a finger in a slow, sweeping motion toward the people around him, he spoke.

"Repent or reap the whirlwind you have sown!" The words were clearly audible over the Response Units throughout INterface. "God is not mocked; The Lord Jesus lives! Accept Jesus Christ as your Savior and Lord and turn from the son of perdition! Jesus is the Way, the Truth and the Life. No one comes to the Father but by Him! Repent! Accept Christ!"

The mob would no longer be restrained. Stones flew toward the center of the circle where the men stood. But they were no longer there!

The astonished people surrounding the pile of stones recoiled, their expressions open-mouthed, fearful. The sky suddenly darkened, and terrible, wicked streaks of jagged lightning cut blindingly against the billowing blackness. Thick gray-white objects as large as cannon shot rained on the hapless would-be executioners and the controllers, and they fell while the hailstones crashed with thunderous noise. The screen went black.

Everyone in the room watched in silence while the screen filled again with the pyramid symbol. Karen started to speak to Jacob but he was no longer by her side.

She found him huddled over a small table, reading.

"Dr. Marchek's Bible?" she looked over his shoulder, seeing the Scriptures underlined in red. "Does it have something to do with those men?"

"Listen to this... It's in the Revelation, chapter 11..." He quickly ran his index finger beneath the words and Karen tried to follow, but gave up, instead giving her full attention to his reading of the passages.

"And I will give power unto my two witnesses, and they shall prophesy a thousand two hundred and threescore days, clothed in sackcloth.

These are the two olive trees, and the lampstands standing before the God of the earth.

And if any man will hurt them, fire proceedeth out of their mouth, and devoureth their enemies; and if any man will hurt them, he must in this manner be killed.

These have power to shut heaven, that it rain not in the days of their prophecy; and have power over waters to turn them to blood, and to smite the earth with all plagues, as often as they will.

And when they shall have finished their testimony, the beast that ascendeth out of the bottomless pit shall make war against them, and shall overcome them, and kill them.

And their dead bodies shall lie in the street of the great city, which spiritually is called Sodom and Egypt, where also our Lord was crucified.

And they of the peoples and kindreds and tongues and nations shall see their dead bodies three days and a half, and shall not permit their dead bodies to be put in graves.

And they that dwell upon the earth shall rejoice over them, and make merry, and shall send gifts one to another, because these two prophets tormented them that dwelt on the earth.

And after three days and a half the spirit of life from God entered into them, and they stood upon their feet and great fear fell upon them who saw them.

And they heard a great voice from heaven saying unto them, 'Come up here.' And they ascended up to heaven in a cloud, and their enemies beheld them.

And the same hour was there a great earthquake, and the tenth part of the city fell, and in the earthquake were slain of men seven thousand; and the remnant were terrified, and gave glory to the God of heaven."

Jacob looked away from the book for a moment, deep in thought, then reread part of the Scriptures silently.

"I just can't accept that. It's nonsense!" Karen said, then watched and heard him read in a whisper. *"...And their dead bodies shall lie in the street of the great city, which spiritually is called Sodom and Egypt, where also our Lord was crucified..."*

"Jerusalem! Come on!" He rushed from the room and into the adjoining one, where the INRU screen's video was split into two images. The larger segment showed the pyramid symbol; a small picture in the lower right corner displayed a confused scene in which controllers rushed about, weapons poised, searching the bodies and rubble of the stones for the two men who had vanished before the sudden hailstorm struck.

"Is this just coincidence? Like all the rest that's happened?" Jacob said.

"I don't know, Jacob. I've never believed all that religious garbage. Not even Dr. Marchek could convince me that."

"But you see it for yourself, Karen. You saw them vanish the same as I did!"

They watched an angry-faced Controller charge the camera, which was obviously hand-held, causing the small picture in the corner of the INRU screen to become a jumbled blur, then white out with electronic snow.

"I'm not saying there's nothing unusual going on in all this. There's never been a situation like it in history. But it's just the inevitable outcome of a dictatorship that has at its disposal unprecedented technologies, Hitler... the Nazis.... would've probably come to this, or maybe worse, if they had the technology Krimhler and INterface has available to them for controlling people. The eschatologists or whatever they were called during that period, no doubt proclaimed the Nazis to be the end-time dictatorship... Hitler, the Antichrist."

"You sound like Uncle Conrad," Jacob said.

"And you've been sounding like Hugo Marchek."

"Yeah... Somehow things got turned around, didn't they?" He pulled her to him and they looked into each others' eyes, sharing the special emotion there had been little time for until this moment.

"You still like me?" He brushed her lips lightly with his.

"A little, maybe." She smiled, her eyes glistening with tears. She held his face between her hands and kissed him, then looked into his eyes again. "I love you, Jacob Zen. Nothing can ever change that."

"No... We can't let anything change that, no matter how much everything else gets turned around," he said.

They kissed again and he felt her quiver. "Are you okay, Sweetie?" He tried to blanket the cold fear he sensed in her by embracing her more tightly.

"If we weren't so caught up in it... weren't so much at the center, knowing what's happening to the world, maybe it could be like it used to be for us," she said, putting her face on his shoulder and looking away, wishing.

"But we are at the center, and if for no other reason, that's why we have to try to understand what's going on. We have to be able to agree, or at least try to agree, about the nature of what we're facing, so we can fight it with the strength of our combined wills. This thing will tear apart anything or anyone, who fights it with anything less than its one and only solution."

"And that's to be found in the Scriptures?"

"I'm absolutely sure it all fits together. The Bible, Marchek told me, is a living entity, not just a great work of literature. The living Word of God himself. *'In the beginning was the Word and the Word was with God, and the Word was God.'*

"The Word says that Jesus of Nazareth was, is, the Christ. He and the Holy Spirit are One with the Father. The Trinity... the perfect Good. And the perfect Good is the only thing greater in power than the absolute evil. Jesus Christ is the only being who can and will put an end to Herrlich Krimhler and INterface... To the genocide."

Karen held him tightly. "I'll accept it because you accept it. I can't say I find it easy to believe everything about these prophecies. About Herrlich Krimhler being some end-time Antichrist. But I believe in you, and in your faith in all the things you say."

Jacob took her hand and spoke earnestly, gently. "No,

Karen, not me. It's man's belief in man... thinking that he can solve all of mankind's problems, that brought us where we are now. That's why the world has turned to this maniac to save them from the problems they've brought upon themselves. It's God, not man, who has the answers. Do you understand the things I'm saying?"

"I'm trying, Jake."

"It's a one-on-one situation. The individual and God. No one can make the decision but the individual whose immortal soul is beckoned by God's Spirit to accept Christ. Without Jesus Christ, one's soul is lost for eternity. We must accept Christ and refuse the mark of the beast, the symbol of INterface and the controls that go with it. We must reject the Antichrist system to the end."

"The end of what?"

"Either the end of this age, the period of tribulation, which is to last a total of seven years — three-and-a-half of which, I believe, might have already passed — after which Jesus Christ will return at the end of the world's last battle at Megiddo."

"Armageddon?"

"Yes, Armageddon."

"It's all so totally foreign to all I've ever been taught and believed, Jacob. Knowing we're together and that Conrad and Kerry and other good, sane people have faith in our effort, gives me something to hold onto while I try to absorb all the things you've told me. We've got to hold to each other and our friends through this, don't we? Human beings still need other human beings. Things haven't changed that much, have they?"

He felt her convulse again and tried to warm her after gently kissing her, feeling the softness of her hair, smelling its fragrance.

"It's time to be on our way," Conrad Wilson said, putting his head through the doorway. "Everything's plotted. They'll know the plane is missing by now, so we've got to move quickly."

Wilson stood to one side of the doorway, allowing them to pass on their way out of the room, then carried Karen's luggage to the top of the steps leading to outside, where another man took her bags.

"I've some last-minute things to attend to here, Jake. I'll join you on board in a minute," Wilson said, patting his foster son on his shoulder, then watching them hurry toward the clump of trees and the jet sitting in the opening just beyond.

A few seconds later, having returned to a room near the back of the underground facility, he heard the four engines of the plane stir to life and settle into their idling whine. He put the thick attaché case on the single bed and opened it, then sat on the bed beside the case while expertly manipulating its contents. The adjustments made, he carried the open case into the adjoining room and slipped a small black device into the INRU unit. He activated the Unit by pressing two buttons within the case in his lap, causing the screen to snap to life. A dark-skinned woman gazed at him and spoke in a business-like manner.

"Stand by, sir. You are priority for Interact One."

The picture changed to that of a flat, brilliantly illuminated map of the world, overlaid with white gridlines and dotted with various points of light that represented major cities and population centers. On either side of the map, INRU monitors were alive with video from each of the INterface capitals.

There materialized the image of a man upon the gigantic map. He was young, bronze-skinned, with thick, black hair swept precisely back on either side of the handsome, symmetrical head. The eyes, as dark as the hair above the smooth, tanned forehead, projected commandingly from the almost too-perfect face.

"Is all as it should be?" the deep voice, seemingly older than the one to whom it belonged, said in English.

"It is, Sir," Conrad Wilson replied with confident, reportorial inflection. "Everything has come together as envisioned from 'The Plan's' inception."

"You have accomplished your duties faithfully, but there is yet much to be done to assure that my enemy cannot complete his objective. The agents of his birth and fulfillment will be slaughtered where they nest like rodents infesting a world which must be purged of them forever!"

Herrlich Krimhler stood and walked to his right, his image disappearing from the center of the map. Wilson's INRU screen then showed Krimhler walking to a position in front of the world map.

"We know the Jews are here." Krimhler pressed a button and the map changed, the area of Jordan enlarging greatly, filling most of what formerly was representative of INterface in its totality. "And we know they are most likely here, in the area known as Petra." He made another adjustment on the control board in front of him and the map changed again, the specific area enlarging within the Jordanian enlargement. "The Holy One..." The words burst from his mouth with hatred, "thinks they are hidden from me, and that the prophecy will be fulfilled. But, thanks to 'The Plan,' and to your ward, Mr. Zen, here is where the fulfilling of the prophecies end, and my kingdom... My Father's kingdom... begins!"

"I am prepared to carry out this last portion of my assignment, my Lord," Conrad Wilson said, bowing his head and closing his eyes before lifting his face again to see the young man, whose features were animate with excitement.

"Yes!... Yes! Follow this Jew ward of yours into the bowels

of the world, where the excretion awaits its flushing. Then my world shall be purged of their defiling stench!"

"How can we be sure they can be located? All we have are the somewhat sketchy directions of those two Jews. Did they divulge additional information before they were turned over to the people?"

"This is no concern of yours! Yours is only to do as you are directed! You will not question me! Do you understand?! No one will question me!" Krimhler's glee had turned instantly to screaming rage; he slammed his fist into the control board repeatedly. Wilson bowed his head. "I am sorry, my Lord. I did not mean to question..."

"From the time the child was placed in your responsibility when its mother was dispatched, this moment has been the purpose of his continued existence... and yours. Do you not know that?" Krimhler's voice calmed while he spoke, finally leveling at consoling volume and tone.

"His every movement was orchestrated — from his placement into the United States diplomatic service, to his being made to sense collusion against his nation, to his meeting the women operatives, to his being hated as our greatest enemy — all aimed at bringing him to this hour. A Jew, meeting the two preachers from the so-called Holy One. Being accepted by the underground Jews because they trust him... because they perceived him as also a victim of INterface. So that now I shall learn, through Jacob Zen, of their place, which they stupidly believe I will not be able to locate."

Krimhler's features seemed to grow darker, his expression hardening, and he slammed his fist against the control console again.

"Now do you think we cannot accomplish so simple a thing as following your deluded little Jew into the rat's nest, which this God of theirs will surely open to him after all the trouble he has taken to lead him there?"

Wilson did not answer, but nodded, with closed eyes, his fawning agreement.

"There has been no greater slaughter in the history of this world than will take place when they are found! Go now! Accompany Jacob Zen to the fulfilling of his purpose for being allowed to live to this moment... And question your Lord no more!" along with that!"

* * *

CONRAD WILSON NUDGED Jacob's knee with his fingertips, his voice still jovial. "Oh, lighten up, Jake. I know you're talking about this newfound religion of yours." He gestured toward the book Jacob held open in his lap. "The pilot you're talking about sits at the controls a few miles above our present altitude."

Jacob said nothing in answer to Wilson's teasing words, choosing to let his troubled thoughts take refuge in the words underlined in Hugo Marchek's old Bible. He read the words, hearing Marchek's accented voice in his mind's ear. *"Trust in the Lord with all thine heart, and lean not unto thine own understanding. In all thy ways acknowledge him, and he shall direct thy paths."*

Kerry Vinchey grabbed instinctively for the controls when the shrill, pulsating sound pierced his ears through the headphones. The electronic guidance-locator screen near the center of the complex middle control console blazed red with warning that the H-9 had been locked onto and was being tracked. Vinchey pushed a button on the left grip of the control and spoke into the headset's microphone.

"Buckle up! Somebody's onto us!"

Moments later, Jacob was at his side, strapping himself into the seat next to Vinchey.

"What do you think you can do up here?" Vinchey said,

glancing at Jacob, then at the glowing screen whose warning continued to be punctuated by the high-pitched sound. The pilot pushed a nodule that silenced the noise.

"I'll fly this thing for you if I have to," Jacob joked weakly, his eyes scanning the incredibly intricate agglomeration of buttons, dials and toggles.

"If that happens, them trying to shoot us down will be among the least of our worries," the pilot bantered somberly, searching for the instruments that could jam the enemy's fix on the craft. "Not working! It's inoperative!" he said angrily, trying again to activate the jamming device.

"What's happening?"

"The jamming's totally gone. It's not even hooked up!"

"What does that mean?"

"It means I can't confuse them. They'll lock onto us... hit us whenever they choose. I checked this out a couple of times in the preflight. Somebody has disconnected it since then."

"What can we do?"

"You know that God you've been telling me about? It's time to give Him a call. We're sitting up here like a carnival shooting gallery target." Kerry glanced at Jacob, then back to the instrument panels when he thought he saw his friend's lips moving in silent prayer, as suggested.

"It's almost black down there," Jacob said moments later, straining to look out the right corner of the windshield. "How far are we from the spot you've programmed us to land?"

"We're about five minutes away. But it's taken some kind of wind to stir that much sand and dust." Kerry looked out the left side of the windshield past the nose of the aircraft, then turned to Jacob.

"You'd better go get them prepared, Jake. If they don't get us first with surface-to-air missiles or with fighters, we'll have to take our chances with that turbulence down there. There is a positive side."

"What's that?" Jacob said, hurriedly unbuckling the seat harness.

"Like you said, if the dust cloud is high enough, and we can get into it quickly enough, we'll have good cover. They won't be able to follow us in too closely. Their pursuit aircraft can't maneuver safely under conditions like those down there. The H-9 can... I hope. And, if it's not too rough, our terrain-reading and landing computers will get us to our touchdown spot in good shape."

Vinchey gripped each side of the control tightly and called over his shoulder to Jacob, who stopped to hear the pilot's words before ducking through the cockpit's doorway. "Tell them to expect a sharp turn and steep descent. Let me know when you're strapped down."

Karen clutched Jacob's hand when the plane banked to the right and plunged toward the swirling darkness of the storm below. All bodies strained to battle the negative gravity force being exerted, fighting the sensation that their stomachs were, invading their throats.

"It's all right, Kay... It's all right," Jacob said soothingly to her while he fought his own urge to gasp for the breath that had left him somewhere several thousand feet above. "We'll be coming out of it in a second or two."

"Reminds me of my first and only time on the Coney Island coaster," Conrad Wilson wheezed from his seat, his face increasingly crimson against the silver-white hair, eyebrows and mustache. "On that occasion I had a pretty girl like Karen holding my hand, Jake. Wish I had one now!"

The plane's angle of descent moderated, the scream of the powerful engines and the stress on the airframe vibrating the craft while it struggled to come out of the dive. The bird shuttered and popped, as if, Jacob thought, the wings had snapped or were in the process of snapping from the fuselage. When the H-9 leveled off, it was buffeted wildly from side to side, rocking violently, almost doing a complete roll, it seemed, while Vinchey fought to stabilize it in the vicious winds of the desert storm.

The engines surged and pulsed when Vinchey applied power, then throttled back before throttling up again, trying to maintain controlled momentum and altitude.

"One thing for sure, folks," the pilot said over the intercom, straining between words, "they can't know exactly where we are in this stuff. Looks like we're okay now."

Seconds later, the jet slowed to barely controllable forward movement, the Harrier machinery pushing jet exhaust hard against the desert floor, toward a landing that Vinchey hoped would be within tolerance. When the bird thumped hard but safely against the sand, the flyer let his intensity seethe in exhalation through his clenched teeth. He relaxed his grip on the controls, then cut the engines.

"Terrific job, my friend!"

Jacob's hand slapping against his back brought full realization of the ordeal he had brought them through. His joints ached, his temples pounded with each beat of his heart.

"Yeah... thanks. But I think we should both be giving that compliment to whoever you talked with just before we started down through this stuff..."

The hot sand had blasted the exposed areas of skin nearly raw during the first several hundred meters of their trek against the wind that raged at them from the south. But the storm was dying, and they moved with greater ease.

"We'd better get a reading!" Kerry Vinchey shouted above the howl, pulling the compass from his pocket and squinting while holding the instrument near his face, away from the wind and sand.

Jacob, with Karen clinging to him, pressed against his friend to hear his assessment.

"We're headed a little to the north! The wind's pushing us off course! We'll have to stop to get our heading more often!"

They shuffled through the drifting mounds in the new direction Vinchey pointed out. The wind no longer blew a steady gale, rather came in powerful bursts, occasionally subsiding to a less impeding level. Vinchey, in the lead, stopped again after they had traveled another 300 meters.

"We're almost there!" he shouted to Jacob. "Less than half a kilometer, I'd guess!"

The density of blowing sand thinned while the storm's power quickly spent itself. Their view of what lay ahead became more defined. Jacob could see the tops of the ridged terrain standing in dark maroon relief against the dust-choked, orange sky. Somewhere ahead they would find the canyon's opening, the narrow pathway leading into Petra, the ancient rose-red city carved into the cliffs by a people who could not have fathomed the purpose their backbreaking labors would serve at this most crucial juncture of human history. Jacob mulled the thought while the party again trudged through the dunes. Hugo Marchek's God was indeed the true God. To know such endings from such beginnings.

The wind was alive with new sounds that vibrated the earth beneath them. A familiar pounding that grew painfully louder with each thumping noise it made.

"Choppers!" Kerry Vinchey shouted, pointing to the sky behind them. The huge, black helicopters were above them, sweeping low then encircling them, settling, finally, on the sand mounds that surrounded their captives. Seven INter-face controllers spilled from the bird nearest the group and trotted toward them, automatic rifles at the ready.

Karen pressed tightly against Jacob, who put his arms around her and kissed her check. His own fears were devoured by the agony of knowing there was nothing he could say to give solace, to reassure her. INterface had again anticipated him, had outwitted and outmaneuvered him. Nothing left of his carefully conceived and executed plan but the small prayer he almost unconsciously let slip from his spirit, toward Heaven. "Dear Father, save us."

The troops' leader approached Kerry Vinchey, the INterface soldiers moving to positions that would allow them to cover the others. "Do you have weapons?" the darkly-clad man demanded in English spoken with a German accent.

When Kerry said nothing in response, the INterface officer clubbed him with the rifle butt. The soldier held the muzzle of the weapon to the pilot's temple while Kerry supported his weight on hands and knees against the sand.

"Please answer..." the man said in pseudo-polite inflection. "Or I will be obliged to blow your head from your shoulders."

"Leave him alone."

Jacob knelt beside his friend and steadied him by holding Kerry's shoulders in his grip. "We don't have any weapons."

"They have no guns, Colonel," Conrad Wilson said, stepping between the soldier and the fallen man. "Let him get to his feet."

"Sir!" the officer said in a military manner, then stood at parade rest. Jacob looked upward, into his foster father's eyes.

"Sir?" Jacob said incredulously. "Kerry gets hit with a rifle butt for not answering, and you are called 'Sir' when you give this animal an order?"

Wilson ignored Jacob, turning instead to the soldier. "Are the forces ready?"

"Yes, sir! They await your orders, sir." Jacob's emotions blurred with senses darkening inner rage, the abject bitterness of ultimate trust betrayed.

"Why?" he asked softly, his eyes again meeting those of Conrad Wilson.

"There are some things greater than we are, Jacob. We must take second place to them. Our needs, our feelings, are of little matter when considered alongside the eternal." The wind had grown strangely calm, as if the storm, which had not lasted quite long enough to provide the cover needed to get them safely to the canyon city just ahead, had never happened at all.

Now, a deep rumble took the place of the former wind's shrillness, the sound of mechanized war machinery on the move, toward them, toward Petra. "Even if you had made it into those caverns, Jacob, the tanks and artillery would have ended your rebellion against the inevitable kingdom that is coming upon the planet. Your God would not be able to save you and Karen and the rest when the deep-penetration, smart bombs pierce through the cliff tops."

"Why? You must know who you're serving."

"You've read Milton, you know why. Better to rule in Hell than to serve in Heaven," Wilson said with resigned irony in his voice. "At any rate, I've cast my lot, and we must, as I said, put our parochial interests aside. I am sorry about you and Karen. But I am comforted by the fact that your fate will be less agonizing than will that of the foolish masses cringing in those caves."

The rumbling grew louder, and now dust, which had settled after the abrupt end of the storm, could again be seen billowing skyward in the distance. A storm of even greater fury drew closer by the second, a man-made maelstrom intended to flush its victims in a flood of violence gushing from the satanically enraged INterface fuehrer. Jacob's diffused thoughts were suddenly synchronized into one thought, galvanized by Conrad Wilson's words: "...the foolish masses cringing in those eaves."

Jacob's recall came to him in the unforgettable, unmistakable voice of Hugo Marchek, while his mind's eye reread the passage from Revelation, chapter 12, verses 14-16 in Marchek's Bible,

"And to the woman were given two wings of a great eagle, that she might fly into the wilderness, into her place, where she is nourished for a time, and times, and half a time, from the face of the serpent. And the serpent cast out of his mouth water like a flood after the woman, that he might cause her to be carried away by the flood.

And the earth helped the woman, and the earth opened her mouth and swallowed up the flood which the dragon cast out of his mouth."

"Time, and times, and half a time," Jacob thought Three and one-half years....

The woman — the nation Israel — who delivered the Savior — Jesus Christ — the man-child whom the serpent — Satan — hated above all else. The flood — the onstorming INterface assault force! The prophecy of the 12th chapter of Revelation being fulfilled before his astonished eyes!

Jacob felt a rush of renewed strength. "Stay close to me," he whispered to both Kerry and Karen, while he continued, with Karen's assistance, to help the pilot to his feet. "Be ready to move fast when we've get the chance."

The armored vehicles and tanks shook the earth while they drew to within a kilometer. A fighter-bomber shrieked overhead less than 1,000 feet above them, and in the next instant the face of the cliff that guarded the ancient city of Petra erupted, the blast sending huge fragments of rock high into the air, outward, and to the desert floor below. Two jets followed closely behind the first, and the rocks again burst violently when the bombs struck.

"Look!" Karen's wide eyed command caused Conrad Wilson, Jacob, and Kerry Vinchey to turn their attention from the next set of attacking jets, to the top of the cliff, which exploded upward. A thunderous blast drew gigantic boulders and molten rock several hundred meters into the air. The pilots, unable to react in time, flew the planes into the spewing inferno and instantaneous oblivion.

Jacob's legs suddenly trembled, the earth beneath him seemingly turning to liquid. Debris rained around them, while the earth quaked mightily, opening wide fissures that bubbled with lava and expelled acrid smoke that made it difficult to see more than a few meters, in any direction.

He held tightly to Karen while the shaking became more violent. "Don't let go!" he shouted to her, at the same time scanning the area around them for Kerry Vinchey. "Kerry!"

"Here, Jake!... I'm here!" The pilot came through the veil of smoke, reaching to take Karen's offered hand. "Let's head for the cliffs, Jake!" he urged, tugging Karen toward the rocky area beyond the big helicopters, half-swallowed now by huge cracks in the still-shifting earth. "Jacob!"

Conrad Wilson's weak-voiced cry was barely audible through the great noise and commotion taking place around them. Jacob strained to see through the swirling smoke and ash. "Jake! Over here!"

Jacob knelt on one knee in front of the old man, when he saw that Wilson was wedged in a fissure barely wide enough to trap a man's body. "I'll get you out! Take it easy, I'll get you out."

Smoke and gasses arose from the crack that entrapped Wilson, causing both Jacob and the old man to fight for breath while the younger man tried to free his foster father. Kerry Vinchey tried to lift Wilson from behind, without success.

"Never mind, boys... It's over for me," Wilson said. "But not for you!" He pulled a pistol from somewhere within the fissure and thrust it in Jacob's direction, causing Jacob to jerk instinctively, away from his foster father. Before Vinchey could react from behind, Wilson fired two shots in rapid succession.

Jacob was hit from behind, the blow knocking him forward on his knees. The body of the black-uniformed, INterface storm trooper rolled from Jacob, the soldier's face streaming blood from the two holes Wilson had put in his forehead. The dead Controller's hand still clutched the Uzi that had been aimed at Jacob's back.

Conrad Wilson winced, the pistol dropping from his hand. His expression became more relaxed. "Jake, I am sorry... Son. Forgive me."

When Jacob grasped his foster father's hand and arm, the earth convulsed violently, knocking Karen and Kerry Vinchey off their feet and causing Jacob to lose his grip on Wilson.

"Uncle Conrad!" Jacob crawled forward in a desperate attempt to grab the old man, whose eyes bulged widely when the earth fissure closed momentarily, crushing him, before opening wide, causing his lifeless body to slip just beyond Jacob's grasp into the boiling regions below.

"We should be going, Jacob," Karen said after a few moments of emotion-charged silence, gently pulling him away from the chasm. The tears came not from the gasses and smoke that engulfed them, Karen knew while she and Kerry walked Jacob from the abyss, but from love only a son could have for a father lost to him forever.

They moved past the broken places in the earth, past the mangled machinery of war that partially jutted from the cracks in the Jordanian desert's floor. They moved with growing resolve, toward a new beginning, when things would be made right again by the One who had brought them safely this far.

Hugo Marchek's voice again whispered in Jacob's spirit.

The words from the old Book were true. They were absolutely true! *"For then shall be great tribulation, such as was not since the beginning of the world to this time, no, nor ever shall be."*

"It is even the time of Jacob's trouble, but he shall be saved out of it."

A LOOK AT: THE RAPTURE DIALOGUES: DARK DIMENSION— THE SECOND COMING CHRONICLES

BY TERRY JAMES

Set in the era from the 1947 Roswell UFO incident, to the terror attacks of 9/11, "The Rapture Dialogues" sets the stage for biblically prophesied events.

USAF Fighter pilot James Morgan finds himself in supernatural conflict that suctions his wife, Laura and daughter, Lori, into clandestine governmental intrigues of terrifying dimension.

Mark Lancing, a young Marine fighter pilot, finds his life intertwined with the plight of the Morgans, through a growing love for Lori, night-marish intrusion by hellish creatures and explosive involvement with Israel's spiritual and physical wars for survival.

Prophecy expert Terry James offers a stark vision of the future that combines government conspiracy theories, UFO mythology, spiritual warfare and end-times prophecy in a prescient tale eerily reminiscent of the times in which we live.

AVAILABLE NOW ON AMAZON

ABOUT TERRY JAMES

Terry James is author, general editor, and co-author of numerous books on Bible prophecy, hundreds of thousands of which have been sold worldwide. James is a frequent lecturer on the study of end time phenomena, and interviews often with national and international media on topics involving world issues and events as they might relate to Bible prophecy.

He has appeared in major documentaries and media forums, in all media formats, in America, Europe, and Asia.

He appeared in the History Channel series, The Nostradamus Effect.

He is an active member of the PreTrib Research Center Study Group, a prophecy research think-tank founded by Dr. Tim LaHaye, the co-author of the multi-million selling "Left Behind" series of novels. He is a regular participant in the annual Tulsa mid-America prophecy conference, where he speaks, and holds a Question and Answer series of sessions on current world events as they might relate to Bible prophecy.

Terry James has been blind since 1993 due to a degenerative retinal disease (retinitis pigmentosa). He uses the Jobs Accessible Word System (JAWS) –which is voice synthesis— to write and conduct business over the Internet.

His former profession was in public relations, advertising, marketing, and publicity and promotion.

He received his education from Arkansas Polytechnic

Institute, Memphis Academy of Arts, and University of Arkansas at Little Rock.

He served in both corporate and government positions for 25 years, before becoming a full-time writer.

James also served in the United States Air Force from October 1966 through October 1970.) He served at Randolph AFB, Texas, in the T-38 section, a mission dedicated to training pilots in high-performance jet fighter-trainers.

Terry James and his wife, Margaret, live near Little Rock, Arkansas.

SEE MORE GREAT TITLES BY TERRY JAMES ON
christiankindlenews.com